New Free Chocolate Sex

Also by Keith Lowe

Tunnel Vision

New
Free
Chocolate
Sex

A NOVEL

Keith Lowe

ATRIA BOOKS

New York   London   Toronto   Sydney

ATRIA BOOKS
1230 Avenue of the Americas
New York, NY 10020

This book is a work of fiction. Names, characters, places
and incidents are products of the author's imagination or are
used fictitiously. Any resemblance to actual events or locales
or persons, living or dead, is entirely coincidental.

Library of Congress Cataloging-in-Publication Data
Lowe, Keith, 1970–
New free chocolate sex : a novel / Keith Lowe.—1st Atria Books hardcover ed.
p. cm.
ISBN 0-7434-8209-3
1. Chocolate—Fiction. I. Title.
PR6112.O84N49 2005
823'.92—dc22
2004055056

First Atria Books hardcover edition February 2005

10 9 8 7 6 5 4 3 2 1

ATRIA BOOKS is a trademark of Simon & Schuster, Inc.

Manufactured in the United States of America

For information regarding special discounts for bulk purchases,
please contact Simon & Schuster Special Sales at 1-800-456-6798
or business@simonandschuster.com

For my mother and father

New

Tiny acorns may grow into mighty oaks, but cocoa beans become chocolate, and that is a more miraculous process by far.

Chapter one

If the universe were made of chocolate, this is what it would look like. A limitless expanse of darkness. Stardust made from cocoa powder and the tiniest flakes of grated Ghirardelli. A firmament sparkling with a million individually foil-wrapped Hershey's Kisses. The whole of creation infused with the aroma of chocolate bars with ethereal names: Dove, Sky, Milky Way. Vast chocolate planets hanging in the chocolate sky: Jupiter with its giant red spot picked out in glacé cherries, Saturn with its rings made of brittle caramel, Venus built entirely from pure white chocolate. The asteroid belt filled with éclairs and profiteroles. And in a sort of interstellar joke, Mars would be constructed entirely of Mars bars, the red planet rendered a light chocolate brown for all eternity.

The Earth itself would be the center of this universe. Its continents would be made of vast slabs of chocolate originating from exactly the places they represented. Mighty America would be built from Snickers and Hershey's bars, and Reese's peanut butter cups; Europe would be made of Kit Kats, and After Eights, and gianduia and huge blocks of Lindt and Godiva; Australia would be made of Top Decks. Africa, South America, and Asia would be built from cocoa beans—billions upon billions of them—raw, unprocessed, and glued together with millions of gallons of dark cane-sugar syrup.

Geographical features would be lovingly sculpted from the most appropriate materials. Toblerone triangles would form vast mountain ranges, tipped with white chocolate snow and forested with trees made from chocolate Pixy Sticks and Big Hunk bars. Rivers of chocolate liqueur would flow through boulders of Baci and Ferrero Rocher down to carved chocolate seashores, where oceans of Nutella would lap thick, viscous waves upon cocoa powder beaches. At the poles there would be icebergs and glaciers made from rich white chocolate ice cream. At the equator there would be volcanic springs giving forth geysers of hot drinking chocolate. It would be a beautiful world, rich and soft and sweet, lit by halogen lamps and saved from melting by a refrigerator deep within its core.

. . .

At the moment, and for the next two days, the capital of this chocolate world is New York City. People from all over the planet have convened in this metropolis to attend the International Chocolate Trade Fair, and to sample the vast array of chocolate available in the city. They try everything on offer, from the Sacher torte in Madison Avenue's most exclusive eateries to the sugary sweetness of Betty Crocker's Black Forest gâteau available in all the local delis. They sample the delicacies of the French patisseries in SoHo. They eat chocolate bars from the Korean delis in the East Village and compare the mousses in the Four Seasons with those from Gristede's. It is a three-day orgy of chocolate.

New York has been chosen as the venue for the Trade Fair because it consumes so much. It doesn't matter if the fair is in town or not, chocolate is always here. And it is omnipresent. It takes pride of place in the pantries of the Upper East Side brownstones and in the kitchen closets of the Washington Heights projects. There is chocolate on the lips of vacation lovers. There is chocolate in the hot drinks of cold retirees sipping on oblivion. There is chocolate around the mouths of Park Slope schoolkids, and on the sticky fingers of ten-year-olds selling stolen cell phones to tired commuters outside Pelham Bay Park subway station. There is chocolate in the smiles of brokers at the New York Stock Exchange. There is chocolate in the desk drawers of secretaries, chocolate on the bodies of glamour models posing for top-shelf magazines, chocolate in coffee breaks, chocolate on dinner dates, chocolate in factory cafeterias and on boardroom tables, chocolate in the hands and hearts and mouths of just about everyone who has seventy-five cents to spend on a snack, or fifteen bucks to spend on a few moments of luxury.

The International Chocolate Trade Fair is being held in the Jacob K. Javits Convention Center on the west side of Manhattan. It is 9 a.m., and the fair has just opened up. Hordes of people have braved the April rain to stand in line for the entrance, their umbrellas jostling with one another like octagonal lily pads floating on the surface of the wet city streets. Once through the doors the umbrellas are shaken and folded and wielded like batons by enthusiastic owners eager to fight their way through to the sweet-smelling displays and the smiles of the salespeople at their booths. Near the entrance a restaurateur is arguing with a rather large woman who has flourished her umbrella a little too enthusiastically, scratching his face below his left eye with one of the spokes. He proclaims loudly that a woman like her shouldn't be at the fair. He tells her that with a butt like hers she should steer clear of chocolate altogether.

Farther in, the crowds are calmer, lulled perhaps by the sweet chocolate aroma that fills the building like some sort of invisible fog. Their movements are sluggish. They seep from display to display, drinking in the seemingly unlimited variety of chocolate products: chocolate wedding cakes, chocolate escargots, chocolate tennis rackets, chocolate trees with truffles as fruit and large, sculpted chocolate shavings as leaves. There is even a stall where you can have business cards made from chocolate, and where, for a small fortune, you can have a large slab of chocolate carved into your own portrait.

Farther in still there are the food stands, where the less well-informed parts of the crowd quickly learn that not all chocolate is sweet. Here hapless mothers try to convince hyperactive children to try chocolate curries or mole sauces or black polenta flavored with cocoa. Immigrants from Mexico are happy here. Others are less certain— the more adventurous try samples before buying a full meal, while established chocophiles shy away from the unfamiliar foods, having already gorged themselves on the sweeter products they came here for.

In the middle of the hall, at the very epicenter of the chocolate industry, there is the sculpture of the chocolate universe. Here no one moves at all. They merely gape at the grandeur and the vastness of the giant structures and wonder aloud what the world would be like if it truly were made of chocolate, if everything around them were edible and sweet, if they themselves were made of chocolate—living, breathing chocolate beings with bones made of peanut brittle, muscles made of sponge, and hot fudge sauce flowing through their chocolate veins. At over ten yards tall and almost twenty yards across, it is the largest chocolate sculpture ever made: a colossus that has attracted the attention of newspapers from around the world. As a piece of art it is intriguing; as a piece of engineering it is a marvel. But its greatest success is as a piece of advertising. A rumor is spreading among these people already that at the end of the exhibition the chocolate universe will not merely be dismantled but consumed. Visitors on the last day will be able to break off pieces of the very fabric of the cosmos and take them home: a piece of Pluto, a piece of Orion or the Great Bear or the Crab Nebula. The organizers are expecting a rush for parts of the sculpture of Earth itself. Switzerland and Belgium, they predict, will be the first to go.

. . .

Sitting beside this vast chocolate sculpture is a woman. She is not like the other people here. She has no umbrella. She has no raincoat, and her clothes are unseasonably thin, as if she has been caught off-guard by the weather outside. Her blouse and her light cotton sarong are well made, but very crumpled, as though she has been sleeping in them. At her feet is a small but tightly crammed backpack, at which she glances occasionally to make sure it is still there. She has big blue eyes, but they have the tired look of someone who has been awake for most of the night. Her face has been tanned to the color of light caramel by some far-off sun, and her blond hair bleached to the color of cocoa butter.

She is quite unlike almost everyone else here, but what truly marks her out in the crowd that has congregated at the center of the International Chocolate Trade Fair is that she alone is not marveling at the vast sculpture she sits beside. In fact, she is not even looking at it. She sits with her back to it, as though she finds the very thought of such opulence distasteful.

Opposite this woman, across a short span of empty floor space, a man is watching her. His gaze is not that of a predator, but rather the look of someone accustomed to being bored by his surroundings, who has just caught sight of something unusual. He is standing at one of the larger trade stands, surrounded by posters and leaflets and stacks of big, glossy catalogs. Like all the other men standing around him, he wears a sharp suit and a professional smile, but unlike them he does not look as if he is here to talk to any of the passersby. It is obvious that he does not need to sell his products, that he leaves this to others while he keeps his eyes on the bigger picture. Only today his eyes are *not* on the bigger picture. They are resting on the woman with the backpack, and smiling sadly as if the memory of something dear to him has just entered his mind.

He only gets to look at her for a few short seconds. Suddenly, as if deciding that she has had enough, she lifts her bag from the ground and swings it onto her shoulders. As she stands up, her eyes lock with those of the man at the stand, just for a moment, but then both of them look away to other, more inconsequential things. It is embarrassing to hold the eyes of a stranger for too long. It implies intent. It implies commitment.

When the man at the booth looks back, she has disappeared. In her absence, all that is left is the sculpture. Somehow it looks incomplete now that she is gone—less impressive, less marvelous. The crowds of openmouthed tourists move on and are replaced by new ones. Fresh blocks of chocolate are consumed. New candy wrappers are discarded and trampled into the exhibition hall's floor. The man at the stand turns back to the group of colleagues who surround him and forgets that the woman was ever there.

Before him, the sculpture continues to draw the crowds. A group of New Jersey schoolkids wander past and take photographs, and their teacher smiles, because he knows that their cameras are not equipped with good enough lenses to fit the whole sculpture into one picture. At best they will come away with mere details, or panoramas they will have to piece together like jigsaws later. None of them will show the chocolate universe as it really is, and the full grandeur of the piece will be lost.

Chapter two

Samantha Blackwood gathered her things and got ready to go. She couldn't wait for Paul much longer—she needed to get out of here. Something about this place was oppressive. It was too big, too overwhelming, and compared with what she had just seen in Africa, the excess of the place, the pure gluttony of it all, was absolutely terrifying.

There were children here—fat, whining children—begging their parents to buy them chocolates that cost more than the average West African family's entire weekly income. She watched them. The ones who didn't get what they wanted threw tantrums, as if being denied something that was absolutely essential to their existence. In the end they all got what they screamed for. There were kids eating enormous chocolate bars everywhere she looked. She saw one girl tease her brother so mercilessly that *she* had a chocolate bar while *he* didn't that Sam almost applauded when the boy thumped her. He didn't manage to get a piece of his sister's chocolate though—his parents intervened too soon for that—and he was forced to watch as the girl ostentatiously licked it in front of him.

The adults were just as bad. Some people here spending literally hundreds of dollars on chocolates, as if doing so were the most natural thing in the world. She had seen one man buy a gigantic Toblerone, so large that he had been unable to carry it and was forced to ask the people at the booth to arrange for it to be delivered. She had also passed an ADULTS ONLY stall, where she had seen a couple laughing nervously over one of the chocolate "novelty" items: a large chocolate penis sculpted to look uncannily like the real thing. The saleswoman was giving them some bullshit about how she had modeled it herself by hand, and how chocolate was the most sensual material for a sculptor to work with. Sam had watched in amazement as the man handed over seventy-five bucks to the saleswoman, while his girlfriend continued to giggle sensuously. *Seventy-five* bucks! As if the same effect could not be bought for the price of a king-size Mars bar.

At times in the past she might have laughed at behavior like this, but this morning she was too tired to find it anything but repugnant. After three weeks filming conditions on African cocoa plantations the sheer indulgence of a place like this was difficult to take. The only reason she and Paul had come here at all was to see if it would be worth filming tomorrow, and they had ascertained that almost immediately. Images of Americans guzzling chocolates, images of Western kids whining for more candy, and the hideous opulence of the sculpture that was the centerpiece of the whole fair—all these would make great footage when placed next to the poverty and child slavery they had filmed in Africa. But that would be tomorrow. Right now she needed to get out of here.

She'd only just got off the plane from the Côte d'Ivoire a couple of hours ago. She needed to get home and catch up on some sleep.

.   .   .

Reaching into her pocketbook, she pulled out her cell and dialed Paul's number. He was over ten minutes late now, and Sam knew that if she didn't call him, she could be waiting here all morning. He was probably so caught up in the spectacle of this place that he'd forgotten all about her.

She sat there, listening to his line ringing, trying not to be annoyed with him. She was beginning to think it had been a mistake to get involved with Paul. It was all very romantic while they were thousands of miles away, but now that they were back in New York, things were different. The old boundaries were already beginning to reassert themselves. She had felt it on the airplane home: a tightening in the way they spoke to one another—a return to the same stilted conversations about work that had made her feel so uncomfortable on the way out. It would be easy to blame it all on him, but she was just as bad. She was closing up, just as she knew she would, sooner or later.

When he finally answered the phone, she hesitated a second before saying, "Hello? Paul, where are you?"

"Near the Nestlé stand. I've just spoken to the marketing guy there —he's agreed to give us an interview next week."

"Oh," said Sam, "great."

Paul began to babble. "This place is an absolute gold mine, Sam! Every chocolate company in the world must be here. Some of the displays are incredible. I've been taking some footage with the digital camera, and the shots I'm getting are amazing. I can't wait to get the crew here tomorrow."

"You're *filming?*"

"Yeah."

"But I thought we were only scouting the place out. You were supposed to meet me back at the sculpture"—she looked at her watch—"fifteen minutes ago."

"I know. I'm sorry, I got sidetracked."

Sam let out a deep sigh. She knew something like this would happen. "Can't we leave the filming to Mark, tomorrow? He is the professional, after all." She paused. "And anyway, this is our last day together."

"Don't be silly—we'll be seeing each other tomorrow."

"That's not the same and you know it."

The other end was silent for a moment, and Sam had the feeling that she had stepped over some hidden line. "Listen," said Paul, "all I'm doing is getting a little extra footage, just in case. At the very worst it'll be good to show to Mark, so he knows what kind of thing I have in mind. Why don't you come and join me while I'm finishing up?"

"I don't know, Paul. I'm tired. I need to go home."

"I'll be done in a half hour. An hour at most."

"Yeah, right. I've heard that before."

"Honestly. Just one hour. And then we can go back to my place."

Sam hesitated once again, before saying, decisively, "No, I think I should just leave you to it."

"Well, if you're sure . . ."

"I'm sure. You go and do your filming. I'll see you tomorrow."

She switched off her phone and sat for a few moments, staring out into the mass of chocolate stands. From this angle it looked like some sort of upscale shantytown, a parody of the markets and villages she had come across in West Africa. There were the same market stalls, the same bright colors, and logos—logos everywhere. Somewhere in among all this, Paul was switching on his digital camera. She could just imagine him, zooming in on some display of chocolates with all the intensity of a freshman film student. He'd probably forgotten about her already.

Perhaps it was her imagination, but she was sure she had heard a note of relief in his voice when she had said she was going home. It wasn't surprising, she supposed. They had spent the last three weeks virtually in each other's pockets—eating together, sleeping together, spending twenty-four hours a day in each other's company. To begin with, this had been partly for Sam's safety—West Africa was no place for a white woman to go wandering around alone. It was also part of their cover: they were pretending to be tourists, husband and wife, dumb choco-holics making a pilgrimage to the plantations where their object of desire was first grown. But after a while she had grown used to Paul's constant company. And since they were sharing rooms, and even occasionally beds, getting together for real had seemed like only a small step.

She should have known that things would look different in the sharp electric lights of Gotham—not just to him, but to her as well. She would have been kidding herself if she didn't acknowledge that she too felt relieved to be on her own once more.

She took one last look around the hall. The kids she had been watching earlier were fighting again, and their father, losing patience, had started shouting at them. A group of students had just entered the hall and were staring at the sculpture behind her. Some of them started taking photographs. It was time to go.

It was just then, as she was reaching down to take hold of her backpack, that she caught sight of a face in the crowd. It was a man's face. Unlike most of the other people here, he wasn't smiling—in fact, his face was pretty expressionless—peaceful, and perhaps a little sad. He was standing at one of the trade stands, surrounded by grinning colleagues, who all looked as though they were about to congratulate him on something, but he didn't look as though he felt like being congratulated at all. It was a strange sight and didn't seem to belong with all the other things that were going on in the hall.

Sam got the impression that the man had been gazing at her for a while—but as soon as she caught his eye, he turned away, embarrassed. She stood for a second longer, waiting to see if he would turn back. He was a good-looking guy, in an olive-colored suit. He had really been *staring* at her. For some reason she found herself wondering why Paul had never looked at her like this—but the thought made her feel slightly anxious, so she pushed it quickly from her mind.

Turning away from the man, she began walking purposefully toward the exit, and a few moments later as she stepped out onto Eleventh Avenue, she had forgotten him altogether.

Chapter three

Earlier in the day, before the International Chocolate Trade Fair opened to the public, the exhibition hall at Jacob K. Javits Convention Center was already buzzing. Most companies started setting up their booths at around six, just as Sam's flight from the Côte d'Ivoire was coming in to land at Kennedy airport. By the time Sam was standing in line at passport control, the world's entire population of chocolate PR people was gathered in the exhibition hall, putting up posters and making the last alterations to the displays of each of the stands across the floor. Promotional catalogs were being stacked on tabletops. Boxes of samples were opened and their contents arranged in elaborate displays. Salesmen tightened their ties, saleswomen applied their lipstick, and smiles everywhere became polished and professional.

The Trundel & Barr stand was in the center of the hall, close to the sculpture of the chocolate universe. It was built in the shape of a crescent and painted almost entirely in gold and red—the T&B colors. At one end of the crescent was a store, selling the full range of T&B chocolate goods, and there was also a row of printed boards that explained the history of the company and described the chocolate-making process at its factory outside Baltimore, Maryland. At the other end of the crescent was a meeting area. And in the center, suspended several feet above the ground, there was an enormous map of the world molded out of T&B milk chocolate. Apart from the brightness of the colors, it was this chocolate map that most caught the eye—it was a deliberate attempt to mirror the sculpture that was the centerpiece of the fair. The message was simple. In the chocolate universe, Trundel & Barr was not only a large and relatively important satellite, it was also a world all of its own.

. . .

As the doors of the exhibition hall finally opened, and the crowds (Sam among them) swarmed into the center of the fair, a group of five or six people gathered at the front of the T&B booth. They obviously all knew each other—they were smiling, and making jokes about a man in their midst. This man was the center of their attention. He was wearing an expensive olive-colored suit, and unlike any of the others he had a frown on his face.

"No," he said, with the firmness of someone who is fed up with being asked, "I'm not doing it."

"Go on, Matt," his colleague Grant was saying, "we could do with something to get us in the mood."

"I don't want to," said Matt firmly.

"You did it last year," said Claire, another colleague.

"And the year before that," said Grant.

"It'll entertain us all while we wait for the stand to get busy."

Matt Dyson looked at the group that had gathered around him with amazement. "Jesus, this is like being back at high school. I told you, I'm not doing it. I'm not in the mood."

"But you *have* to do it," tried Phil, T&B's corpulent sales director, "it's a tradition at the trade fairs now."

A few more people came over at this point, to find out what all the excitement was about. Among them were Jo and Andrea, two MBA students who had agreed to help out with the booth as interns. Jo, the more attractive of the two, sat on the edge of the table halfway between Phil and Matt.

"What are you talking about?" she said. "What's a tradition?"

Phil motioned toward Matt. "This man is an utter genius. You can point out anybody in this place, and he'll be able to tell you exactly what chocolate they buy."

"Come on, give me a break," said Matt.

"In fact, not only can he tell you what chocolate they buy, he can tell you everything about them—what newspapers they read, what they have for breakfast in the mornings—everything. It's incredible. He's like a mind reader. Every year we pick out a few people in the crowd and get him to tell us about them. He has to guess what chocolate they'll buy, and if he gets it wrong, he has to buy us all a drink. He never gets it wrong."

"That sounds like a very impressive skill," said Jo, turning to smile at Matt. "How do you do it?"

Matt looked into her eyes. She was an extraordinarily pretty woman. She had the sort of beauty that hit you instantly—all shiny blond hair, flawless teeth, and long, perfect legs.

Her eyes held his own for a second, before flicking down to his mouth and back up again. She was flirting with him! Thirty seconds she had been here, and already she was flirting with him. He responded automatically, as he knew he would, by showing off.

"It's a knack," he said, smiling a deliberately modest smile. "It's just a matter of paying attention. Anyone can do it . . ."

"Not like you they can't," said Phil. "Don't be fooled by his modesty, Jo. All our most successful products are down to this guy. He knows what people want. I tell you, it's uncanny how much he can tell about people just by looking at them. It's like he's got a direct line into people's souls."

Jo smiled and crossed her legs. "And you can do this with anyone?"

"Well," said Matt, "pretty much anyone, yes."

"Go on," said Phil, "test him out. Pick someone in the crowd. Anyone you like."

Jo turned away, almost reluctantly, and looked out across the floor full of chocolate shoppers. The whole group waited expectantly for her to make her choice. Finally she pointed out a man in a Burberry jacket, who was dragging a bored-looking five-year-old son behind him. "How about him?" she said.

"Here we go!" said someone in the group.

"Pay attention, girls," said Phil to Jo and Andrea. "You're about to get an education."

Matt watched the man in the Burberry jacket for a few moments as he marched across the floor. There was something peculiarly determined about his stride, unlike the reluctant steps of his son, who was lagging behind him at arm's length.

"Well," Matt said, "he's certainly on a mission. Look at the way he's walking. There's something single-minded about him, as if he knows exactly what he wants. His son is looking over at us—*he* wants to try our chocolate, just like all his friends at school do. But his dad's not interested in what his son wants. He's not here to indulge his son, he's here to educate him."

Matt paused for a second to watch the way the man pushed his glasses back onto the bridge of his nose: they weren't designer glasses —they were functional, solid. Matt noticed for the first time that the man was carrying a newspaper and a whole stack of leaflets in his free hand.

"I think he works in the media," Matt continued, "possibly publishing. The most important thing in life to him is *knowing things,* and he wants his son to know things too. When the boy's older, his dad will educate him about wine, and about food and art and music. But since he's only five, he's going to start him off with chocolate. He wants to show him that there's more to life than Snickers bars. He wants to give him something made by Lindt. Or maybe something really exclusive. Valrhona! That's where he's going. The Valrhona stall."

While Matt had been talking, they had all been watching the man and his son. There was a large group of them now, all waiting to see if Matt was right. Sure enough, the man in the Burberry jacket walked straight to the Valrhona stall and started talking to the sales attendant there.

"Amazing!" said Andrea, Jo's less attractive friend.

"That's my boy!" said Phil, the sales director, slapping Matt firmly on the back.

"Okay, okay," said Jo, obviously a little put out, "I've got another one. How about . . . *her.*" She pointed to a woman by the enormous sculpture in front of them.

Matt looked at her. She was in her thirties. She was wearing pink leggings and a light plastic raincoat. She was slightly overweight, alone, and a little desperate-looking.

"Right," he said. "I can tell all kinds of things about this woman. She works in an office, probably as a secretary or as someone's assistant. She is constantly overlooked for promotion despite being far more competent than the people she works for. She probably drinks chardonnay because it's the only wine she knows the name of. She doesn't read newspapers, but loves magazines, and has a whole stack of them at home because she can't bring herself to throw them away after she's read them. She buys *Billboard* chart music—her favorite singer is Norah Jones—and occasionally she ventures into a bookstore to buy something pink off one of the front tables. When it comes to chocolates, I'd say she goes for a combination of quantity and quality—she won't waste money on Lindt or Valrhona, but chocolate is definitely one of her treats in life. I reckon she'll go for one of the top to midrange assortments—something like Godiva. And she won't stop until she's finished the box in one sitting."

They all watched, as the woman reached into her shoulder bag and pulled out a small, gold cardboard box.

"Is that a Godiva box?" said someone behind Matt.

"I don't know, but it's definitely an assortment."

"Jesus, look at her go!"

The woman was stuffing the chocolates in her mouth one by one, until her mouth was so full she couldn't even chew. A couple of Matt's colleagues cheered.

"What did I say, girls?" said Phil. "This man can read people like a book."

Jo looked up at him with her big brown eyes. "That's unnerving," she said with a pout. "Can you tell as much about me?"

Matt looked down at her perfectly manicured nails, and the way she tapped them restlessly against the tabletop. "Maybe not quite as much," he said, and held her eye for as long as he could without feeling uncomfortable—which in the end turned out to be not very long at all.

"Do another one!" shouted one of the people at the back of the group.

Matt laughed and looked at his crowd of colleagues. "Don't you all have meetings to go to?"

"Just one more?"

"I've got one for you," said the less attractive Andrea. "That woman there, the one on the other end of the bench, talking into her cell phone."

Matt turned and looked over to where Samantha Blackwood was sitting. "No," he said instinctively, "I've done enough for one morning."

Protests rang out all around.

"What's the matter?" said Jo. "Don't you think you can make it three in a row?"

He took a deep breath. "Okay," he said, "but this is the last . . ."

He turned back to the woman on the bench. She had put her cell away now, and was looking around the hall. She didn't look like anyone else at the fair. To start with, she wasn't dressed for a day out at a chocolate fair—she was wearing a sarong and carrying a backpack and looked as if she'd be more at home in a youth hostel in Bali than at a trade fair. And yet, something about her seemed too groomed, too sharply focused for a hippie traveler. Unlike everyone else here she looked totally uninterested in any of the products. She didn't appear to be taken in by the glitz. In fact, she was not really looking at the products at all, but seemed to be doing exactly as he was doing—people-watching. For a second it crossed his mind that she might be a trend-spotter for another chocolate company, someone employed to observe the habits of shoppers and report on how better to lure them into buying their products. But then why the backpack? Why the sarong, when it was a wet, cold day outside?

"Well?" said Jo expectantly.

Matt hesitated. "Right . . . well, she's . . . she's . . ." He couldn't think of anything to say.

"Don't tell me she's got you stumped!" said Phil. "I never thought I'd see the day!"

"Give me a chance," said Matt, irritated.

At this point the woman stood up and slung her backpack over her shoulder. As she did so, her eyes locked with Matt's for a few seconds. Cold blue eyes—eyes that were not amused. Embarrassed, he turned away.

"The champion is defeated!" said Phil, ruffling Matt's hair. "Well done, Andrea. No one's ever managed to do that before."

Gradually the crowd of Matt's colleagues dispersed and went back to their duties. Some customers came to the stall, so Jo and Andrea suddenly found themselves busy, and Matt was left alone.

He turned back toward the bench by the sculpture, but the woman was gone. He returned to scanning the crowds, particularly the people gathered around the other end of the Trundel & Barr stand, but for some reason he no longer felt comfortable. He couldn't quite put his finger on what it was—perhaps he simply didn't like having found himself so easily at a loss—but something was definitely wrong here now. Something, somehow, had been spoiled.

• • •

Later on that morning, he wandered over to the bench where the woman had been sitting. Turning his back to the chocolate sculpture, just as she had done, he sat down. It was strange looking at the fair from this angle. He was used to sitting inside his booth looking out—now, with the positions reversed, he could see what the customers saw, and it didn't exactly inspire him. There were stands as far as he could see— temporary structures, designed so that they could be put up and taken down with the minimum of effort, all of them brightly colored, all of them shiny. And there, right at the front of them all, was his own stand: Trundel & Barr.

He sat for a few minutes, looking, before he noticed one of the MBA students walking past him. It was Andrea; she was obviously on a coffee break.

"Andrea," he called as she walked past, "are you busy?"

The girl looked at her watch. "Not for the next five minutes."

"Can you come out here for a second? I've got something to ask you."

Andrea stepped over to the bench and joined him.

"Look at our booth," he said. "What do you see?"

Andrea sat down alongside him and contemplated the Trundel & Barr stall for a few moments. She was a large woman—not fat exactly, just buxom—and since Matt was positioned in the middle of the bench, she was forced to sit quite close. He thought of moving up to give her more room, but hesitated just too long, then decided that moving up now would only draw attention to their proximity. It was better to try to ignore it.

"Well," she said thoughtfully, "first of all I see the T and B colors, which really stand out. Then I see the map of the world, and the counter down the other end with all the displays. I also see lots of people buying our chocolates down there, which is a good sign. And then I see the names of our products along the top. All in all I'd say it was a pretty good exercise in branding. Beats the other stands here hands down."

Matt nodded, then folded his arms. "You don't think it looks a little . . ." He thought for a second. "I don't know . . . cheesy?"

"It looks mass-market, if that's what you mean."

"Exactly!" Matt smiled. "You've hit the nail on the head. It looks mass-market!"

"Is that bad?"

"No. It's not bad. It's just, well, good to remember occasionally, I suppose. You can't please all of the people all of the time."

He could feel his arm pressed against hers, and the feeling made beads of sweat break out across his forehead. He didn't know what was wrong with him today—he was acting like a horny teenager. Perhaps it was just the buildup of anticipation: he had been preparing for today for over three weeks now, and it seemed somehow wrong that the day should not be marked by something big, something momentous.

"You know," said Andrea, "what you did earlier was very impressive. I mean, I know you didn't have a chance to do that last woman, but even so . . . How do you do it?"

"I told you at the time, it's just a knack. I'm a marketer. It's my job."

"I've worked with other marketers, and I've never seen anyone else who can do that."

"Well," said Matt, "perhaps they haven't been marketing as long as I have. I've been doing it since I was a child. It's what I've always done. Ask me any advertising slogan from the 1970s onward, and I can tell you those too. And when it comes to chocolate, I can tell you the history of just about every company in the world."

The girl looked at him curiously, then glanced at her watch. "I should get back. My break's over."

She smiled hesitantly before standing up and turning to walk back to the booth. Matt watched her for a moment. She might not be as attractive as her friend, but she had a definite wiggle to her walk that was kind of sexy.

"Andrea," he called after her, "look, I was wondering what you were doing this evening. It seems a shame just to go straight home after work, and I was thinking . . . well, do you want to have dinner with me?"

She stood there looking back at him, an uncomfortable expression on her face. "I can't really. I mean . . . I have a boyfriend."

"Of course you do," said Matt sadly as she walked back to the stand. "Of course."

Chapter four

New things do not stay new forever. In marketing terms nothing is worse than a long, lingering death: it is better to kill something off with a bang while it's still fresh in people's minds. At least that way you might make the headlines.

On the last day of the International Chocolate Trade Fair, in the afternoon, the organizers announced over the loudspeakers that the enormous sculpture in the center of the exhibition hall would not be packed away at the end. Instead, anyone who wanted to could break a piece off and take it home. As a souvenir.

At first there was no reaction in the crowd. One or two of the people who had been admiring the sculpture sighed sadly and remarked that it was a shame that something like this could not be given a permanent home. Most of the kids in the hall merely looked around at their parents, refusing to believe that they were even allowed to go near the chocolate universe. There was a low fence all around it, and signs telling you to keep clear.

Only when one of the women in the crowd stepped across this fence did the rest of them begin to move toward the sculpture, slowly at first, and then in a huge rush. Parents and children alike hurried forward to see if they could get their hands on the best parts, either to take home as trophies or to gobble down, there and then, while they tried to pocket more.

The first countries on the chocolate globe to go were Switzerland and Belgium; then went Italy and France and Germany and the rest of Europe. America was popular with children, who were delighted that they could break off such enormous chunks intact. Despite being the most beautifully sculpted, most of the southern hemisphere was discarded as people scrambled upward to the north of the chocolate world. The more ambitious reached literally for the stars, clambering onto each other's shoulders to pluck the tiny foil-covered Kisses from the sky. One teenager grabbed hold of Jupiter and brought it tumbling onto the exhibition hall floor—a scramble quickly developed to salvage all the chocolate possible before the remainder was trampled into the floor and left to melt into a sticky brown mess, punctuated by the occasional glacé cherry.

Once the crowd finished, virtually nothing was left. The universe had literally been consumed. A few Matchmakers lay uneaten at the back of the stand that used to support the sculpture. A pool of melted white chocolate marked the place where Antarctica used to sit, and pieces of Saturn had been crushed into the bench where Sam had sat down on the first morning of the fair.

Soon after the fair closed, even these tiny remnants disappeared, swept up by the cleaners and taken away along with all the debris from the trade stands: crumpled leaflets, order forms and business cards, empty food containers and discarded chocolate wrappers. By nine o'clock that evening, after the stands had been dismantled and everyone had gone home, even the one or two mice that scurried out into the hall under the cover of darkness were unable to find a single morsel. The chocolate universe had gone, as completely as if it had never existed.

Free

The production of chocolate is essentially violent. It begins with the cocoa pod being sliced from the tree with a machete and smashed open with a wooden club. Then its beans are ripped out and left to ferment in a pile of cocoa pulp. After a few days these beans are dried and sent thousands of miles across land and sea to factories in the West. There they are broken, alkalized, roasted at a temperature of 250°F, and ground to fine powder. This powder is then shoved into a press where it is squeezed until most of the fat is squashed out of it. Afterward it is crushed once again with various other ingredients and sent through vast spinning machines to an enormous tank, where a giant granite roller breaks the mixture down even further until each remaining particle is a mere hundredth of a millimeter in size.

What is left at the end of all this cutting, smashing, roasting, and crushing is almost unrecognizable from the humble plant that started the process, growing in the shade of the cocoa plantations. For most of its journey, the bruised and battered cocoa has been bitter, acidic, and unpleasant. But somehow, at the very end, something magical is released—like a genie being set free from its bottle—and what began as a mere handful of beans is transformed into the deep, smooth majesty of one of the world's richest foods.

Chapter five

It was Monday morning, and Sam was sitting by the telephone in her hallway feeling uneasy. There were two moments in life when you were supposed to tell your best friend *everything*, without leaving out any details: the moment when you first got together with a man, and the moment when you split up with him. It was so easy to be dishonest about what happened in between (and God knows she'd lied enough about that in the past); but the beginning and the end—the alpha and omega of relationships, when things were too new or too old for there to be anything to lose—*that* was not to be withheld.

When she'd called Rachel just now she had fully intended to tell her all about Paul. She had envisaged one of those conversations you saw in Hollywood teen movies—two girls, each in impossibly pink bedrooms, sharing every detail of a vacation romance over the phone with squeals of "No! . . . You *didn't!* . . . And what happened next?" But even when she was a teenager, Sam had never really acted like that. And after what had happened with Cameron last year, she had lost her enthusiasm for gossiping about her love life. So in the end she had said nothing.

Even when Rachel had asked after Paul directly, Sam had avoided the issue. "Paul?" she'd said innocently. "Oh, he's away in New Orleans, filming at a chocolate company there. So I'm free all day. Maybe we could meet up for lunch . . . ?"

She hadn't lied, exactly—just avoided telling the whole truth. But even so, it left her feeling dishonest, as if she had something to hide.

. . .

Sam had known Rachel since she was thirteen. They had been friends since a time before boyfriends, when the two of them were still blank slates, with no messy breakups behind them, no expectations of disappointment, and no biological clocks counting up the years lost by every squandered opportunity. In those days they cared more about their test scores than they ever did about boys. Love, romance, sex—all of these were merely rumblings on a distant horizon—something they noticed and even talked about occasionally, but never seriously believed was coming their way.

They were in the same class at high school, but their friendship had only really grown because of Sam's family problems. Her parents used to have regular fights, and since Rachel lived on the same block, Sam used to retreat to the safety of her friend's house until things calmed down. They would do their homework together and gossip about their schoolmates, and hot lead singers, and TV shows—anything to fill the time until it was safe to go home. Sometimes Sam would even stay over. If her parents were ever anxious about where she was, they never showed it—they were too involved in their own problems to worry about her.

Sam never told Rachel about the things her father said and did to her, but she had the feeling that Rachel knew about them instinctively. She was less taciturn about the way her father treated her mother. She would sit up at night on Rachel's bed and describe the way he undermined her mom at every opportunity, criticizing her endlessly, and shouted at her with such bitterness that it made Sam wonder how they had ever gotten together in the first place. And then she would hold Rachel's hand and vow that she would never get married as long as she lived, because she didn't want to end up like her mother.

In the following years Sam and Rachel became inseparable. The boys at school used to joke that they were like Siamese twins—you couldn't date one without the other also tagging along. It was an exaggeration, of course—they both knew exactly when to make themselves scarce, and when to hang around and make a nuisance of themselves—but there was an element of truth about it too. Sam could get very jealous when her friend spent time with someone else. It didn't matter if it was a boy or a girl—seeing Rachel talking and joking with another person could send her into such a sulk it frightened her. Once she had even struck out at a girl called Kirsty, simply because Kirsty and Rachel had gone shopping together without asking Sam along too. She apologized later, and all was forgiven—but even so her jealousy still scared her. Rachel was the only person who had ever shown she cared about her. She couldn't bear the thought of losing her to anyone else.

At the time Sam had dreaded to think what it would be like when Rachel finally found a boyfriend. Sometimes she even dared to say as much—or at least hint at it—but her friend always dismissed the possibility with a frown. "Don't be stupid," she'd say, *"you'll* have a boyfriend long before I ever will." And Sam would laugh and pretend to be reassured, when in fact she found her friend's reaction confusing.

One afternoon, after a similar conversation, she asked Rachel what she meant by this. It was the beginning of summer vacation, and they were sitting in Rachel's bedroom, bathed in bright, sharp sunshine, and listening to the music charts on a portable radio. The radio DJ was just beginning the countdown to the number one record. Through the door, at the other end of the apartment, Rachel's mom was dusting the family photographs that she kept on a table by the entrance to the living room.

"Why do you always say that?" Sam said. "Why do you think that I'll have a boyfriend before you?"

"Because you will."

"But why?"

"Just look at you. You're much prettier than me. And you're . . . you know." Rachel sighed and glanced down at Sam's body. "All the boys talk about you. You could probably have any boy in our class. Or the class above."

"But I don't *want* a boyfriend." She looked anxiously down at her body. She still felt awkward, and gangly, but she knew that her figure was more developed than that of any of the other girls in her class, and she could already pass for someone at least three years older. It felt like an impossible burden. While all the other girls seemed to be straining toward adulthood, bragging about their periods and their new bras, Sam desperately wanted the process to stop, or at least slow down.

They lay there for a while on Rachel's bed, listening to the music on the radio—love song after love song, drifting through the sunshine. It was Sam who spoke again first.

"Why do people fall in love?"

"I don't know," said Rachel. "So they can get married, I suppose. And have kids."

"Doesn't seem like much of a reason to me. You can do all that without being in love. Look at my parents."

"But people *like* being in love. That's what everyone wants."

"Not me," said Sam. "When I grow up, I want to be free. I don't want to end up stuck to a man just because I once fell in love with him."

At the other end of the apartment Rachel's mom was working her way slowly from one photograph to another, wiping off the dust with a dry cloth. Sam turned on her side so that she could watch her, wishing with all her heart that her own mother could be so solid, so patient, so utterly and beautifully normal.

. . .

Almost twenty years later, Rachel was still Sam's touchstone with normality. Rachel had normal parents, who didn't fight, and who allowed her to get on with her life without criticizing her all the time. She had a normal average job, and a normal average home. Even her partner was normal and average—Andy was a responsible, devoted husband whose only real quirk was an unhealthy interest in baseball stats. It hadn't surprised Sam when her friend had got married soon after her thirtieth birthday—that was the normal way of doing things. And now Rachel was pregnant, just as any newlywed should be. She was one of those people who did everything the way it was supposed to be done, and who seemed to exist in harmony with everything around her. Sam envied her the beautiful regularity of her life.

They had arranged to meet at a restaurant in Midtown. Rachel had been feeding Sam's cat while she was away, so Sam had offered to buy her lunch as a way of saying thank you. It was a good excuse to spend some time together and catch up on news.

Her friend was already at the restaurant when Sam got there: she was sitting in a seat by the window, sipping a glass of seltzer water, looking big and round and radiant.

"Look at you!" said Sam, gazing down at her pregnant belly. "You look fantastic!"

Rachel beamed and rested her hands on either side of her bump. "Thanks. Apparently the pregnant look is in this season."

Sam sat down opposite and smiled warmly across the table at her friend. She couldn't take her eyes off her belly. It was so *big*. It was so *there*. "I can't believe how much you've grown in the last month! Last time I saw you, you were like a beanpole."

"Okay, you skinny bitch," said Rachel, grinning, "a little less of the belly talk, please. And if you start asking me about whether we've thought of any names for the child yet, I'm out of here. I've had the same conversation every day for weeks, and it's beginning to drive me nuts."

Sam held up her hands. "Fine by me!"

"I don't want to talk about childbirth, breast-feeding, diapers, breathing techniques, or even those cute little baby clothes that make them look like tiny little adults." Rachel listed each item on her fingers as she spoke. "In fact, if you can steer the conversation away from babies altogether, you'll be a friend for life."

Sam laughed. "Perhaps it would make it easier if you told me what you *do* want to talk about."

"I want to talk about you, of course! I want to hear all about Africa. What was it like?"

"Interesting." Sam blushed and thought immediately of Paul. "Interesting in all kinds of ways."

"Sounds like you have some stories to tell me!"

"I can do better than that." Sam reached into her shoulder bag and pulled out a small pack of pictures. "Photographic evidence!" She handed the pack over to her friend.

For the next few minutes they went through Sam's pictures, talking excitedly about her trip. Most of the photos were of conditions in the cocoa plantations, although Sam had removed some of the more gruesome shots before coming—pictures of prison cells and mistreated children—because she didn't think they were appropriate for a light-hearted lunch date with her pregnant friend. But there were also some snapshots of the jungle and the beaches and the sunsets. And, occasionally, one of Paul.

She was wondering if now would be a good time to mention what had happened between them, but before she could decide, they were interrupted by the arrival of the waiter. Rachel already knew what she wanted, so Sam was forced to put her pack of photographs down and pick something at random from the menu. By the time she had chosen, the will to divulge her secret had evaporated.

"Oh," said Rachel, "before I forget . . ." She delved into her coat pocket and pulled out the spare keys to Sam's apartment.

"Thanks," said Sam. "How was it? I hope my cat didn't give you any trouble?"

"She was fine. But you'll never guess who came around while I was feeding her . . ."

"Who?"

"Your mother. I was just about to go when she rang the doorbell. It was handy actually. I'm not supposed to go near cat shit, so I managed to convince her to change Cleo's litter tray for me. But she really didn't want to. You should have seen the look on her face."

Sam could easily imagine it. She had seen that look on her mother's face a thousand times: scornful, disapproving, but also faintly pathetic, as if a part of her truly believed that clearing up after someone else was all she was good for.

Sam let her friend continue for a time, before finally interrupting her. "What did she want?" she said bluntly.

"I'm not really sure. Just to see you, I suppose. She seemed . . . upset."

"My mother is *always* upset. More to the point, she's always upset *with me*. It's a perfect way for her to ignore her own problems."

"Yeah," said Rachel, "well, that's mothers for you."

"But not all mothers are married to people like my dad. She only ever comes to see me when they've had a fight. It's like she wants me to make it all better somehow." Sam stopped, suddenly aware that she was raising her voice, and took a deep breath.

"Actually," said Rachel, "now I come to think about it, I reckon she was probably just worried about you."

"Worried? Why?"

"Well, she said she'd called you a couple of times, but you hadn't answered. I don't think she knew you were away."

"Oh. Oh, dear . . ."

"Didn't you tell her?"

"I didn't want to worry her. You know how she gets if I ever go anywhere she thinks is dangerous." Sam sighed resentfully. "I suppose I'd better phone her."

They paused for a moment while the waiter brought Sam a glass of wine. He glanced at the two of them as he refilled Rachel's glass, smiling indulgently at her bulge.

"So," said Sam, once he had gone, "what did you talk about? I suppose she questioned you all about me?"

"No more than any mother would have done."

"And I suppose she wanted to know your opinion on why I don't have a man?"

Her friend grinned sympathetically. "She might just have *touched* on that."

"Jesus, the woman is a nightmare!"

"She didn't seem like she was prying, Sam, she was just concerned, that's all. She *is* your mother after all—that's her job."

Sam didn't want to argue, so instead she tried to make a joke out of it. "Gee, Rachel, anyone would think you're about to become a mother yourself."

Rachel took a sip of her drink and looked across the table at Sam. "It's not the sort of thing I'd normally say, but maybe your mum's got a point. It would be nice to see you with a boyfriend again: it might restore your faith in human nature a little. They're not all like Cameron, you know."

"That's easy for you to say," said Sam, nodding down at her friend's bump.

"Well, it's true."

"And anyway," said Sam recklessly, "who's to say I haven't got my eye on someone already?"

"Oh, yes?"

"I might do."

Rachel's face broke out into a broad smile. "Tell me more! Is it someone I know?"

"No," said Sam flatly.

"Oh, come on! You can't just drop something like that and expect me not to want to know all about it. Who is he? What's his name?"

Sam hesitated. "I can show you a picture if you like . . ." She picked up the pack of photos again and flicked through them until she found one of Paul. "It's the guy I went to Africa with. The one who's the director of the documentary."

"Your director? Isn't that a bit like sleeping with your boss?"

"I'm freelance. I don't have a boss."

She handed the picture to her friend and watched anxiously as Rachel looked at it. Almost immediately she regretted not picking out a more attractive one. Paul looked a little dull here. He was standing outside a government office in Abidjan, with an expression on his face that was just a little too intense.

"So what's the story?" said Rachel. "Did he take advantage of you?"

"Not exactly . . ."

"Ah, I see! So *you* took advantage of *him*."

"No! It just sort of happened, that's all. I mean, we were sharing bedrooms occasionally anyway. And most of the rooms only had double beds. And since we were pretending to be married when we went to the plantations—well, things just sort of fell into place."

"*Very* convenient."

"Yes," said Sam. "Like you say—convenient."

She forced a smile. Even to her own ears she didn't sound enthusiastic. In the past she would have gushed forth with all the details about what she thought of him, how they'd gotten together—that's what she'd done with Cameron—but for some reason today she simply didn't feel like it.

Her friend seemed to sense something was wrong. She was looking at her with a worried expression on her face. "Are you sure about this, Sam?"

"Of course. Why not? *You're* the one who says I should get myself a boyfriend."

"Yes, but you've got to work with this guy. What happens if it goes wrong? And anyway, I thought you said before you went away that he was a . . . workaholic."

"Well, he's not exactly perfect, if that's what you mean," said Sam.

"But he's a nice guy. And we get on well with each other. We've just spent three weeks together without arguing once."

She paused for a second, trying to think of something else nice to say about Paul, and she noticed that Rachel was still looking skeptical. All of a sudden Sam felt uncomfortable, and more than a little foolish.

"Look," she said frustratedly, "if I hang around for the perfect man, I could be waiting forever. At least he's single, which is more than I can say for most of the men I meet. And he's in the industry, so he'll understand if I have to work long hours. He's right for me in lots of ways."

Rachel's face softened. "Well . . . good for you, Sam," she said at last.

But Sam could tell she didn't really mean it.

•   •   •

After a while their food arrived. For the rest of the meal they talked about Rachel and her pregnancy. For all her protestations earlier, Rachel seemed more than happy to speak of childbirth *and* breathing techniques *and* names for the baby. When she talked about seeing the scan of her child for the first time, her face lit up in a way that made Sam's heart want to burst. But while Sam felt happy for her, she also felt dreadfully jealous—because for all her own newspaper columns and TV documentaries and journalistic fame, all she actually wanted was what Rachel had: a husband, a family, and a simple, quiet life surrounded by people she loved.

Later, when she got home, she tried to reassure herself by calling Paul. She wanted to hear the sound of his voice once again, just to remind herself of why she'd gotten together with him. She knew she wasn't in love with him—it was far too early for anything like that. And besides, she had made herself a promise long ago never to fall in love with a man again. But there must have been something between them, on those hot African nights last week, for them ever to have found themselves in bed together.

Not until Paul's voice mail kicked in did she remember he'd gone away for the day, filming in New Orleans. It crossed her mind, suddenly, that it would have been nice if he had thought to ask her along too. The French Quarter, just the two of them—it would have been romantic. They could have spent the night and carried on where they

had left off in Africa. She would have liked the opportunity to fall just a
little in love with him.

Reluctantly, she left a message for him, asking if he wanted to meet
up sometime this week. And for the second time today she put down
the telephone with a sense of unease in her heart.

Chapter six

What is love, anyway? Sam was beginning to wonder if it really existed
these days. There was a time, once, when she'd believed in a romantic
ideal; but nowadays love seemed more like something that had been
invented to sell champagne and roses. Love wasn't merely an emotion
anymore. It was a brand concept.

That evening, as she was going through her many piles of research,
she came across a document proclaiming the discovery of the secret of
love. It was a press release from Trundel & Barr advertising their new
product—a chocolate bar called Bliss. According to the copy, love was
not complicated at all: it was simply a state of mind brought about by a
chemical imbalance in our brains. Like most natural highs, it could be
reproduced artificially, and this was what T&B claimed they had done.

Apparently, chocolate naturally contains a variety of stimulants and
mood enhancers that happen to be the same chemicals that are released
in the brain when we are in love. In their new product T&B had
increased the levels of some of these naturally occurring chemicals.
With the Bliss bar, they said, not only could you enjoy the smooth, sensual taste of dark chocolate, but just a few bites was enough to fill you
with an overwhelming sense of well-being—not unlike the feeling of
being in love.

When Sam first read this, she wanted to laugh: there was no earthly
way that chocolate was going to be a substitute for love—this was just
the modern equivalent of some medieval potion. But later, after she'd
had time to think about it for a while, she found herself feeling deeply
angry at the claims. Was the world really so cynical now that people
might believe this, that the answer to all their problems could be con-

tained inside a chocolate bar—that money *could,* after all, buy you love? It was bad enough that companies tried to tap into our deepest emotions to market their products—now it seemed they were trying to acquire those very emotions themselves and sell them back to us at a profit.

And besides, who was to say love was such a perfect, blissful state anyway? Sam had fallen in love three times in her life, and it had never brought her anything but pain. The first time was when she was sixteen—a disastrous crush on a boy in the class above, which had ended when she stumbled across him in the changing rooms with his hand up another girl's sweater. The second time was a few years later, at college—eight months of passion with an English exchange student, which had fizzled out in an agonizing succession of phone calls after he'd returned to his hometown in England. And the last time was with Cameron, a little over two years ago. That was the most painful of all.

She picked up the press release and shoved it back on top of one of her piles. She was angry—not so much at the press release now as at herself. She had only started going through her papers in the first place as a way of taking her thoughts away from Paul—and yet here she was, allowing her mind to wander into *far* more dangerous territory.

Deciding that it was time she stopped for the night, she closed the lid of her laptop. Some things were better not mixed with work—and Cameron was top of the list. So, leaving her papers where they were, she stood up and went through to the kitchen to pour herself a glass of wine.

. . .

She hadn't thought about Cameron properly for months—it was the one thing she normally tried to avoid if at all possible. Even now, after nine months, it was still difficult. Rachel had a theory that every time you split up with a man, you lost a piece of yourself—like two plants that had become so intertwined that the only way to separate them was to cut off the tangled parts. It was a nice theory, but Sam wasn't so sure. She had lost large parts of herself *long* before she'd found the courage to split up with Cameron: they had been yanked out of her by the roots. The nine months since then had been one long process of trying to recover those parts, reclaim them for herself.

She'd first met Cameron a couple of years ago, in the bar where he worked. He was a brash, good-looking Australian man who flirted with her as he served her drinks. She ignored him at first, of course—barmen always tried their chances—but there was something different about this one, something commanding, masterful. And also something perhaps a little dangerous. Despite her reservations she found herself going back to his bar on other nights as well, and returning his flirtation. It made her feel deliciously wanton, flirting like this with a total stranger. It made her feel liberated.

After a week or two, she finally summoned the courage to go to his bar on her own. She told him that she was just passing and had simply stopped by for a drink, but Cameron was no fool, and he knew that this was his opportunity. Somehow he managed to convince the bar manager to give him the rest of the night off. That was one thing she noticed about him straightaway: nobody ever seemed to be able to say no to Cameron.

From the very beginning, their affair was nothing like any other relationship she'd had. There was none of the tentativeness she normally had, none of the holding back until she knew him better—she just dived right in, almost without thought for the consequences. After that first night together she blew off some of her work, just so that she could spend more time with him. They spent most of the next three days in bed. It was like the beginning of an addiction: she lost count of the number of times they made love. Neither she nor Cameron wanted to stop, and only when they were both spent would they roll apart and lie naked on top of the covers, smiling at each other through an exhausted haze.

No matter what Sam thought about the freedom of remaining single, she would never feel as free as she had during those frantic periods of lovemaking. It was as though her body had opened up, unfurled itself like a snowdrop, and bared her naked soul to the world. After just a couple of days together there was nothing she would not let Cameron do to her. All modesty, all inhibition, had disappeared—she had become an animal, answering only to instinct and leaving her rationality to soak away into the bedsheets with her sweat. She had lost all self-consciousness. It was as if she no longer had a self to be conscious of. It was as if she no longer existed.

Cameron finally left her apartment after the third day, taking Sam's phone number with him and promising to call in a day or two. Afterward, Sam slept for a straight fourteen hours. Only when she woke up, groggy and sore, did she finally pull herself together: it was like waking up from a dream, or perhaps some inordinately long drug binge. Only the mess in her apartment gave away the reality of the last three days. It was difficult to know whether she felt good or bad about it—all she knew was that, like it or not, she was definitely going to be seeing more of Cameron. It was almost as if she had no choice in the matter.

.　.　.

From the outside, their relationship must have seemed perfect. In all the time they were together, they never argued in public. They never contradicted one another or interrupted each other's stories. Neither were they *over*affectionate in a way that might make other people uncomfortable—they got the balance just right. And they smiled a lot. In fact, when other people were looking, their smiles never wavered.

Right from the start Sam refused to say anything against Cameron, not even to her friends. At times when a whole group of them were sitting around a table gossiping about their boyfriends, all Sam had to say was how good Cameron was in the kitchen, how good he was around the house, how good he was in bed—what an all-round passionate, considerate partner he was. Not everyone believed her of course. No man could be *that* perfect, they'd said. But then Sam had simply changed the subject and slowly withdrawn from the conversation, leaving her friends to assume, somewhat bitterly, that she was so drenched in domestic bliss that she had no need to say anything more.

Only her closest friends began to notice the change in her. Sometimes one of them would comment on how nervous she appeared, or how quiet, and she would have to spend ten minutes trying to be vivacious to make up for it. Once Rachel had even commented about the bruises on Sam's arms—*those* had been awkward to explain away. But in general she managed to avoid making people suspicious. Besides, as her relationship with Cameron progressed, Sam began to see less and less of her close friends. It seemed to be the simplest way of avoiding difficult questions.

Sam's mother and father were more easily convinced. When Sam and Cameron visited them for Thanksgiving dinner, her parents welcomed Cameron more enthusiastically than she'd ever seen them welcome anyone else. Her father gave up his chair for him and sent her mother out to open a bottle of their best wine. And he offered Cameron a cigar. Sam didn't even know her father *smoked* cigars.

"You must be special," said her father, as he wrapped his lips around the end of a half corona. "Samantha has never brought any of her boyfriends home before. I was beginning to think she was ashamed of us."

"More likely she was ashamed of *them*," said Cameron, and the two of them had laughed. "Actually," Cameron continued lightheartedly, "Sam's never had a boyfriend before me. I'm her first."

Her father's eyes glinted. "Now I know for a fact *that's* not true."

For the next half hour they discussed Sam as if she weren't there, trying to outdo each other with feats of verbal cruelty dressed up as humor. Sam was used to standing up to her father, but facing the two of them together was more than she could manage. So she held her tongue and let them make jokes at her expense. Her father obviously liked Cameron. He seemed to have recognized him as a kindred spirit.

Her mother said nothing to defend her, of course—she had learned through years of experience never to interrupt her husband. And besides, she too seemed to have fallen under Cameron's spell. Later, in the kitchen, she had nothing but praise for him.

"It's so good to see you settling down at last," she told Sam, as she was preparing a sauce for the turkey. "I was beginning to think you'd never find yourself a man."

"Why? I've had plenty of boyfriends before—whatever Cameron seems to think."

"Yes, but no one serious. No one who knows how to deal with you."

"*Deal* with me . . . ?"

"You know what I mean. You can be a little wild sometimes, and he seems to be able to handle you, that's all."

Her mother lowered her eyes, turning back toward the cooker and her sauce.

Sam watched her resentfully. She couldn't help noticing that she was wearing a high-necked sweater, despite that it was unbearably hot in the kitchen. Her mother always wore clothes with high necks and long sleeves. She liked to keep herself covered up.

Without really knowing she was doing it, Sam began to roll up the sleeves of her own shirt. "And what makes you think I *need* handling?" she said deliberately.

"Every woman needs to be handled just a little bit."

"You mean like dad handles you?"

Her mother didn't reply.

"Is that what you want for me, Mother?" said Sam angrily.

"I don't know what you're talking about."

"Yes, you do. You know exactly what I mean."

Her mother turned to rebuke her, but as she did so she noticed Sam's arms, and she stopped. A look passed between them that was unlike anything they'd ever shared before, and for a moment Sam allowed herself to hope that her mother would answer her, that they would finally be able to talk to each other, honestly and openly. But then her father came into the kitchen, looking for a corkscrew. Sam immediately pulled her sleeves back down over her arms. Her mother turned away once more, without saying anything, and went back to stirring her sauce. And the moment was lost.

• • •

As far as the rest of the world was concerned, the next logical step in their relationship was marriage. So it came as a shock when, a year and a half after they'd first met, Sam finally threw Cameron out of her apartment. To her friends, who knew nothing of what went on behind those walls, it seemed like a pointless, self-destructive act. Her parents acted as if it didn't make sense at all. Her mother cried copiously, as though the breakup were her own personal tragedy, and her father called Sam a fool for getting rid of the one man who would put up with her.

None of them knew how desperate she had to have been to risk breaking up with Cameron. Sam still marveled that she'd ever had the strength to do it. It hadn't simply been a case of telling him it was over—he had ensconced himself in her apartment, and in her thoughts, as if they both belonged to him by right. Removing him wasn't a matter of mutual agreement—she'd had to carve him from her life, then weather a storm of threatening notes and phone calls that had lasted for months. She still remembered the sound of him beating on the front door of her brownstone, waking the neighbors and promising to break it down if she didn't open it—and also the ominous silence on the nights when he *didn't* come around, as she waited, sleeplessly, for the sound of his footsteps on the street outside.

Admitting that their relationship had failed was almost as painful. Even now, she found it difficult to tell people the truth about Cameron: she had spent so much time dressing their relationship up like a box of chocolates that lying about him had become second nature. So while she told Rachel the full story, and also one or two of her other female friends, she let everyone else think that she and Cameron had split up amicably. She felt ashamed to say any more. She didn't want people to think of her as a victim.

Nine months later, and she rarely let herself think about Cameron—not properly, intimately, as she sometimes did with her other ex-boyfriends. She had locked him out of her head just as she had locked him out of her apartment all those months ago. But every now and then he broke back in again—as he had tonight when she was reading that damn press release—and it felt as if she were allowing herself to be violated by him all over again.

. . .

That night she dreamed she was back at the Chocolate Fair. She was hiding from someone—she wasn't sure whom—and to escape she had climbed up the sculpture in the center of the hall. The chocolate globe, she discovered, was hollow, and so she crawled inside and sat there, waiting for whoever it was to give up looking for her. Although she could hear the person outside, walking around the hall, she felt safe inside her globe. But then she looked down to find that the heat given off by her body was beginning to melt the chocolate she was sitting on, and there was a danger she would fall through. With a sinking feeling she realized she couldn't stay there forever, that sooner or later she would have to come out . . .

She woke up feeling anxious, and inexplicably angry. She lay in bed for a while, trying to calm herself down by watching the shadow of the tree outside move across her second-floor window. It formed a lacelike silhouette on her curtains, every branch and every leaf moving independently of the others in the breeze, yet simultaneously interconnected with one another. She found the shadow patterns they made soothing. She told herself she had nothing to be angry about. It was only a dream.

Later, when it was light, she got up to make herself breakfast. As she sat down at her desk, the first thing she noticed was the piece of paper on the top of the pile—the ad for the Bliss bar, with all its extraordinary claims. Sam stared at the press release for a long time before screwing it up into a small ball and throwing it away.

Chapter seven

Later that morning Sam sat down to make some phone calls. The first one was to Nestlé. That was the easiest—Paul had already organized an interview with their public relations executive, so it was simply a matter of setting up the time and date. Her next phone call, to the Mars Corporation, was similar. The last, and most difficult, was to Trundel & Barr, the company whose press release she had come across yesterday. T&B was famous for being unfriendly toward journalists, so Paul had left this one to Sam. He figured that she would be much more likely to charm them into doing an interview than he would. But even before she spoke to them, she was already having trouble—despite over an hour of Internet searching to try to find a contact name in T&B's public relations department, she had drawn a blank. Even the other chocolate companies she'd spoken to were unable to give her a name. So in the end she had no choice but to go in cold.

"Hello," said Sam, once the receptionist answered, "can you put me through to your PR department, please?"

"We don't have a PR department. What is your inquiry about?"

Sam hesitated. "Well, I'm making a TV documentary about chocolate, and I'm looking for someone I can interview."

The voice on the other end went silent for a second, before saying frostily, "I'm afraid you're wasting your time. T and B doesn't give interviews. Perhaps you should try one of the other chocolate companies. Cadbury's perhaps. Or Nestlé."

"But we really had our hearts set on *you,*" said Sam, trying to sound as charming as she could. "We love your products, and we thought we'd rather give you the publicity. Our documentary is going out on national TV and we're expecting viewing figures in the millions. It could be a great opportunity for you, as well as for us. If you could just put me through to the person in charge of—"

"Like I said," the receptionist interrupted, "we don't give interviews. Now if you'll excuse me, I have a call on another line."

The phone went dead. Sam pulled the receiver away from her ear and looked at it. "I don't believe it," she muttered to herself. "The bitch hung up on me!"

Determined not to be outdone, she put the phone back on the hook for a moment, before picking it up again and redialing the number. The same voice answered.

"Hello," said Sam, "I was just speaking to you a moment ago. I think you must have cut me off by mistake."

"There was no mistake," said the receptionist. "I thought our conversation was over."

"Well, it *wasn't* over. I want to talk to someone about doing a TV interview. If you don't know who that person might be, I'd be grateful if you could put me through to someone who does."

The receptionist sighed, as if Sam's persistence was beginning to bore her. "As I explained before, we don't do interviews at T and B. That's company policy."

"Yes, but—"

Sam didn't have time to finish before the line went dead once more. "Hello? *Hello!*"

There was nothing worse than having the phone hung up on her. As far as Sam was concerned, it was the highest form of rudeness—worse by far than turning your back on someone or refusing to shake her hand. At least if someone snubs you to your face, you can still *say* something back—but when someone hangs up on you, there is nothing you can do. In that single action all opportunities both for reconciliation and for revenge are immediately snuffed out.

Of course, you can always call back, and this is what Sam now did. As she dialed the number this time, she punched the digits in hard, jabbing each button with her finger the way she'd like to be jabbing the receptionist's chest.

Once again the same voice answered, irritating in its cheeriness: "T and B, good morning."

Sam gritted her teeth. "Didn't anyone tell you that it's rude to hang up on your customers?"

"Yes, but you're not a customer. You're a reporter."

"But I'm a customer as well."

"Oh," said the receptionist smugly, "so you have a *customer* inquiry now. If you like, I can put you through to one of our sales team—"

"No," said Sam angrily, "I don't want to speak to your sales team. I want to talk to someone about an interview."

"I keep telling you, we don't do interviews. If you can't understand a simple thing like that, then I'm afraid you're not much of a reporter."

By now Sam's patience had just about run out. "Right, that's it. Give me your name, please."

"What do you want my name for?"

"I want to make a formal complaint."

"Fine," said the receptionist, "in that case, my name is Minnie."

Sam wrote the name down. "And your surname?"

"Mouse. That's spelled *m-o-u-s-e.*"

"Minnie Mouse. Very funny."

"Thank you," said the receptionist, and hung up once again.

Sam sighed angrily and replaced her phone on the hook. There were moments in life when there was nothing for it but to concede defeat.

. . .

For the next few minutes she sat back in her couch and tried to think what to do next. No way was she going to let a receptionist get the better of her—that felt like an embarrassment. It was one thing to be turned down by the managing director or the press officer, but Sam hadn't even *got* to them. She had been knocked out in the first round. It seemed, therefore, that she would have to use more unorthodox methods.

As she sat there, wondering how to bypass T&B's receptionist, she sorted through in her mind all the pieces of information she knew about the company. They were an unusual firm. Unlike all the other big-name chocolate companies, T&B was still family owned, which meant it didn't follow any of the normal company rules. According to hearsay, Nathan Trundel, the great-grandson of the original founder, governed the company like a despot. There were rumors about him strutting around the office, dictating people's jobs to them, and firing workers on a whim. The T&B offices were not supposed to be a very cheery place to work.

And apparently it wasn't only the office staff who were discontented. Sam had read a report recently that T&B also had problems with their industrial workforce. They owned a large chocolate factory somewhere in Maryland, and the workers there had been threatening to strike for a while now—she wasn't entirely sure of the reasons why. Something to do with pay and conditions, she presumed.

What else did she know about the company? She knew their products—a variety of chocolate assortments, bars, cookies, and ice cream. She knew from their press release that they were launching the Bliss bar in a couple of weeks. And she knew that they had attended the International Chocolate Trade Fair at the Javits Center, because she remembered seeing them there. But apart from snippets of information like these, Sam didn't actually know that much about the company. If they were *always* as unfriendly toward journalists as they had been to her, then it was a miracle that even these details had reached her.

These were the things Sam thought about while she sat on her couch, beside her telephone. She went over her conversations with the receptionist in her head once more and realized that she now knew a fresh piece of information: T&B didn't have a PR department. That meant that the people she wanted to interview must call themselves something else—publicity, perhaps, or marketing. If she called back later, then that was whom she'd ask to speak to. She knew she'd get there in the end. She just had to bide her time, that's all.

. . .

She waited for half an hour before calling the company back. When she did, she disguised her voice slightly, so that the receptionist wouldn't recognize her.

"Hello," she said, "I'm calling from the exhibition hall at the Jacob K. Javits Convention Center. Your company attended the Chocolate Trade

Fair last weekend—you had a stand near the center of the hall, didn't you?"

"I think so, yes," said the receptionist.

"Well, one of your publicity people left his cell phone in our office. I'd like to return it to him if I can. Could you put me through to him?"

"We don't have any publicity people here. You're probably thinking of our marketing department. I can put you through to one of the assistants if you like?"

Sam was determined not to be put through to anyone until she at least had a name. "No, this guy wasn't an assistant. He was the boss."

"You mean Matt Dyson? Our marketing director?"

"Yeah, that's the guy."

"I'm afraid he's not in today. But if you give me your name, I can get him to call you back."

"Don't worry," said Sam hurriedly, "I'll call him another day. Matt Dyson, you say?"

"Yes." The receptionist's voice became suddenly suspicious. "Why don't you give me your name so that I can tell him who called?"

"It's okay—I'll just call back. Thanks, you've been a great help."

"Who is this?" said the receptionist bluntly. "Are you the woman who called earlier?"

Sam put the phone down without answering, and as she did so, she couldn't help smiling victoriously to herself. Touché, Minnie Mouse, she thought. You're not the only one who can hang up on people.

Chapter eight

Paul did not share Sam's sense of victory over T&B's receptionist. When she went over to his place that evening, it was clear that he had been hoping for bigger things.

"So," he said, almost before she'd stepped through his front door, "did you manage to get an interview out of them?"

"Not yet."

"No?" He sounded disappointed. "Oh, well . . ."

"Don't worry, I'll get there in the end. Now that I've got a name to work on."

"Well, you'll have to be quick about it. If we're going to interview them, it's got to be next week. Our schedule's tight enough as it is."

Sam took her coat off and followed him in. This was not the sort of welcome she had been expecting. When Paul had invited her over this evening, she had hoped that he was planning to treat her to a romantic dinner. Tonight was the first time they'd been alone together since they'd got back from Africa, and she was looking forward to putting their documentary aside for the evening. But as he led her into his apartment, it became clear that Paul had other ideas. He had obviously been hard at work all day, and it didn't look as if he was planning to stop now on her account.

She followed him through to the living room. She couldn't help being a little surprised at the state of the place: last time she'd been here it had been as tidy as a show home—but tonight it looked more like some kind of student dormitory. Papers were strewn out across the floor—some of them in neat piles, but many more in random heaps, as if they'd been cast there from a height. The coffee table was covered with library books, held open with paperweights and half-full cups of coffee—and over on the couch Paul's laptop was humming quietly, its screen displaying his Internet-browser home page.

She hovered beside the door wondering where to put herself. She was feeling less comfortable with every moment that passed. She had gone through her entire wardrobe this afternoon trying to find the right dress for the occasion—but now that she was here with Paul, in his scruffy jeans and T-shirt, she felt completely overdressed. Not that *he* seemed to notice, of course. He hadn't given her a second glance since she'd come in.

"Make yourself some coffee if you like," he said, as he stepped through his mess of papers toward the couch. "You know where everything is."

Sam smiled grimly and went through to the kitchen.

.   .   .

While she waited for her coffee to brew, Paul talked to her through the doorway. Apparently he had spent most of the afternoon trawling through the Web for reports on slavery, and information about the chocolate industry in general.

"I can't believe what a dirty history chocolate has had," he was saying. "It seems to have been tied up with slavery ever since the stuff was invented. First the Aztecs enslaved their own people, then the Spanish enslaved *them,* then the rest of the world joined in and enslaved half of Africa. Did you know that in the eighteenth century over one hundred thousand slaves were transported across the Atlantic every year, just to work on the cocoa plantations? I tell you, if I'd been told things like this when I was a kid, I don't think I would ever have eaten a chocolate bar again."

Sam came back in with her coffee and looked around the room. "Is there anywhere to sit?"

Paul cleared a space on the floor beside him and carried on. "Take a look at this." He reached for one of the books on the coffee table. "It's a history of slavery. I thought maybe we could interview the author—get a bit of background on the subject to start the film off. What do you think?"

Sam sat down next to Paul and pretended to look at the book. She was beginning to wish she hadn't come. "Yeah," she said, after flicking through it for a while. "That sounds like a good idea."

"Look at this bit," he said impatiently, reaching forward to turn the pages for her. "Everybody thinks slavery finished after the Civil War, but it didn't. Not in the *chocolate* industry. There were still slaves on cocoa plantations in some parts of West Africa until well into the twentieth century. And I'm talking about *official* slaves here. Sanctioned by colonial governments."

Sam looked him straight in the eye and shut the book. "Paul, I thought you invited me here tonight to have dinner with you."

"I did. I thought we could order in pizza and eat it while we go through these documents."

"Can't we leave the documents to another time? I haven't seen you for three days."

"Exactly—we've got a lot of catching up to do." He frowned awkwardly and took back the book from her. "Don't worry, we'll have a break later on. Work first, rest later. We've got a lot to get through this evening. We have to wrap up all the filming by the end of next week, and we haven't even finalized our interview schedule yet . . ."

There was no point in arguing. She knew from experience that he would carry on with or without her—nothing could stop Paul from working once he'd gotten started. If she wanted him for herself, then she would have to wait until later, when they had a break.

. . .

For the next two hours they sorted through Paul's piles of papers, setting aside all the information they might be able to use and discarding the rest. The reports were from all over the world: data on women's chocolate cravings in South America, papers on tooth decay from Japan, statistics on cocoa prices from the London stock exchange, and company accounts from chocolate companies just about everywhere. Enough information was here to make a whole series of documentaries.

Not until past ten o'clock did Paul finally agree to order the pizza. By the time it was delivered, Sam was suffering severe hunger pangs.

"Do you always eat this late?" she asked, tearing herself off a large slice.

"Sometimes. Sometimes I don't eat anything."

"Really? Why?"

"Well, sometimes I forget."

Sam laughed. "How can you *forget* to eat?"

"Easily—if I'm busy doing other things."

"But that's terrible! That shows you're not looking after yourself."

"Oh, I don't think it's going to do me any harm if I miss a meal every now and then. Half the world's population goes without an evening meal. And besides, Westerners eat too much anyway. There are more calories in one of these slices than most people get in a whole day."

Sam looked at him and shook her head. "Amazing. Even *eating* is political with you."

"Especially eating."

She watched him as he put down his pizza and began to expound on the injustices of food distribution. There was something of the zealot in Paul tonight. He seemed to have an appetite for politics that far outweighed his hunger for anything else. While his food lay virtually untouched on his plate, he had been consuming political issues in vast chunks all evening—and here he was, eager for more.

Sam remembered a time several years back when she'd found such passion attractive in a man. Nowadays she merely found it confusing. How could anyone be so utterly sure of himself? She herself had doubts about almost everything she did. She even had doubts about Paul.

"Did you know that in the States, we throw away forty-three thousand tons of food every day?" he was saying now. "And that's not including household waste. While half of Africa regularly suffers from famine, we trash vast amounts of food without giving it a second thought."

It was time to put a stop to this. Nervously, she moved closer to him, until their shoulders were almost touching. "Tell me," she said, pushing her doubts aside, "are you this passionate about everything?"

"Of course. About the things that matter, anyway."

"And what about things a little closer to home?"

He smiled, then reddened slightly, as if suddenly aware of how close her body was to his own. "We should get back to work."

"We're on a break, remember?"

"But we've got a lot to get through."

"It can wait."

She took hold of his hand and, after a moment's hesitation, leaned forward and kissed him clumsily on the cheek.

She suddenly felt foolish. For some reason, what she'd just done felt hideously inappropriate—more like some schoolgirl making a pass at her teacher than a woman kissing her partner. And he was her partner, wasn't he? Or was it still too early to say that?

For a moment she almost thought he was going to pull away from her, pretend she hadn't kissed him at all so that he could get back to his papers. But then, at last, he tilted his head and put his lips against hers.

· · ·

After a while they moved to the bedroom, where they undressed each other with inept, amateurish fingers. She had a terrible time fumbling with the buttons on his jeans, and the zip on her own dress caught halfway down, forcing her to wriggle out of it like a circus performer extracting herself from a straitjacket. By the time they climbed into bed, Sam was feeling self-conscious. In Africa everything had seemed so automatic—sex had simply *happened,* without the need for any of this. In comparison, things tonight were just a little . . . heavy-handed.

She was telling herself that a little awkwardness was natural, that the first time now they were back home was bound to be strange, when suddenly everything went wrong. It happened when she reached out to grasp his shoulders with her hands. She wanted to inject some urgency into the proceedings, but as she clutched his flesh in her hands, Paul immediately let out a yelp.

"What are you doing!"

"I'm not doing anything," said Sam.

"Yes, you are! That *hurt.*"

Pulling away from her, he turned on the bedside lamp. A smudge of blood was at the top of his chest. Sam glanced at her hands and found blood on the ring she wore on her middle finger. Somehow the metal must have nipped his skin.

"I'm sorry," she said. "Here, let me kiss it better."

"You've *cut* me," said Paul incredulously. "You've actually *cut* me!"

"It must have been my ring. Don't worry—I'll make it up to you."

He rolled away and sat on the edge of the bed. "You should be more careful with your damn jewelry."

"Come on, Paul, it was just an accident. Come back to bed."

"I'm sorry, Sam, but this isn't working." He picked up his jeans from the chair beside the bed and began to pull them on. "We should have stuck to business."

He stood up and walked through to the next room. Sam watched him through the doorway as he wandered over to the couch and sat down among all the papers they had been studying just fifteen minutes ago.

"You can't just leave me here like this," she called out after him, incredulous. "Paul, please come back to bed."

"Look," he said impatiently, "did you come over here just to have sex, or to do some work?"

"To do some work, naturally . . ."

"Well, in that case let's get down to it. We can forget this ever happened. We've got plenty of stuff to sort out here—if we go through it together, we can get it all finished tonight . . ."

. . .

Sam left him talking to himself. Wrapping the bedsheet around her, she stepped past him and made her way down the hall to the bathroom. She couldn't control herself for much longer than it took to lock the door behind her. Sitting down on the lid of the toilet, she buried her face in her hands and sobbed for a while, as silently as she could manage.

It wasn't sadness she was feeling, or loss, or even sexual frustration. She was angry at herself for ever having let her guard down. After what had happened with Cameron she had promised never to let herself be so vulnerable again—and yet here she was, sitting in the bathroom sobbing her eyes out, just like in the old days.

In some ways this was *worse* than the old days. Violent womanizer that he was, Cameron had never abandoned her halfway through making love. He would have scoffed at the very idea of allowing something as small as a scratch from her ring to get in the way of their mutual pleasure. He would have just carried on and tended to the scratch later.

Sam blew her nose on a piece of toilet paper. To her utter surprise she found herself missing Cam, just a little bit. She remembered the feeling of peace she'd always had after they'd made love—those glorious moments after climax when everything in the universe felt as though it had effortlessly slotted into its proper place. For all his other faults, Cameron had always been the perfect gentleman after sex. Sometimes he would massage her, delighting in the satisfied noises she made beneath his hands; sometimes he would go to the kitchen and bring her food or coffee or wine. The unspoken understanding between them was that no matter what happened in the rest of their lives, this was always *her* time. It was Cameron's way of repenting for all the things he did to her.

Perhaps, subconsciously, this was what she'd been looking for tonight: not sex so much as the chance to feel important once again. She wanted the opportunity to feel that she was the center of someone's world—even if it was only for a few minutes. But she wasn't the center of Paul's world and never would be. The only thing that existed for Paul was work.

She let herself cry for a while, but after a few minutes, when she decided that she'd cried enough, she took a deep breath and shoved her anger back down into the pit of her stomach. Wiping the tears from her face, she stood up and began to slowly unwrap the sheet from around her. She suddenly had the urge to wash herself, scrub the remnants of Paul's touch from her body, so she dropped the sheet on the bathroom floor and stepped into the shower.

• • •

Later, when she was clean, she went back to the bedroom to get dressed. Paul was still in the living room, poring over his papers, but as she entered, he looked up from them suddenly. "There you are. I've been waiting for you."

"Oh, yes?" said Sam, still hurt. "And why's that then?"

"I just . . ." His eyes flicked down to her towel and back to her face again. He looked uncomfortable, perhaps even regretful, and for a moment Sam thought he might be about to apologize. But then he composed himself. Holding up a sheet of paper, he said matter-of-factly, "I want you to take a look at our interview schedule when you're ready. There are one or two things we need to finalize."

Sam shot him an angry glance. "You're telling me," she said dryly.

She tried to close the bedroom door behind her but it was stiff, and a whole pile of books was in front of it, so she was obliged to leave it open while she started putting her clothes on. Not that Paul was paying any attention to her, of course. His head was buried obstinately in his papers once more, just as it had been when she'd first arrived.

"We're interviewing the antislavery protesters tomorrow," Paul called through to her, as she stepped quickly into her underwear. "And then next week we're taking on the chocolate companies: Mars on Monday, Nestlé on Tuesday, Cadbury on Thursday morning, and Kraft Jacob Suchard in the afternoon. All we need now is your interview with Trundel and Barr."

"Don't worry," said Sam angrily. "I told you, I've got a name to follow up—someone called Matt Dyson."

She started pulling on her dress.

"You're not going, are you?" asked Paul, finally looking up at her.

"No, Paul, I'm not going."

"I just thought for a moment . . . since you were getting dressed . . ."

She glared at him. "I don't know about you, but I generally work with my clothes *on.*"

Only her stubbornness prevented her from leaving. She certainly *wanted* to go—and she could tell by Paul's face that he was feeling just as embarrassed as she was. But she knew that however bad she was feeling now, it would only be worse if they left it until tomorrow. It was better to do what Paul suggested—pretend nothing had happened, get back to work.

Resolutely, she returned to the living room. Holding her dress against her knees, she sat down—not quite so close to him as before—and peered over at the piece of paper on which he'd written their interview schedule. When Paul held it out toward her, she didn't hesitate before reaching to take it from him. But she was careful this time *not* to let their hands touch.

Chapter nine

Later that night, in the cab home, Sam looked at the ring on her middle finger. It was still a mystery to her how she had managed to cut Paul's skin with it. Was it the stone that had cut him? Or perhaps the metal claw that held the stone in place? She pulled the ring to the end of her finger and held it up to the light, just to check that no remnant of Paul's blood was still there—but of course her shower must have washed any blood away.

For a while she admired the way the streetlights played across her ring. The unusual piece of jewelry had two bands of silver, twisted around a yellow gemstone. It wasn't a real gem, of course, just a cheap semiprecious stone—but it was striking nevertheless, in a gaudy sort of way. It was cut like a diamond, with facets that scattered the light in all directions, and no matter how long Sam stared into the middle of it, she never managed to see through to the metal that held it in place. She admired it for that—its ability to hide its depths.

She still remembered the day when Cameron had given her this ring, on her birthday, about four months after they had first started seeing each other. He had been cute about the way he did it—presenting it to her in a jewelry box over dinner as if it were an engagement ring rather than merely a birthday present. She half-expected him to drop down on one knee as he held it out to her. The idea was ridiculous, of course—Cameron wouldn't get on his knees for anyone, no matter what the occasion. But even so, he had been solemn about the way he'd presented it over the table. He said it would mark a turning point in their relationship. And looking back on it now, it seemed that he had been right.

As she pushed the ring back down toward her knuckle she wondered why she still wore it. She certainly didn't keep it for sentimental reasons—in fact, it brought back many more unpleasant memories than good ones. But perhaps those memories themselves were the reason she kept it on her finger. Perhaps she wore it because she didn't want to forget what Cameron had been like, so that she would never make the same mistakes with a man again.

She dropped her hand back onto her lap and went back to watching the world as it passed by the windows of her cab. And as she traveled through the midnight streets, she played with the ring on her finger. She twisted it around a few times, then rubbed the stone against the palm of her hand, just to see if it was sharp in any way. But it was as smooth as ever, and she still couldn't see how it could possibly have cut Paul's chest. As far as she could tell, there was nothing dangerous about her ring at all.

.   .   .

The first time Sam ever had a taste of Cameron's darker side was six months after they'd got together. It was late at night, and he had come back slightly drunk from the bar where he worked. They'd been arguing over something—Sam couldn't even remember what—and Cameron had turned and cuffed her around the face. She didn't see the blow before it struck her. His hand seemed to come out of nowhere, swiping her face and knocking her over onto the couch. She didn't scream or cry out. She didn't even strike him back. The shock of the blow left her vaguely paralyzed, both in her mind and her body, and rather than railing against the violence of his blow—rather than being outraged that her lover could find it in him to actually *hit* her across the face—she found herself absentmindedly clutching her jaw and wondering why his blow hadn't hurt more than it did.

He apologized profusely, of course, claiming that it had been a mistake, and Sam let it pass, because she wanted to believe him. And besides, she had probably provoked him—she knew she could be unbearably argumentative sometimes. Later, after they'd made love, they even joked about the incident, as if it were some one-off freak accident that would never happen again.

The second time was more serious. A few weeks later, during a louder argument, Cameron lost his temper completely and hit Sam not once but several times: across the face at first, with an open hand, and then with a closed fist against her arms and body. It was so unexpected that she barely had the presence of mind to protect herself, and by the time he stopped she had bruises all over. She said nothing about it afterward—she was so shocked she didn't know what to say. She couldn't bring herself to believe that this new violent streak was anything but a temporary aberration—Cameron wasn't anything like her father. Things would be back to normal again soon.

A few days later she went out for a drink with Rachel. Her friend noticed the bruises on her arms and asked how they had happened, and for a few seconds Sam considered telling her everything. But in the end she just shrugged and mumbled some excuse about falling over in the shower. She didn't want Rachel to think badly of Cameron—after all, he was the perfect boyfriend most of the time. And, if she was truthful, a part of her didn't want to acknowledge her own weakness. Not to Rachel, not even to herself.

Over the next few months this became part of her routine: she and Cameron would argue, he would hit her, and Sam would spend the next few days trying to come up with plausible excuses to explain away her injuries. She started wearing long sleeves to cover up the bruises on her arms. She started wearing dark glasses. And eventually she began avoiding her friends altogether. It was easier to spend time with strangers—people who wouldn't ask questions.

For months she lived a double life. Professionally she was going from strength to strength—she had her own column in one of the nationals now, she was getting a lot of freelance assignments, and she was even starting to do some television work. She fought other people's causes for them with a passion that was uncompromising, and she was beginning to get a name for herself as someone who was always willing to stand up for what she believed in. But her personal life was a mess. She was often reluctant to go back to the apartment, for fear of what might be awaiting her there. Her most common emotions were dread and guilt and self-loathing. And when she got home to find that, after all, Cameron was in a good mood, she was so overcome with gratitude she almost felt as if she were in love with him again.

Of course, she knew that things couldn't go on like this forever. Sometimes she fantasized about breaking up with Cameron. Sometimes she imagined what it would be like to stand up to him in the same way she'd been standing up to other people all her life—but as soon as she saw him, all her resolve just melted away. It was as if he had some kind of mesmeric power over her. It was as if the very masterfulness that had attracted her to him in the first place now had her in thrall. She despised herself for submitting to him the way she did. She felt like her mother—a doormat—only worse, because she at least should have known better. She should have seen it coming.

. . .

As summer approached, Cameron started staying out longer, and drinking more. And the more he drank, the more violent he became. In June he hit her so hard across her left ear that it rang for a month. In July he cracked two of her ribs. But she had begun to regard such injuries as a hazard of everyday life, and she was almost numb to his beatings now. What upset her more was that he had all but stopped making love to her.

A part of her knew exactly what was going wrong. She had long suspected that a man with Cameron's sex drive couldn't possibly be satisfied by a single woman. He'd even told her that she was inadequate for him, several times. But even so, she couldn't bring herself to believe that he was being unfaithful to her. Sex was the only part of their relationship that still brought her any pleasure at all—she didn't think she could bear it if he started giving that to someone else, leaving her with nothing but kicks and punches. So when he got back late at night wearing his T-shirt inside out, she convinced herself that he must have left home like that earlier, without either of them noticing. And when she found lipstick on his clothing, she told herself it was perfectly innocent: he worked in a bar—he had probably picked up the lipstick from a glass, accidentally, when he was clearing up at the end of the evening. There was an explanation for everything.

In the end, inevitably, she blamed herself for his lack of interest. She wasn't exciting enough. She wasn't inventive enough. To reawaken their sex life, she started waiting up for him at night, greeting him at the door in her underwear, or with nothing on at all, so that he could take her right there in the hallway. She wore sluttish clothes around the apartment, bending over provocatively before him whenever she could or accidentally brushing past him with her breasts or her bottom. She played sex games with him. She tied herself to the bed, crawled around for him on all fours, kissed his shoes and begged him—literally begged him—to make love to her. There was nothing she would not do to debase herself as long as it got Cameron where she wanted him.

At first her strategy seemed to work: Cameron stopped going out at odd hours, he stopped drinking so much, and for a while he even stopped hitting her. And though it was exhausting for Sam always to be playing this role, always having to come up with new ways to keep Cameron happy, she was sure it was better than losing him altogether. Besides, when he was making love to her, he couldn't also be beating her up—except in the spirit of the game, of course.

And then, one day, when she was hanging up Cameron's jacket, a pack of condoms fell out of the pocket. It was open, and two were missing. The sight immediately shattered all her illusions: she and Cameron had never used condoms, not since the week they first met. In that instant she finally allowed herself to see what had been going on—the man was insatiable, and she was powerless against him.

For a long while she sat on the edge of her bed, staring at the pack in her hand. Was this all she was worth? Did Cameron have so little regard for her that he could no longer even be bothered to hide the evidence of his infidelities properly? She couldn't believe she had finally come to this. She felt as if she were imprisoned in some long, complicated dream that refused to end no matter how hard she tried to wake up.

Rolling over onto her side, she put her face in her hands and lay there, for a very long time, trying to figure out what to do.

. . .

When Cameron came home later that evening, Sam went back to his jacket and retrieved the pack of condoms. She waited until he had gone and opened himself a bottle of beer, and once he was comfortable, once he was sitting down in front of the television, she dropped the pack on the coffee table in front of him.

"What's that?" said Cameron.

"That is what *I* wanted to ask *you.*"

"Don't fuck around, Sam, I've had a busy day."

"They're yours. I found them in your jacket pocket."

Cameron went silent and simply sat there, staring at the television screen.

"There's a couple missing," said Sam, raising her voice.

"Yeah, so?"

Sam grabbed the remote and switched the television off. She was shaking. "You've been sleeping with someone else, haven't you?"

"Don't be silly—"

"You've been fucking some other woman, and I want to know who she is, and how long you've been seeing her. I can't believe you've done this. After all I've had to put up with—"

"After all *you've* had to put up with!" Cameron stood up, suddenly angry. "What about everything I have to put up with? What the hell were you doing going through my pockets anyway?"

"I was just hanging your jacket up . . ."

"So? That doesn't give you the right to check up on me."

Sam stared at him, aghast. How on earth could he possibly think *she'd* done anything wrong? He was trying to twist it around, just as he always did. Only this time she wasn't going to take it. She turned to face him square-on, and trying hard to keep her voice under control, she said, "That's it, Cam. I can't take this anymore. It's over."

He glared at her. "What are you talking about?"

"I mean I can't live like this. I've had enough. It's over." In an effort to emphasize the point, she took hold of the ring that Cameron had given her for her birthday and pulled it off her finger. Without taking her eyes off Cameron's, she dropped it on the coffee table.

Cameron looked absolutely livid. "Put that back on."

"No."

She could have run away at this point. She could at least have ducked or put her hands up to protect her face, but she didn't want to give Cameron the satisfaction of seeing her cower. So instead she caught the full force of his blow on her cheek. She felt an intense pain shoot through her mouth as she fell to the floor on the other side of the coffee table.

"Put it back on," said Cameron again, and once again she said, "No."

He kicked her legs, then her butt, and when she tried to stand up again, he kicked her hard in the ribs so that she stumbled forward and collapsed in the middle of the room. She could barely breathe. With a few vicious blows the man had beaten all the strength out of her.

"Put the ring back on."

"Please, Cam!"

He skipped across the room and kicked her again, hard, repeating his order like some sort of mantra, and when this time she didn't answer, he knelt down and struck her in time with each word: "Put . . . the . . . ring . . . back . . . on!"

To Sam's surprise she started to laugh. How could she possibly put the ring back on if he kept on hitting her like this? She was nowhere near the table now—if she was going to put his damn ring back on her finger, he was going to have to give her a chance. The whole thing was absurd.

Her laughter seemed only to make Cameron more angry. Grabbing hold of her hair, he hauled Sam to her feet, and as soon as she was standing, he delivered another vicious blow to the side of her head. This time something inside her face let out a loud crack. As she fell to the floor, a searing pain shot through the numbness in her cheek. She tried to cry out, begging him to stop, but her words came out sounding like meaningless gibberish. To her terror she found that she could no longer move her jaw—her lips could no longer form syllables—and the only thing she could voice to express her panic was a loud, formless groan.

Clambering to her knees, she started crawling back across the room toward the coffee table, but before she got there, Cameron started laying into her once again, kicking and punching her repeatedly. He screamed obscenities at her in such an endless stream that after a while she could no longer make out what he was shouting—and each time she tried to pull herself a little closer to the table, he hit her again. For a moment she thought she'd never make it back to the table: she was on the verge of blacking out. Even when she finally did, grabbing the ring from the tabletop, he didn't seem to notice and carried on hitting her and screaming at her just as before—she had to hold the ring up in front of his face to get him to stop, shove it back onto her middle finger right before his eyes. Only then did he finally stop beating her.

At last he let her move slowly away from him, and as she did so, he stood up straight and gazed at her with disgust. "Go and clean yourself up. You look terrible."

Terrified, but grateful that her ordeal was at last over, Sam got to her feet and hobbled through to the bathroom. All she could do now was pray that Cameron didn't follow her there.

．　．　．

Later that night Sam went to the hospital. She went by herself because, as Cameron said, it would look suspicious if he went with her. Her story this time was that she had been mugged. She left her bag at home, in an effort to lend her story authenticity.

The doctor told her that she had dislocated her jaw, and while by some miracle none of the bones in her face were broken, some tissue was damaged, and it would take weeks before the swelling in her cheek would subside. Her ribs were bruised, but not broken this time, and some of the hair at the back of her head had been ripped out when Cameron had used it to pull her up.

Aside from this the worst injury she had was to her finger. In her hurry to shove the ring back on, she had failed to realize that her finger was already broken, and she had made the break worse. The doctors couldn't treat it until the ring was back off her finger again. They were going to cut it off, but Sam was so terrified of what Cameron would do to her if she came back from the hospital without it, she refused to let them do anything that would damage the ring. When they started to insist, she took hold of it herself and, gritting her teeth against the pain, squeezed it over her swollen knuckle.

Later, when they had finished giving her ice packs and painkillers and x-raying and bandaging her, one of the nurses took her upstairs to see a counselor called Kiki. Sam tried to protest, of course, saying that she was okay, that she didn't need to see a counselor, but the nurse kept insisting. In the end Sam gave in. She was too tired to argue.

Kiki was a thin, tired-looking woman who didn't look as though she could stand up to one of Cam's blows, let alone the beating Sam had just had. She tried to get Sam to admit to being battered by her partner, but Sam stubbornly refused to do so, even when Kiki told Sam that she could help, that there were ways to get rid of Cameron, legal ways, if only Sam would trust her.

Sam knew that Kiki was only trying to help, and somewhere deep within her she was grateful, but she was glad when Kiki finally gave up and allowed her to go home. She didn't want to resort to the police. She realized that she was being foolhardy, but she wanted to deal with this situation on her own. She needed to win back her self-respect, by herself, without any interference from outside. And she knew that if she *didn't* do so by herself, then she would never be free.

That evening she went home with her head in bandages, and two of her fingers strapped together with a splint. She still wore Cameron's ring, but now it was on her other hand. As she caught a cab back to SoHo, she couldn't stop looking at it on her finger—twisted and gaudy and impossible to forget.

.   .   .

A few days later, while Cameron was out at work, Sam gathered together all his things and put them in cardboard boxes. She was scrupulously fair about it: anything that they had bought together she counted as his and packed it up with the rest. She put all his clothes into shopping bags and went through the laundry to make sure she didn't miss a single item. She unplugged the portable television he had bought for the kitchen, removed his toiletries from the bathroom, packed up the glasses he'd brought home from the bar. She went through the whole process calmly and dispassionately, as if she were packing for a vacation rather than a breakup, and when she had filled several bags and four or five cardboard boxes, she took them outside and left them in the hallway. Then she bolted the door and went to bed.

She was woken at three by an enormous crash against the door to her apartment. As she got out of bed the sound came again, the sound of someone hurling his body against the door. This time it was followed by a frustrated scream, and Cameron's voice calling her a fucking-bitch-whore-slut and vowing to kill her. The sound filled her with an almost uncontrollable rage. Shaking, she marched through to the kitchen to grab a knife and the rolling pin. As she did so, she heard Cameron's body hit her front door again, this time accompanied by the sound of wood splintering.

She was glad he was almost through. As soon as the door was broken, as soon as she saw him entering her apartment, she would bludgeon him with her rolling pin for all she was worth, and if that didn't work, then there was still the knife. She stood in her hallway waiting for the door to fall in, almost willing it to fall in and give her the opportunity to finish this whole saga off. But the door never did come tumbling down, because that was when her neighbor, Malcolm Butler, came to her rescue.

She wasn't sure who it was at first because she had never heard him say so much in one go. But it obviously had to be him—he was the only man who lived in the building. His voice was quiet, almost nerdy, but even so was somehow authoritative. It certainly stopped Cameron in his tracks.

She still remembered the exact words that voice said: "If you don't stop hitting that door right now, I'm calling the cops."

"I'll hit any door I fucking well please," Cameron shouted back at him. "This is my home!"

"No," Malcolm Butler's voice said firmly, "that is Miss Blackwood's home, and it looks like you are no longer welcome."

There was a long silence now. Sam stood staring at her semi-splintered door, trembling. Just one more push, she was thinking, just one more push and he'll be in, and she could beat him for all she was worth, just as he had beaten her. But the push didn't come. She waited for several minutes, until she heard shuffling from outside, and the sound of someone dragging plastic bags down the stairs. He was going. Cameron was finally leaving her.

She sat in the hallway for several hours after that, her knife and her rolling pin on the floor beside her. She even fell asleep at one point, only to wake up again with a frightened shriek as she fumbled about in the dark trying to find her weapons. Her shriek echoed as if she were in a cave, and for once she found the sound reassuring. The hallway was empty, and Cameron was gone.

The next day she had her door fixed and fitted with strong security locks. She thought about going upstairs to thank Malcolm Butler for coming quietly to her rescue, but breaking several years of neighborly silence would be difficult, and she was still feeling slightly vulnerable. And besides, a definite part of her resented his interference. She had almost wanted Cameron to break the door down, so that they could finish the whole sorry affair, with the rolling pin and the knife, one way or the other. Malcolm Butler might have saved her life, but he had denied her an outlet for the rage that had been building within her for months.

Of course, the battle wasn't quite over yet. Cameron wasn't going to let her go so easily. He came back that night, and every other night that week, and shouted up to her from beneath her bedroom window. Sometimes he waited for her outside her apartment building, and she soon developed the habit of scanning the street every time she left the building, just to make sure he wasn't lurking somewhere behind a parked car. For the next few months he called her every day—sometimes two or three times a day—begging her to take him back, then throwing abuse down the phone at her when she refused. He wrote her threatening emails. Once he even cornered her at the offices of one of the magazines she worked for, and she had to get the security guards to take him away. Eventually she was forced to take out a restraining order against him. It was the only way to stop his harassing her.

Even now she wasn't completely free of him. Sometimes she still found herself sitting up at night, listening out for strange noises in the street outside. And when she came home late, like tonight in her cab, she always had a good look up and down the street before she approached the door to her brownstone—it was automatic.

Worst of all, she still found herself missing him occasionally, as she had in Paul's bathroom this evening. That was probably the real reason she still wore his ring: some perverse part of her was still attached to Cam. And at times, in the small hours, in the dark, she believed that a man like Cameron was all she deserved.

. . .

That night, when she went to bed, she took off Cameron's ring—just to see what it felt like. She placed it on her nightstand and lay for a while, staring at her finger. She had never taken Cam's ring off before—not since the night at the hospital. Underneath where the ring had been was a pale band of skin: shiny skin—the sort of flesh that only babies have. Her finger looked suddenly naked and unprotected—but also new, as if it had once been cut off and had only now, miraculously, grown back.

She glanced over at the nightstand, then back at her hand, before turning the light off. For a while she lay there trying to ignore the strange naked feeling of her finger. It reminded her of what it felt like to swim in the sea without a bathing costume on—deliciously free, but at the same time anxious, as if some strange, unseen creature in the depths were more likely to bite her now that her last flimsy piece of protection was removed. After a few minutes she slid her hand under the pillow, but it still felt strange. Then she tried wrapping the edge of the comforter around it. Eventually she reached out to the bedside table in the darkness. Sliding the ring back onto her middle finger, she felt comfortable once more, able at last to fall asleep.

Chapter ten

Sam slept fitfully that night, her slumber punctuated by a series of vivid and disturbing dreams. By the time she awoke, late on Wednesday morning, her pillow was damp, as though she had been sweating profusely into it all night. She was groggy and tired. She felt as if she'd hardly slept at all.

Reluctantly, she dragged herself out of bed and got up to make herself breakfast. She had a busy day ahead of her. In two hours' time she was supposed to be going to an anticapitalist rally with Paul, to interview a group of antislavery protesters there. She had a whole pile of research to get through this afternoon—papers she had brought back from Paul's in the cab last night. And worst of all, she should really think about calling her mother at some point. After what Rachel had told her on Monday, she felt obliged to phone her mother, just to let her know that she was back in town, and that everything was okay.

Sam hated calling home. It was never a particularly rewarding experience. If her father answered, they might end up arguing with each other; and if her mother answered, then Sam would probably have to listen to her crying and bemoaning that Sam never told her anything anymore. Sam's mother didn't just put her on guilt trips—she put her on whole *journeys* of guilt that could last for days, or even weeks. So in the end she decided to leave phoning her mother until another time, when she had a little more energy.

Instead, after breakfast, she decided to call T&B. She still had to see if she could secure an interview with their marketing director. Sitting down at her desk, she picked up the phone and dialed the number she had noted down from their press release two days before.

At the other end the phone started ringing, and Sam prepared herself to speak to T&B's receptionist again—Minnie Mouse, or whatever her real name was. She was going to disguise her voice once more, just as she had done yesterday morning, and hope that the woman wouldn't recognize her. She waited for ten rings, then twenty—but not until she was about to give up did somebody answer. In the end all her preparation was pointless, because the voice that wished her good morning was not the receptionist's after all: it was a man's voice—deep, rich, and sonorous.

"Hello," she said timidly, "I was wondering, could you please put me through to Matt Dyson."

"No problem," said the voice at the other end, "I *am* Matt Dyson."

"You are?" For a moment Sam was thrown slightly. "I'm sorry, I was expecting to have to speak to your receptionist. I didn't know I had your direct number."

"Actually, you've called my assistant's number, but since she's not here to answer, you've got me."

Sam looked back at the phone number in her notebook and realized that it was slightly different from the number she'd dialed. She'd transposed two of the digits by mistake—and by some stroke of providence or sheer good luck, it seemed to have given her a direct line into the marketing department.

"Are you still there?" said the voice on the other end.

"Yes, of course. Sorry, you've just caught me by surprise, that's all."

"Well, now that you've got me, how can I help?"

Automatically, Sam started her spiel. "My name's Samantha Blackwood. I'm shooting a documentary for the New Horizons television channel about how chocolate is made, and I've heard that you're bringing out a brand-new product soon. It would be good for us to get a behind-the-scenes perspective on what it takes to produce a chocolate bar. So I was wondering if it would be possible to interview you about it."

"I'm afraid we don't normally give interviews, Ms. . . . I'm sorry, what did you say your name was?"

"Samantha Blackwood."

There was a slight pause on the other end of the line. "That's not the same Samantha Blackwood who has a column in the *New York Times Magazine,* by any chance?"

"Yes, that's me."

"Oh." The line went quiet for a few moments.

"What's the matter?" asked Sam, unnerved by his silence. "Don't tell me—you can't stand the *Times.* And you loathe the way I write."

"No, not at all. It's just a little strange—I mean, I read your column every week it appears, but I never expected to be getting a call from you. It's like suddenly getting a phone call from the police."

"The police!" She laughed. "I've been compared to a few things in my time, Mr. Dyson, but never that!"

Matt Dyson laughed too, and it seemed that the momentary tension had dispersed. "Well, it's not so far-fetched, is it? After all, your newspaper presents your column as if it were society's conscience. And everyone I know who reads it either loves you or hates you. That sounds just like the police to me."

Despite herself, she couldn't help feeling flattered. The man was talking as though he sat down with a group of his friends every weekend to discuss Sam's writing, when she knew that such a thing was impossible. It was only a small column hidden away among the magazine's ads—not something that would set the world on fire. But anyway, she appreciated the compliment.

"What about you?" she said, trying not to sound as if she were fishing for more. "Are you a lover or a hater?"

He paused for a moment, before saying, "I like to think of myself as someone who reserves judgment. A detached observer, if you like."

"You disappoint me, Mr. Dyson. I like to provoke a reaction."

"I'm sure you do." A note in his voice was almost flirtatious. "If it's any consolation, I've got a friend here at work who also reads your column. He will quite happily sit at his desk and shout at the newspaper as if it were some sort of personal affront. He does it every week. I think he'd miss you terribly if you ever went away."

"He sounds like he needs help."

"Yes, I think we can safely say that Phil needs help."

"So, anyway," she said in an attempt to get the conversation back on track, "the next question is whether any of this is going to prejudice you against giving me that interview. It should be good publicity for you. The documentary is going out on New Horizons in a few weeks' time, so it should coincide with the launch of this new chocolate bar of yours."

"Oh, dear. I'm afraid I'm going to have to disappoint you a second time. You see, as I said earlier, we have a company policy of never giving interviews to anyone."

"Not even the police?"

"*Especially* not the police."

Sam started playing with her pen nervously. She hated to think that after having lucked her way into a phone conversation with this man she wouldn't be able to capitalize on it. "Is there no way I can convince you otherwise? I'm pretty harmless really, and unless you've got something to hide, I don't see how the publicity could do you any damage."

"I don't know . . ."

"How about if we met up for a drink somewhere near your office. I'm sure I'll be able to talk you into it if you give me a chance."

"Just a drink?"

"Yes. Or if your resolve is very strong, maybe two drinks."

He laughed. "Okay, I'll meet you for a drink. But only so that I can tell my friends I once met Samantha Blackwood."

Sam smiled. "Sounds good to me."

They arranged to meet on the weekend, on Sunday, when they were both free of other work commitments. He suggested a bistro in the Village on the grounds that it served good wine and good food—and Sam was quick to agree.

"I'm looking forward to meeting you, Mr. Dyson."

"The feeling is mutual."

.   .   .

Sam sat back in her chair, smiling gently to herself. For some reason she felt a lot better now that she'd talked to Matt Dyson, and faintly pleased with herself. She was looking forward to seeing the look on Paul's face when she told him she was meeting this man for a drink. Who said she couldn't get an interview with T&B? Sure, she might not have secured it yet—but she was halfway there. A little charm could go a long way.

Actually, Matt Dyson had been pretty charming himself. He could certainly give Paul a few lessons on how to treat people. There hadn't been even a hint of embarrassment when he had flattered her about her newspaper articles, and he had agreed to meet her as though he genuinely thought it an honor. If his marketing was half as engaging as this, then it was no wonder that T&B was such a successful company.

She glanced across her desk at all the research notes she had on T&B, and suddenly she found herself frowning. Maybe it was prudent to remember that Matt Dyson was a marketer. He must be used to handling journalists. She remembered the press release she had read the other day—the one about T&B's new Bliss bar—and it crossed her mind that he must have produced it. Her good mood faded slightly. Perhaps Matt Dyson was not all he seemed.

But there was no time to brood. The clock on her desk caught her eye—she was supposed to be interviewing in just over an hour. Pushing her thoughts to one side, she stood up and made her way through to the bedroom. It was time she got ready to go uptown.

Chapter eleven

She caught the subway to Times Square. She had been looking forward to this anticapitalist rally for days now—everyone had. It was the big media event of the moment. For the past week all the newspapers had been filled with speculation about what would happen—there had been discussion pieces about the aims of the march, interviews with protest groups and businesses and police representatives, retrospectives on the Seattle riots in November 1999—the list was endless. Sam herself had been commissioned to write an opinion piece for a national newspaper this weekend—but of course that was not her primary reason for being here. She was supposed to be interviewing a small group of antislavery protesters who were taking part this morning. Paul had found them through one of the many websites devoted to chocolate and coffee production and had arranged to interview them here. Later, after the interview was over, he was hoping to film them in and among the main rally.

. . .

Times Square did not look anything like it normally did on a Wednesday morning. There was no traffic on the streets, and many of the stores were literally boarded up—enormous sheets of plywood had been placed over their plate-glass windows. The whole area had a shabby, broken-down feel. It looked more like a rough neighborhood in an outer borough rather than midtown Manhattan's shopping heartland, and the strange, end-of-the-world atmosphere was unlike anything Sam had experienced before.

As she walked up Broadway, toward the place where she'd agreed to meet Paul and the camera crew, she surveyed the other people on the street. Instead of shoppers there were *anti*shoppers: students wearing T-shirts with political slogans, aging hippies with garlands of flowers around their necks, people in fancy dress. One woman was dressed as a fairy, roller-blading down the center of the street and waving her wand at many of the cheering passersby. A group of men walked past wearing bandit masks. They were smoking large cigars and handing out Monopoly money to everyone they came across. The carnival atmosphere made Sam smile, but also left her feeling slightly nervous because she wasn't sure quite what to expect next. She got the feeling that *anything* could happen.

She finally found Paul a few hundred yards up the street, outside a luxury chocolate store. He wasn't happy. Apparently the main march was on its way up to Forty-second Street now—they could already hear the sound of whistles and drums being beaten in the distance—and

Paul was worried that if they didn't get filming over with soon, then the sound would be too loud to continue. "We should get the show on the road," he said. "Now."

"Who am I interviewing?" asked Sam.

"That woman over there. Her name's Amy. She's their spokesperson."

Paul pointed to a woman who was talking with some of the others in the protesters' group. She was young, probably in her early twenties. Her brown hair was braided into scores of tiny plaits, some of them interwoven with red, blue, and green strands—they made her look like a colorful rag doll. She was wearing a tight pink T-shirt, with T&B ARE SLAVE TRADERS printed in large letters across the front.

While Paul helped the other two set up, Sam went to introduce herself. "Hi, I'm Sam. I'm going to be interviewing you."

The woman held out her hand. "Pleased to meet you, Sam." She had a large, pretty smile.

"The others are just setting up now, so I just thought I'd let you know what we're going to do. We're going to have to be reasonably quick, I'm afraid, because when the main rally gets here, there will be too much noise, but we should be able to get everything done in time."

"Fine by me," said Amy. "I know what I want to say, so just stick me in front of a camera."

"You're not nervous at all?"

"What's there to be nervous about? If I say anything too contentious, you'll probably cut it anyway. I know you've got your own agenda, so I figured I'd just say whatever I wanted to say, tell the truth, and then leave it to you. As long as I get my T-shirt on television, I don't really care."

Sam smiled. "I take it you've done this before then."

"Whenever they let me."

She took Amy forward to where Paul and the others were setting up. They stood her in front of a stand while Mark the cameraman took some light readings. Then they made her say something into the microphone to take some readings of her voice. And after a few minutes they were ready.

. . .

They began the interview with a few simple questions, as they always did, to put Amy at ease. But after a couple of minutes it became obvious that Amy was quite at home already. Sam took an instant liking to the woman. She was eloquent, sure of herself, and truly passionate about what she was saying. And she was a natural in front of the camera: her words were clear and bold and spoken with conviction—there wasn't the slightest hint of hesitation in her voice. Sam couldn't help wondering if her own voice sounded nearly so confident.

"We in the West have pretty cozy ideas about chocolate," the woman was saying. "We think of it as something comforting, something to give to our children as a treat. Unfortunately, the reality for thousands of people who work on cocoa plantations is far from cozy. While children *here* are happily spending their allowance on chocolate, children in West Africa are being sold into slavery in order to produce it."

"Can you tell us something about the scale of the problem?" said Sam.

"According to Unesco, there are over fifteen thousand child slaves in the Côte d'Ivoire alone. They work on cocoa plantations for upward of sixteen hours a day, seven days a week. They are beaten and abused as a matter of routine, and many of them are malnourished. And that's just the Côte d'Ivoire. Mali and Benin also have a major problem—and as the poorest countries in the region they are also where a large proportion of these child slaves come from."

"Do you have any idea of how much a slave costs in West Africa?"

"Yes. Most of these kids are originally bought for as little as fifteen bucks each—that's the price of about twenty-five chocolate bars. Fifteen dollars for a human being. Life in West Africa really is cheap."

Sam asked her a few more questions about slavery, and the conditions on cocoa plantations. Most of it was information she'd heard before, and material she'd filmed for herself in Africa, but it was always good to get someone else's opinions on film. And Amy had a way of putting things that was not only succinct but evocative.

"I suppose the big question," asked Sam, "is *why* is this happening?"

"Well," said Amy, "I'm afraid the answer is that we *like* it like that. As with everything in this world, it all eventually comes down to money. We have an insatiable desire for chocolate in this country, but we want it *cheap*. The only way we can get cheap chocolate is if we drive down cocoa prices. Low cocoa prices mean low profits for plantation owners, which means they employ slaves rather than paying their workers. There's a direct link between our own desire for cheap goods and the conditions that these people have to suffer."

"So what can we do about it?"

"All we can really do is put pressure on the chocolate companies to change things. They are the *only* people who have the power to do anything about it. The big companies have turnovers far greater than most governments in the area, so they have a lot of clout. But unfortunately, most of them seem reluctant to act."

"But what *can* they do?"

"They can do plenty. They could put pressure on West African governments to introduce antislavery measures. They could send their *own* inspectors to check conditions in the plantations they buy their cocoa from. They could boycott farms they know to be disreputable. There are all sorts of things they could do, but they don't want to do any of them because they cost money.

"What *we're* trying to get chocolate companies to do is to pass this cost on to us. If they raised the price of chocolate, they could easily afford to take these measures and still keep their profits intact. And I'm not talking about a massive hike in prices here. If we were to increase the price of the average chocolate bar by a single cent, then these companies could raise hundreds of millions of dollars for local economies in the developing world. A *single* penny. Nobody here would notice the difference, but I can assure you that the difference in Africa and South America would be enormous.

"It's about time we all realized that *nothing* in this world is free. There is always someone, somewhere, who is paying the cost. And at the moment, when it comes to chocolate, the people who are paying are not us, but child slaves. How can any rational person possibly think that's right?"

. . .

As the anticapitalist rally got closer, they decided to finish the interview. They could see the procession coming up Broadway, and the noise levels were rising. Paul wanted to get some shots of Amy and the other protesters among the main crowd, to show that this antislavery campaign was part of a much larger movement, but first they would have to wait for the procession to reach them. It was big, and it was already deafeningly noisy, but it was also slow.

While they waited for the protesters to draw closer, Amy took Sam to one side. "I just wanted to say thanks, you know, for filming us. It's difficult getting publicity, especially when there are a thousand other groups fighting for the same space." Amy gestured toward the approaching crowd.

"Well, it's a story that needs to be told," said Sam. "I should be thanking you. You're good in front of the camera. You should see some of the people I have to interview . . ."

The other antislavery protesters were picking up their banners now and getting ready to join the procession. Amy introduced Sam to a couple of them—a student called Toby whose face was thick with acne, and a crusty-looking man in his thirties called Vince.

"So I take it you lot must come to this kind of march all the time," said Sam by way of conversation.

"Not that often," said Vince with a smile. One of his front teeth was missing. "Normally we prefer more *direct* action."

"Oh, yes?" said Sam. "Like what kind of thing?"

"Oh, nothing too serious," said Amy hurriedly. "We just make a bit of a nuisance of ourselves, that's all."

"Commercial disobedience," said Vince enigmatically.

Sam looked from Vince to Amy and back again. She got the feeling something was going on here that she didn't quite understand, and her interest was certainly aroused.

"For example," explained Amy, "this week we're targeting Trundel and Barr. We're going to protest outside their offices next Wednesday, make some noise, and perhaps do one or two other things to make their lives miserable."

"Yes, I noticed you're not exactly fans of T and B." Sam nodded to the slogan on Amy's T-shirt: T&B ARE SLAVE TRADERS. "Why them, rather than anyone else?"

"Because they're worse than anyone else."

"Really?"

"Absolutely. The whole industry is shady, but most chocolate companies have sold off their cocoa plantations years ago, so they can at least *claim* that conditions are nothing to do with them. But T and B still owns cocoa plantations across West Africa. Not only that, but they are notorious. T and B are one of the few chocolate companies left who still have a *direct* link to slavery."

Sam stared at the woman. "Are you sure about this?"

"Positive."

"How come we've never heard about this before?"

"Because T and B is still a family-owned business. It's not a public company, so it doesn't have to publish company reports."

"That's unbelievable . . ." For a few moments Sam was lost for words. Thinking quickly, she said, "Listen, I don't suppose you'd be prepared to say all this on film, would you?"

"Sure. Why not?"

"Well," said Sam carefully, "there is a possibility we might get into trouble. T and B is one of the biggest chocolate producers in the country, and it's not going to take kindly to accusations like this. It's going to want to discredit you if it possibly can. But we should be okay as long as we have incontrovertible proof." She paused a second. "You *do* have proof, don't you?"

Amy hesitated. "Kind of."

"What do you mean, kind of?"

"To tell you the truth I'm just going on what I've been told by a friend of mine. But he works for Unesco, so he should know."

"And does *he* have proof?"

"Probably. I mean, I think so." Suddenly Amy didn't look so sure of herself. "He's away in the Côte d'Ivoire at the moment, but I can give you a phone number if you like."

"Listen," said Sam, "whatever you do, you should keep this quiet— just for the moment. There's no sense in inviting a libel case until we've got all the information."

"But what about our protest?" said Vince. He looked sullen, as if he didn't like being told what to do.

"Trust me—just wait for a while. Then I'll give you all the publicity you need."

As the procession finally reached them, they were engulfed in the din of the crowd. It was far bigger and far noisier than Sam had expected, and the sound of all the drums and whistles, punctuated by the shouts and chants of the various different groups within it, was deafening. Sam could see Mark and Paul up ahead, scurrying along in front of the group, filming them as they made their way up Broadway. Amy joined the crowd now too, but before she did she scribbled down her friend's phone number in Africa on a book of matches and handed it to Sam. And then she was gone, swallowed up among her friends.

. . .

Later, while the others were filming, Sam pulled Paul into the privacy of the doorway of the chocolate store and told him what Amy had said.

"This could be big, couldn't it?" said Paul.

"Are you kidding? This could be a scoop."

"So how are we going to follow it up? If T and B is as guilty as she says it is, it's not exactly going to publish the information."

"I could look them up on the Internet if you like," said Sam.

"And I could ring this guy in Africa."

"The newspaper archives might have something on them. If I can get hold of some newspapers from the Côte d'Ivoire, there might be something about T and B there. And then there's always . . ." She stopped.

"There's always what?"

"Well, it all depends on what happens on Sunday, when I meet this Matt Dyson guy. If I can get him to agree to an interview, then there's a chance we could make him admit something on film."

They looked at each other. Sam could feel the excitement growing between them. There was something conspiratorial about standing in the doorway together like this, as the importance of their story ballooned before them.

Paul gazed at her, his eyes lingering on her lips for a second. "You know," he said after a while, "I've been thinking about what happened last night, and . . . well, maybe I was a bit hasty. You know, when you cut my shoulder . . ."

Sam smiled cautiously. "Yes, you were."

"Listen, can we forget that yesterday ever happened and start over? I was hoping perhaps we could get together again, maybe tonight. We could see what information we pick up this afternoon, and compare notes . . ."

She paused for a second. She knew that it would be a mistake to go back to Paul's place again—especially after last night's fiasco—but then, what other offers did she have? She had nothing to lose. All the same, no way was she going to make it easy for him. "I'm busy tonight," she lied. "Perhaps sometime next week."

Out in the street the procession passed in a loud, chaotic whirl. Sam watched as the hordes of people wandered by, and she noticed suddenly that many of them were dancing. In among all the slogans and banners, people were swaying and gyrating to whatever rhythms they could hear in the chaos—whistles blowing, drums being beaten, and later a sound system playing distorted dance music, much to the glee of the swirling crowd. For a moment she had a real urge to step out into the street and join them. But then Mark returned with the cine camera, and Colin with the sound equipment, and it was time to get back to work.

Chapter twelve

Matt Dyson had arranged to meet her at a simple-looking bistro in the Village, with large wooden tables and large windows looking out onto a busy street. As Sam entered the room, she realized that she had absolutely no idea what T&B's marketing director looked like. She had a vague mental image of a businessman—someone fat and aging in a suit, with cheeks full of broken veins—but no one here looked even remotely like that. Most of the tables were occupied by groups of thirtysomethings enjoying a lazy Sunday-afternoon drink together, or middle-aged couples sharing their Sunday newspapers across cups of hot coffee.

She was just about to ask after him at the bar when a waiter tapped her on the shoulder. "Excuse me, but is your name Samantha Black-wood?"

"Yes."

"Mr. Dyson asked me to bring you to him once you arrived."

The waiter took her across the bar to a table near the window. The man sitting there had his back to the room, so Sam was not at first able to tell what he looked like, but she could see straightaway that he was not dressed in a suit: instead he had on a simple pair of jeans and an unironed blue shirt. She chided herself for her preconceptions—it was the weekend, after all, and even a high-profile businessman would not feel the need to dress formally on a Sunday.

Only when the man stood up to greet her did she discover the full extent of her misconceptions. Matt Dyson was not the slightest bit portly. He was nearer to thirty than to fifty years old, and far from having cheeks full of broken veins, he was actually quite handsome. He had the most beautiful brown eyes, boyish, tousled hair, and a large smile that Sam found immediately disarming. There was also something vaguely familiar about him, although in the confusion of the moment she couldn't quite put her finger on what it was.

"Well," said Sam, as he introduced himself, "I have to say that you're not at all how I expected you to be."

His grin broadened. "If it comes to that, then neither are you. There's no picture of you in the *New York Times,* you know."

"So what did you think I'd look like?"

"You wouldn't like it if I told you. You should understand that most of the journalists I come across are male, alcoholic, and just a little sour. Compared with them, you're a breath of fresh air."

Sam laughed. "Believe me, I can have my sour moments."

They sat down, and as they ordered themselves drinks, Sam studied his face for a few moments. She definitely recognized him from somewhere. There was something about those eyes . . .

"So," said Matt Dyson, turning back to face her, "who would have thought I'd be spending Sunday afternoon sharing a drink with a famous journalist?"

"That works both ways. Who would have thought I'd be spending Sunday afternoon with a titan of industry?"

"Come on," he said modestly, "I'm sure you meet businessmen like me every day of the week."

"Businessmen, yes—but not like you." Inexplicably she found herself starting to blush. So she covered up by saying, "Tell me something—have I met you before? You look familiar for some reason."

"Well," he said after a pause, "we didn't actually meet . . . but, yes, you have seen me before."

"I have?"

"Yes. It was at the International Chocolate Trade Fair. Had I known who you were then, I would have come over and introduced myself."

Sam frowned, trying to remember.

"It was on the first morning," he explained. "You were sitting on a bench by the centerpiece, with a backpack by your feet. When you got up to go, you looked straight at me—gave me a withering look, actually—and then made for the exit. That's not the kind of effect I usually have on people. At least, not before I've even spoken to them, anyway."

"My God," she said, a smile breaking out over her face, "I thought I recognized you!"

"Well, I'm glad to see I haven't had the same effect on you the second time around."

"Sorry about that. I wasn't walking out because of you. It was that place that made me want to leave, and that hideous chocolate *thing* in the middle of the hall. It all made me feel a little sick."

"Not your kind of thing?"

"Not really."

"No," said Matt, "me neither."

She smiled at him again, although this time her smile was a little guarded. She remembered seeing him at the fair now—surrounded by all those other people. She recalled his expression, and the embarrassed way he turned away when she caught his eye, almost as if he had been hiding something from her.

For a while they talked about inconsequential things—the Chocolate Fair, the restaurant they were in, the kind of people who came here to enjoy the afternoon—and slowly Sam began to relax once more. However Matt might have seemed at the Chocolate Fair last weekend, there was nothing embarrassed about him now—in fact, he seemed open, and genuine, and she was beginning to enjoy his company. It felt nice to be sitting in a bar, chatting, drinking. Sam couldn't remember the last time she'd gone out on a Sunday. She missed going out like this, and it seemed a shame that she was here to work and not merely to chat the afternoon away. She had to remind herself that Matt Dyson worked for one of the most unethical companies in the chocolate industry—she wasn't here to get to know him, but to ensnare him.

"So," he said after a while, "tell me about this documentary of yours. What's it about?"

"Oh, you know," she said, trying to sound nonchalant, "it's just a program about chocolate. It's a behind-the-scenes look at the world's favorite confection: how it's made, where it comes from, how it's sold—that kind of thing."

"Do you mind me asking who else you have approached?"

"Not at all. I've spoken to all the usual suspects: Mars, Nestlé, Cadbury . . ."

"In that case what do you need *us* for? They're all much bigger players than T and B is—we couldn't possibly hope to compete with them."

"Well," she said, thinking quickly, "of course, normally we wouldn't bother approaching you. But when we heard about the fact that you were going to launch a brand-new product . . . what's it called—the Bliss bar? . . . well, when we heard about that, we changed our minds. We figured that this could be good for both of us—we get to talk to you about what it's like to launch a new chocolate bar, and you get a whole load of free publicity."

"It all sounds like a good idea, but like I told you on Wednesday, we have a company policy of not giving any interviews to journalists."

"I know, but I was kind of hoping I might be able to change your mind."

He sighed heavily. "Well, it's not really up to me. You see, this is something that the owner himself has decided. Nathan Trundel doesn't want anyone in the company to talk to the press."

Sam smiled as sweetly as she could manage. "Well, in that case perhaps *you* could change *his* mind."

Matt smiled back at her and said nothing for a few moments. Once again Sam got the impression that he knew more than he was letting on—the way he held her gaze was somehow unnerving, and she had the uncanny feeling that those big brown eyes of his could see right through everything she was saying to the *real* reason she wanted an interview.

Eventually, to her relief, he looked down at his hands and the Bloody Mary he was clutching. "Let's put all this aside for a moment," he said. "I want to hear more about you. It's not every day I get to chat with a newspaper columnist—especially not one of your caliber. I want to know what makes Samantha Blackwood tick."

Sam was thrown for a moment. "I don't know what to say. I mean, what do you want to know?"

"Perhaps I should explain myself. I'm quite an admirer of yours. I have been for some time. I don't generally have much time for the newspapers—but your column is something I make sure I never miss. There's a hard edge to everything you write that I find intriguing—it doesn't matter how seemingly harmless the subject matter is, you always manage to pierce through to something darker lying just beneath the surface. It's quite a talent."

"Well, thank you. I'm flattered."

"It's I who should be flattered. When you said you wanted to interview me, I was amazed that I could have done anything to attract your attention. But then, I suppose it's not really me you're interested in, but chocolate."

"Yes," said Sam. "I mean, obviously you're a high-profile figure in the industry—but the documentary is about chocolate in general."

Again those eyes fixed on hers—not piercing so much as engulfing. "In that case, tell me this: What is it about chocolate that so interests Samantha Blackwood?"

"Well . . . it's an innately interesting subject."

"Is it?"

"Yes. It's the world's favorite flavor. It arouses inordinate passion in people everywhere. What subject could be better?"

He leaned forward, resting his glass on the table before him. "Samantha." He paused. "Can I call you Samantha?"

"Most people call me Sam."

"Okay, Sam, why don't you tell me what this is *really* all about?"

Sam swallowed hard. "I don't follow you. . . ."

"Come on! You're not a hack journalist—and you don't want to make some fluffy documentary about chocolate. You're after something."

She looked into his eyes and realized that she had to make a decision fast. Either she kept up the deception, made out that her documentary was perfectly innocent, or she told him the truth and prayed that he would still want to be involved. Each option had its risks. If she told him the whole truth, he might well back out of the interview there and then. On the other hand, if she wasn't straight with him from the outset, then that could lead to complications later, and possibly even a legal challenge to stop any interview from being aired. Her head told her to equivocate a little, try to change the subject and buy herself some time to think; her heart told her to be direct with him. She liked this man. She wanted to trust him.

Eventually she looked away. "Like I said, it's just a perfectly innocent documentary about chocolate," she lied. "Behind the scenes with Willy Wonka."

"Is that all?"

"Sure, that's all."

Matt folded his arms with a frown. "You know, Sam, you're not the only one who's able to dig things up with a bit of investigation. It's relatively easy to find out all kinds of things if you know the right people, and the right questions to ask. For example, when I called up your TV station yesterday and asked them the title of the documentary you're working on, they told me that it was not really about chocolate at all, but about working conditions in the cocoa industry."

Sam sat back in her chair, avoiding his gaze. She felt like a high school girl who had just been caught cheating on a final exam.

"I don't appreciate being lied to," he continued, "and much as I admire your journalism, I cannot agree with your methods."

"So I suppose that means you're not interested in giving me an interview then?" said Sam sullenly.

"I don't see how I *can*. I mean, if you've lied to me on this, then how can I trust you on anything else?"

Sam sat there for a while, feeling small, before finally resigning herself to having failed. She had tried to deceive him, and he had seen through her. There seemed little point in staying. "Well, I suppose that means our meeting is over."

"Yes," said Matt, "it does look that way."

Reaching back for her shoulder bag, she made ready to go. "In spite of everything," she said, "can I just say that it was a pleasure to meet you."

"It was a pleasure to meet you too."

"And I'm sorry if you think I'm untrustworthy. Perhaps if T and B were a bit more trustworthy themselves, I would have approached things a little differently. You work for a very shady company, Mr. Dyson, and no matter how much you don't like me lying to you, it's nothing compared with the way your company does business."

"I don't know where you get your information from," said Matt, looking genuinely surprised. "As far as I'm concerned, everything we do at T and B is perfectly aboveboard."

"Yes, well, that's where you're wrong."

She picked up her drink and finished the last few drops.

"There's just one other thing I want to know," she said as she stood up to go. "If you already knew what my documentary was about, then why did you agree to see me today?"

"Like I said, I wanted to meet you, that's all."

"You never were going to give me an interview, were you?"

Matt shrugged and made a regretful face.

Sam paused for a second before saying, "You might not like being lied to, Mr. Dyson, but I don't like being taken for a ride. I don't know if you think it's funny to summon me here on a wild-goose chase, but I don't."

Matt started to say something, but before he could, she placed a twenty on the table, turned her back on him, and left the bar.

. . .

As she stepped out onto the street, the first thing she did was take out her cell phone and call Paul. She thought of telling him what had just happened, but she didn't want to disappoint him, so instead she simply asked him for a couple of phone numbers.

"What's going on?" said Paul. "Have you had your meeting with Matt Dyson yet?"

"Yes. I'll tell you about it later. But in the meantime can you text me the protesters' phone number, and also that phone number in Africa they gave us. There are one or two things I want to sort out with them."

"So is T and B going to do the interview?"

"I said I'll tell you about it later."

"Right," said Paul, disappointed. "So that means they've turned us down."

"Don't worry, I've just had an idea. We'll get our interview. Now just text me those phone numbers."

She rang off and waited for the text message to arrive. Her blood was up now. Companies like T&B relied on people like Sam to roll over and give up—well, she wasn't going to oblige them. She could smell a scoop here, and she wasn't going to let the opportunity pass her by. If Matt Dyson wouldn't give her an interview, then she'd have to go straight to the top of the company, to Nathan Trundel himself. And since the softly-softly approach hadn't worked, then perhaps she'd have to try something else.

She smiled to herself. She knew she had a fight on her hands, and it felt good. Matt Dyson might have thought he'd seen the last of her, but he didn't know what he was letting himself in for. She would get an interview out of T&B if it killed her.

Chocolate

The product we know as chocolate today is very different from the substance consumed by the Mayans and Aztecs five hundred years ago. For the ancients, cacahuatl was only ever really a drink. It was made by pulverizing a few cocoa beans, perhaps adding a little maize or chili, then mixing it with water to make a bitter, frothy, and slightly acidic liquid. Generally only the oldest, driest, stalest cocoa beans were used to make this drink. The Mayans and Aztecs used cocoa as a form of currency, so to grind up your best beans and drink them was effectively like swallowing money.

To the sensitive taste buds of Europeans, such drinks were foul in the extreme, and it took a great deal of European effort and know-how to convert what they thought of as primitive concoctions into something a little more palatable. The first thing the invading Spanish did to the drink was to add sugar. A while later, a Dutch chemist discovered that treating cocoa with alkaline salts made it taste milder and much less acidic. An Englishman invented the first industrially produced eating chocolate, and a man from Alsace came up with the idea of mixing it with milk powder. Then a Swiss man discovered that rolling it beneath giant granite rollers for up to three days smoothed out the grittiness of the mixture. The whole process was imported to the United States in the nineteenth century, where chocolate was produced on a scale the Aztecs could not even have imagined.

Today's chocolate is the result of several centuries of such refinement. Unlike the drink of the ancients, our product is always sweet, always smooth, and always delicious. It can be either liquid or solid, or anywhere in between the two. It can be molded and shaped into any form we choose, from simple slabs to giant and elaborate sculptures. We even have chocolate bars that can be stored in temperatures of up to 125°F without melting. Due to North American and European intervention, chocolate is now consumed all over the world and is probably as perfect a product as it can ever be.

And yet our enthusiasm for the substance is still only a pale shadow of the veneration with which the ancient Mayans viewed their humble drinks. Bitter as their chocolate was, they still drank it with as much pleasure as we have when we swallow our own perfect morsels. The difference is that their pleasure was not merely physical. To them, chocolate was a life-giving substance of enormous religious and cultural significance. It was never merely a snack. It was the food of the gods.

Chapter thirteen

Matt Dyson was a marketing genius. Everyone said so, even those who didn't like him. He could sell radios to the deaf. He could sell hamburgers to vegetarians. If he wanted to, he could make computer nerds seem cool, and grandmothers seem sexy, and politicians seem credible. But more important, since he worked for a confectionery company, he could make the world seem sweet. He had the ability to make people's doubts melt away and turn their wishes, desires, and aspirations into pure milk chocolate.

Everybody in the chocolate industry knew this. It was why he had been headhunted to work at Trundel & Barr in the first place. It was why he was paid more than any of his predecessors had been, despite being the youngest marketing director ever to have worked for the company. It was also why Matt hadn't had a proper night's sleep in over five years, why he stayed at work late almost every night worrying over marketing plans, and why, since the day he'd started working for T&B, he hadn't taken even half the vacation he was entitled to.

He hadn't gotten where he was without working hard. In fact, he had gotten here by sacrificing most other things in life: family, friendship, even love. Matt's last girlfriend, Sophie, had walked out on him saying that she spent more time with her hairdresser than she spent with Matt—if she'd wanted to have a relationship by email, plenty of Internet sites were far more satisfying than he was. And though he had fought with her at the time, because what she was saying was undoubtedly unfair, a small part of him suspected that she might be right. If he was to be the marketing director of one of the world's major chocolate producers, then perhaps that was simply the price he had to pay.

. . .

Whenever anyone asked him the secret to his success, he always said the same: it was a passion for the product. You didn't make it in chocolate marketing unless you knew what you were talking about. Or more than that—you had to *care* about what you were talking about. It wasn't enough merely to live and breathe the stuff, you had to *want* to live and breathe it, every hour of every day of every year. If that wasn't a sacrifice you were prepared to make, then you were in the wrong industry.

Matt had embraced chocolate far more wholeheartedly than he had ever embraced Sophie. He knew all its idiosyncrasies—what temperatures it preferred, what humidity it liked, and what ingredients it blended with best. He knew its history, how it was made, and how it was used; he even knew its chemical composition. He could taste it like a vintner tastes wines, picking out each of the different notes on his palate: the flowery flavor of Guanajan *criollo* beans, the pungent fruitiness of Madagascan *trinitario,* and the spicy tang of Brazilian *forastero* beans. But what truly inspired him was not the actuality of chocolate, but the *potential.* What got him out of bed in the mornings was not merely a dessert or a snack to eat between meals—it was the concept, the dream, the ideal that chocolate represented. For a marketer like Matt, chocolate was probably the perfect product. It could be bent to any occasion, be it Mother's Day, Easter, or Christmas. It could mean whatever you wanted it to mean: a way to say thanks, a gesture of love, an invitation to sex. The potentials were endless. Chocolate was luxury. It was sensuousness and sweetness and innocent joy. It was to be adored and worshiped and yearned for and enjoyed with an abandon people normally reserved for the bedroom. Chocolate was the stuff of dreams. And as the marketing director of one of the country's biggest confectioners, Matt saw himself as its special envoy, serving up those dreams to the world, in blocks, chips, powders, sauces, and individually wrapped, bite-size portions.

.   .   .

Matt had been surrounded by chocolate all his life, and in a manner of speaking, the substance was in his blood. When he was a child, his father had owned a candy store in Boston, so he had grown up surrounded not only by chocolate but by confectionery of all kinds: everything from Fun Dips to Old Fashioned Sticks and giant Easter eggs filled with toys and games. As soon as he could walk, his father had put him to work in that store—stacking shelves, running deliveries, even working the till. His mother had died when Matt was a little boy, so there was nobody else to help out. It was just Matt and his dad, selling candy by the ounce and struggling to make ends meet.

It was an unusual childhood, surrounded by big glass jars full of candy, laid out on shelves like surgical specimens. Whenever Matt wasn't in school, he was in the store, helping his father. He worked every evening, serving out Jelly Belly beans, Life Savers, and Charleston Chews to whining kids who didn't have enough allowance to buy what they really wanted. And while his friends went out and played soccer on the weekends or met girls or even just stayed at home watching Saturday-morning television, Matt was stuck behind a counter talking to old women for whom the event of the year was to bring their grandchildren to the store and set them loose among the boxes of Blackjack taffy, jujubes, and Cherry Heads.

Being a kid in a candy store wasn't all it was cracked up to be. There was no point in running amok stuffing your face full of fudge when you were surrounded by the stuff every day of your life. Matt didn't really like fudge, anyway. In fact he didn't really like most candy. Having been encompassed by it for most of his life, he saw it for what it really was: something adults used to occupy their kids' mouths, shut them up for a moment, distract them from the boredom of day-to-day life. There was nothing to aspire to in a bag of Twizzlers, or a pack of Starburst. There was no magic in toffees or mints or Bonkers fruit chews. All they did was rot your teeth and make you hyperactive. Matt would sooner have sat down with a bag of sugar and a spoon.

In fact, out of everything that Matt's father sold in that store, chocolate was the only product Matt had any respect for. For some reason, chocolates were always in a class of their own. Unlike the other candies, they had wonderful, evocative names, like Butterfinger or Bounty bar or 3 Musketeers. A whole group of chocolates even had cosmic names: Mars, Milky Way, and Sky bars—you could travel to the end of the universe and back with just one bite. Unlike other candy, chocolate was always associated with special occasions—weddings, christenings, Valentine's Day, or Christmas. Nobody gave you licorice on your birthday—why would they?—but chocolate was a different matter. Chocolate was special.

Everything about the substance was enchanting. Its taste wasn't just sweet like most of the other products in the store, it was also smoky and tangy and somehow *rich*. Each chunk was the perfect size to press against the roof of his mouth, and when it melted—slowly at first, then faster—waves of intense flavor would burst over his taste buds, filling his mouth with an almost physical sensation that lingered there long after he had swallowed the first chunk and turned his thoughts greedily to the next.

No situation in life was so good that the addition of chocolate couldn't make it even better. It was a treat whenever he did exceptionally well at school and a comfort for less happy times, such as the day his grandpa died or when he broke his arm playing soccer. When so much else was missing in his life, chocolate was always there. It was the frosting on every cake, ever present, like a friend or a guardian angel, escorting him through life.

. . .

Whenever he spoke of his childhood, which wasn't often, Matt always presented it as a happy time, a time when he had begun to learn the tricks of his trade, and when he had first formulated all his hopes and dreams. But in truth, beyond the occasional clandestine chocolate bar in the back of the store, there hadn't been much space for hopes and dreams—just the hard reality of having to sell as much product as possible to pay the bills.

"Always make sure the customer buys something extra," his father would say to him. "I don't care if they've only come for a Bounty bar, they're not leaving this store until they've also paid for a pound of toffee. We need the money."

There were numerous ways you could get people to buy more than they originally came in for, and his father had a different strategy for every different kind of customer. Since kids were his main source of income, he had a whole range of ways to deal with them. With the more timid, he'd simply bully them into taking more than they'd asked for—fill their bags with too much, then charge them for the extra. With the more streetwise, he'd reason with them, tempting them with products they'd never considered trying before. Dime bars might be cheaper, he'd say, but premium butterscotch was much *better*. And who wanted to suck lollipops like some *baby,* when you could have a more grown-up, and more expensive, bar of Toblerone instead?

With adults, his methods were a little more sophisticated. He flirted outrageously with the mothers who came in, flattering them on the way they looked, and telling them how slim they were, just so that they wouldn't have any objections when he offered them boxes of chocolate assortments to take home. "If you weren't married, Mrs. Jones," he'd say, "I'd buy you a box of chocolates myself!" And whether it was the twinkle in his eye that convinced them or something else, they would leave the store with a small treat for the children and a large one for themselves, because today they felt they deserved something nice. They owed it to themselves.

The easiest people to bamboozle were always fathers—particularly fathers with daughters. With fathers, their pride sold them: both pride as a parent and as a provider. "What an *adorable* little girl you have, Mr. Smith," Matt's dad would say. "You'll be wanting something special for *her.*" And if Mr. Smith disagreed, he would look shocked, as if denying the poor child half a pound of fudge was tantamount to child abuse.

Matt had watched these routines so often that he knew them by heart, and he knew exactly what line his father would take as soon as a customer entered the store. It all seemed so transparent to Matt that he couldn't believe people still fell for it. But they did, every day, almost without fail.

While Matt couldn't hope to match his father's performance with most candy, he did begin to develop a sixth sense when it came to chocolate. By the time he was a teenager he was able to guess with almost total accuracy what kind of chocolate any given customer would like. He could also sense intuitively how much they were prepared to spend—a talent that impressed even an old professional like his father. Knowing how far a customer would go gave you an invaluable advantage—if they didn't reach their limit, it was always just possible to bring to their attention an extra little something that they might not have realized they wanted.

These were some of the tricks of the trade Matt learned. He also learned how to display goods, what colors sold your products, the psychology of pricing, and of bargaining, and of value for money. These weren't formal lessons of the sort he received in high school. They were just the things he picked up in passing—techniques that seeped into him by being constantly surrounded by them.

Even now Matt still remembered what his father had once said to him when he was only twelve years old. "Selling," he'd said, "is the most important thing you will ever learn. Forget schoolwork. Forget math and geography and history and science. Compared to what you will learn with me, they're all useless. I'm going to give you the best education a boy could ever hope for. I'm going to make you into a salesman."

Twenty years later, when Matt became the marketing director for one of the world's biggest confectionery manufacturers, it seemed that the old geezer had kept his promise after all. While Matt had few friends, no lover, no wife, and no children—while he was overworked and lonely and constantly tired—he had undeniably been turned into one of the best salesmen of his generation. He was a selling machine, born and bred, with marketing strategies in his veins and a heart made of pure milk chocolate.

Chapter fourteen

At the end of last year, Nathan Trundel, chairman and owner of T&B, had taken Matt aside and asked him to think of some ideas for a new chocolate bar. He didn't give Matt any kind of brief. He didn't seem to care what kind of chocolate bar Matt came up with just so long as it expanded the company's product portfolio. The wily old man seemed to sense that he could squeeze much more work out of Matt if he didn't make any suggestions and just left him to his own devices, allowed him to invest a little of himself in the project.

Matt set about the task with an enthusiasm he hadn't felt since he was a little boy. This was his opportunity to create something unique, something inspirational, something to delight people everywhere. This was the one chance he had to leave his mark on the world. And besides, since Sophie had left him, he had been struggling to fill his time with anything worthwhile—this, at least, would keep him occupied. So for the next couple of months, just as Nathan Trundel knew he would, Matt buried himself even deeper in his work. He came into the office on weekends, stayed late every night, and slowly his blueprint for a new chocolate bar began to take shape.

Coming up with the actual product was not that difficult. Ever since he was a boy, Matt had daydreamed about what he would put in his own bar. He knew exactly which ingredients worked best together, and which combinations to avoid. In the end, for simplicity's sake, he made his new chocolate bar as pure as he possibly could. He would put flakes of nuts inside, and tiny pockets of cookie and nougat to give it texture, but essentially it would be a straightforward block of chocolate, high in quality, with a high percentage of cocoa solids.

In a way, the product was irrelevant—there were only so many combinations of ingredients, and all of them had been used a dozen times before by other manufacturers. Far more important was the marketing concept, and this was what kept Matt busy for so long. He knew he had to come up with a strong idea—something that would capture people's imaginations—otherwise it would never get off the ground.

For a long while he struggled to think of anything, but then he remembered something Sophie had told him—long ago, when they had first gotten together—and it immediately gave him inspiration.

. . .

Sophie was the only woman Matt had ever come across who knew as much about chocolate as he did. She could match him point for point on the history of cocoa and could just about equal him when it came to tasting the different varieties. However, while most of his knowledge revolved around marketing the product, Sophie's interest was almost entirely sexual.

Their first date together was in an expensive Mexican restaurant, where cocoa featured heavily on the menu. They ordered chocolate soup, and Mole Poblano de Guajolote. They shared a bowl of thick cocoa chili. And while they lingered together over a rich chocolate mousse, she told him all about the chocolate sex secrets she'd discovered.

"Did you know," she said, "that cocoa contains a chemical compound called anandamide, which has similar effects on the brain to cannabis." Then she smiled seductively and added, "It heightens bodily sensations."

According to Sophie, chocolate was a regular cocktail of aphrodisiac substances. When you eat enough of it, the caffeine and theobromine it contains begin to stimulate your nervous system and heighten your awareness of physical sensations. You start to feel butterflies in your stomach. Soon your pupils are dilating, and your heart rate speeds up, pumping greater amounts of blood around your body. Within a short time, your body begins to feel primed for action.

If you are not in the mood, then plenty of substances in chocolate can *put* you in the mood. The high sugar content triggers the release of endorphins in the bloodstream, giving you a warm glow inside. Then there's tryptophan, which is related to the drug Ecstasy—it helps to give you that chocolate "loved-up" feeling. And just when you're beginning to feel emotionally and physically stimulated, another chocolate chemical kicks in—phenylethylamine. This is the substance that your brain produces when you're in love, which swamps your pleasure centers when you're having sex, and which peaks when you orgasm.

Throughout history all the most sexually liberated people have known of chocolate's aphrodisiac properties: Casanova used to woo all his women with chocolate before he bedded them; Madame du Barry gave it to all her suitors; and even Montezuma, the king of the Aztecs, used to drink a cup of the stuff every time he entered his harem.

"But the most important reason why sex and chocolate go together," said Sophie as she licked the last bit of mousse from her spoon with the tip of her tongue, "is the anticipation they both cause. Even before you take that first delicious bite, you know exactly what to expect. Your taste buds are already totally aroused."

The memory of their conversation had finally given Matt the inspiration for the concept behind his new chocolate bar. The Bliss bar would be aimed exclusively at the Ecstasy generation: clubbers, eighteen-to-twenty-five-year-olds, and all who fantasized about losing themselves in hedonism. All the psychotropic ingredients of chocolate would be listed on the packaging, just as Sophie had listed them to Matt, and it would be marketed in nightclubs and at rock festivals, at strip shows and backstage parties, in the music press and in adult magazines. In short, it would be chocolate's answer to sex and drugs and rock 'n' roll.

While the link with recreational drugs would be fairly heavily implied, the main thrust of Matt's marketing efforts would be focused on sex. They had already filmed a range of TV commercials featuring seminude couples in scenes reminiscent of the food episode in *Nine and a Half Weeks*. They'd had talks about sponsoring television shows with adult content, and their billboard posters showed close-ups of women in various postcoital poses with the caption "Blissed out."

To add credence to the claims made in the ads and on the packaging, Matt commissioned some independent research into the effects of chocolate on the libido. Needless to say, he was disappointed when he discovered that chocolate wasn't quite the aphrodisiac Sophie had claimed it to be. It turned out that cheddar cheese had more phenyleth-ylamine than a bar of chocolate. A cup of tea had more caffeine, and the traces of tryptophan and anandamide were so small they barely regis-tered. One of his researchers calculated that he would have to eat three thousand Bliss bars for it to have an aphrodisiac effect. But as Sophie had so rightly pointed out, none of this mattered if the expectation was there. As with all marketing, it was image that counted: anything could be a turn-on if you believed enough in its power to excite. And besides, Matt *knew* chocolate was sexy. He had seen it, in Sophie's greedy eyes that first night, every time she'd wrapped her lips around her spoon.

.   .   .

Despite a few personal reservations, Nathan Trundel authorized pro-duction of the Bliss bar straightaway. Though he didn't really approve of sex or drugs or rock 'n' roll, he realized their sales potential. He also saw the potential of selling to eighteen-to-twenty-five-year-olds: not only did they set the trend for the rest of the market, but curiously, no other chocolate bar on the market was aimed specifically at this demo-graphic. So chances were good that the Bliss bar might end up a money-maker.

To Matt, however, Bliss was far more than this. In some ways his cre-ation was a culmination of all that he was. It was also a tribute to the only woman he'd ever had a lasting relationship with. He watched its market trials with the same interest a father has as he watches his child's first steps. He lay awake at night planning for its future and formulating schemes to ease its path through the dangerous world of confectionery marketing. He worried inordinately whenever the slightest thing threatened its development—a problem with the packaging or a holdup with the advertising agency. Or suspicious phone calls from Samantha Blackwood wanting to interview him about company practices.

As the launch date approached, he found himself feeling more anxious than ever. He couldn't shake off the feeling that something was about to go terribly wrong. His colleagues told him not to be so jumpy: the Bliss launch was less than a month away now—what could possibly happen? But Matt had had this feeling before. It was the same feeling he'd had just before Sophie left him—the sense that more was going on than he fully understood. And this time he knew better than to ignore it.

Chapter fifteen

It was eight o'clock on Monday morning. Matt was thinking about Samantha Blackwood, and trying unsuccessfully to catch a cab. It wasn't the first time he'd thought about her this morning—in fact, ever since she'd walked out of the bistro yesterday, he had been unable to get her out of his head.

As he hurried along Canal Street waving halfheartedly at every cab that passed, he tried to turn his mind to other matters. He had plenty of other things to worry about. He was late for work, for one thing. They were launching the Bliss bar next month, so the coming weeks were going to be busy. But no matter how often he tried to divert his thoughts, he just couldn't concentrate on anything but Sam. She was like some irritating song lyric that refused to go away.

What kept coming back to him was how *personally* she had taken his refusal to do an interview with her. He couldn't understand it: it was as if he had insulted her somehow, just because he'd said no. Sure, he had caught her lying about her motives, which must have been a little embarrassing. And he had wasted her time by enticing her to come and meet him when he'd never intended to give her an interview. But the look on her face when she told him she was investigating his company—the look of pure disgust—well, that was completely out of proportion.

It was a shame, because until the issue of an interview had come up, he and Sam had actually been having a pleasant time together. Their conversation had been relaxed, almost effortless—it had been nice to sit in a bar and talk about something other than work. She wasn't bad looking either. Buried beneath that scowl was a pretty face: full lips, plump cheeks, enormous blue eyes—nothing out of place, not even the small scar beside her left eyebrow, which had crinkled slightly every time she became animated. Yes, there was definitely something interesting about Samantha Blackwood. But then she had gone all weird on him, and vengeful, and their meeting had ended on a distinctly sour note.

Matt trudged toward Broadway, turning their conversation over and over in his head. He was just thinking to himself that he must have had a hundred conversations with journalists since he'd been working for T&B, and that none of them had stuck with him quite like this one had, when he found himself walking past a florist. He stopped outside it for a second, staring at all the brightly colored flowers in the window. Since he was looking for a way to lay his thoughts to rest—and since he was in an impulsive mood anyway—he momentarily abandoned his journey to work and stepped inside.

"Excuse me," he said, stepping up to the counter where an old lady was cutting the leaves off a few stems, "can I have some . . ."

He looked about him and suddenly realized that he didn't know what most of these flowers were called. Not wishing to appear stupid, he simply said the first name that came into his head: "Some roses, please. Red ones." And then he added recklessly, "A dozen."

The old lady took out a pen and began to write on a form. "A dozen red roses," she murmured. "And who are they being delivered to?"

"Her name is Samantha Blackwood, and she works at New Horizons— you know, the TV station. I think she's freelance, though, so perhaps you could give the station a call and find out where they should be sent."

"No problem at all, sir. And would you like to send any message with them?"

Matt paused for a second. He hadn't thought about a message.

"Here," said the lady, passing him a card, "since you're here in person, you can even write it yourself."

Matt stared at the card and tried to think of what he would write. Perhaps he could say that he had enjoyed their meeting. Or he could say that he hoped next time they could meet in social rather than professional circumstances. But then, that might give her the wrong impression. Really, all he wanted to do was to let her know that no harm had been intended in his actions. Taking the pen from his inside pocket he wrote simply, "Sorry I couldn't do your interview—and thank you for indulging me."

A few minutes later he left the shop and found himself a cab. He was now even later for work. And if the purpose of buying Sam flowers was to exorcise her from his thoughts, then it hadn't worked. But somehow he felt better anyway, and as he stepped into his taxi, he was satisfied that he had probably done the right thing.

.   .   .

Matt arrived in the T&B offices at twenty after nine. As he made his way through the sea of desks and workstations toward his own department, he could see his assistant, Claire, hovering in front of his office. She stepped forward to greet him, and Matt could see immediately that she was anxious.

"Mr. Trundel is looking for you," she said in a lowered voice. "He's in your office."

"Oh, yes? What does he want?"

"He didn't say. But he looks pretty pissed."

"I wouldn't worry about that," he said reassuringly. "The Walrus always looks pissed."

"Not like this morning." Claire shot an anxious glance toward Matt's office door. "Matt, I think you'd better go in and see him. He keeps calling me in and demanding to know where you are. I didn't know what to say."

Matt looked at his assistant's worried face and smiled. "Now don't you worry about the Walrus. He's just a bully, that's all. How long has he been waiting?"

"About twenty minutes."

"Well then, another couple of minutes won't make much difference, will it? So why don't you tell me what we've got planned for today, and I'll go in and see him in my own good time."

Claire smiled nervously and gave him a quick summary of his appointments for the day—a phone conference with the manager of the chocolate factory, lunch with a TV producer, a departmental meeting this afternoon. "Oh, and a woman called for you this morning."

"A woman?"

"Yes. She said she was a journalist, but she wouldn't leave her name. She said she'd call back another time. I figured she must be some secret admirer of yours."

Matt smiled to himself. The flowers must have arrived at Sam's workplace already.

"And talking of secret admirers," said Claire, "Mandy's been hanging around again."

Immediately Matt's smile faded. Mandy was one of the sales administrators, who, much to the amusement of the rest of the office, had an obvious and rather embarrassing crush on him. "What did she want?"

"Oh, nothing much." Claire grinned. "I suppose she was just hoping you'd walk by, that's all."

"Well, I'd appreciate it if you'd warn me next time she comes around. Working in this office is difficult enough without people like Mandy lurking around you—"

Their conversation was interrupted by the sound of an angry voice, bellowing from inside Matt's office. "Dyson! Is that you I can hear out there?"

Matt frowned. "I suppose I'd better go in and see him," he said with resignation. "Hold my calls for the moment, okay? And if Mandy comes wandering past again, tell her I've left the company."

He gave his assistant a tentative smile and stepped reluctantly toward his door.

. . .

Nathan Trundel was called the Walrus not so much because of his massive bulk as because of the way he moved. Most excessively fat people tend to sway down a hallway, swiveling their bulk around first one foot then the other, the same way you would move a heavy filing cabinet from one end of the room to another. The Walrus, on the other hand, tended to jerk his flesh forward as if he were moving not on legs but on giant flippers. His thick white mustaches hung down from his upper lip like two miniature tusks, and as he hauled his bulk through the offices, he wheezed and grunted as if the effort of movement forced him to make small, animal noises. The nickname Walrus served to ridicule all of these characteristics simultaneously. But at the same time it marked the respect, and even the fear, with which the rest of the company viewed their owner and managing director: his mere presence in a room was intimidating. Needless to say, nobody ever called him the Walrus to his face.

When Matt stepped into his office, he found the Walrus sitting in *his* chair, behind *his* desk, going through a pile of *his* papers. He wasn't entirely surprised. It was the Walrus's company, after all, and he treated everything as if it belonged to him—the furniture, the paperwork, even the employees. Plus, given his size, Matt's chair was the only one in the room big enough to support his bulk. Had he sat on any of the chairs Matt reserved for guests, he would probably have engulfed it entirely.

"Is this when you *always* arrive at work?" the Walrus barked as Matt entered the room.

Matt walked calmly to one of his guest chairs, on the other side of the desk, and put down his coat and briefcase. "Now come on, Nathan," he said calmly. "You know as well as I do that I work longer hours than anyone here."

"That's not the point. What happens if someone needs to get hold of you at the beginning of the day? I've been waiting here for twenty minutes."

"Well, I'm sorry about that. I had some things to do on my way here this morning. A public relations matter."

The Walrus scowled and stroked his tusklike mustaches thoughtfully. "Public relations, eh?" he said, as if expecting Matt to elaborate.

Realizing that his boss probably wouldn't see buying flowers as a good use of company time, Matt looked back at him and said simply, "Yes."

"Well, it's funny you should mention public relations, because that's exactly what I came to see you about. Tell me, Dyson, how are your interview skills?"

"Fine, I think."

"Good. Because you're doing one on Wednesday morning."

"Okay," said Matt unsurely. "Who are we interviewing?"

"We're not interviewing anyone. We are *being* interviewed. Or rather, you are."

"I don't follow you."

The Walrus stretched out in the chair (as much as it was *possible* for someone of his bulk to stretch out on a chair of limited size) and fixed Matt with his piercing Walrus eyes. "I've had a long conversation with a journalist this morning. My assistant has been putting the woman off for days, but somehow she's managed to get hold of my direct line. A most persistent person—admirable in some ways, I suppose. Anyway, she is making a television documentary about the chocolate industry, and she wants to ask us all about the way T and B does business. So I volunteered you."

"A journalist . . . ," Matt began, his heart sinking. "I don't suppose this woman is called Samantha Blackwood by any chance?"

"Yes," said the Walrus, scrutinizing Matt's face, "she mentioned she knew you."

Matt hesitated for a few moments. "I'm afraid I can't really talk to her—not in a formal interview. You see, I've already refused her once."

"Well, I've just unrefused you."

Matt stared at his boss, wondering if this was some kind of joke. He couldn't do an interview with Sam now—not after the way their meeting had gone yesterday. But the Walrus wasn't the kind of man to make jokes like this, and Matt knew that he would have to come up with some other way to get out of it. "Look, can't someone else do this interview? Only I'm frantically busy with this Bliss launch at the moment—"

"Everyone's busy," the Walrus interrupted. "And besides, you're the closest we have to a public relations executive. You'll do admirably, I'm

sure." He looked around the room smugly, obviously pleased with himself for having put Matt in his place. "I think it's probably best if she interviewed you in here, don't you? It's big enough for a camera or two, and it's nicely out of the way of the rest of the office . . ."

He went on to extol the virtues of Matt's room almost as if he were considering requisitioning it for himself. Only once he had got on to praising the positioning of one of the promotional posters did Matt finally pluck up the courage to interrupt him.

"Hang on a second. I hope you don't mind me asking, but is this a change of company policy? I mean, I was under the impression we never gave interviews to journalists."

"We don't, only in this case, we do. Let's just say that this particular journalist has convinced me that it would be in the company's best interests."

"Why? What makes her so special?"

Nathan Trundel shifted slightly in Matt's chair, and his air of smugness diminished somewhat. "Well . . . it seems she has managed to unearth some information about T and B that might be a little bit sensitive. Under the circumstances I believe that it would appear churlish to turn her down." He smiled. "Think of it as an exercise in damage control."

"And this sensitive information? What is it?"

"Ah, well, I'm afraid I can't really tell you that. It's rather delicate, you see. The fewer people who know about it the better."

"But . . ." Matt was temporarily lost for words. "But . . . how am I supposed to prepare for an interview if I don't even know what I'm defending myself against?"

"Don't be so dramatic, Dyson! You're not *defending* yourself. You're just there to answer a few questions, that's all. And if possible to squeeze in the odd plug for one of our products."

"But what happens if she asks me about this 'sensitive information'?"

"Simple. Deny knowledge of everything."

The great man started to expound upon the art of interviewing—which was fairly ironic, considering that *he* had instituted T&B's "no interview" policy in the first place—and Matt was forced to sit and listen to him pontificate. The more he talked, the more difficult Matt found it to quell his rising resentment. How was he going to have any credibility with Sam now that she had successfully gone over his head? And as for telling him to deny knowledge of whatever gripe she had with the company, wasn't that the most effective way of making him look like an idiot?

It was a relief when the Walrus eventually got up to go. Matt watched as he disengaged from the chair and jerked his body toward the door. After he had gone, Matt carried on sitting in his guest chair for a while, thinking about what the Walrus had said. He couldn't help wondering what this "sensitive information" could be. Since Sam's documentary was about working conditions in the chocolate industry, he assumed it must be something to do with that—but what could possibly be so sensitive that the Walrus wouldn't even tell him what it was? He knew there had been some trouble at the factory recently—in fact, the workers there were about to hold a ballot over whether to go on strike—but that was common knowledge. And besides, it was certainly not worth making a full-length TV documentary about.

Standing up, he walked to his door. "Claire," he called, "I want you to cancel my lunch. In fact, cancel all my appointments for today—and bring forward that departmental meeting as early as possible. There's something I want to talk to you all about."

Leaving Claire to organize it, he returned to his room and sat down at his desk, this time in his *own* chair. Somehow it didn't feel as comfortable as it once had. His boss's weight seemed to have squashed all the stuffing, compressed it into a hard ball in the center of the seat. Matt shifted about on it for a few seconds, but no matter how he positioned himself, he couldn't avoid this ball of stuffing—it jutted up between his buttocks making it impossible to get comfortable.

Cursing his boss, Matt wheeled his chair to the other side of the desk and replaced it with the one he had been sitting on earlier. It was smaller, and less impressive, but at least he could sit on it without wincing.

. . .

Late that morning, Matt's colleagues filed into his office for their earlier-than-usual departmental meeting. One by one they pulled up Matt's guest chairs and arranged them in a sort of uneven crescent in front of his desk. There were five of them: the two marketing managers, Maya and Grant; the assistant manager, Alex; Claire, his own personal assistant; and they were joined this morning by Phil, the sales director, who grinned at Matt widely and perched himself on the corner of the windowsill.

"Right, everyone," said Matt as they settled down, "I'm afraid we have a little situation on our hands. Some of you might be aware that we've been fielding calls from a journalist for the past week—a woman who wants to interview us about our trade practices. Well, I met her for a drink yesterday afternoon and thought I'd managed to put her off— but now it seems that we're giving her an interview after all. Nathan Trundel agreed to it this morning. She's coming here bright and early on Wednesday with a film crew, and she'll be interviewing me right here in this very room."

"So you're going to be a film star!" said Alex with a smile.

"Not exactly. More like the fall guy. Samantha Blackwood doesn't like T and B, and I think I can safely say that this is going to be a hostile interview."

"Why?" said Maya. "I mean, what's she got against us?"

"That's what I want to find out. Perhaps you could give New Horizons another call, and this time don't allow them to be vague—find out as much as you possibly can. Samantha Blackwood is out for our blood, and I want to know why. What information does she have on us, and how is she planning to use it? We advertise on New Horizons, so they should tell you everything we want to know—if they don't, then maybe you could subtly let them know that there are plenty of other TV channels that we can advertise with. Oh, and while you're at it, ask them when this documentary is due to be aired. If it coincides with the Bliss launch, we could be in for a rocky ride."

Next Matt turned to the assistant marketer. "Alex, I want you to get our researchers on the case. Get them to find out all they can about Samantha Blackwood. I want to know what newspapers she writes for, what stories she's covered recently, where she travels to, who she talks with—anything that could give us a clue as to what she's got against us. Gather together as much information as you can and get it to me by tomorrow evening. If she's going to be interviewing me on Wednesday, I want to be ready for her.

"As for the rest of you, I want you all to carry on as normal. But if Samantha Blackwood or indeed any other journalist calls, then I want you to put them straight through to me. Is that clear?"

The crescent of faces before him all nodded.

"Good, now are there any questions . . . ?"

. . .

The rest of the departmental meeting went as normal. They talked about the Bliss launch for a while, before reviewing all the advertising slots they had secured. They were just moving on to the issue of how a strike at the chocolate factory might affect their Bliss promotions when they were interrupted by a noise coming from outside the office.

It was an unusual sound—the noise of human voices crooning. This sort of noise usually only happened when a roomful of women were joined by a friend carrying a newborn: assorted oohs and aahs mixed in with the occasional excited cry of delighted surprise. Everyone turned instinctively to the door to catch what was going on, but whatever was happening was doing so just out of view.

Irritated at the interruption of his departmental meeting, Matt stood up and went to the door. To his surprise he saw Debbie, the receptionist, walking straight toward him carrying a large bunch of roses. She was surrounded by four or five other female employees, each of them craning her neck to get a better look. Among them was Mandy, the sales administrator who had a crush on him—unlike the others, who were smiling dreamily at the romance of it all, she had a hard-looking sneer on her face.

Matt had originally intended to close the door and get on with his meeting, but since the whole group seemed to be heading straight for his office, he simply stood there and waited for them to arrive.

"They're pretty," he said as Debbie came and stood in front of him. "Who sent you those?"

"Actually," said Debbie excitedly, "they're for you."

"For *me?*"

"Yes. There's a note here with them—do you want me to read it?"

"No, no," said Matt hurriedly, "I'll read it."

He took the roses from her arms and carried them through to his office. To his irritation he noticed that the group of women didn't move—they hovered around the doorway as if they were about to join his meeting. For a moment he thought of shutting the door, so that he could read the note in private, but since his office was already full of his colleagues, he figured that privacy was a luxury he was not destined to have. So, reluctantly, he plucked the envelope from the midst of the flowers and opened it.

"Well?" said Claire excitedly as Matt turned the note over in his hand.

"It's just a note from our market research agency," Matt lied. "They wanted to wish us good luck with the Bliss launch next month."

A disappointed sigh came from the assembled group—all except Mandy, whose face finally softened with relief.

With apparently nothing to get excited about, the women dispersed from Matt's doorway and went back to their desks. Matt also wrapped up the departmental meeting—they had covered pretty much everything they were going to talk about, and after this distraction it would be hard for them to focus. One by one they filed out of his office, leaving Matt alone with his bouquet of roses.

"I'll get you a vase for those," said Claire as she stepped through the door.

"Thanks."

"Did you see the look on Mandy's face? You should have told her they were from a secret admirer. That would have got her off your back for good."

Matt smiled weakly. "I wouldn't bet on it."

. . .

Once they had all gone, Matt picked up the bunch of roses and stood them up in the corner. There were twelve of them in all—lush, red flowers with petals that looked as though they were made of velvet. A couple of them were still just buds, delicate new blooms that had hardly had the opportunity to unfurl—but most of them had already opened, coquettishly displaying their brilliant crimson folds. Here in his office they looked distinctly out of place.

He looked once again at the note. On one side it carried his own handwriting, saying, "Sorry I couldn't do your interview—and thank you for indulging me."

On the other side it said, in bold cursive letters, "Apologies accepted. See you on Wednesday."

It was, effectively, a declaration of war.

Chapter sixteen

At six o'clock, just as the rest of the office was packing up to go home, Phil came and put his head around Matt's door. Matt was sitting with his head in his hands, looking at all the paperwork he still had to do before he could leave the office.

"I'm not interrupting, am I?" said Phil, stepping into the doorway.

"No. No, not at all. I was just . . . thinking."

Phil came in. "I was wondering if you fancied coming for a drink, that's all. After work."

"What time are you thinking of going?"

"In about five minutes. It's been a long day."

Matt thought for a second before saying, "I think I'll give it a miss this evening, Phil. I've got to catch up on all this damn paperwork."

"That can wait until tomorrow, can't it? Come on—you look like you could do with a drink." Phil smiled archly. "Mandy will be there . . ."

"Well, in that case I'm definitely not coming."

"Now, Matt, how can you be so heartless? The poor woman's besotted with you—and all you can do is dismiss her without a moment's thought. I think it's about time you gave her a chance." Phil grinned. "And besides, you'd be doing me a favor. I've got fifty bucks in the sweepstakes saying that you'll finally get it together with her this week."

Matt ignored him. Phil was always making jokes about Matt and Mandy. "I'm sorry, Phil. I'm far too busy tonight. If you want to go out with Mandy then fine, but I'm staying here."

"Come on, Matt. To tell you the truth, I don't really understand what you've got against the woman. I mean, she's single, isn't she? She's intelligent. She's got a *great* body . . ."

"Yeah. And she's also pushy, ruthless, and won't take no for an answer. That's not the sort of woman I want to get involved with."

"I'm not suggesting you get *involved* with her. Just come out with her tonight, have a good time. Remember what that is?"

"Of course. I'm just busy at the moment, that's all." Matt turned back to his desk with its mountain of papers.

Phil gave a deep, frustrated sigh. "Matt, I'm worried about you. I know you've had a rough time with women in the past, but that's no reason to lock yourself up in here with your paperwork the whole time. You're young, free, and single. You're successful. You've got money. Hell, you're even good-looking. You know how many men there are out there who would kill to be in your position? And what are you doing? Staying here every night, working. It's such a waste."

Phil came and sat down on the chair beside Matt's desk. "Do you remember that intern we took to the Chocolate Fair?"

"Which one?"

"The one with the blond hair, and those amazing legs . . . Jo, that was her name. She was more than interested, Matt. She was hanging on your every word. I tell you, she was like a ripe peach, just waiting for you to reach out and pluck her. But what did you do? Nothing!" Phil shook his head. "It breaks my heart, seeing opportunities like that go to waste."

"Then why didn't you go for her yourself?"

"She wasn't after *me*. Besides, I had my eye on her friend. And I would have got her too, if you'd kept your end of the bargain."

"My end of the bargain?"

"Yes! You're my partner, remember? My wingman! Together we score, divided we crash and burn! If we'd been working *together* that day, you would have gone home with the blond, and I would have gone home with the brunette. But you had to go and let me down."

Matt thought back to the Chocolate Trade Fair, trying to recollect what these two women looked like. He could remember the brunette all right, with her nice smile and her long dark hair—and he also remembered that she'd told him she had a boyfriend. But for some reason he couldn't recall her blond friend. In fact, the only blond woman he could picture at the moment was Sam Blackwood. She too had been at the Chocolate Fair.

"Well," he said acidly, turning back to his paperwork, "maybe I just decided I don't like blonds."

Phil leaned forward toward him across the desk and said in something approaching a whisper, *"Mandy's* not blond."

"I'm not coming out," said Matt assertively. "I've already told you, I've got work to do."

"Just this one time?" Phil begged. "You'd be really helping me out. I need someone to keep her occupied while I talk to her friend. And, oh, Matt, you should *see* her friend!"

"No! I'm not doing it."

Phil tried again. "I'll share my winnings with you. All you have to do is kiss her, and I'll give you twenty bucks."

"You mean . . ." Matt looked at his friend in surprise. He thought Phil had been fooling around earlier. "You mean there really *is* a sweepstakes?"

"Yeah. Bob Pagano from accounts has organized it."

"Twenty dollars," Matt said incredulously. "You'll have to do better than that."

The sales director sighed once again. Obviously he wasn't going to get anywhere, so he stood up to go. At the doorway he paused for a second, looking back to where Matt was already going through a pile of invoices. "One day I'm going to stop asking you to come out, you know that?"

"I know. I'll come next time, I promise."

And with that Phil left the room.

. . .

Matt put his head back in his hands and stared at all the paper on his desk. He was glad his friend had gone. Ever since Sophie had left him, Phil had been coming around, trying to cheer him up, trying to get him out on dates—and while Matt appreciated the sentiment, it only really made him feel more lonely than he already was. He didn't want to spend his evenings hitting on virtual strangers, and he wasn't interested in one-night stands. He missed Sophie terribly—but going out for the evening with some pushy sales administrator wasn't going to change that, no matter how good-looking she was.

He cast his mind back to the last time he'd gone out with Phil. It had been a few months ago on the night of the office holiday party, and Matt had been terribly, terribly drunk. By a cruel coincidence their holiday party had fallen on the anniversary of the night when Sophie had walked out on him. Not only that, but he had been avoiding calls from his father in Boston all week, and he was about to spend Christmas on his own. All in all he was having trouble working out what exactly was worth celebrating.

The party itself had been a fairly low-key affair: no fumbling with secretaries in the stationery closet, no throwing up all over the company accounts, or photocopying your butt and sending it to the Walrus in the office mail—just a few party hats and a civilized meal in one of the larger Midtown restaurants. Whatever jollity there was seemed forced, and Matt felt maudlin the whole evening. So when Phil suggested they go out after the party and "find some real action," Matt had simply shrugged and followed him to a local bar. It was better than going home.

By two o'clock in the morning he was sitting in a heap at one of the tables trying to focus his eyes on the breasts of the woman sitting next to him. Phil had managed to ensnare a couple of girls at the bar and was now trying to impress them with stories of the mountains of chocolate he sold every month. Strangely, it seemed to be working. Matt had no doubts at all that it was only the chocolate that got them interested. Had Phil been a salesman of plumbing supplies, they probably wouldn't have given him a second glance.

They ended up taking the two women to a hotel somewhere on Seventh Avenue. "They're *sisters*," Phil whispered to Matt in the cab on the way there. "Who knows, if we get lucky, maybe later on we can swap."

Phil was happy to fumble with the older of the two on the couch in the suite, so Matt had the luxury of taking his woman to the bedroom, where they had perfunctory, forgettable sex before falling into a drunken sleep. For all he enjoyed it, he may as well have been asleep throughout the whole thing. It was almost as if he weren't really there, as if he had switched off at some point in the bar, leaving his body to go through the mechanical actions of sex. Compared with the nights he'd enjoyed with Sophie, or indeed any of his other girlfriends, it was not only passionless but soulless.

Matt woke up at about six. He was disoriented and unbearably thirsty. He got up and stumbled through to the bathroom where he drank several glasses of water and almost immediately threw them back up. His head was pounding, and he was breaking out all over in a cold, slimy sweat. He drank two more glasses of water, and this time managed to keep them down. Then he went back to the bedroom and got dressed.

He knew he should have woken the woman before he went or at least have left her a note, but he simply didn't feel capable. Looking at her lying in the bed, he barely even recognized her. It would be embarrassing to pretend he was interested in her, and besides, he couldn't think of anything to say.

On his way out he bumped into Phil—great, fat, white Phil—who came walking down the hallway in his underwear. "Was that a great night or what!" he said brightly, pausing outside the bathroom door. "We should go out together more often."

Matt grunted something in response and started toward the door.

"Hey, where are you going?"

Matt gave him the only answer he could think of. "Office. Something I forgot to do. Tell . . ." He paused, trying once more to remember the woman's name.

"Courtney?"

Matt nodded. "Tell Courtney thanks."

And with that he left.

. . .

Matt had been using work as a reason not to go out with Phil ever since. Paperwork was generally a good excuse, because it was almost always a genuine one: this evening, for example, Matt stayed at the office for another three hours, digging into the mountain on his desk. For all its global power, T&B had never quite managed to outgrow the narrow-minded bureaucracy of the family-owned business that it was. There were forms here for everything: invoice forms, marketing plans, messenger authorizations, budget planning schedules—they all needed

double-checking, and they all needed to be signed. Matt was determined not to leave his desk until it was all done—but even so, a definite
part of him despised all this paperwork and wanted to gather it all
together, carry it to the window, and drop it all, like in a ticker-tape
parade, on the traffic below.

Chapter seventeen

Maybe Phil had been right, after all. Maybe he should try to get out
more, forget about work for a while and have some fun. He was certainly finding it hard to focus on his papers. He kept finding himself
staring at the vase of roses in the corner of his office and daydreaming,
asking himself if this was all his life would ever have to offer him: a desk
full of paperwork and the return home to a cold, empty apartment. But
no matter how long he stared at the roses, he couldn't find the answer
there. They merely stared back at him, silently mocking him as he
reluctantly turned back to his work.

At least when he'd been with Sophie there had been someone to
come home to in the evenings. She may not have been perfect, but she
had made life interesting—to say the least—and that had to be better
than the way things were now.

He smiled sadly to himself. What he missed most about Sophie were
her quirks: the way she twitched in her sleep, the way she twirled her hair
absentmindedly while she read, the way she always went to the bathroom
after meals and came back smelling of fresh mint toothpaste, as though
she were terrified that he might not want to kiss her anymore if she didn't
clean her teeth. And the way she sometimes insisted on smearing herself
with Nutella when they made love, as if it were the chocolate that turned
her on as much, or even more, than he did. She had always had a strange
relationship with chocolate. She kept secret stashes of the stuff hidden
around the apartment—he had found one or two of them by mistake
while he was looking for other things. But then, who was he to criticize?
His relationship with chocolate wasn't exactly normal either.

Matt wondered if there was such a thing as a perfect woman. When he was a teenager, he used to think so. He had imagined her a thousand times, in his bedroom over his father's store. He knew exactly what she would look like: tall, slender, with a body like a polecat; dark, almost black, hair down to her shoulders; a perfect oval face; enormous brown eyes that smiled at him and made him feel comfortable, happy, warm. And it wasn't just her physical attributes that he listed to himself. She would be enthusiastic, resourceful, gentle, and unafraid. She would not be too proud to look after him once in a while, and she would not be ashamed of letting him look after her too. She wouldn't be a pushover, that was for sure—Matt wanted a lover who challenged him occasionally. She would be able to make him forget himself and live life as though the past and the future no longer mattered.

For the first six months of their relationship, he'd thought Sophie was all these things and more. He had blinded himself to her faults, simply because that was easier than confronting them. Perhaps if he had allowed himself to be a little more aware of what she was *really* like, then he would never have invited her to his father's that Christmas. He might have avoided putting so much temptation in her way. He might have been able to help her, rather than frightening her off.

. . .

At the time, taking her up to his dad's store had seemed the most natural thing in the world. They were about to spend Christmas with Sophie's parents, so it only seemed fair to spend a weekend with his father too. Matt had even been looking forward to it. It had been years since he had taken a girlfriend home, and it felt somehow significant—not only for his relationship with Sophie, but for his relationship with his father too.

They drove up to Boston on Friday afternoon and arrived at around seven, just as Matt's dad was shutting up the store for the evening. It was strange for Matt, wandering into that store. Every time he went back, he was always surprised at how little the place had changed. It was like walking into a time warp: there was the same glass counter, filled with trays of liqueur chocolates and pralines and expensive truffles from Belgium and France; the same lines of shelves on which candies of all descriptions were displayed in glass jars; the same loose-candy area at the back of the store, where all the cheapest candies were displayed in plastic boxes so that the local kids could rummage in them without disturbing the wealthier customers at the front. Apart from a few Christmas decorations, and a window display to reflect the season, nothing had changed since Matt had stood behind that counter himself, serving out bags of candy by the ounce to his classmates.

Needless to say all his fears about how Sophie and his father would get on were for nothing. As soon as Sophie walked through the door, his father was all over her, shaking her hand and smiling and offering to take her coat. Sophie also seemed enchanted—not only by Matt's dad, but by the place itself.

"What a lovely store you have!" she said once the introductions were over. "It all looks so exciting!"

"Why thank you," said Matt's father, looking genuinely pleased.

"And look at this beautiful window display! It must have taken you hours."

Matt turned to look at the front of the store, where his father had constructed a winter scene: Alpine gingerbread houses, snowcapped mountains made of white chocolate truffles, fir trees made from licorice and green marzipan, every branch positively dripping with mints and fruit pastilles. Sophie's gaze was firmly fixed on the piles of truffles. Her eyes lit up at the sight of all the chocolate piled layer upon layer, and Matt couldn't help feeling a rush of desire rise as he watched the expression of sheer joy spread across her face.

Matt's father seemed charmed by Sophie's enthusiasm. "Come, come," he was saying, "I know you're not *really* interested in all my amateur sculptures. You're just flattering an old man."

"Oh, but I am interested! Honestly. I'd love to see you at work."

"Well, if you really mean it, then perhaps you can give me a hand tomorrow. You can help me make some chocolate figures to put at the front." He smiled at her and Sophie grinned back, as if such a prospect genuinely excited her. "But in the meantime why don't you come upstairs to the apartment and make yourself comfortable? I've got some dinner prepared, and a bottle of wine in the refrigerator. You can keep me company in the kitchen and tell me all about what my son has been getting up to recently."

Taking Sophie's arm in his hand, he steered her gently away from the window. She went along with him, but not without shooting one final, lustful glance back at the chocolate display. Something about her reluctance to withdraw intensely disquieted Matt. She seemed to have to tear herself away, and he was relieved when at last they climbed the stairs at the back of the store, leaving all the chocolate out of sight behind them.

That evening Matt saw a side to his father he'd never noticed before. There was none of the stilted sales talk that marred their own conversations, none of the hidden rivalry and constant striving to prove each point as it was raised. Instead he was charming, enthusiastic, and truly interested in Sophie's opinions. He asked her all about her work and her family and where she grew up. And in return he seemed quite happy to answer her endless questions about all the candy he stocked in his store.

He had cooked them a simple but delicious meal, and Matt, who knew what a poor cook his father normally was, appreciated the effort he must have put into it. Sophie didn't eat much of it of course—she was always on some diet or another. His father looked genuinely upset at her apparent lack of appetite, and so Matt was obliged to make up for it by serving himself an extralarge second helping.

After dinner they got the family photo albums out. As he opened the cover of the first one, the old man grinned at Sophie. "If you want to know what Matt's *really* like," he said mischievously, "take a look at this!"

He held open the album and showed them both a picture of Matt as a three-year-old, standing naked in a paddling pool in the backyard, a golden arc shooting across the photograph as he unself-consciously pissed over a pile of empty chocolate boxes. For the next half hour or so they laughed together over pictures of Matt as a child, stuffing his face or playing with toys or crawling between stacks of products in the storeroom. There were lots of pictures of him when he was small, but fewer and fewer as he got older. Apparently there had never been time to take photos when he was a teenager—he and his dad always seemed to be busy in those days, serving customers in the store.

"Who are all these people?" asked Sophie, pointing to a picture of a group of vacationers having a picnic on the beach.

"That one's me," said Matt's father, "and Matt's the one with the pail and trowel, of course. The man next to me is my father. He used to work in the Hershey's factory on the production line, churning out

Hershey's bars by the thousand. So, you see, confectionery really is in our family's blood."

"And who's the woman?"

Matt froze for a second, wondering how his father would react, but the old man merely paused for a moment before saying, "That's Matt's mother."

Sophie leaned a little closer to have a look. "Why, she looks just like me!"

"Yes," said Matt's father succinctly, "she does a little."

He turned the page to reveal a picture of Matt clutching a teddy bear and launched immediately into a story about how Matt had once lost that bear in the supermarket—apparently he had cried so hard that his father had had to put an ad in the local paper for its return. Sophie made a weak joke about how Matt obviously hadn't changed since he was a toddler, and while Matt laughed, he wasn't really paying attention. He was still thinking about the picture on the previous page.

· · ·

That night Matt and Sophie went to bed in Matt's old room. Sophie wanted to make love, but he refused—the idea of having sex while his father was just two doors down the hallway was faintly disturbing—so instead they decided simply to go to sleep, curled up together in the same small bed Matt had used as a teenager.

For a long while he lay awake staring at the old ceiling of his room. The anxiety he had felt earlier still hadn't gone away despite the ease with which his father and Sophie had got on together. For some reason he felt uncomfortable about how the evening had gone. He hadn't really said much all night, just watched as the other two swapped anecdotes about him all evening. His dad had spent much of the time describing Matt's childhood in a way that seemed to bear little relation to his own memories, and though he had been the center of attention, at the same time he had also been an invisible bystander—a spare part, unnecessary to the smooth flow of the conversation. As he finally slipped off to sleep, he did so with the vague feeling that something hadn't been quite right all evening—something he didn't fully understand.

He awoke, with a start, at about two in the morning. The first thing he noticed was that Sophie was no longer there. Her side of the bed was cold, so obviously she hadn't been there for a while. His father had thoughtfully hung a dressing gown on the back of their door for them, but when Matt looked up at his moonlit room, he noticed also that this was gone. For a while he simply lay there, too sleepy to get up. Then he heard a sound on the stairs outside his room. He waited awhile, but when Sophie didn't materialize, he got up to investigate.

He opened the door to find his father standing outside on the landing, with a large metal crowbar in his hand. "Dad? What are you—?"

"Shhh!" he whispered. "Listen! There's someone downstairs, in the store."

Sure enough, the sound of someone opening and shutting a drawer drifted up the stairs toward them. Quietly, Matt's father began to descend, holding his crowbar aloft like some sort of club. Matt followed him, his anxiety becoming almost unbearable.

When they got to the bottom of the stairs, Matt half-expected his father to leap out into the store, wielding his crowbar with a scream— but actually all he did was turn on the light. As he stepped up beside him, Matt prayed that the person in the store would be a burglar. But in his heart he knew that it wouldn't be.

Sophie was standing behind the glass counter, staring at the two of them with an expression both of guilt and of abject fear across her face. Her hands, and her mouth, were completely covered in melted chocolate, and from the way she was struggling to swallow, plainly her mouth even now was completely full. On the counter in front of her were two large trays of truffles—one of them had been almost completely consumed, while the second still had several rows of truffles left.

"What are you doing?" said Matt.

"It's obvious what she's doing," said his father, "she's eating all my stock!"

"Yes, but"—Matt hesitated—"there must be a *reason*."

Sophie tried to say something, but her mouth was so full of chocolate she couldn't speak.

"If you were so hungry," said Matt's dad grumpily, "then why didn't you eat the food I cooked you?"

Sophie, unable to swallow, was forced to spit a large lump of melted chocolate into her hand. She looked up at Matt's father, and for a few seconds Matt thought she was going to say something. But then she simply burst into tears and ran right past them both, her dressing gown swinging open as she stumbled blindly up the stairs.

Matt and his father simply stood and watched her.

"What's got into *her?*" his dad said.

"She just likes chocolate, that's all."

"I'll say! She's finished off at least a half pound there. Those are my most expensive truffles too—and she was stuffing them down as if they were loose candy!"

"Don't worry, Dad, I'll pay for them."

"That's not the point. If she wanted to try my chocolates, then why didn't she just ask?"

Matt sighed. "I've got a feeling it's not quite as simple as that."

Together the two of them trudged back up the stairs. Sophie had locked herself in the bathroom, so while his father went back to bed, huffing loudly as he did so, Matt sat down in the hallway beside the bathroom door and started trying to coax Sophie out. He spoke to her gently, his face close to the handle of the door. She didn't say anything back to him. Every now and then he heard the faint sound of sobbing through the door, and occasionally the toilet would flush, but nothing else.

She didn't emerge for more than half an hour. When she did, she had the faintest and shyest of smiles on her face. Her breath smelled of fresh mint toothpaste, of course, but this time, as Matt leaned forward to kiss her gently, he could just about make out the smell of something else behind the mints—something harsher, and more acidic.

. . .

Matt decided never to mention what had happened that evening, but even so Sophie dumped him only a few days later. She told him it was because he worked too hard. She said she couldn't live with a man whose career was more important than she was. She said she had to think of her own career, her own life, instead of always seeing to the needs of someone else. It was an easy excuse.

He gave her a couple of days to get over it before he called her, but she didn't answer the phone. He went around to her apartment, but she didn't seem to be in, and when Matt tried his key in the door, he found that she'd changed the locks. Next he tried phoning her at work, but they told him she had just taken two weeks' vacation and wouldn't be back until well after New Year's. Eventually, in desperation, he rang her parents, only to be told that Sophie didn't want to speak to him, and that if he called there again, they would get their number changed. It seemed she was serious after all.

That Christmas was the most miserable one he could remember. He spent the day watching reruns of old comedy shows on cable, and drinking cup after cup of coffee until he was so wired he could barely sit still. He couldn't escape from the image he had of Sophie spitting out that ball of chocolate into her hand. The thought made him feel slightly sick—and he felt desperately sad at the thought of how wretched Sophie must have been to have crept down into his father's store like that. Something must have driven her to do it—perhaps the stress of going to visit his dad, or the strain of having to keep a smile on her face while he forced them through the family photo albums. Or perhaps she had felt rejected when Matt refused to make love to her in his old bed. A thousand things could have triggered her binge, and he turned them all over in his mind one by one—but for some reason the only one that kept returning was the thought of his dad, grumbling about how she hadn't eaten his spaghetti and meatballs.

Late that Christmas Day, once his coffee jitters wore off, Matt ate a plate of cold pasta left over from the night before and opened a carton of ice cream. Sometime after dinner the phone rang—it was his dad. He left it to the voice mail. Christmas or not, his father was the last person in the world he wanted to speak to.

Chapter eighteen

The next morning, as with every morning, the T&B offices in Rockefeller Center opened for business at nine o'clock. As the staff began to arrive, all over the building the noises of morning began to sound: the click of desk lamps turning on, the crackle of static as each computer screen came to life, the electronic purr of fax machines turning out sheet after sheet of paper. Across the company, telephone receivers were raised and replaced, as each of the forty-seven office employees at corporate headquarters checked, and deleted, their voice mail messages. In the kitchen, a coffeemaker was bubbling, and the first row of cups for the day lay in wait.

These were the normal sounds of the T&B offices—gentle, reassuring, but also somehow purposeful. Only when they all simultaneously stopped, around nine thirty, did people notice that they had ever been there in the first place. Suddenly the phones stopped ringing, the faxes stopped whirring, the keyboards stopped rattling. It was a shock that no one was expecting—the removal of all the background noise in the office. As the offices ground to a halt, forty-seven T&B employees sat at their desks, staring at each other aimlessly, and wondering what on earth was going on.

· · ·

Matt didn't arrive at work until past ten o'clock. He had just finished a business breakfast with a movie producer, and it had left him in a bad mood. He had wanted to secure a sponsorship deal for one of T&B's brands, but after three croissants and five cups of coffee he had got nowhere and had been obliged to arrange another meeting in two weeks' time.

He was so preoccupied with this that he didn't notice the uncanny quietness when he entered the offices. In any case, he barely had time to register the lack of noise—as soon as he walked through the door, he found himself face-to-face with Mandy. The sales administrator occupied one of the desks closest to the entrance, and the speed with which she rose to greet him suggested that she'd been keeping an eye out for his arrival.

"Hi, Matt," she fluttered at him, "how are you?"

Matt tried to force a smile. "Fine thanks. How are you?"

"Okay. I was just thinking about those flowers you were sent yesterday. They were quite something. I thought for a moment you had some secret admirer."

"Now, Mandy, you know as well as I do that there's nothing secret about any of my admirers."

She pouted at him and sidled around her desk until her body was blocking his path. "You know, it's a shame that your market research agency sent those flowers to you. They're wasted on a man. Any woman would be proud to receive a bunch of flowers like that."

Matt tried to keep the irony out of his voice. "Would she now?"

"And perhaps—if she was asked—she might also like to go out for a drink with you sometime."

"Mandy, I'm shocked at you," he said with mock firmness. "You know perfectly well that it's against company policy for staff to fraternize in that way."

"We don't have to tell anyone . . ."

"To be honest, Mandy, I'm far too busy to think about that sort of thing. We're launching Bliss next month, and until then I'm flat out. We all are . . ." He stopped, noticing for the first time the lack of noise in the office. He looked around the room. Instead of all the activity that was normal at this time of day, everyone seemed to be standing around aimlessly, chatting to one another over the partitions that separated their workstations. He could see Claire and Alex on the opposite side of the office, hanging around Claire's desk. Something about the way Alex was sitting on the desk, slouching back against the wall, looked particularly purposeless. "At least, I *thought* we were busy. What's going on?"

"Oh," said Mandy uninterestedly, "all the computers are down. Apparently someone was trying to hack into them. Some protest group."

"What kind of protest group?"

"How should I know?" She pouted at him and tried to change the subject once more. "Listen, I was talking to Phil yesterday, and I was thinking, maybe we could all go out for a drink sometime. Phil said you were too busy last night, so I was thinking perhaps we could make it another night this week. I've got a friend who'd be just perfect for Phil—we could make it a double date."

Matt was barely listening. "I'm sorry, Mandy," he said quickly, "but I've got to go."

He hurried past her, being careful not to get too close, and strode away across the office. Why wasn't anyone working? Not a single phone was ringing—in fact, apart from the sound of human voices, the place was virtually silent. Something important was happening here, and he wanted to find out what it was.

"Heh!" Mandy called out after him. "What about that drink?"

Matt ignored her. Heading for his own department, he made his way to the desk where Alex and Claire were sitting so disconsolately.

"What's going on?" he said as he approached them. "What's all this I hear about some protest group?"

Claire, who was examining a piece of paper in her hand, looked up at him. "You know how you said you wanted us to be the Nike of the chocolate world? Well, apparently we already are." She held up the piece of paper. On it was typed in big bold letters:

STOP SLAVERY NOW

"This came by fax," she explained. "In fact, hundreds of them came: they've blocked up all our fax machines."

"Who's sending them?"

"Some group called the Anti-Slavery League."

"Who the hell are they?"

"I don't know, but whoever they are, they're not just blocking our fax machines. They've also been phoning, constantly, so our switchboard is jammed. Not only that, but they've been trying to hack into our computers. IT Support say they've breached our firewall, so we've all had to log out while they shore up security. It's been quite a morning."

"How long's this been going on?"

"Well, I've been here since nine, and I haven't been able to get any work done so far. According to IT, our computers aren't going to be up and running for at least another hour or so."

Matt took the piece of paper from her hand. "Stop slavery now," he read. "What are they going on about?"

"Apparently we exploit third-world labor."

"Really?"

"That's what they're saying."

"T and B has a whole load of plantations in Africa," said Alex. "There's another fax here explaining it all." He held up another piece of paper and smiled, as if thoroughly pleased with himself.

"What the hell are you smiling about?" said Matt angrily. "We're launching a new product next month. If this gets out, it could be a PR disaster. Who are these people? The Anti-Slavery League—I've never heard of them."

The others looked at him blankly.

"Has anyone informed Nathan Trundel of what's going on?"

"Mr. Trundel is in Baltimore today," said Claire. "He's negotiating with the factory workers over the strike they're proposing."

Matt sighed in frustration. "Okay, Claire, I want you to join Debbie on the switchboard and find out whom we're dealing with here. Is it a big organization? Are they just a bunch of students doing this for fun, or do they mean business? And what *exactly* are the charges they're leveling against us? Talk to them if you can, and find out what they want. If we can nip this in the bud, then we need to. As soon as possible."

Next he turned to Alex. "While Claire's doing that, I want you to find out as much as you can about our plantations. Who runs them? What are the conditions like? If there's something crooked about them, I want to know what it is, and how we can change it.

"This is not a game, guys—we've got a fortune riding on this launch. If this becomes news, we could lose millions. If it ever made it onto television . . ."

He paused for a second, midsentence. For a moment a terrible thought had crossed his mind. Only yesterday the Walrus had told him Sam Blackwood had "sensitive" information on the company—and now, suddenly, antislavery protesters were sending them faxes. Wasn't that just a little coincidental?

"Now I get it," he muttered. *"She* must be behind this."

"Who?" said Claire. "Who's behind this?"

Matt looked up at her. "That damn journalist. She said she'd make life difficult for me, and now she's doing so. Anti-Slavery League, indeed! They're probably just friends of hers." He paused for a moment, thinking, before heading toward his office.

"So what do you want us to do?" Alex called out after him.

"Get me Samantha Blackwood's number."

"But how?" said Alex. "All our phones are down."

"Here, use this." Matt threw Alex his cell phone. "If she's not in the directory, then try New Horizons. If they can't help, then try the newspapers. In fact, you can try a detective agency for all I care. I don't give a damn how you get hold of her—I want to talk to her. Now."

He stormed into his office and shut the door. Throwing his coat and his briefcase onto one of his spare chairs, he sat down at his desk before realizing that there wasn't actually anything he could do. Without a computer, and without a phone, he was virtually redundant. He cursed loudly and sat there, glaring impotently at the bouquet of flowers that still stood in the corner of his office.

. . .

It only took Alex five minutes of phoning around to get Sam's number. Surprisingly, one of the newspapers was quite happy to give him not only her cell number but also her address, and as he handed Matt back his phone, he had an air of triumph about him, as though he had just performed some minor miracle. Matt ignored his satisfied grin and took back his phone, and the piece of paper on which Alex had scrawled Sam's details. Then he shut his door again and sat back down.

As Matt dialed the number, he tried to keep himself calm. There was no point in losing his temper—that wouldn't get him any-where—and since she was obviously a slippery character, it was worth keeping his wits about him. But for some reason, the sound of her voice when she answered left him feeling immediately irritated once again.

"Mr. Dyson!" she said delightedly. "How are you?"

"Not very happy."

"I'm sorry to hear that! I suppose you must still be angry with me about this interview thing. It was a bit sneaky to go over your head, I know, but you really left me no choice—"

"Cut the bullshit, Sam—you know exactly what I'm calling about."

Her voice suddenly lost its chirpiness. "No, actually, I don't think I do."

"Come on, Sam, I'm talking about the Anti-Slavery League."

"What about them?"

"Friends of yours, are they?"

"I've interviewed them, yes, but . . . How do you know about them?"

"How do you *think* I know about them? They've been making our lives a misery all morning. They've hacked into our computers, they've blocked all our communications, they've been sending us threatening faxes . . . This is harassment, Sam, and if you don't call them off *immediately,* I'm going to have to call our lawyers."

"But it could be anyone doing those things. How do you know it's the Anti-Slavery League?"

"Because their name is written large all over the faxes they've been sending us. Along with some allegations that we use slave labor to harvest our cocoa."

"They *told* you that! Why the stupid . . ."

Matt paused for a moment, realizing suddenly that he had hit a nerve. "Is that what your documentary is all about? Our plantations?"

"Didn't Nathan Trundel tell you?"

"Mr. Trundel doesn't tell me anything."

"I see . . ." There was silence for a few seconds before she said, "Listen, I'll try to phone these protesters and get them to stop, but I can't guarantee anything."

"Good. Thank you."

"But let's get one thing straight. Just because I'm helping you out this time, it doesn't mean I'm on your side. If I had my way, there would be people attacking your company all day, every day, for as long as it takes to make you change your working practices. I want you to understand that I'm not doing this because I agree with you. I'm only doing it because I want you for myself."

"Fine. Now let me tell *you* something. If you air this on your TV documentary and *any* of it turns out to be untrue, then our lawyers will be all over you like a rash. We will sue you, New Horizons, the Anti-Slavery League, and anybody else we can think of. And we'll keep on suing until there is nothing left. Do I make myself clear?"

"Abundantly. And in return I will publicize every writ and every allegation as and when it happens."

"Fine."

"So we understand each other then?"

"Yes."

"Good," said Sam. "In that case I'll see you tomorrow morning, bright and early, for our interview."

She rang off, leaving Matt alone in his office, staring at his cell phone and wondering how she had managed to get the last word.

Half an hour later all the malicious faxes and phone calls suddenly stopped, and the office returned to normal. Everyone went back to his or her desk, the computers were switched back on, and the T&B offices began trading again, just as though nothing had happened in the first place. As Matt watched this process occur before his eyes, he couldn't help feeling annoyed that Sam had been able to make this happen when he himself had been powerless to do anything. But at the same time, deep down, he had to admit that he was impressed.

Chapter nineteen

A principle in chocolate manufacturing says that unless the basic ingredients are right, nothing will be right. If you start production with a bad set of cocoa beans, then a chain reaction sets in: the beans won't roast properly, the liquor will be gritty and acidic, and when it is finally mixed with all the other ingredients, the whole batch will taste sour. A bad set of beans can ruin a whole vat of chocolate. In other words, if one thing goes wrong at the start, a million things go wrong at the end.

It should not have come as a surprise, therefore, when Phil knocked on Matt's office door and told him the bad news. T&B's human resources problem, it seemed, did not end in Africa.

"You remember the workers at the factory were having their ballot today?" said Phil. "Well, I've just had a call from Hector Gonzalez at the factory: they've voted overwhelmingly in favor of going on strike. From five o'clock this Friday the factory will be shutting down completely for the weekend."

Matt stopped what he was doing and stared at his colleague, speechless.

"I say good luck to them," Phil continued. "The Walrus has been screwing them for years. Did you know the temperature in some of those rooms gets up to one hundred and ten degrees some days? All because the Walrus refuses to install proper air-cooling systems. If it was like that in these offices, then I'd probably go on strike too."

"Jesus!" said Matt. The implications of this news were only just beginning to sink in.

"And Hector Gonzalez was telling me they had all the telephones removed from the factory floor—just to save money. So if someone has an accident, they have to go all the way over to the factory offices to call an ambulance. It's scandalous, really."

"Jesus. What the hell are we going to do?" Matt had been all but ignoring everything Phil was saying.

Phil looked at him, confused. "Do? About what?"

"About the Bliss bar, of course. If they go on strike this weekend, that's going to ruin all our plans for the launch."

"Oh, that. Don't worry about the launch. I'm sure it will be fine."

"But we've got to get the product shipped to all the stores in time. There's no point in launching the damn thing if nobody can find it in the stores—that's the fastest way to kill a product I know."

"It will be fine," said Phil again.

"It had better be. This could ruin Bliss forever."

Phil looked at him curiously. "Matt," he said slowly, "it's only a chocolate bar."

The words stung. Only a chocolate bar! Phil had known him for five years, and yet he still didn't know what Matt was about. "Look," he said angrily, "next time you speak to Hector Gonzalez, tell him I'm coming down to see him on Friday, before they all walk out. I want to find out exactly what's happening to our stock. Actually, forget that—I'll call him myself and tell him. And while I'm at it, I'll tell him exactly what I think of their strike."

He slumped back in his chair, aware that Phil was staring at him. "Sorry," he said after a few moments. "I guess things have been getting to me a little recently."

"You've been working too hard."

"No, it's not that. It's this interview business."

"Why don't you tell me about it?" Phil sat down on the chair across from Matt. "Come on. You've been acting like a real pain in the ass recently—I want to know what's going on."

Reluctantly, Matt told him about Sam. He told him all about their meeting, about how the Walrus had compelled him to go through with the interview tomorrow, and how Sam had some sort of damaging information about the way the company plantations were being run. "And now I've got to sit through this interview without giving anything away, while this goddamn journalist woman makes me look like an idiot on camera."

"I see," said Phil thoughtfully. "So it's a personal thing."

"No, it's not . . . ," Matt began, but then he saw the skeptical arch of Phil's eyebrows and stopped. "All right, so I suppose it is personal. It's bad enough that I've got to do this interview at all, but she's going to ask me a whole load of embarrassing questions which I have absolutely no way of answering."

"Well, in that case I would have thought the solution is obvious. *Don't* answer them."

"What do you mean?"

"I mean that if she asks you about our plantations, give her an answer about how wonderful our products are. It's simple. Don't answer her questions."

Matt sighed and thought about it. "I don't know, Phil. I don't want to come across like some politician."

"Better that than a slave trader. Listen, this journalist wants you to go down. For all I know she might have a point about the way T and B does business—but it sounds like she's trying to pin the whole thing on you personally. She wants to make you look like some evil business-man, some fat cat out to screw the world's poor. She should be inter-viewing the Walrus, not you."

Matt shrugged, as if to say, "You're telling me."

"Not only that," Phil continued, "but *she's* the one who gets to edit the film—so she can do anything she wants to make sure you come across badly. I figure the best you can do is think of something nice to say about our products and use that as your answer to everything she asks. And I mean *everything* she asks. Just repeat the same thing again and again until she gives up and leaves you alone."

"You mean, kind of like a broken record?"

"Exactly. It's a technique I always used for dealing with complaints when I was working door-to-door. If you just repeat yourself, it'll grind even the hardest people down."

Matt looked at his friend with a new curiosity. "You know, Phil, sometimes I can't figure you out. One moment you're bemoaning the plight of our factory workers, and the next moment you're just as ruthless as the worst of us."

Phil shrugged. "It just depends whose side I'm on, that's all."

"And what makes you think this broken-record technique of yours will work?"

"Nothing." Phil smiled. "But if it will stop you acting like such a stressed-out son of a bitch, then surely it's worth a try."

A few minutes later Phil went back to work and left Matt alone to ponder the things he'd said. Matt was by no means convinced, but at the same time he did feel better. Regardless of whether Phil's idea was a good one, it had had the desired effect. As he picked up the telephone to call Hector Gonzalez, the factory manager, he no longer felt any of the anger that had first filled him when he'd heard the news about the strike. He merely made an appointment to come down to the factory on Friday afternoon and left it at that. Pure and calm and simple.

That evening he prepared for his TV interview as carefully as the circumstances would allow. He listed all the company's achievements to date and committed them to memory. He looked up a few things about the company's history and got his assistant to dig out some figures regarding their employment practices at the factory. Since there didn't seem to be any information about this supposed cocoa plantation of theirs, he read up a little about cocoa farming in West Africa, to familiarize himself with as many of the relevant issues as possible.

By the time he went to bed that night, he was probably as well prepared as he could be, and he felt quietly confident that he would be able to handle anything Sam Blackwood threw at him. But even so, a nagging doubt was still at the back of his mind: Weren't there just a few too many variables about this interview that were beyond his control? So far, nothing in his dealings with Sam had gone according to plan. Whether tomorrow would be any different, only time would tell.

Chapter twenty

On Wednesday morning Matt woke up early. He couldn't help feeling terribly nervous about what lay in store for him today. He had never been on television before, and while he knew rationally that he would be fine, that one of his many talents was his ability to put forward a professional facade, a part of him somewhere was absolutely terrified of making a fool of himself.

To make himself feel a little better he decided to dress himself up in all his best clothes. Taking his time, he selected his brightest white shirt from the pile of clothes in his bedroom. Then he got out his best suit and his favorite tie and his newest, most polished shoes. He told himself he was just being vain, but really he knew it was more than that. Somewhere in the back of his mind was a vague notion that if he at least *looked* okay, then perhaps what he said on film wouldn't matter quite so much.

. . .

It was a gray morning outside when Matt finally left his loft apartment. While some patches of blue were in the sky above him, thick, ominous clouds were hanging where the sun should have been, giving his street an unreal light. It had obviously rained during the night: the trash, which had been blowing about the street for the past two days forming piles inside all of the doorways down the block, was glued down to the wet paving stones, forming a patchwork of garbage. Matt walked over drink cartons and chocolate wrappers—even some of Trundel & Barr's own chocolates, he noticed—and, carefully avoiding the dirty puddles, made his way up to Canal Street to catch a cab.

It was almost eight forty-five by the time he reached Rockefeller Center. As Matt walked across the plaza, he ran through a list of possible questions in his mind, in preparation for his interview. He was so absorbed that he barely noticed the group of people outside the building. There were six of them, standing patiently beside the entrance. One, a man, was holding a video camera, and as Matt approached, he peeled away from the main group and began filming him. Matt broke off his thoughts about the interview for a moment to wonder what was going on. Was this Sam Blackwood's film crew? They didn't look much like a film crew: they were a motley group—one of them even seemed to have a couple of front teeth missing. And besides, he couldn't see Sam among them. Perhaps the man with the camera was just a tourist and was trying to get some local color before filming his companions— though why a crowd of tourists would want to video themselves out- side Trundel & Barr's offices was a mystery to Matt.

What he didn't notice was that, while the man was filming, one of his companions was reaching into his bag to pull out a small object. He waited until Matt got a little closer before hurling it at him. The first Matt knew about it was when the object hit his body: first he felt the sting of contact, then a deeper, more bruising pain, and finally, as the object broke open across his chest, there was the stench.

Shocked, both by the smell and by the fact that this man had thrown a rotten egg at him in the first place, Matt turned toward his attacker. He was greeted with another egg, which this time hit his leg, and then a tomato, which exploded across his white shirt and dripped onto his pants. Suddenly the whole group was attacking him, pelting him with eggs and mushy fruit—one of them even squirted him with a bottle of chocolate sauce. Powerless to defend himself, all Matt could do was hold up his briefcase and protect his face. And then, just as quickly as it had started, the hail of food stopped.

In utter confusion Matt lowered his briefcase and stared blankly at the group. His first thought was that there must have been some sort of mistake, that they must accidentally have taken him for someone else. Surely they can't have wanted to attack *him*. Or perhaps he had done something to insult them somehow? Perhaps, as he'd hurried down the street, he had made some inadvertent hand signal or facial expression that they had found offensive, and this was their way of punishing him for it. But none of them *seemed* to be particularly offended—in fact they all looked fairly nonchalant, as if throwing food at strangers on the street were perfectly normal behavior.

One of them, a young woman with her hair in hundreds of tiny plaits, was stepping toward him now, solemnly holding something out to him like an offering. In his confusion, Matt thought it must be some sort of gift, a consolation for having covered him in food. He looked down at it. It was something made of pastry, and cream, the sort of thing you'd find clowns throwing at each other at the circus. He only recognized what it was when it was too late, as the woman raised her offering to shoulder height and placed the pie squarely in his face. As he stepped back, blinded by a medley of pie and whipped cream, he felt the woman press something into his hand: a folded piece of paper.

.   .   .

By the time he had wiped the cream away from his eyes, the woman and her friends were gone, scattered in all directions like broken glass. He could see the woman running off toward Sixth Avenue, while the man who had thrown eggs at him was disappearing into the promenade leading toward Saks. In fact, the only one left was the man with the film camera—he was looking at Matt now with a barely suppressed grin covering his face.

Wiping his hands on his pants, Matt looked down at the piece of paper that had been thrust into his hand and slowly unfolded it. There, written in neat, bold capital letters, were three words: STOP SLAVERY NOW.

Chapter twenty-one

He stood on the street for a few moments, staring at the piece of paper, stunned by what had just happened. There had been a moment, in the middle of it all, when Matt had felt like laughing: it had all taken place so quickly—first the eggs, then the tomatoes, then the pie—it must surely be some sort of prank. But now, as he looked about him for confirmation of the joke, there was nothing funny about it all. Apart from the grinning cameraman, few people were on the street, and none of them were laughing. Those walking past avoided looking at him, as if they thought he were some sort of madman. Even those in the line of traffic inching its way along Fiftieth Street ignored him—everyone was too busy trying to get to work.

He glanced down at his clothes. His suit was ruined. His bright white shirt now looked like a Jackson Pollock painting, and chocolate sauce completely covered his favorite silk tie. Not only that, but the stench coming from where the rotten eggs had burst on his pants was almost unbearable. Slowly, as the shock of what had just happened wore off, he was filled with a strong sense of injustice: Who the hell *were* these anti-slavery people? And what did they have against *him*? It was one thing blocking T&B's phones and fax machines yesterday, but this was in a different league. This was personal.

Turning his back on the street, Matt slopped his way into the lobby of the building. All he wanted now was to get to a bathroom as fast as he could.

. . .

He decided it was probably safer to walk up the stairs than to take the elevator—that way he was less likely to bump into anyone he knew. It was bad enough having to put up with the stifled giggles of the security guards on reception—if any of his colleagues saw him like this, they'd be merciless. And as for Sam and her camera crew, what would *they* say? He could just imagine Sam's commentary as they filmed the pieces of tomato sliding down his shirt: "You? A marketing psychic? A cultural fortune-teller? Well, you didn't see *that* one coming, did you?" That goddamn woman. He was willing to bet money that she was behind this in some way.

Squelching his way through the door at the back of the lobby, he made his way bitterly up to the third floor. When he reached the top of the stairs, he had a quick look around the elevator area, just to make sure no one would see him, then hurried over to the double doors that led into the T&B offices.

He pushed the doors open just a fraction and looked through them, over toward the marketing department. He was hoping that he might be able to sneak into his office without anyone seeing him—he had a spare tie in one of his desk drawers, and an old jacket was hanging on the back of his door—but straightaway he could see that he was too late. Standing beside the door to his room was a man Matt didn't recognize. He was unpacking piles of sound equipment from a series of cases, and a cine camera was sitting in the doorway beside him. There were people in Matt's office as well. Every now and then he saw a flash of blond hair through the glass partition. It seemed that Sam had arrived early. She was sitting in Matt's office, waiting for him.

Most of Matt's colleagues hadn't arrived yet, but he could see that Mandy was already at her desk. Being careful not to draw the attention of the soundman, Matt called gently over to her. "Psst!" he hissed. "Mandy!"

The girl looked up at him, and immediately her face dropped in confusion. "Matt?" she said loudly.

"Shhh!" Matt beckoned frantically for her to keep her voice down. "Come over here!"

Tentatively, Mandy left what she was doing and came to the door. She put her hand over her nose as she did. "Goodness!" she said as she stepped through into the elevator lobby. "What happened to you?"

"It's a long story," said Matt miserably. "Those damn protesters, the ones who sent all those faxes yesterday—they threw eggs at me!"

"You stink."

"I know." He reached into his jacket pocket and pulled out his wallet. "Look, Mandy, I need you to do me a favor. Can you go over to the men's outfitters on Forty-fourth and buy me a new shirt and a pair of pants? I need something to change into."

He pulled out all the cash in his wallet—about seventy-five dollars—and shoved it into the woman's hand. Mandy looked at the money, and slowly her expression changed from one of concern to one of suspicion. "Oh, I see, it's like that, is it? Yesterday you virtually ignore me—but now that you *want* something from me it's a different matter."

"Please, Mandy . . ."

"Don't you 'please, Mandy' me. You've been treating me like I'm invisible for weeks now. All I want is a little respect, that's all."

"But I do respect you." Matt glanced anxiously back at the door to the offices. The rest of his colleagues would be arriving soon—or worse, Sam or one of her film crew might come into the lobby. He thought quickly. "Listen, why don't you go and pick up those clothes for me, and then perhaps we can think about going out for that drink you mentioned yesterday."

Mandy eyed him suspiciously. "You mean with Phil? And my friend?"

"Yes. Or . . . or we could just make it the two of us, if you'd prefer."

"You mean, like on a date?"

"Yes."

Mandy's face hardened once again. "You're only asking me because you want me to do something for you."

"No, I'm not."

"You are. You're using me."

Matt swallowed hard and did his best not to rush his words. "Mandy, would I do something like that?"

She paused, and for a horrible moment Matt thought she would not only refuse him, but give him back his money and tell him to go and buy his own shirt and pants. The way he was feeling, he would probably have deserved it too. But then suddenly she sighed and said, "Okay, I'll get your damn shirt and pants. What size are you?"

"Mandy, I could kiss you!"

"Not while you look like that you couldn't. Now just tell me what size you are and I'll see what I can do."

He gave her his best guess at his chest and waist measurements and told her to find him in the men's room when she came back. Only when he was sure she was gone did he turn on his heels and head straight for the bathroom door.

• • •

The first thing he did was to wash the rest of the whipped cream from his face. Taking off his jacket, he filled one of the sinks with water and began to scrub his cheeks with his fingers. After a few minutes he had managed to remove the worst of it, although some cream had become encrusted in his hair, and he ended up having to put his whole head in the sink to rinse it off.

His clothes were just as bad. A tomato had exploded on his neck and then flopped down inside his suit, leaving a bright orange stain right down his shirtfront—he could even feel where a few seeds had worked their way under his collar. Taking off his shirt, he started to rinse off the juice that had seeped through his clothes to his chest. Just as he was doing this, stripped to the waist in front of the mirror, the door opened and the Walrus himself walked in.

"Dyson!" he said, surprised to find anyone in the bathroom, let alone a seminaked marketing director. He looked Matt up and down, obviously searching for some explanation for his state of undress. "I suppose you . . . um . . . I suppose you must be getting changed for your interview?"

"No," said Matt coldly. "I've just been attacked by a bunch of protesters outside. They threw eggs at me. I've had to send out for some new clothes."

The Walrus looked him up and down, as if assessing the damage. "Yes, security warned me that there had been some trouble outside."

"Why didn't you tell me there was a problem with our plantations? That's what they're angry about. And I suppose that's what this damn interview's about as well."

"There *isn't* a problem with our plantations."

"Then why are these people throwing eggs at me?"

"Because they're misinformed. It's up to you to let them know they're wrong—*that's* what the interview's about. Talking of which, you'd better hurry up and get changed. I saw the camera crew setting up in your office."

Matt's heart sank. "But I can't do the interview now!"

"Why not?"

"Just look at me! I'm a mess!"

"But I thought you said you'd got yourself some new clothes."

"Yes, but—"

"Well, that's okay then. Once you've got changed, nobody will know the difference. You can put the clothes on expenses, naturally."

The Walrus shuffled past him and squeezed his bulk into one of the cubicles to relieve himself. Matt stood for a while, staring at his dripping face in the mirror and listening to the thunderous noise of the great man pissing. Surely he couldn't be serious about Matt going through with this interview? He'd assumed the Walrus would simply cancel it, make Sam reschedule for another day. It would be difficult to keep a professional facade after all that had happened—surely the Walrus could see that? If it had been up to Matt, he would have postponed the interview indefinitely—kept Sam at arm's length until he knew more about what she'd dug up.

Eventually Nathan Trundel reappeared and took his place at the next basin to wash his hands. As he did so, his eyes met Matt's in the mirror. "I'm relying on you this morning, Dyson. I don't want any scandals in my company, and I want you to do whatever needs to be done to avoid them. Is that clear?"

Matt swallowed hard. "You mean you want me to lie?"

"There you go again, being all dramatic. Of course I don't want you to lie! There's nothing to lie about." The Walrus looked away slyly. "But I'd hate to think that this journalist woman might be able to get the better of my marketing director."

Matt thought of Samantha Blackwood bitterly. It was her fault he was in this mess in the first place. "Don't worry, I'm not going to let *her* get away with anything."

"Good!" The Walrus dried his hands on a paper towel, before throwing it carelessly in the vague direction of the trash can. "Well, I know you'll want to get on, so I'll leave you to get changed. But I shall expect a full report about how it all went later on this morning."

And with that he left the bathroom.

. . .

Matt stepped over to the old chair that was sitting by the door and slumped down onto it. What the hell was he going to do? It was all very well pretending that everything was okay, but it blatantly wasn't. He had no idea what sort of questions Sam was going to ask him, or how he could possibly defend T&B against her accusations. If only the Walrus hadn't found him in here—then he could just have canceled the interview, called Sam on his cell and told her to postpone it. But now that the Walrus had told him to go ahead with it, it was too late. To cancel *now* would mean disobeying his direct instructions.

He sat for a while, cursing himself for ever agreeing to go ahead with this scheme in the first place, until a sudden knock on the door made him jump to his feet. Afraid that it might be one of his colleagues, he hid himself in the doorway of one of the cubicles. Tentatively he called out, "Come in?"

The bathroom door squeaked open a few inches, and a face appeared in the gap. It was Mandy.

"Oh, it's you!" said Matt, relieved. "Have you brought the clothes?"

She held out a pair of cheap pants on a hanger and a plastic pack that contained a shirt. "I hope they'll fit you. You didn't tell me what neck size you were."

"Come in, quick—before someone sees you!"

Mandy stepped into the room. She looked him up and down, her eyes lingering wantonly on his bare chest and dripping face. "I'm not sure I should be in here," she said coyly. "What would people say?"

"You're right," said Matt, glancing nervously at the door. He walked across the room and, taking hold of the chair he had been sitting on just a moment ago, wedged it under the handle.

"My my," said Mandy, "the *lengths* some men will go to, just to be alone with a woman."

"I'm not trying to be alone with you, Mandy, I'm just trying to make sure we don't get caught." He took the shirt and pants from her and placed them on the side by the sink.

"I feel very *naughty* being in here," said Mandy. "I mean, if you think about it, this could look quite embarrassing, couldn't it? Me being here in the men's room, I mean. With you. Alone."

Matt started to undo his belt, then stopped and glanced up at the sales administrator. "Do you mind?"

"You don't have to be shy with me!"

Matt folded his arms and looked her straight in the eye, until eventually she shrugged and turned her back to him.

"Are you always this coy?" she said.

Matt scowled in her direction—she was obviously enjoying this. Taking off his pants, he picked up the new pair she'd brought him and held them up to look at them. They were made of cheap blue polyester—the kind of pants only mailmen or people in Burger King wore. Still, he could barely expect more for the amount of money he'd given her.

He was just about to start putting them on when he heard voices outside in the lobby. One of them seemed to be that of the Walrus. Matt's mind raced—what if he decided to come back in? What if he found Matt in here, almost naked, with one of the female sales administrators? Or worse still, what if it was one of Sam's camera crew?

"If you like, I can take your dirty things down to the cleaners for you," Mandy was saying now. "I'm happy to help. And besides, I can keep the ticket as insurance, in case you try to wriggle out of our date."

"Keep your voice down," Matt whispered nervously, "there are people outside."

"It's okay, they can't hear us."

At that moment the handle turned, and the door jammed against the chair—someone was trying to come in. Matt froze for a second and glanced at Mandy—making a quick decision, he grabbed hold of his companion, thrust her into the cubicle by which she was standing, and quickly shut the door behind them.

Unaware of what was going on, the girl let out a startled cry, followed by a satisfied giggle, as if this were what she had planned all along.

"Shhh!" he hissed. "They'll hear us!"

"What's the matter? You've got nothing to be ashamed of." She pushed her body closer until she was pressed right up against him.

Matt thought for a moment of putting his hand over her mouth, just to make sure she shut up, but in the end he figured that would only provoke her. He clutched his new pair of polyester pants to his chest— they were practically the only thing separating him from Mandy now—and prayed that the newcomer would finish his business and leave the bathroom without ever knowing Matt was here.

He listened as the footsteps approached the cubicle door. Slowly, quietly, Matt reached out toward the lock, but before he could push it home, the door swung open. There, standing before him, was Phil.

Mandy took one look at her boss and slowly separated herself from Matt. Then, giggling coyly, she squeezed past him and hurried out of the bathroom. Phil watched her go, his face a mixture of astonishment and sheer glee, then turned back toward Matt, shaking his head all the while.

"It's . . . er . . . ," Matt mumbled, "it's not what you think."

Phil grinned and shook his head once again. Turning away, he reached into his jacket pocket and put something down on the side, before following Mandy out of the bathroom.

Matt struggled into his new pants as quickly as he could and stumbled out of the cubicle. There on the wet tiles beside the sink was a crisp, new twenty-dollar bill.

Chapter twenty-two

When Matt walked into the office, he felt anything but ready for an interview in front of television cameras. He had just spent the last five minutes sitting in one of the toilet cubicles, his head in his hands, trying to calm himself down. And while it had worked, in general, he was still far from comfortable. Apart from anything else, the clothes Mandy had bought him had turned out to be slightly too small for him—so while his new pair of pants fitted him around the waist, their legs didn't quite reach all the way to his shoes; and although the label on his shirt claimed it was the correct chest size, it still felt tight, and the collar was too small for him to do up the top button. Anyone who'd never met Matt would probably never have noticed anything wrong—but Matt noticed, and it made him feel self-conscious, restricted, trapped.

To make things worse, Samantha Blackwood was looking immaculate. Last time they'd met, she'd been dressed casually—but today she was wearing an elegant black suit and a blue silk blouse that looked so soft, so shimmery, that he almost had the urge to reach out and touch it. The rest of her was all neat blond hair and big blue eyes. If it hadn't been for the remnants of some past smile lines around those eyes, she would have looked like some Swedish ice maiden from an art-house movie.

He found her in his office, waiting impatiently for him to arrive. Three other people were with her: one of them, presumably the soundman, was kneeling near the window holding what looked like a giant guinea pig impaled on a stick; the other two were hovering over a camera, checking lighting levels in the room.

Sam did the introductions. "Matt, I want you to meet Paul, our director . . ."

Matt and Paul shook hands.

" . . . and Colin, our soundman . . ."

Matt and Colin shook hands.

" . . . and Mark, our cameraman."

Matt recognized the man from outside—the one who had been filming him getting pelted. He leaned forward a third time to shake hands. As he did so, he felt the buttons straining on his shirt, and he hoped he didn't look too ridiculous in his impromptu outfit.

"We're going to have to hurry, I'm afraid," said Sam. "We were expecting you here half an hour ago."

"Yes, well," said Matt, shooting a sideways glare at the grinning cameraman, "if your protester friends hadn't attacked me outside, then perhaps I might have turned up on time."

Matt looked back at Sam, expecting her to explain their involvement with the protest group and perhaps even apologize for it—but she had already turned away.

"May as well get the paperwork done straightaway then," said Paul, the director. "We have to rush off soon, so if you would sign this release form . . . it just states that you agreed to be interviewed and are allowing us to broadcast it."

Paul shoved a piece of paper toward him. For a moment Matt began to read it, but then he figured that since he didn't have much choice about this interview anyway, he might as well just sign it and hand it back.

"So," said Sam, "we'd better get started. Would you like to sit down— make yourself comfortable?"

Matt looked at his chair, tucked away behind the safety of his desk. "How about I sit *there*—that looks like the best place, don't you think?"

"No," said Paul, "the background's a bit boring there—just your computer and the window. What do you think, Mark?"

"Light's not as good that way," said the cameraman. "The best place to sit would be"—he looked around briefly—"there." He pointed at the chair without any armrests—the one that the Walrus had sat in on Monday morning. "That way you've got the chocolate poster behind you."

Matt looked at the chair. He had to admit that the background did look better that way—the big, colorful poster provided a perfect backdrop, and what's more, it had their logo written large on it. If the idea was to publicize their brand, there wasn't really anywhere *else* to sit.

Reluctantly he stepped over to the chair and sat down. He shifted around for a few moments, trying to get comfortable and wondering what on earth he was doing here. He couldn't remember any of the things he had prepared himself to say yesterday. All he could remember was Phil's "broken-record technique."

"Okay," said Sam. "Now remember always to look at me when you answer the questions—pretend the camera's not there. And try not to move about too much, or it'll look wrong. Okay?"

"Okay."

"Right, so when the camera's rolling . . ." She looked over at Mark, the cameraman, who nodded. "So," she said in a professional-sounding voice, "tell us something about Trundel and Barr."

Matt smiled in what he hoped was a winning way and launched into an impromptu speech about the company. "Trundel and Barr is one of the oldest and biggest family-run chocolate companies in the United States. Like a lot of the chocolate companies that grew up at the end of the nineteenth century, it was founded on philanthropic ideals—decent wages, decent living conditions for its workers, and so on. We produce forty-five different chocolate products, although we're about to add to that in a big way with the launch of our new chocolate bar next month."

He paused to give Sam the chance to say something along the lines of "Oh, yes? And tell me about this chocolate bar . . ." But at that point there was a loud crash from just outside Matt's office.

"What the hell was that?" said Sam, standing up to look through the glass partition.

Matt didn't need to stand up—from where he was sitting, he could see Claire on her hands and knees, gathering up the stack of files she had just dropped. "That's my assistant, trying to cope with all the extra work she has to do while I'm tied up talking to you."

"Is she always that clumsy?"

"No," said Matt angrily. He could feel the collar of his new shirt sticking slightly on the back of his neck, and he suspected that he must somehow have missed a piece of tomato when he was washing earlier.

"Well, as long as she doesn't do it again, I suppose we can cut that bit out." Sam looked at the director, who nodded. "So, let's get back to the interview. Where were we? Oh, yes . . . These ideals you mention. Do you think they're still alive today?"

"Ideals?" said Matt.

"You said the company was founded on philanthropic ideals."

"Oh, yes, sorry."

"So do you think they're still alive today?"

That slightly strained, irritated quality had returned to her voice. Matt remembered what Phil had told him yesterday: *Think of something nice to say about our products and use that as your answer to everything she asks.*

"Certainly they are," he said. "We still have the same ideals, and the same delicious recipe for the soft milk chocolate people everywhere know and love."

"And do you think the workers at the factory would agree with you?"

"I'm sure the factory workers adore our chocolate just as much as everyone else."

"No, I mean about the existence of your philanthropic ideals."

"Oh, that. Yes, I'm sure they do."

"If that's the case," said Sam with a satisfied smile, "perhaps you can tell us why your factory workers are going on strike this weekend."

"Well," said Matt guardedly, "there seem to have been one or two misunderstandings between us and our workforce. Obviously I can't go into that for legal reasons. But I can tell you all about our new chocolate bar—"

"They said to me a few days ago that they were going on strike because Trundel and Barr was breaking the philanthropic principles the company was founded on."

"Well, it's a great shame if they think that, because it's not true." Matt was starting to get frustrated. He didn't seem to be very good at this broken-record technique of Phil's. He had meant to keep repeating the merits of T&B chocolate, but Sam kept drawing him away from the subject. Somehow his concentration seemed to have gone: all he could focus on was the sticky feeling on his collar. As casually as he could, he reached up and wiped the tomato from the back of his neck and, pretending to have an itch on the back of his leg, rubbed it off onto his new polyester pants.

"Don't do that," said Sam.

"Don't do what?"

"Rub your leg like that—it looks like you're fidgeting, like you're not really interested in the interview."

"Oh, sorry." Matt glanced quickly down at his hand to make sure he had rubbed the tomato off.

"You *are* still interested in doing the interview, aren't you?" The irritation in her voice was becoming quite marked.

Matt turned back to her. "Pardon?"

"You're not even listening!"

"No, I am. Sorry. I am listening."

"No, you're not. Wasting my time last Sunday was one thing, but making me waste the time of a whole camera crew is a totally different matter. Now, are we going to do this damn interview or not?"

Part of Matt was tempted to take her up on her offer, call the whole thing off, say it was all a dreadful mistake. But somehow he didn't think he'd hear the last of it. "Yes," he said, "let's get on with the interview."

"Okay." She calmed herself down again, flattening out one of the folds in her elegant black jacket. "Right, are we still rolling? Good. So, *as I was saying,* the factory workers told me they were going on strike because Trundel and Barr was breaking the philanthropic code the company was founded on."

"That's totally untrue," said Matt decisively. "We have always been committed to good working conditions, just as we are committed to making luscious, thick milk chocolate that melts on your tongue—"

"They said you were planning to shut down parts of the factory and relocate the cocoa processing to West Africa where you would be able to exploit cheap labor."

"Well, like I said, I can't really comment on any of that. I don't want to jeopardize any of the negotiations that are taking place between us and the factory workers. All I can say is that nobody else makes confectionery like our factory does, as I'm sure you'll agree every time you taste the soft, velvety texture of our latest—"

"If we can stick to the subject for a moment," said Sam, "we have obtained documents which prove you are planning to move part of your operation to the Côte d'Ivoire. What sort of effects do you think that will have, not only on your workers here, but on the area you're moving into?"

"Well," said Matt carefully, unable to think of any way to twist the question around to the delights of T&B chocolate, "I imagine that if we were to relocate a small portion of our processing to West Africa, it would bring enormous economic benefits to the area."

"With all due respect, isn't that what Nike and Gap said in the 1990s when they outsourced the production of their clothes and shoes to Southeast Asia?"

"With all due respect to *you,* this is all just hypothesis. We haven't moved any part of our factory to West Africa yet, and we may not ever do it, so there's not really any point in talking about it. At the moment we are concentrating all our efforts on producing some of the most delicious chocolate bars in the world, made out of the finest ingredients: cocoa from Africa and South America, almonds from Turkey, raisins from California, and rich, thick caramel from the West Indies."

He took a deep breath and immediately felt a ripping sensation on his front. As nonchalantly as he could, he glanced down at his shirt: a small tear had developed beside one of the buttons where the cheap fabric was stretched taut across his chest. The button itself was straining against the buttonhole. For a brief moment he had the urge to yank that button off altogether, put his fingers into that small hole beside it, and rip it open properly, once and for all. But instead he narrowed his shoulders slightly and made his breathing shallower and prayed that nothing would aggravate the tear until after the interview was over.

"Okay," continued Sam, "you may or may not move your factory to West Africa. But you do already have plantations there, do you not?"

"Yes, apparently we do."

"And it would be fair enough to assume that if you did move more of the production process to that part of the world, your working practices would be the same as in the plantations."

"That would be a reasonable assumption," said Matt carefully, "although"—he paused for a moment, trying to think of something to cover his bases—"although, we are about to review the way our plantations are run."

"Well, that's probably a very good thing. Because I was at one of your plantations in the Côte d'Ivoire a month ago, and I found children as young as seven years old working fourteen hours a day there, seven days a week."

"Really!" said Matt before he could stop himself. He was finding it hard to concentrate on keeping up his professional facade. "I mean, that's certainly not something that should be happening. Why didn't you tell us about this as soon as you found out?"

"I'm telling you now."

"Good, then we'll look into it and see if we can put it right."

"But surely it shouldn't be up to journalists like me to find these things out. Surely you should be aware of these things yourself and make sure they don't happen in the first place."

How did he get himself into this? He felt that he should explain that it really wasn't his fault, that he was only the marketing director. He would be quite happy to answer questions on sales figures or on chocolate trivia—but beyond that he was useless. "Of course it's up to us to sort things like this out," he said. "And we're going to. Which is why . . . which is why we're going to do this review I told you about."

He shifted uncomfortably on the chair, trying to find a position where the lumps of stuffing didn't dig into him.

Sam's eyes turned to daggers. "Will you stop fidgeting for a minute? You're moving in and out of shot."

"Sorry."

"And while you're at it, can you take your hand away from your chest. You look like you're doing an impression of Napoleon."

"Anything *else?*" asked Matt darkly.

"You could try answering my questions for a change, instead of going on about how lovely your damn chocolate is."

"Well, if you asked me questions I *could* answer, it might help. I'm only the marketing director, for God's sake—I don't know the first thing about our plantations in Africa."

The director, who had been looking puzzled for the last few exchanges, interrupted. "Er, can we get back to the interview?"

"Sure," said Sam, "if he'll stop playing games with me."

"Games? I'm not playing games!"

"Of course you are. You've been playing games with me ever since I first met you."

"Well, what about you?" said Matt, suddenly indignant. He pointed to the roses in the corner of the room. "I bought you flowers, and you didn't even have the grace to accept them."

"Those flowers were just something to buy me off."

"I wasn't trying to buy you off! It was supposed to be a peace offering."

They sat there, glaring at each other for a few seconds, before the director stepped in again. "The interview? We're still rolling, you know."

"Sorry," said Sam.

"Yeah," said Matt. "Let's just get this over with."

Sam gathered herself together again. "So, Mr. Dyson, what do you have to say about the contrast between our own children and the children in West Africa?"

"In what respect?" said Matt carefully.

"Well, don't you think it is particularly poignant that Western children think nothing of eating chocolate bars that the children who work on the cocoa plantations would have to save up for weeks to be able to afford?"

"Obviously it's one of the world's great injustices that we in the West are so prosperous, while those in Africa live with such great hardship. But we can only hope that in time, and with investment from companies like Trundel and Barr, the situation in West Africa will change. It would be wonderful if in the future children there could also enjoy the mouthwatering effects of some of our new milk chocolates—"

"Oh, you've got to be kidding!" cried Sam.

"What? I'm only wishing them the same economic benefits we have."

"The world begins and ends with chocolate for you, doesn't it."

"Well," said Matt smugly, "surely that's why you're interviewing me."

Sam sighed. "I give up. You obviously just want to talk about your products, so why don't you? Go on—I'm giving you a free rein. Get it out of your system."

"If you insist . . ."

"Just get on with it!"

"Okay, in that case I'll tell you about this new chocolate bar we're launching." This was it—at last he'd be able to say his piece. He doubted they'd show any of it in the documentary, but that seemed irrelevant now—he simply wanted to say what he had intended to say and get this whole interview over with.

"The Bliss bar will be a whole new concept in chocolate. We're not going for the same old thing chocolate companies have been doing time and time again. This is going to be something completely *new* . . ."

He looked at Sam—her eyes seemed to have glazed over, as if she wasn't listening to him anymore. She made an almost imperceptible nod in the direction of the cameraman, who leaned forward and switched his camera off. The soundman also got the message and began packing up his microphones. Despite this, Matt carried on. He had something to say, and he was going to say it, whether they recorded it or not.

"Bliss will be made out of all the ingredients our customers find most sensual: the hard, sweet taste of almonds from the East; tiny pockets of biscuit and nougat for texture; and the yielding velvet of thick, dark chocolate. It will be an experience like none you've ever had before. The combination of rich nutrients and sugars, and high concentrations of cocoa, are specially put together to release feelings of well-being when you eat it. This chocolate will absolutely live up to its name. It will make you feel new again. It will make you feel blissfully free!"

Suddenly everyone was standing. Sam was glaring at him with something akin to hatred in her eyes—the director was hovering next to her and he too looked thoroughly fed up. Even the cameraman's grin seemed to have waned somewhat. Matt supposed he should have been feeling victorious—after all, Phil's repetition technique seemed to have had the desired effect—but somehow he couldn't make himself feel good about it. Instead he felt rather empty.

"Right," the director said to Sam, "I think it's about time we made a move, don't you?"

"Absolutely," said Sam.

Paul held his hand out toward Matt. "Thanks for the interview. It has been . . . interesting."

"Hah!" snorted Sam from beside him.

Matt ignored them. He was gazing past them, wondering what on earth was going to happen now. At the other end of the office he could see the Walrus maneuvering his enormous bulk between the desks. He seemed to be heading toward Matt's office—presumably to get a report about how the interview had gone.

. . .

Once Sam and her film crew had left, Matt decided it was about time he too made himself scarce. He could see that the Walrus was halfway across the office now—but fortunately he had become sidetracked in a conversation with one of the accountancy staff. Matt knew he should really stay around to tell him how things had gone, but he had already had a battering today in more ways than one, and he wasn't sure he could cope with one of the Walrus's tantrums. Grabbing his briefcase, he stepped out of his office and over to his assistant's desk. "Claire, I suddenly don't feel that well."

"Yes," said Claire after a brief pause, "you look a little pale."

"I think I had better go home." Reaching into his polyester pants pocket, he pulled out Phil's crumpled twenty-dollar note. "Can you do me a favor please and give this to Phil?"

Claire took the note from his hand and raised her eyebrows questioningly.

"He'll understand," said Matt. Picking up his briefcase, he headed straight for the door. He did not look back.

Chapter twenty-three

Image is everything, Matt knew that better than anyone. If you can convince people that your product is a success, then it will become a success. And if you tell them that what you are selling is unique, that it will change their lives, then many people will buy it simply because they want to believe it's true. As long as the idea is strong enough, nobody cares about the reality, because everyone wants to buy into the image.

It's not just products that are sold on their image. Matt had been living on *his* image ever since he graduated from business school. He was the man who brought chocolate fantasies to life; he was the bright young star who could turn a company around with a single marketing campaign. He was the mind reader who could tell exactly what brand of chocolate you ate just by looking at you. This wasn't simply the image he projected to the world—over the years he had gradually come to believe in it himself. As far as he was concerned, he had *become* the image. And yet somehow, in one short morning, something had happened to puncture Matt's idea of himself. As he stepped out of his office just after ten thirty, he was no longer the bright young star he had been when he woke up. For the first time in his life he felt like a fraud.

Despite the discomfort of his new clothes, Matt didn't want to go home straightaway: the thought of being by himself in his apartment made him feel slightly desperate. So instead he walked down to Bryant Park and sat for a while among the office workers, tourists, and hobos. Then, later, he went to a bar and bought himself a succession of drinks, which he consumed while watching a couple of unemployed men playing pool. It felt somehow appropriate.

He didn't get home until late that afternoon. Slumping down in his armchair with a bottle of beer, he switched on the television only to see a sight that made him want to choke: himself. *He* was on television. There he was, dressed in his best suit, strolling across Rockefeller Plaza toward his office; and there were the protesters who had been standing outside the building this morning—he recognized the woman with the braids in her hair. Matt's heart sank because he knew what was coming. He wanted to turn the television off, pretend that none of it had happened, but for some reason he knew he was powerless to do so. Instead he just sat and watched and waited.

While this morning it had all seemed to happen in slow motion, on the screen everything hit him in quick succession: first the eggs, then the tomatoes, then the chocolate sauce, and then—after a brief pause— the cream pie. A commentary was running over the top of the pictures. Matt thought he recognized the voice, but not until the film cut to pictures of the reporter did he realize who it was. And at that point the telephone rang.

For a moment he sat and stared at the phone, as if surprised to find that he still owned such an object. But then, shaking himself, he reached over and picked it up.

The voice on the other end was the same as that on the television.

"Hello, Matt?" said Sam. "Listen, there's something I should warn you about . . ."

Matt took the receiver away from his ear and stared at it for a second, before reaching down to replace it on its crook. "Amazing!" he said out loud. The woman was shameless.

Taking a large sip on his bottle of beer, he switched the TV over to the Cartoon Network. That, at least, would be safe.

When the telephone sounded again, he thought about leaving it, but after it had rung four or five times, he gave in and picked it up.

"I take it you've seen the news then?" said Sam. "I just wanted to explain that it wasn't my fault. I mean, I know I'm the reporter, but . . ."

Matt put the phone down again. How on earth had she gotten hold of his number? He had made a point of ensuring it was unlisted. She must have gotten it from the office somehow. Matt made a mental note to tell Claire never to give his home phone number out, not even to people inside the company.

When the phone rang a third time, Matt picked it up instantly. "What do you want?" he said curtly.

"You're a very rude man," said Sam, "do you know that?"

"Rude!" Matt spluttered. *"You're* calling *me* rude?"

"You've put the phone down on me twice now. That's rude, and it's cowardly."

Matt couldn't believe his ears. "Cowardly? Now you're calling me cowardly as well?"

"I certainly am. Just because you're not man enough to listen to what I've got to say, it doesn't mean you can just cut me off like that in mid-sentence."

"Hold on a minute, I must have got something wrong here. Not only have you convinced a rabble of students to pelt me with eggs this morning, and not only have you filmed that and broadcast it across the entire Eastern Seaboard, you're now questioning my *manhood?*"

"I'm just saying that you're rude, that's all. I called to apologize, and to explain, but you won't even give me a chance."

Matt took a deep breath. "Okay then, apologize."

"Pardon?"

"You said you called to apologize, so here's your chance. When you're ready. Just fire away."

Sam paused for a moment. "I don't feel like apologizing now."

"Well, in that case, I've nothing more to say to you."

Matt put the receiver down a third time. He did it gently, with an air of triumph, but he was actually fuming. How dare that woman phone him up to tell him off! And after all that she'd done! He was just about to take the phone off the hook when it rang yet again.

Without hesitation he picked it up. "Oh, what now?"

"You did it again! That's *three* times!"

"Perhaps if you didn't call me every thirty seconds, you wouldn't give me the opportunity."

"Well, this time I'm giving *myself* the opportunity. You're a sad, pathetic wimp of a man, and this is what it feels like to have someone hang up on you."

The phone went dead.

"I don't believe it . . ." Matt glared at the receiver angrily, as if he were staring straight at Sam's face. "You absolute bitch!"

Quickly, he pulled out the piece of paper on which Alex had written Sam's number yesterday and then rang it, jabbing the numbers in hard, one by one.

The phone rang twice before Sam answered it.

"Hah!" said Matt loudly, and slammed the phone down.

Almost immediately it started ringing again. Matt turned up the sound on the television to full blast and put his hands over his ears. "Can't hear you!" he shouted at the telephone. "La, la, la, la, la—can't hear you!"

For some reason it made him feel a great deal better.

.   .   .

After several beers, a couple of large whiskeys, and over five hours of cartoons, Matt went to bed. Although he fell asleep almost immediately, it wasn't a particularly restful sleep. He had to get up a couple of times in the night to use the bathroom, and even when he slipped back into unconsciousness, his sleep was interrupted by countless dreams. The night became a meaningless jumble of candy stores and chocolate sculptures and telephones ringing and Sam's roses and Mandy and Phil and Sophie, all piled up on one another without any narrative to hold them together.

When he woke up the next day, Matt felt exhausted and hungover. As with every other morning this week, the first thought that entered his head on opening his eyes was that only a few days remained before the product launch. But unlike every other morning so far, today he decided he absolutely didn't give a shit.

Before his voice had a chance to lose its natural morning croakiness, Matt picked up the telephone and called Claire's number at work. Leaving a message on her voice mail, he said that he wasn't feeling well and wouldn't make it to the office.

Then he went back to bed for the rest of the day.

Sex

In *Roald Dahl's* Charlie and the Chocolate Factory, *there are chocolate waterfalls. Millions upon millions of gallons of the finest-quality liquid chocolate flow over the edge of a steep cliff and crash into a chocolate river below, only to be sucked up by Willy Wonka's enormous glass pipes for use in the factory.*

Strange as it may seem, most chocolate factories really do contain chocolate waterfalls, but only in miniature. To make a product like a Mars bar or a Baby Ruth, the sweet centers must first be placed on a wire conveyor belt that carries them through a machine called an enrober. This produces a curtain of liquid chocolate, only a few centimeters high. As each of the centers slides through this curtain, it becomes totally immersed. What comes out the other side has been transformed from a fairly ordinary-looking congregation of ingredients into a unified whole—every crack filled and every lump smoothed out by an even cloak of soft milk chocolate.

This is the industrial way of enrobing chocolate products. However, some traditional manufacturers still prefer to do things the old-fashioned way—by dipping each item individually by hand into a vat of tempered chocolate, then leaving it out to dry naturally. The result, they say, may not be quite as uniform, but the process is far more natural, and far more sensual. Sometimes, inevitably, the manufacturer will accidentally dip his thumb into the chocolate at the same time as the product. And though it is forbidden by all health and hygiene guidelines, how could anyone resist the temptation to run a finger across the surface of the warm, yielding liquid and surreptitiously lick off the mixture?

Whichever way enrobing is achieved, its purpose is the same—to smother the other ingredients completely. The chocolate acts as a barrier, preventing moisture or air or even parasites from getting inside the bar. And at the same time, any soft ingredients that might ooze out are held in check. That is the point: once a bar is enrobed, nothing can get in or out. All it takes is just one chink in this chocolate armor, and the bar or the truffle or whatever it is that you want to protect can be completely ruined.

Chapter twenty-four

The chocolate factory lay about 170 miles south of Manhattan, just outside Baltimore, Maryland. It was easy to get to by car: straight down the New Jersey Turnpike, onto the I-95, over the Delaware and Susquehanna rivers, followed by a short drive through the suburbs of Baltimore to the industrial park on the banks of the Chesapeake Bay. It would take Matt less than three and a half hours, door-to-door. But somehow he managed to put the journey off until well into the afternoon, so that, as he drove onto the turnpike just after one fifteen, he began to worry about whether he would make it to the factory in time before the strike began at five. Fortunately the traffic seemed to be fairly light—which, at this time on a Friday afternoon, seemed like a rare stroke of luck.

Then again, anything would have seemed like a stroke of luck after the week he'd just had. The past couple of days had been among the worst he'd ever experienced—worse even than when Sophie had left him. At least when Sophie had gone, he had managed to hold it together enough to go to work every day—but since Wednesday he had struggled even to get out of bed in the morning. He had moved the television into his bedroom and sat in the dark watching cartoons. His bed was a trash can of pizza boxes, cookie crumbs, and cheese wrappers. Beer bottles covered his floor, and the bottle of whiskey that had been half-full on Tuesday evening now lay empty on his nightstand. For two days he had moved only to visit the bathroom or change the CD in his stereo, with the occasional trip to the kitchen to forage for scraps, or to the front door to greet the food-delivery guy. Gradually, as the debris mounted up around his bed, his room began to stink.

It scared him a little how quickly this transformation had taken place. At the beginning of the week he had been a respectable businessman, worrying over the schedule for the launch of a major new product; and yet now he was more like an overindulgent, self-destructive teenager who didn't care about his job and wanted nothing but to eat and drink his way into oblivion. On the other hand, a definite part of him delighted in this slide into decay. He took long and frequent looks in the mirror to see how far he had degenerated, and with a certain amount of glee he watched the successful marketing executive slowly dissolving, to be replaced by a person who looked more like an unemployed bum, with dark rings around his eyes and the smell of stale alcohol rising off his body.

As he drove through the Lincoln Tunnel, he smelled a little better than he had done a few hours ago. Once he'd decided to keep his appointment at the factory, he had been obliged to clean himself up a little. Halfheartedly he'd climbed into the shower and stood underneath its stream for five minutes or so, rinsing the sweat from his skin. He washed his hair, using the excess shampoo suds to lather his body. Then he dried himself off and put on his second-best suit—the one that had been at home while his best suit was being pelted with eggs—and before he knew it, he was ready to go.

He was glad he had arranged to go to the factory today, otherwise he would likely have stayed in bed all weekend. He told himself that his innate sense of responsibility had forced him to pull himself together: he was a chocolate marketer, he had a new product to launch, and his team was relying on him to talk to the factory manager and discover how badly the strike was going to affect that launch. But in reality his sense of responsibility was far more vague than this. He no longer cared about the strike. He barely even cared about the Bliss launch. The only thing taking him down to Baltimore was his arrangement with the factory manager, Hector Gonzalez. Matt hated people who didn't stick to arrangements.

So here he was, crossing the state line into New Jersey, trying desperately to feel like a proper businessman again. It wasn't working, because something had changed inside him—something fundamental. He tried to concentrate on the outside, on all the accoutrements of business— the suit, the tie, the company car—but that didn't work either, because just as he was being handed his toll ticket before getting onto the New Jersey Turnpike, he noticed that he had forgotten to shave. By then it was too late to turn back.

. . .

For Sam, who was also traveling to Baltimore, to interview the striking
T&B workers, the journey to the chocolate factory was even easier. She
caught the two o'clock Metroliner from Penn Station, due to arrive in
Baltimore at nineteen after four. She traveled first-class, simply because
she felt she deserved it—anyway, she was sure she would be able to
claim the money back from New Horizons once her documentary was
finished. Unlike Matt she was confident of arriving at the factory well
before the strike was due to begin. She knew exactly what questions she
would ask the employees as they walked out. And she had a fairly clear
idea in her head what sort of footage they would be coming back with.
Compared to Matt, she was a picture of confidence and control.

That was not to say, however, that she did not have worries of her
own. As she sat in her wide, luxury train seat, she was more than slightly
concerned about not having spoken to Paul or her producer since yesterday lunchtime. Neither had she spoken to any of her protester
friends about how they were going to make it to the factory. Paul had
talked enthusiastically about taking footage of the protesters standing
outside the factory gates giving support to the workers as they walked
out, and ostensibly that's what they had agreed to do—but nothing was
confirmed. Nothing was certain.

Reaching into her shoulder bag, Sam took out her cell phone and
dialed her producer's number. When all she got was his voice mail, she
left a message asking him to call her as soon as possible. Next she
phoned Amy, one of the antislavery protesters, but there was no answer,
so she tried Paul instead.

"Hello?" he said, although his voice cut out for an instant in the
middle of the word, so that what it actually sounded like was "Heh-oh?"

"Paul? Can you hear me?"

"Just about, yes."

"Look, Paul, I'm on the train, and I just want to know what's happening. Are you and the crew coming down to Baltimore as planned?"

"We are," said Paul slowly, "but I'm afraid . . ." His voice cut out.

"Paul? Paul, can you hear me?"

"Hello? Sam? I said . . . until Sunday . . . important . . ."

The line went completely dead. Sam swore and took the cell away from her ear, but when she tried to dial the number again, she found that her phone had run out of juice. Only then did she remember that she'd forgotten to charge it the night before.

"Dammit!" she muttered under her breath. Just when she thought she'd organized everything, something vital always went wrong. Thank God it was only her phone and not something more important—the camera or the sound equipment or something. Fortunately none of that was her responsibility. That would all be waiting for her when she got to the factory.

. . .

As he neared the Baltimore perimeter road, Matt finally hit traffic. At first it didn't seem too bad—the spaces between the cars narrowed a little, and the speed dropped to around forty miles per hour, but he was still moving and he only had another fifteen miles or so to go. But then came a sign saying construction was ahead. Then the traffic slowed even more—thirty miles per hour, twenty, fifteen . . . he could see a string of brake lights turning red before him, and before he knew it, he had stopped dead in the middle of the passing lane.

"Hah!" he spat out loud. It sounded slightly hysterical, even to his own ears. "I knew it! I knew this would happen!"

He put the car into neutral and pulled on the hand brake. It was three thirty. He should still make it to the factory with plenty of time to talk to the factory manager, but even so, it was irritating. Reaching over to the glove compartment, he pulled out his cell phone and called the office.

"Claire," he said, "you couldn't do me a favor and find the number for Hector Gonzalez, could you?"

"Hector Gonzalez?" said Claire.

"He's the factory manager—I'm on my way up there now."

"Okay. Hold on." There was the sound of Claire dropping the telephone onto her desk as she rummaged through her papers to find the phone list. "I can't find a direct line for him, but I can give you the switchboard number if you like?"

"Yeah, that'll do." Suddenly the traffic in front of him started up again. Matt shoved the phone between his shoulder and his ear as he put the car into gear, before driving forward twenty yards or so. "Actually, on second thought, could you phone him for me? Just to let him know that I might be late. It's the traffic, you see."

"No problem." Claire paused for a second. "Matt, are you all right?"

"Sure, I'm all right. I'm great. Why wouldn't I be?"

"Well, you sound sort of husky. And I saw you on the news the other night."

"Oh, you saw that, did you?" Matt swallowed hard. "I suppose everyone in the office saw it. I'm sure they're all talking about it right now, having a good laugh."

"Let's just say you were probably wise not to come in for a couple of days. Especially after that thing with Mandy . . ."

Matt felt the anger rising. "Listen, I didn't come in because I wasn't feeling well. That's all. I don't want anyone to think I was running away. I've just had"—he thought for a second—"the flu. You'll tell them that, won't you?"

"Of course."

"And I'll see you on Monday. Bright and early."

"Sure," said Claire. "I'll make sure Hector Gonzalez gets your message."

He rang off.

"Fuck, shit, fuck, fuck, fuck!" he spat. "Motherfuck!" he added, just for good measure. He threw his phone back into the glove compartment and slammed it shut.

Outside the traffic moved forward another ten yards, then stopped.

. . .

Only two other people were at Sam's end of the carriage: a man and a woman. She thought she would approach the woman first.

"Excuse me," she said, "I don't suppose I could borrow your cell phone for a second, could I? Only, I have an important call to make, and mine has just gone dead. I'm happy to pay for the call . . ." She held out a ten-dollar bill.

"I don't have a cell phone," said the woman. She sat with her arms crossed, holding Sam's gaze, her eyes cold and expressionless.

"Oh. Okay then. Sorry to have bothered you."

She turned to look at the man sitting in the seat on the other side of the aisle, but as she did so, he quickly looked away. Obviously he had heard what she'd said, and equally obviously he didn't want to talk to her. Perhaps he didn't have a cell either.

Sam sat back in her seat and stared out the window. She was sure it would be all right—Paul and the others would be waiting for her at the factory; she would get to ask her questions, film the last piece of footage, and they could finally put this documentary to bed. She had a whole wealth of material to work with now: all the film they'd shot in Africa, pictures from the Chocolate Trade Fair and the floor of the New York Stock Exchange, interviews with everyone from government ministers and chocolate moguls to candy store owners and kids with sticky fingers. She even had the interview with Matt to use if she wanted, although she doubted there'd be any room for that farce once everything else had been edited together.

Besides, she doubted he'd ever forgive her if she put that in the film, not after the way he'd behaved when he saw the news piece the other evening. She thought he'd come out relatively well in it, a normal businessman suffering an unprovoked attack—he had even looked reasonably handsome in his suit—but for some reason he had insisted on finding the whole thing offensive. If only he'd listened to what she'd been saying on her commentary, he might have realized that she was being fairly balanced in her viewpoint—even defending him as being ignorant of what the people outside his office were protesting about. But no. He hadn't listened to any of it, he had refused to let her explain: it was almost as if he *wanted* to be offended. Well, if that was the case, then fine—as far as she was concerned, it served him right. But still, she couldn't help herself from wondering why he was acting this way. He had always seemed so confident on the other occasions she'd spoken to him—arrogant, even.

She stared through the window at the passing scenery. It was a truly beautiful day, and the afternoon sunshine lent even the suburban office complexes of New Jersey a certain elegance. Perhaps when she had finished interviewing this afternoon, she would suggest to Paul that he and the others come out to dinner, to celebrate the end of filming. Perhaps they could go out in Baltimore or even D.C., rather than New York, make it feel a little more special, more like a holiday.

She was interrupted from her reverie by a sound from farther down the carriage. The sound was so familiar that at first it did not impinge on her consciousness, but after a while it finally dawned on her what it was. It was the sound of a cell phone.

She looked down the carriage to see the woman she had spoken to earlier reach into her coat pocket to answer it. As she switched on the phone and put it to her ear, the woman stared back at Sam, her eyes as cold and expressionless as ever.

. . .

Matt finally pulled into the factory parking lot at ten after four, just as Sam's train was approaching Baltimore. As he strode through the revolving doors of the factory's main entrance, Sam had just disembarked and was wondering how long she would have to wait for a taxi. By the time she had caught one and was on her way to the industrial park, Matt was safely ensconced inside the factory meeting room, talking through the ins and outs of chocolate production, and the implications the strike would have on the distribution of his Bliss bar.

Fortunately Matt was out of sight when Sam arrived at the factory gates—there would only have been a scene. Not that she knew that he was there, of course. As far as she was concerned, the only people who would be at the factory were the workers, the antislavery protesters, and her film crew. To her knowledge, Matt was over a hundred miles away, in his office in Rockefeller Center, and it would have come as a shock to her had she known that he was here, in the very building she had come to film outside.

It was less of a shock to discover, when she arrived, that no one else was there. The workers were still inside working. The protesters had not yet arrived. And her film crew was nowhere to be seen. She had known something was wrong, just from her brief and erratic conversation with Paul, and now her worst fears were confirmed. If only she could borrow a phone from someone, then perhaps she'd be able to find out where he was—but she couldn't ask anyone because she didn't want to draw attention to herself.

Shying away from the front entrance, she walked across the parking lot and around the building to the side entrance. This was where the delivery trucks entered and left, and where, she guessed, the majority of the workers would be coming out. If Paul and the crew were going to be anywhere, then this was the place—an ideal spot to interview people before they got into their cars and drove away. But he wasn't here.

Sam stood for a minute or two, wondering what to do next. After a while, since no one challenged her, she wandered through the gateway and into the factory courtyard. It was the only place left that she hadn't searched.

.   .   .

As five o'clock struck, a torrent of people began to leave the building: workers in white coveralls, managers, administrators—everyone. The surge of departing workers was sudden, and the excitement in the air was akin to the atmosphere outside a high school gate at the end of final exams. Matt and Sam both got caught up in it, as they each approached the factory exit from their separate directions. With frightening speed the building was emptying itself, disgorging its employees en masse into the parking lot. The Trundel & Barr factory strike was about to begin.

Chapter twenty-five

In among all the departing workers, unshaven and dressed in his second-best suit, Matt was saying good-bye to Hector Gonzalez. Their meeting had gone well: the factory manager had convinced him that they'd be able to meet production targets despite the strike, and the Bliss launch should go off without a hitch. Now Hector had to hurry off to supervise the evacuation. One of the other managers had just spent the last half hour locking everything up—windows, gates, even the fire escapes—but since Hector was ultimately responsible, he wanted to go around and give it all one quick double check before he too left the building.

Matt watched him scurry off back up the stairs. He could understand why he was so anxious to get the place secure: tonight was probably one of the first times the factory had been locked since it was built at the turn of the last century. It was in use twenty-four hours a day: there was never any *need* to lock it up. He was surprised that Hector even knew where the keys were.

He stood for a while in the archway, watching the streams of men and women flooding past him toward the exit gates. They were smiling, most of them, glad to have finished work for the week, glad of an excuse to avoid their weekend shifts. Or perhaps they were glad to be taking power into their own hands, making a statement to the Trundel & Barr management. To him. He wondered if any of them knew who he was. It must have been pretty obvious by his suit that he wasn't one of them.

As he stood there, watching, a movement to his right caught his eye. He probably wouldn't have noticed it normally, but with so many people moving in one direction, this movement, in the opposite direction, seemed completely out of place. He turned to see a woman, hurrying away through a doorway on the opposite side of the courtyard. She was wearing a black skirt and a white blouse—nothing remarkable, but at the same time nothing like the clothes any of the factory workers were wearing. He only got a fleeting glimpse, but as the door shut quickly behind the woman, Matt was sure he recognized something about the way she walked, the flash of blond hair as she disappeared into the factory. He paused for a moment, but then a nagging feeling got the better of him, and he too hurried across the courtyard.

As he opened the door into the building, he found himself in a wide hallway. The woman was at the other end of it, disappearing around a corner—Matt thought of calling out to her, but realized he had no idea what to say. He didn't even belong here and had no right to challenge random employees of the factory. Instead he picked up his pace, jogged to the end of the hallway, just in time to see the woman entering a room around the corner and shutting a door behind her. Nervously he approached the door. All he wanted to do was see who the woman was. He paused for a moment while he thought about entering, but then decided that if it wasn't who he thought it was, he could always make an excuse, say he'd got the wrong room. So he turned the handle and went in.

He found himself in a small office overlooking some sort of loading bay. On the other side of the office, just beyond a large desk covered in paper, was the woman he'd been following. She was trying the handle of a glass door that led down into the loading bay, but the door was locked. As he entered the room, she turned to him with a startled and somewhat guilty expression on her face. And then, seeing who he was, she let go of the handle of the glass door and stood up straight.

"Shit," said Sam, "I knew you'd seen me."

Matt folded his arms and leaned back against the door he'd just come through. "What the hell are you doing here?"

"I'm covering a story."

"Don't tell me—it's an investigation into loading bays. 'Goods inward—the full story.'"

Sam gave him a mock smile. "Very funny."

"Are you following me? I mean, I can understand you being pissed with me up to a point, but this is turning into a vendetta."

"Of course I'm not following you. In fact, I'm just as surprised to see you as you are to see me. What are you doing here anyway?"

Matt snorted. "Never mind what *I'm* doing here, what are *you* doing here?"

"I told you, I'm covering a story."

"What sort of story?"

"That's none of your business."

"None of my . . ." He unfolded his arms and thrust his hands onto his hips. "I don't believe you. You're trespassing, you know that? Apart from the fact that last time you were covering a story I got a face full of whipped cream, you're here illegally. How did you get in, anyway? I suppose you broke in?"

"I didn't need to break in—I just walked through the door."

"Well, now you can just walk back out of it again."

He stood away from the door and opened it, motioning for her to leave the room. But Sam made no move to go anywhere. She just stood in the corner glaring at him as if she refused to take orders from him on principle.

Matt frowned angrily. This was absolutely typical. "What are you up to? Why are you here just when the place is closing down?"

"I'm . . ." She hesitated. "If you must know, I'm here to meet someone."

"Who? Someone from the factory?"

Sam didn't answer.

He tried again. "It's not more of those protesters, is it?" He saw a flicker pass across Sam's face. "It is, isn't it? It's those goddamn protesters. Just wait until I get my hands on them!"

Sam sighed. "Well, actually, I get the feeling they're not coming after all. They should have been here by now. They were going to stand around the entrance giving support to the workers as they walked out, but it doesn't look as if they showed up. They're not very organized."

Matt looked at her. She seemed genuinely disappointed, but her lips were still pursed defiantly. He got the feeling he wouldn't get anywhere by being bossy. She was the kind of woman who wouldn't get out of the way of a runaway train unless you asked her nicely—and since Matt had no intention of getting locked in with her all weekend, he did his best to control his anger.

"Come on," he said as gently as he could. "Let's get out of here."

She hesitated for a moment longer, as if trying to decide whether she should refuse him once more, just for the sake of it, but eventually she relented. Stepping forward, she walked through the door Matt held open. Matt shook his head angrily and followed her down the hallway toward the central courtyard.

The hallway was quiet. In fact, for the first time since he'd got here, the whole place was quiet: the distant hum of machines had now gone—there wasn't even the sound of voices. The place had a strange, hollow feeling about it, like a high school after all the kids have gone home.

"You know I could have you arrested for coming in here?" he said to Sam as they reached the door back out onto the courtyard.

"Why don't you then?"

He didn't answer, simply opened the door, ushered her through.

"Go on. Arrest me."

"Oh, don't be ridiculous. Of course I'm not going to arrest you."

Sam smiled wryly. "It was you who mentioned it."

They walked across the courtyard toward the archway, but they could see even before they got there that the exit was blocked off: a large, folding metal gate had been drawn across the way out. Matt took hold of the handle and gave it a good hard yank, but it refused to move.

"Hector must have closed off this entrance first," he said. "We'll have to go to the main entrance out the front."

He led Sam down another hallway along the side of the courtyard, then down through another to the lobby at the front of the building. The lobby had a floor-to-ceiling glass frontage, with two big glass doors in it, and a revolving door. Through the glass they could see the parking lot outside. It was virtually empty.

Striding over to the revolving doors, Matt put his hand out to push them forward, but found himself coming to an abrupt halt up against the glass. He pushed again, but the doors refused to revolve.

"That's strange," he muttered. He was beginning to feel slightly nervous now. Walking to the other doors, he tried them each in turn, but they too were locked. He turned to Sam, who was standing behind him patiently. "What time is it?"

"Twenty after five," said Sam. "Don't tell me we're locked in."

"No," said Matt unsurely. "We can't be locked in just yet . . ."

He turned back to the glass doors and rattled them again. Outside he could see someone walking across the parking lot. It was Hector.

Matt stopped rattling the door and started banging on the glass instead with his palms. "Hector!" he shouted. But the man didn't hear him—he just continued walking toward his car, unlocked the door, climbed inside. Matt started to panic and renewed his banging with vigor. "Hector! Hector!"

"Don't panic," said Sam calmly. "One of the security guards will let us out."

"There aren't any security guards," said Matt, "just security cameras."

"But surely there must be someone here? To look after the place for the weekend?"

"I don't know. This isn't a situation that's ever come up before. All I know is that Hector's supposed to be the last man out."

Sam paused for a moment before stepping over to the glass beside Matt and banging on it for all she was worth. They slapped the glass together and shouted, in the vain hope that Hector would notice them as he drove past toward the factory gates. For a moment, as he pulled up just outside the perimeter fence, they thought he'd seen them, but he had only stopped to close the gates behind him. They watched helplessly as he wrapped a big chain around the gates, fumbling for a second as he tried to find the right key for the padlock. Moments later he got back in his car, and then he was gone.

"Great," said Matt. "Fan-fucking-tastic."

"What are we going to do?" said Sam.

"Well . . ." Matt turned away from the window, thinking. "I suppose we could always phone someone. There's bound to be someone at the office who can sort it out. Or we could call the police."

"Okay. Have you got a cell phone?"

"I left it in the car. We'll have to use yours."

Sam made no move to get her cell from her shoulder bag. The sheepish look had returned to her face.

"Don't tell me you haven't got a cell. *All* journalists have cell phones."

Sam reached into her shoulder bag and pulled out her phone to show him. "It's dead. Ran out of power on the train down here."

"Oh, wonderful!" Matt laughed cynically. "Oh, this is priceless!"

"It's okay. There's bound to be a phone in here we can use. Look, there's one on the reception desk."

"It's internal only. That's one of the company's clever money-saving ideas that started the strike in the first place. The only outside lines are in the offices upstairs, and they'll be locked up like Fort Knox."

"Well, we may as well try anyway. It's no good just standing here whining about it."

Matt glared at her. Did this woman have no shame? The only reason they were in this predicament was because she had been skulking around the factory as if she thought she were some sort of secret agent—and now she was accusing *him* of making a fuss.

"Well?" she said after a moment. "Are we going to try out these offices or not?"

Matt didn't really relish doing anything at all if Sam was going to be tagging along, but there seemed to be little choice. The sooner they got out of here the better. So without further discussion he started across the lobby, striding angrily back out toward the central courtyard. Behind him, walking with smaller, faster footsteps, Sam followed.

Chapter twenty-six

The T&B factory was built on four levels. The chocolate manufacturing proceeded from the top down. All the raw, unprocessed beans were stored right at the apex of the building, in vast silos capable of holding several hundred tons of beans among them. On the next floor down, all the winnowing and roasting took place, in giant roasting machines that baked the beans at a temperature of exactly 250°F before moving them on to be crushed and ground into fine powder. On the floor below, the manufacturing was finished. Here the cocoa powder was pressed, filtered, mixed with sugar and milk, refined, and finally conched, before being piped through to the molds and the enrobing machines. On the first floor were the packaging areas, the goods-in and goods-out sections.

The whole lot was built around the central courtyard, and you could see this courtyard from virtually any room in the building. Or, at least, any room that was important. There were plenty of ancillary rooms—laboratories for testing the quality of the beans, meeting rooms, specialized storage spaces for nuts and raisins and milk powder—but anything that wasn't central to chocolate-making was tucked firmly out of the way, on the edges of the building.

. . .

Matt and Sam found the offices on the second floor, up a set of stairs that led off the entrance lobby. They were guarded by a pair of doors made of steel and toughened glass.

"See?" said Matt, turning the metal handle a couple of times. "It's locked."

"And the only phones you have are in there?"

"The only outside lines, yes."

Sam stepped forward and gave the doors a hard shake. She could see a row of desks through the glass, each with its own telephone, and a fax machine on a table by the wall—but no matter how she shook the doors, she couldn't get them to budge. It struck her that this was an apt symbol of T&B's lack of communication with the rest of the world.

What sort of a company locks its telephones away? No wonder the factory workers were on strike—every day they were locked in here for eight hours without the chance even to ring home if they needed to. Even prisoners had the right to a telephone call.

"We'll have to break in," she said eventually.

"How?"

"Well, these doors are only made of glass—they can't be *that* difficult to break."

Matt looked at her and gave a loud snort. "We can't just go around smashing the place up!"

"Why not? Do you have any better ideas?"

He stood there, and for a moment it looked as if he were about to say something, but in the end all he did was shrug, as if to say, "Fine, do what you like."

"So," said Sam decisively, "all we need is something to break it with."

She reached down and took off one of her shoes. Holding it in her hand like a weapon, she warned Matt to stand back, then slammed her shoe hard into the glass. Nothing happened. She tried again, this time with all her strength, but the only thing that broke was the heel of her shoe—the glass wasn't even scratched.

"It's no good," said Matt somewhat smugly. "You need to use something made of metal. Your shoe's not hard enough."

Sam looked around her. "How about that?" She pointed to the other side of the landing, to a metal fire pail filled with sand.

"I was thinking more in terms of a hammer."

"Yeah, well, we don't have a hammer, so this will have to do." She emptied the pail and, carrying it a little closer, hurled it at the glass panel of the left-hand door—but the bucket merely bounced to the floor with a loud clatter. "Jesus, what's this glass *made* of?"

"Here, let me have a go." Matt picked up the pail and slammed it into the glass. When nothing happened the first time, he tried again, and again, until the metal base of the pail began to buckle under the force of his blows. After one final try he gave up and dropped the pail on the floor.

Sam stood for a few moments staring forlornly through the glass at all the office equipment. She felt a small thrill of anxiety flow through her. She wasn't accustomed to being without a telephone. Normally she surrounded herself with them, both at home and at work. They were her principal means of communication and she used them constantly—for interviews, for catching up with colleagues, for easing her sense of isolation. Without a telephone, all safety nets were at once removed. The thought made her feel extremely nervous: if anything went wrong now, there would be nothing she could do.

"Well?" said Matt sharply. "Are we going to stand here all day, or shall we look for a way out?"

Without waiting for a reply, he turned his back on her and walked back down toward the courtyard. She watched him disappear, then gave one last, hankering look at all those unreachable telephones, before hurrying down the stairs after him.

. . .

Over the next two hours Matt and Sam searched through the rest of the factory. They looked in vain for an open door or window out onto the parking lot, but all the windows on the first floor were covered with metal grilles, and those on the second floor had bars across them. Those that opened on the floors above were too small to climb through. All the doors were locked. The fire escapes had chains and padlocks on them. Hector Gonzalez had done his job well.

At one point they did find their way out onto a roof terrace. One of the doors from the roasting area opened out onto the roof of the third floor, and for a moment Sam hoped that there might be some way of climbing down the outside walls to the parking lot. But there was nothing on the walls to cling to, and at three stories up it was far too high to jump safely. She could see Matt's car thirty feet below—the only car left in the parking lot—but there was absolutely no way she could reach it. The one drainpipe from this roof terrace led not to the outside, but to the enclosed central courtyard.

Only after they'd made their way back to the first floor did Matt dare voice what they were both thinking. "Well, it looks as though there's no way out."

They were in a warehouse room downstairs. The large, empty room held nothing but a few cardboard boxes and a mop sitting in a metal bucket. The entire room was painted white. The walls were white, as was the floor, which was made of concrete blocks painted with thick white floor paint. Down the center of the room were four large white concrete pillars, holding up a white ceiling, which was crisscrossed with white-painted pipes. At the opposite end of the room was a large, metal concertina gate—shut, of course—and three enormous windows. The windows, like all the others on the first floor, were covered with metal grilles, and even these were painted white. It looked more like an art gallery than a warehouse.

Matt walked over to the gate and gave it a token rattle, before leaning back against the wall, resigned to defeat. He slid down it until he was resting on his haunches. Sam watched him for a few moments. Something about his deflated demeanor she found immensely worrying.

"I suppose it's too much to expect of your office for them to wonder where the hell you are," she said, "and send someone out here to find us?"

"Far too much to expect. Why would they wonder where I am? I'm not due in now until Monday morning."

"How about your girlfriend or something? Is there anyone who might get concerned about you and call the cops?"

"Nope. No girlfriend. No wife. No kids. How about you?"

She thought of Paul and gave a short, bitter laugh. "I don't think there is anyone who would even notice I'm missing."

"So no rescue parties then?"

"No."

"Then it looks as though we're stuck here for the weekend." He pulled over a piece of cardboard that was lying on the floor next to him and sat down on it.

"So that's it, then? You're just going to give up?"

"Unless you have any better ideas, yes."

"But there must be *something* we can do. I can't spend the whole weekend in here. With you."

"Why not?" he said sarcastically. "Did you have something *nice* planned?"

"Yes, as a matter of fact. I was supposed to have finished filming today. This was going to be the first weekend for months when I didn't have any work on. I was really looking forward to just sitting at home, relaxing, and doing nothing."

"You should be in your element then—there's nothing to do here."

Sam smiled acidly in his direction. "Whoopee."

She leaned back against one of the pillars and folded her arms. The thought of being locked inside the factory for a whole weekend left her feeling panicky. This wasn't supposed to be the way things happened today. She was only supposed to have been here for half an hour, filming the strikers coming out of the factory and perhaps asking them a few questions. If only her cell phone hadn't cut out when it had. If she'd known Paul and the others weren't going to turn up, she wouldn't be here now.

She glanced at Matt. He was sitting on the floor gazing out of the window almost as if he thought he was on vacation—here to look at the view. Every now and then he blinked in the light, like a cat closing its eyes to purr. In a moment all her feelings of panic turned to irritation: of all the people to get trapped in here with, why did it have to be him? Why couldn't she be locked in with a woman—someone whom she could cooperate with? Or if it had to be a man, why couldn't it have been a fantasy figure: Brad Pitt or George Clooney—or better, some escape artist like Harry Houdini. Even being stuck here with Paul would be better than this. At least then she'd get to spend some *time* with him for a change—although, she imagined he'd probably still ignore her in favor of all the filming opportunities this place offered.

"Well?" she said loudly, more as a way to vent her frustration than because she expected an answer.

"Well what?"

"Well, are you going to say something or not? We can't just sit in silence all weekend. We've got to figure out some way to get out of here, and I don't see why I should be the one to do all the work."

"Why not? It was you who got us stuck in here in the first place."

"Oh, yes?" said Sam. "And how did you work *that* out?"

"If you hadn't been sneaking around the place, we would never have been locked in."

"Well, perhaps if *you* didn't lock your telephones away, then it wouldn't make any difference."

Matt stood up now too. "You're the one who can't even remember to keep her cell phone charged."

"Oh, yeah? Well, at least I brought mine with me instead of leaving it in the car. And anyway, it's *your* factory."

"What's that supposed to mean?"

"Well, you should get us out of here. You're the one who knows his way around. You're the—" She stopped herself just in time. She had been going to say "you're the *man*," as if somehow men had the monopoly on being active in a crisis. She was shocked at herself and covered up by starting again quickly. "If we were locked in the offices of the *New York Times,* I wouldn't expect *you* to get us out—*I'd* do something about it. I wouldn't just stand there looking pathetic."

"No, you'd probably make yourself a pain in the ass there as well."

"Better that than giving up without a fight."

Matt glared at her for a few moments, before evidently coming to a decision of his own. Without another word, he sat back down on his piece of cardboard.

"So that's it, then?" said Sam.

"There comes a time when it makes sense to give up. Why fight it? We're here for the weekend, and the sooner we accept it, the sooner we're going to get along."

He turned away from her and went back to staring out the window. Sam watched him for a minute or so before crossing her arms and plopping herself down on the floor with a growl. Frustrating though it was, she had to admit that he had a point. Perhaps it *would* be better just to accept the situation and start thinking about how they were going to make themselves comfortable for the weekend. There seemed to be little they could do to escape now.

As the thought sank in, it sent a shiver like a cold breath down the length of her back—and for the first time this evening she began to feel truly apprehensive. Perhaps if she had been locked in here alone, it wouldn't have been so bad. But she wasn't alone—she was here with a man. There was nowhere to run to, and no one to turn to if things went wrong. She found the sensation disturbingly familiar.

To make herself feel better, she started running through all the positive aspects of her situation. For example, being locked inside a chocolate factory would make an excellent basis for a magazine story. And as far as her documentary went, this was an unparalleled opportunity to have a look around the production line and gain an understanding of the way it worked. But each time she glanced in Matt's direction, she felt a thrill of anxiety pass through her, and all thoughts of her documentary dissolved. No matter how she tried, it was going to be impossible to view this as a solely journalistic experience.

Chapter twenty-seven

Matt sat for a while, staring at the window. The grille over it cut the view up into lots of tiny boxes—lots of blue and gray squares of sky and parking lot. It reminded him of the pictures he used to copy when he was in high school. His art teacher had taught him that it was easier to copy a picture if you drew a grid in pencil over it first, because it cut the picture up into smaller, more manageable boxes—all you had to do was copy each individual square, and once they had all joined up, you had a perfect copy of the whole picture. Matt always used that method when he was copying things in high school, but somehow the copy never came out looking quite like the original. Once he had rubbed away all the pencil grid lines, he was always left with something that looked slightly off, not quite real.

He wondered why the company had opted to put grilles over the windows, rather than iron bars. Perhaps they were easier to install. Or perhaps iron bars had too many bad connotations. Not that it made any difference to him now—he was just as locked in either way.

Sam seemed to be thinking along the same lines. "For Christ's sake, this is unbearable!" she said. "How do people in prison do it?"

"They've got it easy. They're only locked up with a bunch of other criminals—I've got to put up with *you.*"

She stood up. Walking over to the window, she put her fingers through the grille and rattled it. Then after a few moments she swore and rattled it again, violently.

"I suppose that makes you feel better," said Matt.

"The only thing that would make me feel better would be an open window." She let go of the metal grille and hung her arms despondently by her side. "I really don't think we can spend a whole weekend here together. There must be a way out. Somehow."

"Well, if you can come up with something, Batman, I might even consider giving you a lift home in my car."

"Bat*woman*, please."

"Whatever."

She turned away and put her fingers through the grille again. "Anyway, I do have an idea. I think we should try to break one of the windows."

"What's the point of that? We never managed to break those doors upstairs. And anyway, they're all covered in metal stuff—we'd never be able to climb through them."

"But maybe it would set off an alarm or something."

He stood up slowly, wondering if she was onto something. "I don't think there are any alarms. I mean, this building is designed to be in constant use, day and night. There are always people around, tending the machines, packing boxes—they'd never be able to turn an alarm system on without it going off the whole time."

"But there must be some sort of alarm. I mean, what happens if there's a fire?"

The idea hit him like a brick. "Of course! Why didn't we think of that before? We'll set off the fire alarm."

He turned to search the walls for the telltale red box, but there wasn't one. He wandered over to the entrance to the room and looked down the hallway, but there didn't seem to be a fire alarm down there, either. No wonder the workers had gone on strike, he thought—this was downright dangerous.

"Maybe it's automatic," said Sam. "Look, there's a smoke detector up there—maybe that sets off the fire alarm automatically." She pointed to the ceiling, some five or six feet above their heads, where a plastic disk sat nestled among the pipe-work of the air-conditioning system.

"So all we need to do is set it off."

"Okay. How?"

Matt reached down to the floor and picked up the piece of cardboard he'd been sitting on. "If we set fire to this and wave it around under the detector, that should do the trick."

"But how are we going to reach it?"

"You could stand on my shoulders?"

Sam looked at him. "You *are* kidding?"

"Okay—maybe you could *sit* on my shoulders. That should get you up a little farther—and if you stretch, you could probably get the burning cardboard quite close."

"Can't we just go and find a chair to stand on?"

Matt made a gesture around them at the empty room. "There aren't any chairs. Come on, it'll be fine. I'll just crouch down and you can climb on my shoulders. You must have done it loads of times."

"Yeah," said Sam. "When I was *five.*"

"Come on. It'll be fine."

He crouched down on one knee and gestured to Sam to come over.

She hesitated for a second, but eventually stepped over to him. "I don't believe I'm doing this." Rummaging through her bag for a second, she pulled out the book of matches Amy had given her at the anti-capitalist march with her friend's number on it, then grabbed the cardboard from Matt. She had to hitch up her skirt to swing her leg over Matt's shoulder. "I'm going to be too heavy for you."

"You'll be fine. Honestly. You're not *that* fat."

"Thanks," said Sam flatly, and swung her other leg over Matt's other shoulder. Matt wobbled a bit as he grasped her thighs and tried to get straight, but slowly he managed to stand up.

"Right," he said once he was upright, "now light the cardboard."

Sam's shins clamped the sides of his chest firmly, and he could feel her stomach pressing against the back of his head where she supported herself. He didn't feel that she was well-balanced, but he couldn't really tell: all he could see of her was her bare knees jutting out on either side of his chin. It made him nervous, not being able to see her. She was so unpredictable he had no idea what she would do. Once he heard the strike of a match above his head, he started to worry about his hair. It would be just like her to drop the match on his head once she'd finished with it.

"You should shave," said Sam's voice above him. "Your stubble's scratching my legs."

"Well, I'm sorry, but I didn't bring an overnight bag with me."

Sam ignored him. "Okay, it's lit. Now if I can just reach . . ."

He felt her body stretch away from him, as her thighs tightened around his neck. She was leaning heavily on the back of his head now, and it became increasingly difficult to hold her upright. "Hurry up! My shoulders are beginning to hurt."

"Okay, move a little to the right," said Sam. "Yes, that's right. Now this should work."

Matt waited for the alarm to sound, but it never came. Instead, something incredible happened: it started to rain. Accompanied by a scream from Sam, gushes of water poured down upon him, as if the heavens had just opened up—it seemed that all they had succeeded in doing was to set off the sprinkler system. Within moments his sleeves were drenched, and the front of his pants completely soaked through. The rest of him was protected by Sam, who seemed to be acting as a kind of human umbrella, but in only a split second she started kicking him and grasping desperately at his chest and neck. For a moment he thought he would topple over, she was thrashing about so wildly on his shoulders.

"Let me down! Quick! I'm getting soaked!"

As Matt dropped slowly to one knee, Sam scrambled off his shoulders, and the two of them ran for the doorway as quickly as they could. Behind them, the twenty sprinklers jutting out from the pipes that crisscrossed the ceiling were spraying out gallons upon gallons of water. The air was thick with it—monsoon air, too wet to breathe. The floor was already a miniature lake, and a large and growing puddle was in the hallway outside where the water came seeping through the doorway.

When he made it to the hallway, Matt turned to gaze in awe at the torrential downpour they had unleashed. It made him feel slightly nervous—they had done *that!* He hadn't noticed the sprinklers when they were making their plan—just the smoke alarms. Thank God the smoke had only set off the sprinklers in there, and not everywhere else as well.

There was still no sound of a fire alarm. In fact, the only sound other than the hiss of the sprinklers was the sound of Sam cursing loudly beside him. He couldn't help smiling when he saw her—her hair was stuck flat to her head, parted down the center, and her eyes were streaming mascara so that thick black streaks ran down her cheeks. Her white blouse was completely soaked and had become transparent. Matt could clearly see the lace of her bra shining through the material, and the two hard points of her nipples jutting out beneath it.

"Stop looking at me!" Sam shouted at him, pulling her blouse away from her skin as best she could. "This isn't some fucking wet T-shirt competition."

Matt laughed. "I'm sorry. You just look so . . . ridiculous!"

"Oh, great. *Very* funny. I'm soaked through and you're laughing at me. Fucking thanks."

He laughed again. "Sorry, I can't help it."

"Yes, you can. And stop looking at my boobs." She punched him viciously on the chest.

He was surprised by the blow, partly because the rings Sam was wearing made her punch hurt, and partly because she really seemed to mean it. This wasn't merely something to chastise him—her face was distorted with anger. "I'm not looking at your boobs," he said, and shoved her on the shoulder, just to remind her that she shouldn't go around punching people bigger than herself.

His shove only seemed to make her more angry. "Don't hit me!" she said, and punched him again, even harder this time.

Matt shoved her shoulder again. "Don't hit *me!*"

What happened next came so quickly that it was difficult for Matt to make sense of it. As far as he was concerned, they had merely been testing each other out, exchanging restrained blows like a couple of schoolkids whose hearts weren't really in it. Only Sam's heart *was* in it.

Suddenly she was all over him in a flurry of fists and elbows and fingernails, and he could do little beyond merely holding his hands up to protect his face. She was raining blows down upon him from all angles, and barking words at him that he didn't really hear—all he could hear was the sound of her hands, like hammer blows, as they struck the sides of his head. The shock of it, the momentum of this enraged woman as she surged forward into him, made him lose his balance for a moment, and he stepped back instinctively—but the floor was now wet, and before he could regain his balance, his feet had slipped out from under him and he found himself falling.

For one weightless moment the fight stopped. Suddenly Sam's face was merely inches from his own. Her body was pressed against him, her arms were locked with his arms, and for a split second they hung in the air together, more like they were involved in some floating embrace than a fight. It was a pleasant feeling, Matt thought, a taste of something beyond violence, but before he could clutch hold of the sensation, his body hit the concrete—first his hip, then his shoulder and his ribs, then his head.

The pain was not immediate. Matt was barely aware of being hurt at all—more noticeable was that Sam seemed to have fallen with him, on top of him, and was smothering him with her wet, transparent blouse. He had only a second's respite before she began hitting him again, slamming her hands onto the top of his head and his face.

"Don't you ever!" she was shouting at him. "Don't. You. Ever!"

He started trying to push her away from him, but it was difficult to do this while at the same time shielding himself from her blows. Eventually he was forced to grab hold of her arms, but she obviously interpreted this as a kind of a threat, because as soon as he did, she thrust her knee between his legs and into his groin.

It had been so long since anyone had kneed him in the balls that Matt had forgotten what it felt like. Pain resonated through him like the deep sound of a bell, reverberating through his bowels and rapidly squeezing all the breath from his body. Even Sam paused for a second, as if suddenly realizing what she'd just done. Sensing the lull, Matt instinctively lashed out at her, striking her across the face. She rolled away from him to the other side of the hallway. But Matt was no longer concerned about what Sam was doing. Drawing his knees up to his face, he leaned back against the wall and concentrated hard on not throwing up.

· · ·

They sat like that for a long while—Sam slumped on one side of the hallway, rubbing her jaw with her hand; Matt on the other side, his head on his knees. Neither of them spoke. The only sound was the splash of the sprinklers in the room beside them, hissing like white noise pouring from an untuned radio. Matt couldn't even hear the sound of his own breathing. But for the rhythmical rise and fall of his rib cage, it would be easy to believe that he had stopped breathing altogether.

Eventually the sprinklers turned themselves off, leaving nothing but the slow metronomic sound of the drips from the pipes into the lake below. Matt raised his head from his knees. A thin mist still lingered in the air of the hallway, but in the rain-soaked room the air was already beginning to clear. The pool of water, however, continued to grow: it had spread from the doorway and was seeping slowly but resolutely toward Sam's legs.

He was still pretty shaken up. He wasn't sure whether he should be angrier at Sam for attacking him or at himself for retaliating—ever since he was a boy, he'd been taught never to hit girls, no matter what the provocation. He had broken a cardinal rule.

He raised himself gingerly to his feet and gazed grumpily at the woman opposite him. "You okay?"

"No," said Sam simply.

"You're wet. How come you're so much wetter than I am?"

Sam didn't answer, just shrugged and looked away. Her shirt was absolutely sodden, and a small patch of skin was still visible through it where it had stuck to her shoulder.

"Come on," he said, frustrated. "It's cold here. Let's try to find somewhere a bit warmer."

Again, no answer.

"The water's spreading. If you don't move now, you're going to get drenched."

Matt took a few steps back to allow her space to stand up, and once she had done so, he led her down the hallway to another doorway. Inside was a large room, stacked high with boxes. On one side there were two large tables with various tools scattered on them—X-Acto knives, packing tape, yard rules—and beside them were a couple of stools. Matt stepped inside and held the door open to allow Sam in after him.

"You should get those wet things off," he said.

Sam looked at him in contempt. "I am *not* taking my clothes off."

"But you could freeze."

"I'd rather freeze than take my clothes off in front of you."

Matt sighed. "I'm not asking you to do it in front of me." He took his jacket off and held it out to her. "Here—it's a bit damp, but it's better than what you've got on at the moment. You change into that, and I'll go and see if I can find something to wrap around you."

She thought about it for a second, as if unsure what to do, but then took his jacket. Matt left her there to change into it and wandered back out into the chocolate factory.

Chapter twenty-eight

According to Matt's father, people were made up of layers, each one hidden beneath the last, like the layers of an onion or the rings of a tree. On the outside they had a hard skin, all smiles and practicality: they saw to their everyday needs, chatted to their neighbors, did their shopping, ate, drank, slept. Underneath this practical layer was a more anxious person, prone to worrying about trivial things. Beneath the anxious layer there was a lonely one, and beneath that was an essentially frightened person—someone who lived in abject fear that the world would annihilate him or her.

But according to his father's philosophy, the bottommost layer was what he called "the animal." At the core of each and every frightened, anxious, lonely human being there was a beast that required little more than food and sex. There was no one Matt's father welcomed in his store more than the animal, because animals could be relied on to spend far more than all of the other layers put together. Animals left their sensible facades at home and would do anything—fight, cheat, steal, or more important, spend money—to immediately gratify themselves. In marketing terms they were a gold mine.

The only problem with animals was that they were unpredictable. They could turn on you just as quickly as they gave you their loyalty. And when they became angry or unhappy, you could not reason with them the way you could with other layers. Their responses were beneath rationality, and logic had no effect on them whatsoever.

. . .

Matt normally took his father's theories with a pinch of salt, but this evening, as he walked away from the storeroom where he'd left Sam, he finally saw what the old man had been getting at. Somehow Matt seemed to have released the animal in Sam. Something in what he'd said or done had sliced right through all her layers and pricked her at her very core. In his confused state, it was the only explanation he could think of to justify what had happened between them.

He tried to think back to what might have triggered her attack, but none of it made any sense to him: they had got wet, he had laughed at her, and the next thing he knew she had set upon him like a crazy thing, as if she were possessed. He had been *forced* to strike her back. He hadn't wanted to—he had held off as long as possible—but in the end it had been self-defense.

He wandered blindly down the hallway, his head a jumble of disordered thoughts about Sam, about the feel of her body on top of him, about the surge of adrenaline he had felt as he struck the woman's face. He didn't know where he was going. He didn't really care—he simply had to get away, get his breath back, and clear the nauseous feeling he still felt in the pit of his stomach. He had a vague notion that if he put some distance between himself and her, then somehow he would begin to understand things a little better. He didn't seem to have been able to think clearly recently, especially when Sam was around.

After passing through a few of the manufacturing areas and down another hallway, he found himself stepping out through a doorway into the courtyard once again. Sitting down on the step, he took in a deep breath, allowed his lungs to fill with the cool evening air. Only when he let it go again did he allow himself to relax with all the conflicting feelings within him. And that was when suddenly, and quite unexpectedly, he burst into tears.

. . .

He sat there for a while, his head on his knees once more, sobbing quietly to himself until eventually his tears petered out and he felt a little better. He was glad he was alone. He had never liked crying in front of other people, not even as a child, and something about crying in front of a woman was especially embarrassing. That would truly have been the last straw. So far this week Sam had humiliated him, insulted him, possibly damaged his career, and now she had done her best to put him in a hospital as well. It was painful enough to think that she had brought him this low—but for her to see him crying over it would have been more than he could bear.

He hated Sam now more than he had ever hated anyone else in his life. He hated her stubbornness, her refusal just to let things lie. He hated her clever wit, and her smug jokes—always barbed, and always at his expense. He hated her clothes, her hair, and the way she always looked so businesslike, even when she was soaked to the skin with mascara running down her cheeks. He hated her pert breasts and her tight, desirable body, her beautiful lips and her beautiful eyes, and her guarded facial expressions, which, but for one short moment of violence this evening, seemed calculated to *hide* far more than they ever showed. But more than anything else he hated the way that she always managed, without fail, to bring out the worst in him.

As he wiped his eyes angrily on his shirtsleeve, he went over the fight in his head once again. *Why* had they fought? Because she thought he was looking at her boobs? For Christ's sake, her shirt might have been wet, but she had been wearing a bra—it wasn't as if he could see anything. And even if he had been looking at her, he hadn't been doing so the way that she'd meant it, not like some dirty old man—your eyes simply get drawn to something like that whether you want it or not. It certainly wasn't a good enough reason to attack him the way she had.

Perhaps there wasn't any rational explanation after all. Perhaps it was as simple as his father had hypothesized: some people simply had fewer layers covering up their animal core than others. Christ, Matt had certainly seen enough people like this coming into his father's store over the years—women who treated sugar as a balm to soothe all their problems, children who threw tantrums unless they got exactly what they wanted straightaway. Men who threatened violence over the tiniest of discrepancies in their change. But somehow he couldn't quite see Sam like that.

In fact, until this evening Matt had assumed that Sam would be full of self-control. He had put her in the same category as his father— inscrutable, cold, detached. Throughout all the years of watching his father at work in the store, Matt had never seen him display anything of what lay beneath his own surface. Even after the store was shut for the day, he still kept his professional smile on long into the evening, as if he couldn't bear to give away an inkling of what lay beneath it, not even to his own son. That was the same smile Sam usually wore—a generic expression to cover every situation, no matter how distressing or joyful that might be. It suddenly struck him that maybe it was people like this that you should be wary of—not those who were quick to become angry, but those like Sam and Matt's father, who covered all their emotions with a hard, shiny smile. With people like this perhaps all the layers were there for a reason. Strip them away—even by accident, as Matt seemed to have done this evening—and what lay beneath merely exploded under all the accumulated pressure.

And what of Matt himself? Did he fit into his father's theory? It was just conceivable that Sam had pierced through his own protective layers this evening, just as he had pierced through hers. Surely that would make sense of what had happened. She had somehow got under his skin, burrowed to the very core of him, and he had struck out at her to protect himself. The force with which he'd hit her certainly hadn't been inspired by anything rational—something darker, more primeval, was at work than that.

And yet, as he sat in the courtyard wiping his eyes, Matt found it difficult to conceive of himself as made up of layers. He couldn't help thinking that, when it came to him, the truth was far less exotic than his father thought. Perhaps, with Matt, the analogy of an onion or a tree trunk was less accurate than that of an Easter egg—peel back the first layer and there would be nothing beneath the surface at all. Matt would be *all* surface. Inside, where all the other rings were supposed to be, there would simply be a void.

. . .

It was dusk now, and the white walls of the courtyard seemed to glow in the blue evening light. It would soon be dark. As he stood up, he felt the damp cloth of his pants peel away from his legs. He shivered slightly and realized that he was cold. He needed to get out of his clothes into something dry.

Suddenly his mind began to fill with the practicalities of his situation.

He would have to find somewhere to sleep. He would have to find shelter, somewhere to make a bed, somewhere to find some food. He was hungry. He hadn't had a proper meal for days now—if he was going to be staying here for the weekend, then he would have to find something to eat soon. And then there was Sam to think of as well. He had promised to try to find her a change of clothes—she too would be wet and cold.

For a second he regretted having said that he'd come back to her. All his instincts told him that it would be better if they avoided each other for the rest of the time they were stuck in here—but at the same time he couldn't help feeling somehow responsible for her. No matter how unpleasant he found her company, it would be better all around if they could find some way to cooperate with one another, and he knew it was up to him to make the first move. After all, as she had pointed out earlier, this was *his* factory. Whatever happened, they certainly couldn't carry on the same way they had been until now.

Straightening out his wet pants, Matt turned and opened the door once more—the same door, he noticed, that he'd seen Sam disappearing into all those hours before. It was time to pull himself together and start organizing for the night ahead. Wiping his eyes one last time, he looked about him and tried to remember in which direction the warehouse might lie. After a few moments, having found his bearings, he left the courtyard behind him and stepped back into the darkness of the factory.

Chapter twenty-nine

After Matt left her, Sam stood for a while in the doorway of the storeroom. In one hand she clutched the X-Acto knife she had seen on the table by the door. In the other, she held Matt's jacket. She didn't think of changing into it. She didn't think of anything at all—she just listened out for Matt's returning footsteps. She was shivering all over, but she wasn't taking a single item of her clothing off until she was absolutely sure he wasn't coming back.

Unconsciously, she reached up to feel her jaw where Matt had hit her. It ached in the same way that it had ached the last time she had been struck across the face. Perhaps not as intensely, but the quality of the pain was the same—a burning sensation that radiated up toward her ear and down toward her neck. The emotions that welled up within her were the same as well: a feeling of rage, and of helplessness. She moved her jaw back and forth—it was not dislocated, not this time. Matt obviously didn't have the same sort of brute strength that Cameron had had.

She stood, and she listened, waiting for the sound of his return—not because Matt had said he would come back, but because the last time this had happened to her she *hadn't* listened. The last time, in her apartment on the night before she'd kicked Cameron out of her life, she had been more complacent. She had been standing in the bathroom, splashing water on her face, washing the blood from her nose. She hadn't thought to lock the bathroom door. She hadn't thought to listen out for Cam's return. She thought he'd finished with her.

Poor Matt. How was he to know that shoving her shoulder the way he had would awaken all this within her? How could he possibly understand the rage he'd unleashed simply by laying hands on her? It was like being transported back in time. She had attacked him, just as she had always wanted to attack Cameron, but had never had the courage or the opportunity to do so. She had beaten him, hit at his face with clenched fists—and in the end she had made him act as Cameron would have done, made him strike back at her, just as she deserved. In another life she would have felt proud of herself for fighting the way she had. But as it was, she merely felt ashamed. As she stood in the doorway, frightened and alone, she had an overwhelming feeling of worthlessness, as if being used as a punching bag were all she was good for.

．　．　．

It was a long time before she convinced herself that Matt wasn't lurking at the end of the hallway, waiting for her guard to drop. The cold brought her back to her senses. Her shirt was still clinging to her skin, and she realized that if she didn't get out of her wet things soon, she was going to catch a chill.

Reluctantly, she turned away from the door and took a look around her. A window was down at the other end of the room, but the light it gave had become dim—it was almost night. Reaching over to the set of light switches by the door, she turned one on—just enough for her to see her way around. Then she put her X-Acto knife back down on the table and stepped behind a stack of cardboard boxes to get changed.

Now that the light was on, she could see the rest of the storeroom properly, and it turned out to be much bigger than it looked. Behind the boxes the room was rather long, with rows of metal shelving down one side, and the window at the end. The things on the shelves seemed random and unrelated to the function of the factory—a stack of paper, a set of weighing scales, some boxes of envelopes and elastic bands. But the room itself, with its square concrete pillar in the center, was unmistakably the same as all the other rooms in the place. Sam looked around the ceiling to check for security cameras before removing her shirt, and then once again, just to make sure, before taking off her bra. She wasn't particularly prim about nudity, but she was damned if she was going to be a cheap thrill for some security guard. And besides, she still felt more than a little vulnerable. There was something unnerving about taking your clothes off in a factory. It was so impersonal—all concrete floors and breeze-block walls. People kept their clothes *on* in such places.

Still, it felt good to get her wet things off, and away from her skin. She rolled them up to wring the water out of them, then hung them up precariously on the edge of one of the boxes to dry.

Matt's jacket was thick, and not nearly as damp as her own clothes. The silky lining felt soft against her skin. It was strange wearing a man's jacket—it reminded her of her teens, when she used to wear her boyfriend's blazer after school. She had always felt safe in his jacket then, as if he were protecting her from the outside world. Of course, she had long since grown out of such girlish feelings, but there was still something nice about wearing something eight sizes too big—it was cozy, more like wearing a blanket than a jacket. It was like dressing up in your parents' clothes when you were little.

She pulled the jacket tighter around her and sat down on a box to wait for Matt to come back. She hugged herself to keep the warmth in, and as she did so, she felt something press against her chest—something in the inside pocket of the jacket. Reaching beneath the cloth, she pulled out Matt's wallet—a thick, black leather thing.

She didn't open it straightaway—she just held it in her hand, looking at it and feeling its weight. Of course, morally speaking it would be wrong to look inside—but a part of her was still furious with Matt, and after their physical fight outside, she didn't see why she should be bound by any of her normal moral ties. And besides, she was a journalist. She was paid to be curious: no one could seriously expect her to pass up the opportunity to take a peek inside a wallet belonging to the marketing director of a company she was investigating. So, taking a quick look around the corner of her stack of cardboard boxes to make sure Matt wasn't walking through the doorway, she opened it.

For the most part the contents were pretty standard: a couple of credit cards, an AAA membership card, a book of postage stamps. About sixty dollars in cash was in the main pocket, and five or six receipts with explanations scrawled on them in scruffy cursive handwriting—obviously something to do with expenses, Sam thought. What made the wallet seem so bulky was the large number of business cards it contained—twenty-five or thirty at least. Some of them were his own—Matthew Dyson, Marketing Director, Trundel & Barr—but most of them belonged to journalists, public relations people, designers, restaurateurs. She even recognized one or two names—a friend of hers who worked at NBC, for example. But there was nothing really of interest to a journalist—no contact details for drug barons and slave traders, no large receipts from arms manufacturers. In fact, it was pretty much like the contents of anyone's wallet—deeply uninteresting.

She did linger over two things, though—a couple of photographs. The first was a passport photo of him looking moronic, his eyes half-shut, and his mouth open as if he were in the middle of saying something when the picture was taken. She smiled as she looked at it and wondered why he hadn't destroyed it as soon as it was taken. It would have looked great on the company prospectus, this picture: Matt Dyson, Trundel & Barr's moronic marketing director.

The second picture was older and slightly faded—a picture of a woman. In contrast to Matt's passport photo, this woman looked stunning. She was sitting in a large wicker chair on what looked like some sort of deck overlooking a yard—she had long, dark, almost black hair down to her shoulders, a perfect oval face, and enormous hazel eyes, which smiled out of the picture as if imparting some hidden message. Whoever she was, she'd got her expression just right. Whenever Sam had her photo taken, she was always smiling too much or not enough or pouting just a little too obviously. This woman looked natural, comfortable. And happy.

She was just wondering to herself who this woman could be when she heard a noise behind her. Pushing the pictures quickly back into place, she shoved the wallet back into the inside pocket of Matt's jacket and stood up.

"Matt?" she called out, and stepped around the stack of cardboard boxes to catch him as he came in, but the doorway was empty. She walked over and pushed the door open to look in the hallway outside, but no one was there. Funny, she thought—she must be imagining things. Or perhaps it had been her guilt, reminding her that she was looking through someone's private possessions. She returned to her stack of boxes and picked up her shirt to see if she could wring any more water out of it, but then she heard another noise. It was unmistakable this time—the sound of a footstep.

"Matt?" she called again. "Is that you?"

She was answered by silence. Grabbing her bra, she stepped back nervously, toward the door. Something was not quite right here. Where was Matt? Why wasn't he answering? She drew the jacket closer around herself. Instinctively she reached over to the table and picked up the X-Acto knife once more.

To her right, just beyond her field of vision, she caught a glimpse of something moving, a shadow flitting across the wall, and simultaneously she heard a noise behind her. Holding her knife out before her, she spun around as fast as she could, to face whatever had entered the room.

She didn't know what she was expecting—some sort of monster perhaps, a nameless terror resurrected from some old nightmare—but in

the end it was only Matt after all. He was standing in the doorway holding a long white factory coat, and his face was a mixture of surprise and
fear. He took one look at the X-Acto knife in Sam's hand and promptly
turned and left the room, dragging the factory coat behind him.

"Matt!" she called as he disappeared through the doorway. "Matt, wait!"

Dropping the X-Acto knife back on the table where she'd found it,
she hurried out after him.

"Matt! Where are you going?"

"Away," said Matt.

"Why?"

"Because you scare the hell out of me. Because I haven't the faintest
idea what you're going to do next."

She ran after him and put her hand on his shoulder to stop him. He
flinched under her touch and turned abruptly, as if expecting her to follow it up with a blow. Sam took her hand away from his shoulder
slowly. He looked genuinely worried.

"I was scared," she said. "I heard a noise, but I didn't know it was
you."

"Who else was it going to be? There's nobody else here."

"I know." Sam swallowed. "I was just scared. Scared of the dark, I
suppose."

They stood in the hallway for a few moments, looking at each other
in the half-light. Something had changed between them, she could
sense it. For the first time, as she looked at his face, she saw a mirror of
herself—someone lonely and afraid, trapped here for the night and perhaps for longer, uncertain of where to put himself or what to do. It was
a revelation, and though it made her feel less alone, it also made her sad.
This brash, arrogant man was really no different from her after all. He
was just scrabbling about in the dark—raw, frightened, alone.

"Come on," he said eventually, "let's go."

"Where to?"

"To the warehouse," he said simply. "I've found us somewhere to
sleep."

He turned and started walking away from her down the hallway.
Sam put her hands into the deep pockets of his jacket and set off after
him.

Chapter thirty

The warehouse was vast. It was like stepping out of a tunnel into a huge cavern, which stretched so far before them that they couldn't see the other end through the darkness. Massive pallets stacked with cardboard boxes, sometimes ten or fifteen high, formed dark avenues into the gloom, like giant LEGO brick walls, unfinished, irregular. The ceiling, which in the hallway outside had been just above their heads, was now twenty or thirty feet above them. Sam got the impression glass sections were built into the roof, but since night was falling outside, they seemed only to add to the darkness.

The size of the place, the sheer volume of space, was intimidating. As she stepped inside, she had to stop for a moment to acclimatize herself to the change in environment.

"You don't seriously think we're going to sleep in here tonight, do you?"

"Yes," said Matt. "Why not?"

"It's so big. It'll be cold."

"But it has everything we need. We have food. We have cardboard to sleep on, and I even found a pile of old dust sheets in a room over there. Not only that, but there's a bathroom." He pointed to a door in the corner. "I know it's not perfect, but since it's getting late, I suggest we stay here until we find something better. Tomorrow."

Sam stepped forward toward an enormous stack of crates. "What's in all these boxes?"

"What do you think?" Matt went up to one of the nearest pallets of boxes and, taking out his keys, pierced the tape that sealed the box on the top. Opening it up, he pulled out a bar of milk chocolate. "There must be thousands of these in here. Millions. This is like a mountain of chocolate—literally."

Sam came over to him and looked in the box. She was beginning to feel anxious again. Despite all their efforts, they were still locked inside this place until further notice. Chocolate or no chocolate, this was not exactly a happy state of affairs.

"When you said we have *food* here," she said, "please don't tell me that this is what you meant."

"Well, it's not exactly a balanced diet, but it's better than nothing. I tried to find the staff cafeteria, but I don't know where it is. So for the moment, this is dinner." He opened another box—reaching inside, he held up a handful of chocolate bars. "So what do you want: dark or milk?"

"I don't know. Milk, I suppose."

Matt hesitated. "I'd advise you against that. Dark chocolate is much more nutritious. The Aztecs used to say you could march all day on nothing but cacao—they used to give it to their warriors—"

"Please," Sam interrupted, "I'd appreciate it if you spared me the interesting anecdotes." She reached up and took a bar of milk chocolate out of his hand.

Matt sat down beside her and began peeling the wrapper off his own bar. "Why are you so intent on being grumpy?" he said.

"One of us has to be."

"Why?"

"Because we're stuck here. It's dark. We have nothing to eat. And you're being so . . . so damn *practical.*"

He shrugged. "Would you prefer it if I threw some kind of a tantrum?"

Sam looked at him and sighed. "That was cheap." She reached into the box beside her and pulled out a second chocolate bar. She had been planning to start a diet this weekend, to try to get back into the habit of looking after herself. Having nothing to eat but chocolate was hardly a good beginning. On the other hand, it was a good way of cheering herself up. She took a large bite, allowed it to melt slowly in her mouth. Then, because she was hungry, she took another, and another, and another, until she had finished the whole bar.

After a while she said, "I feel sick."

"You should have had the dark chocolate."

"Matt," she said with feeling, "please don't gloat."

"Well, if you won't listen . . ." He got up and wandered off into the gloom. Sam watched sullenly as he walked to a room halfway along the back wall, just along from the bathroom. A light turned on in the room, before Matt reappeared dragging a couple of large sheets of cardboard.

Pulling them over to where she was sitting, he laid them out on the ground, one on top of the other, then returned to the room for some more. He laid the second lot of cardboard five or six yards away from the first.

"You can sleep here," he said, before wandering back to get the dust sheets he'd mentioned earlier. Once these were in place, he disappeared one last time, only to return a few moments later carrying two small sacks, one on each shoulder.

"What's in those?" said Sam.

"Hazelnuts. They're a bit lumpy, but I thought we might use them as pillows."

"You really have thought of everything." She looked at the makeshift bed before her. "This is much better than I was expecting. Thanks."

He sat down on his cardboard and started taking his shoes off. Sam checked her shirt again, but it was still damp, so she was obliged to continue wearing Matt's jacket. She wanted to ask him if this was okay, but was afraid he might want it back—she didn't want to change into some stranger's factory jacket, and she certainly wasn't putting her body under those dust sheets without something to cover her. So instead she said nothing. Kicking off her shoes, she slipped onto her cardboard bed and drew the paint-spattered sheet over her.

She lay on her back for a while, her head resting on the sack of nuts— it was surprisingly comfortable. If she could only forget that she was trapped here, she might even be able to enjoy it. It was almost like camping out—only, instead of hot food cooked over the campfire, she had chocolate. Instead of the sky above her, she had a roof full of windows; and instead of the moon she had a strip light, suspended twenty feet above her by chains hanging from the ceiling.

"Shall I turn the lights off?" said Matt.

"Yes."

Walking back to the double doors, he switched off the single row of strip lights that illuminated this end of the warehouse, plunging the whole place into darkness. Sam heard him shuffle back to his cardboard and lie down on it.

She lay for a while, staring up into the darkness, making no attempt to get to sleep. She wasn't used to going to bed so early—normally around this time she would be settling down in front of her computer to do a little more work or, on a good day, curling up on the couch to watch a film on television. Her body wasn't programmed to switch off at this time. And besides, far too much was going on in her head to go to sleep now. She couldn't help thinking about what had happened earlier—their fight, and the sheer force of the emotions that had compelled her to act the way she had. She was still shocked at herself. Even now a remnant of those emotions was still with her: fear, anger, anxiety, and something else that she couldn't quite put a name to—something that seemed to have filled her stomach with butterflies.

By the sound of things, Matt was also having difficulty getting off to sleep. She could hear his body turning repeatedly on the cardboard a few feet away, trying to get comfortable. Eventually she heard him sigh, then turn toward her.

"Sam?" he said softly. "Are you awake?"

"Completely."

After a couple of minutes of silence, he said suddenly, "Look, I just want to apologize about before, okay? I've never hit a woman before in my life. It's not . . . it's not something I *do.*"

"Don't worry about it. I seem to have that effect on men. It's not the first time."

"Well, as far as I'm concerned, it's the last time."

Sam rolled onto her side. "Don't feel guilty about it, Matt. I've been hit before, so I know how to handle it. My last boyfriend used to beat me to a pulp—what you did was nothing in comparison. And besides, I provoked you. You were just defending yourself."

"Even so . . ." He paused for a while before saying, "This boyfriend of yours—what was his name?"

"Cameron. And if you don't mind, I'd rather not talk about him right now."

"Yes, of course. Sorry. Anyway, I just wanted to say that what happened this evening will never happen again. I promise."

"Oh, really?" She felt a bitterness rising inside her. "Do you want to guess how many times I've heard those words?"

"I mean it. I'll never lay a finger on you again. Ever. Even if you provoke me."

She grunted softly to herself. "I think you're underestimating how much of a bitch I can be." But after a few moments she added, "Thanks for the thought, though."

They lay for a while in the dark, facing each other. Sam's butterflies had increased. She'd never told anyone so bluntly about what Cameron used to do to her. Even when she'd told Rachel, she'd done so carefully, as if saying the words out loud were breaking some kind of taboo. But tonight, for some reason, she had just come right out and said it. It had almost been easy, as if it were someone else's life she was talking about rather than her own.

It felt odd to say Cameron's name aloud. The name had been rolling around her brain so much in the last nine months that she had come to believe it was a word that couldn't be spoken, only thought. She wondered if it would be the same if she spoke about all the things he had done—the violence, the infidelity, the emotional torture he had put her through. Would she be able to say those things out loud as well?

"Matt?" She spoke his name softly, and when no answer came, she said it again louder: "Matt?"

From across the gap she could hear a faint rasping sound—not a snore exactly, but a heaviness in Matt's breath as if he was just entering deep sleep. For a moment she lay there looking at the dim silhouette of his body. But eventually she turned away and shut her eyes, and she too fell soundly asleep.

Chapter thirty-one

That night Matt woke to the sound of Sam screaming. It wasn't a loud scream—not a horror-film scream, but a startled one, full of panic. He opened his eyes. Through the darkness he could dimly make out Sam's form—she was sitting up, frantically rubbing her legs and stamping her feet on the cardboard beneath her.

"Are you all right?" he asked sleepily.

"No!"

"What's wrong?"

"I felt something! Something crawled over my legs!" Her voice was shaking.

"It was probably just a mouse."

"But it was big. It had . . . claws!"

She reached out from the side of her bed and grabbed something—from the sound of it, her shoulder bag—and started rummaging desperately. After a few seconds she seemed to find what she was looking for, and the next moment Matt heard the striking of a match and the whole area around Sam's bed was lit up. He blinked and looked at her face. Her eyes were wide with terror, and tears were streaking down her cheeks. She wasn't looking at him. She was using the match to light up the aisle of boxes around them—she was peering into the gloom, terrified, as if she expected to see a ghost.

Gradually the match burned down and went out. He heard her fumbling with the book before lighting another one as quickly as she could. She carried on peering at the ground all around them and started to sob.

"What's the matter?" said Matt. "Whatever it is won't kill us."

"I hate it here. I'm scared." She let out another sob. "And I want to go home."

"Me too," said Matt gently.

Once again the match went out, and Sam hurriedly lit another.

"You're going to run out of matches soon if you keep doing that."

"I don't want it to come and get me again. I want to see it coming."

Matt watched her panicked face in the light as the match slowly burned down to her fingers and went out. Almost immediately she lit another one.

"Hey," he said, "why don't you come over here? You can sleep next to me."

Sam didn't move. But she seemed to stop peering into the boxes and pallets around them.

"Come on. Bring your things over here. If there's two of us, maybe the mouse or whatever it is will be less likely to come back."

"It was bigger than a mouse," said Sam. "I'm sure it was."

Matt gestured for her to come over. When her match went out, he heard her scrambling to get her things together and then saw her shadow come over and kneel down beside him. He took her matches from her and kept one lit while she arranged her dust sheet around her.

"I'm sorry I woke you up," she said. "You must think I'm pathetic. Scared of a mouse—it's such a fucking cliché."

"Don't worry about it. It's fine."

"But it was definitely bigger than a mouse. It was quite heavy. And it had claws. I felt it run across me."

"I know."

They lay for a while together in silence, her with her back to him. He could hear her breathing gradually slowing, becoming more regular.

"Matt," she said after a while.

"What?"

"Thank you."

He smiled to himself. "You know something, I like you a lot better when you're scared."

"Why's that?"

"You're not nearly so crabby."

"Just pathetic instead."

He smiled again. "Yeah. Just pathetic."

Given her fright, Matt thought Sam would be awake for a while, but she fell asleep long before he did. He had never been good at getting back to sleep once he'd been woken up, whatever the setting—and that he was in a strange place did not help. For some reason he felt alert. His limbs were charged with energy, his senses sharpened. Who knew, perhaps he had taken some of Sam's adrenaline from her, subconsciously taken on her need to keep a watch out for rats. He did not resent her for it. Lying here, awake, keeping the monsters at bay while she slept was nice. It had been a long time since anyone had sought his protection.

He lay on his back listening to the sound of the breath entering and leaving her body. She seemed helpless, lying there, vulnerable—not at all the way she was when she was awake. At least when she was asleep, she wasn't having a go at him about something. And when she was frightened, she became grateful for his company, which was something of a novelty. He had meant what he'd said about liking her better when she was scared—she seemed far more human that way.

He wondered what sort of tirade she would launch upon him tomorrow morning. Perhaps she'd be upset with him for luring her into his bed, as if he'd hidden a rodent in her bedding deliberately. Or maybe she'd claim his jacket, which she was still wearing, was too scratchy, or the dust sheets too dusty, or the cardboard too lumpy; and he would have to do his utmost not to wind her up on purpose, just because he could, because she was so unbelievably touchy about everything. But for now she was silent. He could lie on his back and enjoy the sound of her breathing. He could feel the gentle rise and fall of the back of her rib cage against his arm, let its rhythm soothe him, like the rocking of a child. And slowly, without even trying, he drifted off to sleep.

Chapter thirty-two

When Sam woke up the next morning, she was alone. She had rolled off the cardboard onto the hard concrete floor, and the dust sheets, which she had thrown off in the night, lay crumpled all around her. She was still wearing Matt's jacket. Her shoes and her bag were beside her, and her bra and shirt were still hanging up on the crate where she'd left them last night. In fact everything was there, just as she'd left it, except Matt. Matt was nowhere to be seen.

She sat up, then climbed slowly to her feet. With a quick glance in each direction, she took off the jacket and changed back into her shirt—it was grubby, and a thick brown line of dust was across the back of it, but at least it was dry. And it was hers. It felt good to be back in her own clothes—she felt more in control. Perhaps now she wouldn't make a fool of herself as she had last night. God knows what Matt must have thought of her, sobbing pathetically like some child with nightmares begging to be allowed to sleep in her parents' bed. But then, her fear had been very real—primeval almost. There had been something about the darkness, the feeling of being alone in all this cavernous space, without knowing what lay beyond the feeble light of her frantically lit matches . . .

She shuddered slightly and pushed the memory from her mind. In the daylight her fear looked foolish. It was best forgotten.

Sliding on her shoes, she looked down the giant aisle of cardboard boxes beside which they had been sleeping. For the first time she could see the back wall of the warehouse, not so far away after all. She was tempted to go down there to have a look around, but she did not want to stray too far away in case Matt came back.

The thought reminded her of his absence. She looked around her. Where was the man? Apart from his jacket there was no evidence of his existence.

"Matt," she called out, and then more loudly, "Matt!"

There was no answer—not even an echo. The sound of her own voice simply disappeared into the space of the warehouse, soaked up by all the thousands of cardboard boxes. She walked along the width of the warehouse, looking down each aisle, and when she reached the end, she went to the small bathroom Matt had pointed out to her the previous evening. Afterward, she returned to their bed, in the hope that he might have reappeared—but the bed was just as she'd left it.

"Great," she said out loud to herself, "he's abandoned me."

A voice came from behind her, filled with mock indignation. "Now would I do something like that?"

Turning, she found Matt standing in the doorway that led back to the factory. "*There* you are. What happened to you?"

"I went exploring."

"Well, you could at least have told me. I've been looking for you all over."

"Why?" He smiled sardonically. "Were you worried about me?"

Sam couldn't think of anything to say, so she picked up one of the dust sheets and started folding it. It was a slightly absurd thing to do—the sheets were all hopelessly crumpled and absolutely encrusted in dried paint—but it gave her something to do with her hands while she did her best to avoid Matt's unbearable smugness.

"Well, aren't you going to ask me where I've been?"

"If it will make you happy," she said dully.

"Go on then!"

Sam looked at him. What was this—some game for ten-year-olds?

Putting on a sarcastic smile, she said in her best 1950s housewife voice, *"Hey,* there, Matt! Where have *you* been today?"

"You'll be pleased to hear I've been out searching for breakfast."

"Gee whiz, honey, and did you *find* any?"

"As a matter of fact I did."

Sam went back to folding the dust sheets. "Congratulations. What is it? Chocolate mousse, I suppose. With chocolate whip to follow, all washed down with a nice chocolate milk shake."

"Not even close. How does bacon and eggs sound?"

"Hah!" said Sam, not even bothering to look up.

"Or if you're a vegetarian, there's beans. And mushrooms and tomatoes and toast. In fact there's loads of stuff, but I fancy something fried, don't you?"

She stopped her folding to look at him suspiciously. "Are you trying to be funny? Because if you are, it's not in very good taste."

"I'm not trying to be funny at all. I've found the staff cafeteria—it's downstairs, in the basement below the offices. The kitchens are full of food—there's everything from vegetables to burgers to cookies."

"You're serious?"

"Completely."

She dropped her dust sheet on the ground. "Then what the hell are we hanging around here for? I'm starving."

.   .   .

Matt led her out of the warehouse, across the courtyard, and down a flight of stairs to the basement. There, through a set of doors, they found a large room that reminded Sam of high school: the same off-white Formica tables arranged in rows, the same gray plastic chairs stacked neatly at the side of the room, and at the opposite end a stainless steel counter, with large steel food compartments shielded behind sheets of thick glass.

As she scanned the room, Sam's heart leaped. There, on the wall opposite the counter, was a pay phone. She was about to step over to it when Matt interrupted her.

"I already tried it. It's out of order."

"But surely you can get through to the operator . . ."

"No, it's completely dead."

She glared at him. "Doesn't *anything* work in your company?"

He opened his mouth about to reply, but then stopped, thinking better of it. He turned away and led her toward a door behind the counter. By the splintered wood around the handle, it looked as if Matt had had to break it in earlier.

He pulled the door open and led Sam into a large kitchen.

"What do you want?" he said, walking straight to one of the refrigerators.

Sam came and stood next to him to look inside. She hesitated for a moment, looking at the endless rows of ham, cheese slices, veggie burgers, lettuces, tomatoes, mushrooms, sausages. "Everything," she said eventually. "I want everything!"

. . .

Working in unison, Sam and Matt pulled all the produce out onto the steel counters and began to cook. Pans appeared on the range, sizzling with bacon and sausages and veggie burgers. While Matt fed the toaster with slices of bread, Sam chopped mushrooms and tomatoes for an omelet. They hardly needed to speak as they worked—they simply got on with it, taking up each task where the other left off. In contrast to everything that had gone before, they were a model of cooperation.

By the time they had settled down together at one of the Formica tables next door, they were both ravenous.

"I think this is the best breakfast I've ever had," said Sam, shoveling a large forkful of food into her mouth.

"Me too," Matt agreed, then added, a few moments later when his mouth wasn't so full, "With a fridge packed with food like that, I could happily stay here until Monday."

"Are you kidding? I could stay here all week!"

He laughed. "You've changed your tune."

"Don't listen to me, it's only the food talking."

They smiled at one another as they chewed. They had cooked far more than they could possibly eat in one sitting. Sam was forced to leave half her omelet because she was so stuffed. And while Matt returned to the kitchen to refill his plate, he only managed to finish a small portion of what he brought back. Eventually they were sated. Sam poured them both a cup of coffee and they leaned back in their chairs to digest their food.

"Tell me something," said Sam after a while. "How did you end up working in marketing? I mean, despite the fact that we obviously hate each other, you seem like you could be a nice guy. So what went wrong?"

Matt toyed with his fork thoughtfully for a moment before replying. "Well, firstly, I don't hate you—I just wish you'd lighten up sometimes. And secondly, what's wrong with marketing?"

"Everything."

"Like?"

"Well, for a start, it's shallow."

Matt raised an eyebrow. "Shallow?"

"I mean, you spend huge amounts of money trying to make your product seem as shiny and glossy and sparkly as possible, like it's the meaning of life or something, but when it comes down to it, it's just a bar of chocolate."

"And what's wrong with that?"

"It's obvious, isn't it? You build this thing up to make people think it's going to make them happy. But it doesn't make them happy. People should be free to think about the things that are really going to fulfill them, but instead all they care about is getting a flashy car, or the latest pair of sneakers. Or one of your chocolate bars."

Matt didn't answer for a moment. He just sat there, staring at the tabletop rather unnervingly, like some chess player trying to think through his next set of moves. Eventually he looked up at Sam and said, "Tell me something—when you eat a bar of chocolate, how do you feel?"

Sam was slightly thrown by the question. "I don't get you," she said suspiciously.

"How do you feel? It's quite simple. You take a bite of chocolate, and how do you feel?"

"If you want the truth, I probably feel a little guilty, because I should be on a diet—"

"Oh, well," Matt interrupted, "that's a whole different story, isn't it?"

"But it's a fair point. The only reason women are constantly on diets is because advertising makes them feel bad about their bodies."

Matt leaned forward eagerly over the table. "Exactly! Okay, now go with me on this one. You have taken that bite of chocolate, and you feel slightly guilty because you think you should be on a diet. But underneath that guilt, what do you feel? Do you feel happy? Or sad? Indifferent?"

"Okay," said Sam reluctantly, "I suppose I feel happy. Because I'm indulging myself."

"Just because you're indulging yourself?"

"Well, that and because of the chemicals in chocolate which change your mood."

Matt looked surprised. "Chemicals?"

"Yes," said Sam suspiciously. "The chemicals you mentioned in your press release."

"Oh, those." He shrugged. "Of course, it's true that chocolate contains a few mood-enhancing drugs, but not in enormous quantities. If you really want to know why eating chocolate makes you feel happy, you'll have to guess again."

"In that case I suppose it must just be because it tastes good."

"Come on! Chicken tastes good. Apples taste good. But they don't make you feel like chocolate does."

"Look," said Sam, frustrated, "you obviously have a point to make, so instead of asking me all these questions, why don't you just come out with it?"

Matt smiled. "If you insist."

"Just get on with it!"

"Fine. The only reason you feel happy when you eat chocolate is that people like me spend millions trying to make that happen."

"Oh, please!"

"No, it's true." Matt tapped the side of his head. "It's all up there. For over a century we've been marketing chocolate as something that makes you happy. Everything about it makes you feel good. People buy you chocolate for your birthday. Lovers buy each other chocolate on Valentine's Day. Mothers reward their kids with it. These aren't things that just happened—marketing *made* them happen. You get chocolate on the holidays. Chocolate is sexy—people eat chocolate ice cream off each other's body. When you take that bite of chocolate, all those connotations come to mind—and *that's* why you feel happy. It's got nothing to do with the chocolate itself. It's all because of the image."

"That all sounds *very* virtuous."

"Yes, it does, doesn't it." He sounded smug. "That's the difference between the way we market things and the way other people do. The *dieting* industry has a vested interest in making you feel bad about yourself—they want you to feel guilty when you eat that chocolate. We have a vested interest in making you feel good about yourself. We're the good guys."

"Like Willy Wonka," said Sam sardonically, "spreading your joy across the world."

"Exactly! Effectively, I *am* Willy Wonka. And this"—he gestured around himself enthusiastically—"this is my palace!"

"God, I wish I had a camera on you now," said Sam dryly. "This is truly fantastic. Why weren't you like this on Wednesday?"

"I didn't like you on Wednesday."

Sam ignored him. He might think he could sweet-talk her, but in the end what he was saying was bullshit. "Unfortunately there's a flaw in your logic. Willy Wonka doesn't work in a vacuum. He has competitors—people who want to steal his ideas, people who want to lure away his customers. And it's the same with you."

"So?"

"So everything you've said applies to the chocolate industry *as a whole*. But you don't work for the industry as a whole—you just work for Trundel and Barr. Your job isn't only about promoting chocolate. Your job is to steal the market away from other chocolate manufacturers."

"Of course it is. And we do that by making sure our product is better than theirs."

"But it's not better than theirs, is it? It's exactly the same. There's only a few ways you can combine chocolate with nuts and wafers. So all you do is try to think of ways to convince people that there's something different about your chocolates, when in reality there isn't anything different about them at all."

Matt was beginning to look slightly uncomfortable. "I'm not sure if that's strictly true—" he began, but Sam wouldn't let him finish.

"And because there's nothing much that's different about your chocolates, you have to find other ways to make them stand out. So you sponsor kids' shows on television. You offer free trips to Disneyland and give out all the latest *Star Wars* toys—anything to make your chocolate seem more attractive than the rest."

"But what's wrong with that? It's all added value."

"I'll tell you what's wrong with it," said Sam, getting quite heated now. "The amount of money you spend on this sort of promotion is obscene. For every buck I spend on a T and B chocolate bar, you will spend twenty-one cents inducing me to buy another one. It's the same with all chocolate companies. If even a small proportion of that money was spent on making it a more ethical product, we would live in a much better world."

"Now hang on a minute—"

"And not only that, but who is all this promotional money aimed at? Kids, that's who. Kids are the ones who eat the most chocolate, and they're the ones you're trying to convince. You tell them that chocolate is good for them. You sponsor bogus research which tells them that chocolate is actually good for their teeth. And you bombard them with images to make them think chocolate will make them happy. Your job is basically lying to kids. You're not Willy Wonka—you're more like the child catcher in *Chitty Chitty Bang Bang*."

She stopped to get her breath back. She felt like a balloon that someone had let go without tying the neck—words had been pouring out of her in a rush she had been powerless to stop, and now that they had all come out, she felt deflated and still and almost peaceful. Although she was straining forward over the table, she had nothing more to say, so she sat back in her chair quietly. Raising her cup of coffee to her mouth, she took a large, lukewarm sip.

Matt, who had been pinned to the back of his chair during most of her outburst, sat and watched her. "Feeling better now?" he asked after a few moments.

"Yes, thanks. Much better."

Matt's eyes continued to scrutinize her face as he sat forward and folded his arms on the table. "You've got so much anger inside you," he said coldly. "Why is that?"

"There's a lot to be angry about."

"Maybe, but there's a lot *not* to be angry about as well. You started this conversation by saying you thought I was a nice guy."

"You probably are a nice guy. But you're also a marketing director, which makes you an evil slimeball."

"Thanks. That's very magnanimous of you."

"You're welcome."

Matt sighed. He was obviously irritated. "This might be news to you, Sam, but journalists aren't exactly renowned for their integrity either."

"You're right. We're a bunch of hard-nosed bitches who'll do anything for a story."

"Great. So where does that leave us?"

Sam stood up. "It leaves us with a whole pile of dishes to do."

She gathered together their dirty plates and carried them off to the kitchen, leaving Matt where he was. She couldn't help her small, triumphant smile to herself as she stacked the plates in the sink—there was no doubt that she had won this argument, with points to spare. The poor guy hadn't had a hope against her. She had heard the marketing spin so many times that she'd had answers prepared even before he opened his mouth.

But beneath her smile she also felt a tinge of regret. When she had called him a nice guy at the beginning of their conversation, she had meant it as an olive branch. It had been fun cooking together, and it had been a good meal—they had even smiled at each other a few times. If they were going to spend the weekend together, they could probably do with a few more smiles between them, and a few less arguments.

Still, she thought, it was his own fault for coming up with that ridiculous stuff about making people feel good about themselves. Chocolate companies didn't make you feel good. Chocolate companies just stuffed you full of calories until you were so fat no one but a box of truffles would give you a second glance. She even thought of saying as much as she went back to clear away the rest of their breakfast things, but when she returned to the main room of the cafeteria, Matt was nowhere to be seen. He had taken his jacket and gone.

Chapter thirty-three

Matt had once seen a documentary on television about the history of marketing. It had mapped out the changes in marketing techniques during the second half of the twentieth century and related these to the changes that had taken place in society at the same time. According to the documentary, the massive cultural metamorphosis that had taken place between the 1950s and 1980s was a direct result of the way marketing had shaped our lives.

At the time the show had simply made Matt laugh. It was obvious to him that it had been made by a journalist rather than by a real marketer: the idea that marketers had the power to force such massive changes on society was flattering, but plainly absurd. Hippies, the summer of love, the civil rights movement—all this had been the result of enormous cultural shifts. Hundreds of factors had led to these things happening, and marketing probably wasn't even in the top ten. As far as he knew, the only role that marketing had played was to jump on the end of the bandwagon.

Only *now* did he begin to see the more sinister side of documentaries like this. They simplified things until there was no longer room for anything but black and white, good and evil. Seen through the documentary's lens, marketing was no longer just another job: it didn't merely give consumers what they wanted—it *dictated* those wants in the first place. And according to its manifesto, marketers weren't ordinary people. They were gods laying down rules for customers to live by. Either that or devils, taking away customers' free will and replacing it with the preordained responses of automatons.

Of course, painting marketers as diabolically clever villains was far more interesting than the mundane reality (and Matt knew from experience that most marketers were little more than pen pushers, reeling out the same tried-and-tested campaigns time and time again). That was the problem with documentaries like this—the journalists who had made them were more concerned with entertaining their viewers than with enlightening them. It was the same with Sam. She wasn't interested in presenting a clear, unbiased view of chocolate marketing. She was only interested in making her show sexy. She was only interested in showing the world in black and white.

As he left the staff cafeteria, Matt was angry. It had been nice sitting there with Sam. There had been an animosity between them for too long now, and this morning, at last, he had allowed himself to see her as a companion rather than a threat, as a woman rather than merely a journalist. Her hair was rumpled, her skirt creased, and she had an attractive just-woken-up look about her that made her seem much more approachable than she had been yesterday. He had for the first time seen a spark of something truly exciting in her smile. In fact, this morning was possibly the first time he had ever seen Sam smile without sarcasm, without some barb or immediate defense mechanism popping up to spoil it. He should have known it couldn't last.

He had wanted to show her a world where marketing *wasn't* automatically the work of the devil—where, on the contrary, it was a benign, creative force. But Sam seemed more interested in winning the argument than in hearing someone else's point of view. While Matt had talked of marketing lovingly, Sam could only see it as an aberration, an intrusion. Or worse, as some sort of mind rape, forcing its views on unwilling victims.

In the end he'd had no choice but to walk out on her. He didn't want a repeat of their scene last night. To him, this morning's argument was not much different—only, instead of battering him with her fists, today she was doing it with words. He didn't want to strike back at her as he had done yesterday. And he didn't see why he should have to carry on putting up with all her clever snide remarks. So, in the absence of an alternative, he had simply left her where she was.

He walked up the steps from the basement, and through a doorway that led out onto the courtyard. He found it faintly disconcerting to be in exactly the same place as the last time he'd left Sam alone—it seemed that every doorway in the factory led out onto this damn courtyard. It was sunny and fresh outside—it looked as if it might turn out to be a beautiful day—but somehow Matt didn't feel much like appreciating the weather. Disappointed, demoralized, but glad to be free, Matt meandered across to the middle of the open space and tried to figure out what he was going to do next.

. . .

Downstairs, Sam set about clearing up their breakfast things. She felt angry—almost as angry as she'd felt during their fight last night. She knew she was overreacting, and yet she couldn't seem to do anything to stop herself. She felt wronged. *Nobody* walked out on her like that. And even if they did, they did it in front of her face—not while she was out of the room. Coming back to an empty room like that had been a shock—where the hell had he gone? There was something almost physical about his abandonment, as if he had enforced his absence upon her.

She continued clearing away their breakfast things not because she wanted to, but because she didn't know what else to do. She couldn't go after him because she felt that would amount to an apology—or worse, an admission that she needed his company. And she couldn't go anywhere else either. Only one staircase led out of here. If she walked up it to find him sitting in the courtyard outside, she might just be tempted to start hitting him again. So she was stuck here.

Yet to stay in this empty room was almost unbearable. It was so sparse and soulless—all vacant chairs and identical, institutional tables. The only sign of life was the very breakfast she was now clearing away: a few slices of uneaten toast, some butter and jelly, some fried mushrooms and half an omelet. Sam stacked them all onto a tray and carried them through to the kitchen, then came back for the coffee cups separately. She felt like some kind of waitress in a diner, clearing up after someone else's meal.

She couldn't understand why she felt so bad. She hadn't *acted* badly: they had merely had an argument, that's all. And she couldn't understand why she felt so suddenly alone, either. She was used to being alone. She lived her whole *life* alone, for God's sake. She wasn't one of those people who craved company, who needed to fill every waking moment with hordes of other people—if anything she was the opposite: she sought out solitude. So what was different now?

She stacked away the butter and the jelly in the refrigerator, and also the second half of the omelet Matt had started. Then she turned her mind to the dishes—two plates, two cups, and all the pans and chopping boards they'd used.

"Jesus," she said out loud, "I'm acting like a housewife."

For some reason the thought made Sam feel desperately sad.

.   .   .

When he reached the center of the courtyard, Matt stood for a second, looking for a place to go. In front of him were two doors. The first was the door he'd seen Sam slipping through yesterday evening—the door that led to the goods-in area, the warehouse, and the chocolate manufacturing and molding area. The second, on the other side of the courtyard, seemed to lead only to a set of stairs. Matt looked from one to the other before he finally decided on the second, simply because he had never gone through it before. He wanted to explore somewhere new. He needed to get his mind off things.

Through the doorway, he found a short flight of stairs leading up to the second floor of the factory. At the top of these was another doorway, leading to what could only be the refining room.

The first thing that struck him as he stepped inside was the smell. Everywhere he had been in the factory so far had smelled of chocolate— but here the smell was overpowering. Before him lay the chocolate conches—a succession of eight or ten rectangular vats, each of them holding hundreds of gallons of chocolate. Matt could see the thick brown mixture through the slats of the nearest conche. It was caked all over the metal rollers, large splatters of it at each end where the rollers had washed the chocolate against the ends of the tub as they swept back and forth. Drips of the stuff were even running down the outside of the vats. Chocolate was everywhere.

He was astounded that the workers had left the room like this. He had imagined that they would have finished off a batch of chocolate, then emptied the conches and cleaned them, ready for them to start again on Monday. But instead it looked as though they had simply gone on with their jobs as normal until five o'clock yesterday, then simply switched the machines off and left. He doubted they would be able to use this chocolate when they came back to work. It would all have to be thrown away.

He wandered between the conches, looking around in wonder. Everywhere he looked there were pipes: across the ceiling, along the walls, even across the spaces in the middle of the room. It was like walking into a forest of parallel lines: small silver-colored pipes, encrusted in chocolate, were suspended over the conches as if waiting to pour ingredients into the troughs; larger brown-colored pipes poured down from the ceiling into other pieces of machinery up ahead; small brass pipes ran between machines; enormous, square ventilation pipes ran across the ceiling. Matt had to fight the urge to strike them each in turn, like a child running a stick along a set of railings. He had no doubt that each pipe would sound a different note. They would be like tubular bells, deep and resonant and beautiful.

Just beyond the rows of conches he came out into an open space, occupied by a huge machine. Four or five huge metal rollers, one on top of the other, were suspended in a gigantic metal casing, with conveyor belts and pipes coming out of it, joining it to the other pieces of machinery in the room. Beyond this machine was another, almost identical, and then another. These must be the refiners, he thought, which spun the chocolate sugar mixture between their rollers to break the particles down smaller and smaller.

The next thing he came across was a row of storage vats. There must have been ten or fifteen of them—enormous cylindrical metal tubs, each one five yards high and a couple of yards in diameter.

"Amazing!" whispered Matt as he walked up to one of these vats. He put his hand on the metal casing. How much liquid chocolate would a vat like this hold? Three thousand gallons? Four thousand? "Amazing!" he said again, almost unconsciously. "Absolutely incredible!"

Stepping back, he surveyed the room once more. It truly was a wonder of engineering. When the factory was in action, six or seven different processes were going on in this room simultaneously—everything from pressing and filtering the cocoa butter, mixing it with the cocoa liquor and sugar, refining the mixture, conching it, and storing it in these gigantic vats.

He was suddenly overcome by an urge to see it all in action—rollers spinning, pistons pumping, and everywhere chocolate being poured and spun and stirred. That would truly be a sight to behold. And why not see it in action? If he was going to be stuck in this factory, he might as well find out how it all worked. He could take charge. He could be king for a day, master of all he surveyed, with several hundred tons of machinery all moving in accordance to his whim! Excitedly, Matt set about trying to discover how to turn some of these machines on.

.   .   .

In the cafeteria kitchen Sam was washing the dishes and trying to work out what was wrong with her. What was it about her that made men hate her so much? Was she really so repulsive that the only thing she was good for was a fight—someone to argue with, someone to beat up and then discard, someone to abandon halfway through a conversation or halfway through sex? Was it something that she *did* that made men act like this? Or was she so innately contemptible that they couldn't think to treat her any other way?

As she fumbled her way through the dirty dishes, these questions occupied her mind. She gazed vacantly at the dishwater, as if hoping that the answers might arise from its murky depths. What was wrong with her? She knew she wasn't an unattractive woman. When she was younger, before she met Cam, she had been able to turn heads just by walking into a room. She was intelligent—she had to be, just to get by as a journalist. She had an interesting job, and her career had really taken off in the past couple of years. In fact, in every other sphere she was a success. So why was her love life such an utter fuckup?

It seemed faintly ironic that she should be standing here, washing her way through his-and-hers coffee cups like some paragon of domesticity, when actually she had never managed to hold down a stable relationship in her life. She seemed to get worse as the years went on—nowadays she didn't even seem able to hold down a stable conversation. She found herself getting defensive when it wasn't appropriate. And she went on the attack when that wasn't appropriate either. What was all that stuff she'd said to Matt about his being like the child catcher in *Chitty Chitty Bang Bang?* Where the hell had that come from? She'd only really wanted to point out a few problems with his theories, and instead she'd ended up insulting him.

The problem was that she no longer knew instinctively how to deal with people like Matt. She had hidden herself away from people in general, and men in particular, for such a long time now that she had forgotten how to communicate with them. Almost every conversation she had had in the past year had revolved around her work in some way. She had shied away from social contact, and now in this situation where she was virtually obliged to get on with someone, she didn't know how to act.

She tried to think back to a time when meeting people hadn't been a problem, when talking to them, getting on with them, *liking* them, had been second nature. How had she done it before she'd met Cam? She had a vague notion that she had once been more open with people, and more sharing, but maybe that was just wishful thinking. Maybe she had never been good at it. All she knew was that the thought of opening herself up to Matt made her feel unbearably anxious. It was so much easier just to fight him off, keep him at arm's length with barbed words and insults. She was much more comfortable like that.

With a sigh, she dropped the handful of cutlery she was washing back into the bowl. What was the point? she thought. What was the point of anything?

. . .

Each of the machines had a large red emergency stop button, but no equivalent green button to start them up. He walked all the way around the refiners looking for a switch, but he couldn't find one. He came across an old stepladder beside one of the storage vats, so he climbed up it, looking for a switch on top of the machines—but all he found up there was a little dust, and a lot of cocoa grease. There weren't even any wires he could fiddle with. If he wanted to start this room spinning and whirring, he was going to have to do better than this.

He figured the machinery must have some central control system, so after a while he hurried across the factory floor to the small office he had spied in the corner. When he reached it, he found it full of computers. Some of them looked old: black screens with lines of DOS code written across them in fluorescent green type—the sort of technology that had been state-of-the-art in the 1980s. One of them, however, looked almost the same as the computer Matt had at work: only instead of its screen showing Microsoft icons, it was covered in icons showing different pieces of machinery.

Apprehensively, Matt took hold of the mouse and double-clicked on one of the images. He didn't expect anything to happen, but almost immediately he heard a buzzing sound start up, followed by a clanking, and then a loud whirring noise from down below. Walking over to the doorway, he looked out over the factory floor. Across the length of the room, machines were coming alive, one by one. The conveyor belts on the refiners had started to move—he could see their drums spinning. And in the background, the rollers in the row of conches had begun their relentless movement, swinging back-and-forth across the thousands of gallons of chocolate mixture within their trays.

Matt stood in the doorway of the control room and laughed nervously to himself. He felt like the sorcerer's apprentice. He had done all this! All this movement, all this machinery had been switched on by *him,* with the simple click of a computer mouse. After the silence of the rest of the factory, the noise sounded deafening. It was the sound of chocolate being created, magic being worked, dreams being spun.

Skipping down the steps, he ran down into the midst of it all. He wanted to get a better view—see if he could watch it all, the whole room working at once—so once he was back in the center of the room, he climbed up the metal staircase to the walkway above the chocolate storage vats.

The staircase was steep and slippery, as if the chocolate in the air had condensed on the metal to make it greasy with cocoa butter. Matt almost slipped as he climbed up the stairs. He was saved by grabbing hold of the railing, which was also greasy—it left a smudge on the sleeve of his jacket. But once he was up on the walkway, he could see the whole room, from the entrance on the other side of the conches right to the windows at the far end. In the far corner he could see the longitudinal press, as it squeezed the butter from the ground cocoa nibs. He could see the pipes that led the filtered, deodorized butter to the mixers by the end wall, where it was blended with cocoa liquor, sugar, and milk powder. He could see the belts that carried the mixture from there to the prerefiner and the refining machines spinning below him, then more pipes that took the refined chocolate to the conches by the entrance. And finally the storage vats right beside him, where the finished chocolate ended up. To think that all this went into the creation of chocolate—and not only this, but all the winnowing and roasting and grinding that went on upstairs—it was amazing, mind-boggling! For such a simple product, it had to be one of the most complicated food processes there was.

He rested his hand on the edge of the vat nearest him and was surprised to find it shuddering slightly at regular intervals. At first he thought it must be vibrations from some of the other nearby machinery, but looking around him, he didn't see anything close enough to have this sort of effect—and besides, the shuddering did feel as if it was coming from *inside* the vat.

There was a handle on the lid of the tub. Reaching forward, he grasped it and folded back a large section of the cover to reveal the insides of the enormous container. It was like opening a vast cauldron filled with sweet, dark chocolate—there, a few feet below him, the surface of the mixture shone darkly, reflecting the lights on the ceiling above his head. The aroma was intoxicating—it wafted from the surface of the liquid, making him giddy.

The shuddering was coming from two giant paddles, which rotated about a central column to stir the mixture. Of course! All the cocoa fat would rise to the top, so the chocolate had to be stirred constantly to keep the texture even. He gazed down into the swirling chocolate below. The turning of the paddles was mesmerizing—it was like looking into a huge mixing bowl during the preparation of some gigantic cake.

Instinctively Matt reached down through the opening in the cover to see if he could dip his finger into the chocolate. The surface was a good three feet below him, and he had to stretch to reach it—but the turning of the huge paddles made it impossible to get to the liquid without being caught by them. Looking up, he saw a large red emergency stop button above the vat, with wires leading to the central stirring column. To his satisfaction, when he pressed it, the paddles immediately stopped, leaving a pair of viscous waves to circulate the vat a couple of times before they too died away and three thousand gallons of thick liquid chocolate lay perfectly still.

Once the paddles had stopped, Matt was able to reach down into the liquid and dip his finger in. He was so fully focused on the sweet, shining surface of the mixture that he forgot how slippery the walkway was. As he leaned forward, he was forced to stretch farther than was strictly safe. His weight shifted forward, and the smooth leather soles of his shoes began to slide on the greasy metal. Even before his outstretched hand reached the chocolate, his feet had lost their grip, but it was too late now to stop its happening. As his index finger dipped itself into the thick, dark liquid, Matt lost his footing altogether and toppled forward into the vat.

. . .

Sam was sitting in the cafeteria thinking evil thoughts when she heard the noise of the machinery start up. She recognized it as the same sound that had filled the factory when she had first stepped foot in here yesterday evening. After the virtual silence of the last eighteen hours, the noise was jarring—it snapped her out of herself, reminded her that she was not here alone with her thoughts. Like it or not, she still had to share this factory with Matt.

"That *awful* man!" she muttered with a glance toward the door. What was he up to now? One minute he abandoned her, and the next he was making damn sure that she couldn't forget his presence.

She thought of going to find him, to tell him to turn the machines off *now* and find something quieter to do with himself. But then she realized that that might be playing into his hands. He might *want* her to come and find him, just so that he didn't have to be the one to look for her. Perhaps the best thing to do would be just to ignore it—he'd soon get bored and turn the machinery off again. Why should she be the one to crack?

But eventually her curiosity got the better of her. Truth be told, she was so used to the silence of the factory that the sound of machinery starting up made her a little anxious. Why would Matt have started it? Perhaps some of the workers had come back, strikebreakers who had returned to work for the weekend. Perhaps they had unlocked the gates, leaving the way open for her to go home.

She left the cafeteria and wandered up the stairs toward the sound of the machines. Before long she found herself back in the central court-yard. Her first reaction was to look over at the entranceway to see if it was open, but the metal gates were still drawn, so that ruled out any returning workers. Realistically, the only person who could have turned the machinery on was Matt, and she had no reason to concern herself with it. If he wanted to play with the machines, then that was his busi-ness. He had made it absolutely clear that he wasn't interested in talking to her anymore—if she had any sense, she would leave him to it, try to avoid him for the rest of her time here.

And yet, something about this noise attracted her. She had not seen the factory in action. While making the documentary she had wanted to film the production process, but they hadn't been able to find a choco-late company that would allow cameras into their factories. Matt or no Matt, this would be an opportunity just to see some of the machines in action.

She stood in the center of the courtyard and hesitated. The noise seemed to be coming from the eastern side of the factory. She looked over to that side of the courtyard and saw a doorway there that she had not yet been through.

"Oh, for God's sake, Matt!" she said at last, and stepped decisively toward the door. "You obviously want to get my attention. Why can't you be normal about it?" She opened the door, and immediately the sound became louder. "This had better be good," she said, and started up the stairs.

· · ·

Matt didn't fall into the chocolate straightaway. As he slipped forward, he threw his arms out and grabbed hold of the central column that drove the stirring paddles. Ordinarily he would have been able to pull himself back up from this point, but the metal column was greasy with cocoa fat, and almost immediately Matt felt himself sliding. He tried desperately to grip the pole, hugging it hard to his shoulder with both arms, but he could do nothing to stop his slide toward the sticky mixture.

After a few moments suspended between the edge of the container and the central column, he realized that there was no way out of the vat without first going into it. So, loosening his grip on the pole, he let his legs slide off the side of the container and dropped gently into the chocolate mixture.

As he sank down to his neck, he let out a loud curse, but a few moments later he couldn't help smiling to himself. Of all the ridiculous things he could have done to himself, this was probably the most absurd—but even while he felt foolish, a part of himself was secretly overjoyed, because this would top any dinner-party story he had ever told. He was doing what countless people had only ever dreamed about—lying in a giant bath of chocolate, his entire body immersed in the stuff. He laughed quietly. Opening his mouth, he dipped his face into the mixture and took a gulp. He was swimming in chocolate! He was a human Mars bar!

The chocolate was warm and thick, and sinking into it was a surprisingly pleasant feeling—a little like immersing himself into a bath of warm mud. He had expected it to feel wet, but it didn't—not at first, anyway. It felt more like being gripped by large, warm hands all along the length of his legs and body, holding him fast in the liquid. The only place where it seeped beneath his clothing right away was around his neck—he could feel the greasy, viscous fluid oozing under his collar and dribbling down across his shoulders.

Motion of any sort was actually quite difficult—the thickness of the chocolate saw to that—and since his body was hanging vertically in the liquid, it was hard even to float. After only a few moments he began to feel as if he were being sucked down toward the bottom, and he had to hold on to the stationary paddle to stop himself from sink-ing—but the edge of the tank didn't look so far away, and he was too amused with himself to find any of this alarming. He felt deliciously naughty in a way he hadn't felt since he was in high school. This was certainly not the way for a marketing director to behave! What amused him most was that he was still wearing his suit. While the cleaners were battling to clean his other suit and remove the egg and tomato stains from Wednesday morning, here he was saturating his next suit in chocolate. They were going to think he had some sort of food fetish.

He was also going to have to find something else to wear for the rest of the weekend, which was more of a worry. He certainly couldn't walk around covered in chocolate until Monday morning—he'd never hear the last of it from Sam. He would have to find one of those white coats the workers wore. He wondered if they had matching white pants—something for him to wear on his legs until he got home.

Deciding it was time to get out, he sloshed himself slowly to the side of the tub and reached up to see if he could haul himself out of the chocolate. To his surprise the lip of the vat was a good foot and a half out of reach. He tried kicking with his legs as he would do if he were swimming in water, but the chocolate was too thick, and his kick ended up being merely a vague flop under the weight of the liq-uid. In any case, it only raised him an extra inch or two above the sur-face, before he was sucked back down again to where he'd started from.

Part of the problem was the position in which the paddles had stopped when he'd switched them off. Had they come to rest directly below the opening through which he'd fallen, then he would have been able to push himself up on them and reach the lip of the vat from there. But the paddles were both underneath the covered section of the tub. He tried pushing himself up on one of them anyway, then throwing himself forward toward the opening, but he fell far short, and when he slipped back down into the chocolate, he found himself rapidly sinking without anything to hold himself up with. Panicking, he flailed his arms about at the surface and somehow managed to scramble his way back to the central column.

Suddenly the edge of the vat, which had seemed well within reach when he'd just fallen in, was painfully far away. How on earth was he going to get out of here? He couldn't climb out because it was too slippery, and it seemed that he couldn't jump out either. And yet he had to get out somehow—he couldn't stay here until Monday. The thought of becoming a human Mars bar didn't seem half so funny anymore.

The only person who knew he was in this factory at all was Sam. The thought made him wilt. What was she going to say if she ever found out what sort of a predicament he'd got himself into? Somehow he didn't think she'd be exactly sympathetic. She'd probably laugh at him. She might even write a story about it, make sure he never forgot his embarrassment. What was it she'd said earlier in the cafeteria? Journalists are all hard-nosed bitches who'd do anything for a story. Well, this was a story. This was a reporter's dream.

In desperation he started tugging on one of the stirring paddles to see if he could move it around to the part of the tank beneath the opening—but without the powered rotation of the central column it wouldn't budge.

"Move, you fucker!" he spluttered as he gave the paddle a last, violent wrench, but it was useless.

Eventually he stopped, breathless from the exertion of moving through the chocolate sludge. After a few moments he tried again and clambered up onto the paddle, determined to see if he could stand on it somehow, give himself the leverage to make a proper leap for the edge. He could feel his heart thumping against his rib cage. He had to get out of here! He didn't care how embarrassing it might look anymore—all he cared about was getting out, getting clean. His muscles were so tired now it was an effort just to haul his body up onto the paddle—he had that same aching powerless feeling in the pit of his stomach that he used to get in high school when his phys ed teacher made him climb up the ropes. Desperately he dragged one leg out of the chocolate and swung it over the metal paddle. Holding on to the central column with all his strength, he tried to pull himself into a semistanding position, but no sooner had he hauled his other leg out of the goo than his foot slipped out from underneath him and he fell forward, cracking his head on the metal.

As he flopped back down into the chocolate mixture, he reached out and grasped hold of the edge of the paddle to stop himself from sinking under the surface. He was too tired to do much else.

Swallowing his pride, he called out a single word: "Help." And then again, this time with more conviction: "Help! For God's sake, Sam, come and help me!"

But the sound of the machinery on the factory floor was deafeningly loud, and his voice was also muffled by the vat's cover, which was only open on one side. Even as he shouted he knew that, unless Sam was standing directly above him, there was absolutely no way that she would ever hear his calls.

.   .   .

The sight that greeted her when she stepped into the conching room on the second floor was magnificent. Lined up before her were ten conches, in double rows, their enormous rollers swaying backward and forward in time with one another to grind the chocolate smooth. It was like watching some sort of industrial ballet—everything synchronized, everything in harmony. She watched in awe and cursed that she had not brought the digital camera with her when she came down on the train yesterday—this would make a fantastic image for any documentary. The mechanization of chocolate, the *industrialization* of it—it would have been a brilliant counterpart to the human side of what was happening on the plantations.

Just as Matt had done some half an hour before her, she wandered between all the machines, marveling at their size and the sheer volume of chocolate they processed. The aroma the conches gave off was overpowering. It wasn't an acrid smell, like the smell in one or two of the rooms upstairs they'd passed through yesterday—it was a sweet smell, round, and somehow chewy. It was hot in here too, probably the result of all the friction caused by the motion of the rollers. Sam could feel prickles of sweat forming on her forehead.

Matt didn't seem to be anywhere in sight. She called out his name a couple of times, but her voice was drowned out by all the noise, so she just kept looking. She would probably find him at the back somewhere, pushing buttons and pulling levers—working the machinery without knowing what he was doing, just so that he could pretend he was in control of it all.

She wandered past the refiners, which were still spinning just as Matt had left them. She walked past the control room, but since all she could see in there were a couple of old computers, she didn't really give it a second glance. At the back of the room she walked up a set of steps to a sort of platform where a line of cocoa presses stood. She didn't really know what they were, and despite their grandeur and their impressive size, she didn't really care. All she was interested in was finding Matt— partly so that she could satisfy her curiosity about why he'd turned all this machinery on, and partly so that she could ask him to turn it all back off again. It was horrendously noisy, and she was beginning to be tired of it.

But Matt wasn't here. She walked around the presses, down to the refiners and the storage vats again, and then back out to the conches at the front. Nothing. The man had disappeared.

It crossed her mind that perhaps he hadn't been here at all. Perhaps the machinery was on some kind of timer—it might have turned itself on automatically to prevent all this partially produced chocolate from going to waste. But no—surely that would be dangerous. And she doubted whether the company would allow the machines to work over the weekend without anyone here to supervise them. So then Matt must have been here. Though why he would want to turn on all this machinery and then just leave it was completely beyond her. As it was, the place was like some industrial *Marie Celeste*— everything functioning, everything in place, just abandoned and left to itself.

Well, since Matt obviously wasn't here anymore, she might as well leave too. She had no doubt that he would come back in his own time to turn all the machines off. If she bumped into him somewhere else in the factory, she would damn well tell him to come and turn them off— they were deafening. They spoiled the peace of the place—if they were going to be here until Monday morning, the least they could do for themselves was make the place peaceful.

On her way to the door, she stopped at one of the conches. Waiting for the roller to swing away from her, she reached down and dipped her finger into the mixture, then brought it back up to her lips. Gritty, she thought.

Without looking back, she stepped away from the conche and made her way back down the stairs to the courtyard.

New Free Chocolate Sex

Nothing embodies the spirit of Western consumerism so completely as chocolate. The product is entirely superfluous to our existence, and yet it invokes desire bordering on addiction in those who buy it. It is sensuous and marketed to tap into our deepest erotic wants and needs. It gives the eater an immediate and effective cocoa and sugar high, leaving him or her faintly euphoric—but this euphoria only lasts a short while and can only be won back by eating more chocolate. In this sense it takes built-in obsolescence to its logical extreme—the product requires replacement just a few minutes after it has been consumed. It is perceived as luxurious, and yet it is ubiquitously available at a price that even children can afford. It is the ultimate symbol of instant gratification: available to all, affordable to all, loved and desired by every culture that has embraced it. Only those who are immersed in the chocolate industry itself see it for what it really is: a product, no more no less—soft to the bite, a little sugary, and an unfortunate shade of brown.

Chapter thirty-four

The dilemma, when drowning, is whether to hold your breath before you go under. Do you take one final gulp of air as you slip beneath the surface, a last gesture toward survival in the hope that some miracle will pull you back from the brink; or do you abandon yourself to the grip of the liquid, embrace death, welcome it as it floods through your mouth and into your lungs?

Some would claim that such a choice is impossible, that the survival instinct is too strong: a drowning man automatically clutches to his final breath whether he chooses to or not. Others would say that he never has enough time to think about such things, that he cannot possibly imagine the pain and the sheer surprise of inhaling liquid, that the inevitable happens long before he has been able to consider even a fraction of the implications.

The difference between drowning in water and drowning in chocolate is a matter of how thick the liquid is. Drowning in water is a relatively natural process. After the first gasp beneath the surface, water rapidly floods into your lungs, filling them within moments. The initial struggle for breath is over relatively quickly—once you realize that the only thing passing up and down your windpipe is fluid, you stop trying. Your body floats, weightless in the water; and as the oxygen levels in your blood drop, and your consciousness begins to fade, you are returned to a womblike state. People who have drowned and later been revived often talk of it as a peaceful experience, almost as if the water is reclaiming you for itself.

Drowning in chocolate is a different matter. Because it is so much thicker than water, your lungs would not be able to inhale it properly. There would be no sudden inrush of liquid, just the choking discomfort of the thick, sticky substance seeping down your windpipe. There would be none of the letting go, abandoning yourself into the arms of oblivion. Chocolate doesn't reclaim you, it strangles you, cutting off your supply of oxygen but replacing it with nothing. The man who drowns in chocolate feels none of the peace experienced by the man who drowns in water. The man who drowns in chocolate dies gasping.

For Matt, suspended in a vessel of chocolate liquid without any means of escape, it was hard not to think of such things. For a while he merely loathed the substance, which had got under his fingernails, in his ears and his hair, up his nostrils. But after half an hour or so he began to fear it. All the things that once made chocolate desirable—its thickness, its sweetness, the all-pervasive way it wraps its way around other ingredients—these were the things he began to fear most. Because these were the things that were sapping his strength and dragging him down beneath the surface.

The experience was doubly difficult because he had already imagined being immersed in chocolate a thousand times. He had used the image in countless marketing campaigns over the years: athletes diving into chocolate, blissed-out teenagers basking in chocolate baths, naked men and women cavorting in chocolate waterfalls . . . The contrast between these fantasies and the reality was so great that it was hard not to feel bitter about it. There was nothing blissful about being sucked down by the weight of all the chocolate that clung to his feet and legs. There was nothing erotic about the way he was forced to clutch the stirring paddles, praying that he would have the strength to hold out until Monday morning. He felt choked, claustrophobic, and above all, frightened.

The chocolate itself was becoming more repulsive as every minute went by. It had begun to separate, and all the cocoa butter was floating to the top: what had started as a thick chocolate mixture was rapidly becoming an oil slick, and any movement he made sent scores of shiny ripples across the surface. The chocolate around his legs, by contrast, was getting thicker. It sucked at his ankles, constantly drawing him downward. With every passing moment it was becoming more exhausting just to keep himself afloat.

He considered taking his belt off and strapping his body to the central column above the stirrers—otherwise he couldn't keep himself from sinking. Presumably the separation would only get worse, making it yet harder for him to stay on the surface. Also, without the motion of the stirrers the chocolate might begin to cool and thicken, restricting Matt's movements even further. Only by tying himself to the column would he be able to stay alive.

For a long time he thought about things like this: practical considerations that would make it possible for him to survive in here for two days and two nights. He had long since given up hope that Sam would come to find him. Why should she? He had abandoned her in the staff cafeteria, and now she was abandoning him, unwittingly leaving him to his fate inside this container. Even if she bothered to come to find him, she would never think of looking inside the storage vats, and no amount of shouting on his part would ever rise above the din of the refiners and the conches outside. So all he could do was to try to think of ways to keep himself afloat until Monday morning, and hope that one of the returning workers would eventually climb the stairs to the walkway above the tanks.

The thought raised new fears in Matt's mind. What would happen if nobody *did* climb up here to look? What would happen if they didn't check the tanks before turning the stirrers back on—just shut the lid without looking and left him in there to die like a cat in a washing machine? Surely that would be worse than simple suffocation—being churned and battered until all the breath left your body. He knew it didn't help to think about such things, but he couldn't stop himself. He didn't want to spend his final moments drowning in the very substance that had made him who he was. He didn't want to die gasping.

. . .

He was so involved in these various doomsday scenarios that he almost didn't notice the sound coming from the factory floor outside. It wasn't the sort of sound that would immediately have grabbed his attention anyway. In fact, it wasn't a sound at all, but rather an *absence* of sound—the din of the machines in the conching room seemed to have reduced slightly, as if one of them had stopped or come to the end of its cycle. He listened for a while and had almost convinced himself that he was just imagining things when it happened again—a noticeable reduction in the sound level. When the sound dropped for a third time, Matt's heart rose into his mouth. If this continued, then perhaps he would be able to call for help after all. He had no idea why the machinery was stopping, but it might not be happening by itself. Someone might be *turning* it off.

"Sam!" he called as the noise of yet another machine died down. "Sam, is that you?" He felt the adrenaline rise within him again. Suddenly, he started to shake. In desperation he dipped his free hand down into the goo and reached for his pocket—pulling out his chocolate-covered keys, he maneuvered himself as fast as he could to the side of the vat and started banging his keys against the metal.

At the same time he shouted for all he was worth. "Help! Sam! For God's sake help me!"

He was shouting so loudly he didn't hear the footsteps climbing up onto the walkway by the vats, and he was almost shocked when Sam's face appeared in the opening above him.

"Matt?" she said, confused. "Is that you in there?"

The wave of relief that swept through him was almost orgasmic. "Oh, thank God you're here!" He leaned back against the stirring paddle, exhausted. He felt like crying.

Sam, by contrast, had an irritated look on her face. "I was wondering why you hadn't turned any of the machines off. I had to go around switching them off one by one." The tone of her voice was slightly schoolmarmish, as if Matt had put her to great inconvenience. "What are you doing in there?"

"I fell in," he explained breathlessly. "I couldn't reach the top to pull myself out again. Oh, God, Sam, I'm so happy to see you!"

"And now I suppose you want me to help you out again?"

"Yes. Please."

Sam stood for a moment with her arms folded, before finally rolling up her sleeves. "I don't see why I should help you at all after you walked out on me like that," she said, leaning into the vat. "I came back from the kitchen to talk to you and you'd just disappeared. That was over an hour ago. I've spent all this time wondering where the hell you'd gone."

Matt let go of the stirring paddle and, moving out to the edge of the vat below the opening, reached up toward her as far as he could. It took all his effort just to avoid sinking farther into the chocolate.

As she grasped hold of his outstretched hand, her nose wrinkled in distaste. "You're so *oily!*"

"Be careful," he gasped.

"I can't get a grip. Here, let me grab your wrist." She leaned a little farther into the vat.

"Be careful of the floor up there," he panted. "It's slippery—"

He didn't get to say any more. It was too late. As Sam bent farther forward, she lost her footing—careering forward with a sharp cry, she fell down into the tank on top of Matt. He felt her leg connect with the top of his head, and before he had time to draw breath, he found himself being pushed under the surface, dunked bodily into the depths of the chocolate.

For a second everything was quiet. Immersed in chocolate, suspended in the sweet, warm liquid, it was almost beautiful. He felt supported on all sides to the point of perfect weightlessness, and for a split second it was nearly as if he no longer existed, as if his very essence had melted into the chocolate, become one with its warmth. All his thoughts from earlier returned, and he found himself wondering whether drowning in chocolate *would* be quite so painful after all—but then he heard a rushing in his ears, and almost involuntarily he began to kick out with all his strength. Disoriented, he wasn't even sure which way was up—he stretched his arm above his head instinctively until his hand reached something long and soft. He grabbed hold of it and pulled: a few moments later his head broke the surface, and he was able at last to gasp for air.

Someone beside him was shouting.

"Let go of me! You're drowning me!"

Matt felt a kick. Wiping his eyes, he opened them to find himself back on the surface of the tank. The long, soft thing he had grabbed hold of turned out to be Sam's leg, and she was doing her best to get it back from him—she kicked him again, then started flailing her arms desperately, in an effort to get to the safety of the stirring column.

Matt released her leg and let her pull herself to safety. At the same time he splashed his own way breathlessly back to his paddle.

"*I'm* drowning *you*," he gasped angrily when he got there. "That's rich!"

"You were pulling my leg—"

"Of course I was pulling your leg! You landed on my head! What else was I supposed to do?"

He glared at her. She shrank slightly before him, all her earlier superiority quickly evaporating. The way her face and hair were flecked all over with great globules of chocolate made her faintly pathetic. Save for a few white patches on her shoulders, the blouse she had dried so carefully overnight was now stained almost entirely brown.

"I'm really sorry," she said defensively. "It's slippery up there and—"

"I *told* you it was slippery! I told you to be careful!"

"Yes, but not until it was too late."

"Jesus, Sam! Wasn't it obvious? Anyone with half a brain would have realized that it was dangerous. But, no, you just go and jump straight in!"

She looked away resentfully. "I said I'm sorry," she mumbled. "And anyway, I'm not the *only* one stupid enough to fall in here, am I?"

Matt leaned back against the central column. He was too tired to argue. His limbs felt like lead—they were shaking with exhaustion—and his head was beginning to throb. "How the hell are we going to get out now?"

"Can't we climb out?"

"Of course not! The side is too high to climb."

"Are you sure?"

He glared at her again. "Don't you think I've tried it?"

They fell silent. But after a few moments, determined to prove him wrong, Sam struck out for the edge of the tank. He didn't try to stop her, just watched as she slopped her way forward and stretched up toward the lip of the vat. Her hand didn't reach much more than halfway to the top, and to avoid sinking altogether, she was obliged to slide her way back to the paddle. Determined not to give up, she lifted herself up on the paddle and hurled herself toward the opening up above her, just as Matt had done half an hour ago—and just as Matt had done, she missed by a mile. He watched her sink into the mixture, hold her head desperately above the surface, and struggle back to the middle of the vat again.

"See?" said Matt.

They each clung to one of the stirring paddles, on either side of the central column. They stayed like this for a while, not talking, not looking at each other. Before them the surface of the liquid had turned yellow with all the separated cocoa butter on the top, interspersed with the occasional brown streak where their splashing around had churned up some of the thicker chocolate from underneath. They were both breathing heavily—Sam from her efforts to get to the lip of the tank, and Matt from the continued exertions of spending over half an hour keeping himself afloat. They both gazed at the opening unhappily, as if reaching it were some impossible dream, a glittering prize that would always be beyond their grasp.

Eventually, Sam broke the silence. "I'm sorry. I didn't realize you were seriously in trouble."

"What did you *think* I was doing in here?"

"I'm sorry," said Sam again.

"Anyway, we're both in trouble now."

They fell back into silence for a while, before Sam said, "Look, there are two of us now. Perhaps if we worked together, one of us might be able to reach the top."

Matt shook his head wearily. He was too tired to try to escape again. It was better to conserve energy—God knew they were going to need it.

She tried again. "Maybe I could climb onto the top of this stirrer and jump."

"I've tried that. It's too slippery. I almost killed myself."

"Well, maybe you could hold my legs for me. Or even better, maybe I could stand on your shoulders—like we did yesterday, in the room with the sprinklers."

"Yes—but remember how *that* turned out."

Sam sighed. "All we can do is try."

She was right, of course. It was certainly worth a try—anything was better than staying here until Monday—so Matt dragged himself over to her side of the tank and helped her to climb onto his shoulders. Holding on to the central column, she hooked her leg over his back while he braced himself against the metal. Once she was almost free from the clutch of the chocolate, she managed to stand up, with one foot on his shoulder and the other on the paddle. She steadied herself by holding her hands against the roof of the tank, then transferred her other foot to his other shoulder.

Matt couldn't help having a bad feeling about this. She seemed so *precarious*. She was wobbling dangerously, and he was afraid she might slip and injure herself. It was bad enough being trapped here without having to cope with an injury as well, and the opening still seemed much too far away for her to make it with one jump.

With her weight on his shoulders it was difficult to keep himself afloat in the liquid, and he had to use all his remaining strength to do so. He realized that this might be their last chance for a while—he was too tired to do this more than once. There and then he made a decision. "Right," he said, panting, "when you jump, I'm going to push out away from this column, try to get you as close to the opening as I can."

"Okay, but we'll have to time it right."

"We can do it on the count of three."

With a slight wobble on his shoulders, Sam agreed.

"So are you ready?"

"Yes."

Matt steeled himself. "One, two, *three . . .*"

He let go of the central column and pushed his body forward into the lake of chocolate. At the same time Sam launched herself up off his shoulders, and without anything to support him the power of her thrust shoved him down into the chocolate. He had just enough time to see her propelled into the air before he sank beneath the surface one final time.

He had been concentrating so hard on getting Sam closer to the opening that he had forgotten about himself. Too late, he tried to take a breath. As he opened his lips and inhaled as deeply as he could, his mouth filled with nothing but chocolate and greasy cocoa butter. He quickly spat it out, but then was forced to inhale again. A choking feeling filled his throat, like thick chocolate hands tightening around his windpipe. Gripped on all sides by the liquid, he gasped desperately, instinctively, but he could force nothing into his lungs—his breath was completely smothered. Frantically, he began to kick out with his arms and legs. The rushing sound he'd heard before returned to his ears and became a roar. His limbs became heavy, then numb. And the world went dark.

Chapter thirty-five

Sam threw herself with all her strength toward the opening at the top of the vat. In the end, despite all their worrying, she reached it with ease: she caught the rim of it about chest height and was able to hook her arms over the edge to stop herself from sliding back down. From there, she could haul herself out onto the walkway. Still, her arms weren't as strong as they should be, and for a horrible moment she thought she was going to end up falling back into the chocolate. While she tried to gather the strength to clamber out onto the walkway, it was all she could do to hang there, grunting with the effort of it all.

The way she was forced to clamber out of the tank was enormously undignified. Unable to pull herself up with just her arms, she had to throw her leg up over the side and haul her body up onto the lip—but once she managed to get her waist onto the edge of the tank, the battle was won. Rolling over the edge, she flopped shoulder first onto the metal walkway, dripping chocolate all around her as she went.

"Jesus Christ," she gasped as she landed on her hands and knees. "I need to get to the gym!"

She lay there for a moment or two, getting her breath back, before kneeling up to pop her head over the side of the tub. "I made it!" she said with a triumphant smile, but as she stared back down into the tank, her smile became a frown. Matt was nowhere to be seen.

"Matt?" she called, and then again, more urgently, "Matt!"

Standing up, she leaned forward into the vat, being careful this time not to let herself slip.

"Come on, Matt, don't fuck around! This isn't funny!"

There was nothing. No sound, no movement, not even any bubbles on the surface. It was as if he had never been there in the first place. For a moment she stood there, staring at the chocolate below and wondering what could have happened. Perhaps he'd hit his head on the side of the tank and knocked himself unconscious. Or perhaps he had simply succumbed to the exhaustion. She knew she should be doing something—diving back into the tank to save him or running off to find a pole or a stick for him to cling to should he bob back to the surface. But for some reason, as she peered into the greasy depths of the chocolate, she didn't feel like doing anything. She felt numb.

All about her the factory was silent. It was almost beautiful, this stillness. For the first time since she'd been locked in here, there was no one to argue with, and nothing to disturb her or the peaceful splendor of the place. It would be nice to think that she could have the rest of the weekend to herself, without the constant need to accommodate someone else. She could walk away now, turn her back on the tank and leave. What was it Matt had said yesterday evening? Sometimes it was better just to accept defeat, sit back, and let events take their course.

She stood for a moment, thinking about how she could justify herself to the factory workers when they opened the place up on Monday—but then, she realized, there might not be any need to justify herself. No one need know she hadn't helped him. If she cleaned herself up, she could pretend that she'd never come in here in the first place, that Matt had drowned by himself without her ever having seen him. It would be easy. And even if she were to admit that she had seen him go under, there was no reason why she shouldn't get away with it anyway—neglecting to save someone wasn't the same as actually killing them. She could easily claim she was too frightened to do anything, that panic had forced her into inaction.

As she stood there beside the vat, she noticed the red emergency button above the stirrers, the same as all the other buttons she had used to turn the machines off one by one earlier. It crossed her mind that if she could somehow start the stirring paddles up again, they might bring Matt up to the surface of the liquid. Tentatively she reached forward and pressed the button. Nothing happened. She pressed it again, hard—and then again and again, slamming it with her fist—but the machinery stayed still.

"Jesus, what's the matter with me?" She leaned over the edge of the vat once more and screamed Matt's name as loudly as she could. She was answered, once again, by silence. A surge of fear shot through her stomach. The longer she stood there, the faster the situation slipped away from her. If she didn't do something soon, then there wouldn't be any point in trying. And yet what *could* she do?

Desperately, she turned away from the opening at the top of the vat and looked about her for inspiration. When her eyes alighted on the stepladder on the factory floor, she saw a spark of hope. Reaching over the railings, she grabbed the top of the ladder and started hauling it up onto the walkway. Whatever happened, she was going back into the vat. But this time she was going to make damn sure she would be able to get back out again. She only hoped it wasn't too late.

· · ·

The chocolate didn't feel quite so liquid, or nearly so warm, the second time she entered it. It merely felt greasy, like climbing into a bath of cool oil. Her clothes, which were already saturated with it, stuck to her body once more, clinging to her like Saran Wrap.

The stepladder hadn't reached all the way to the top of the tank, but by jamming it between the central column and the side at an angle of about thirty degrees, she had managed to give herself a platform to climb down onto. She also had something to clutch onto as she ducked her body beneath the surface in search of Matt. She searched with her legs, swishing them around in the mixture until they made contact with his body.

It only took a few moments to find him, suspended limply in the midst of the chocolate. Hooking her feet beneath his armpits, she hauled him to the surface, then used her arms to drag him back to one of the stirring paddles in the center of the tank. She talked to him all the time as she did this—more to reassure herself than anything else, because she was worried about how long he had been unconscious. It must have been at least a couple of minutes since she'd pulled herself back up onto the walkway. How long did it take for someone to die?

"Why do you have to be so damn heavy?" she gabbled nervously as she heaved him across the vat. "We're all right now, I promise—I'm going to get you out of this."

Slowly, she got him back to the center of the vat. By swinging one of her legs over the bottom rung of the stepladder, she managed to free both her hands so that she could haul him up over the stirring paddle.

"Okay, Matt, you can wake up now," she said, shaking him violently. As she did so, she noticed her voice was also shaking. She was feeling unbearably nervous, and her heart was in her mouth—she couldn't help worrying that, after all her hesitation on the walkway, she might be too late.

"Come on, Matt. You can't do this to me now." She slapped his face hard. "Wake up!"

There was still no response. Leaning forward, she put her hand in front of his mouth and nose, but to her utter dismay she could feel no breath entering or leaving his body. She tried to remember what you did to people when they'd drowned, but all she could think of was mouth-to-mouth resuscitation, and that would be virtually impossible in these circumstances—she had to use both hands just to stop him from sliding back into the depths of the mixture. He was slumped forward over the stirring paddle, and even to get around to the other side so that she could face his mouth would be a feat of athleticism.

"Please, don't do this."

Desperately she shook him once again, but his body was completely limp, lifeless. A cold fear rose into her throat: What had she done? Her eyes filled with tears.

"Wake up," she begged, slapping him halfheartedly on the back. And then, feeling suddenly angry, she repeated, "Wake up, wake up, wake up . . ."

As she said the words, she beat his back hard, again and again, with her fist. It never crossed her mind that thumping Matt on his back like this might revive him—when she heard him spluttering mouthfuls of chocolate, she thought it was just the strength of her blows forcing the chocolate out of his mouth. Only once he started to move did she realize he was alive—she stopped hitting him and threw her arms around him instead, holding him so tightly she threatened to drag him back down beneath the surface.

"What are you doing to me?" he gasped after a few moments, his voice little more than a rasping whisper.

Sam didn't answer. Suddenly ashamed of her show of emotion, she pulled away and helped him to get a grip on the paddle. She left him for a few moments to get his breath back, then gently pulled him over to the middle of the tank where the stepladder was jammed against the central column. With a great deal of help Matt climbed onto the first rung of the ladder, and in only a couple of minutes they each heaved themselves through the opening at the top of the tank and collapsed together in a heap on the floor.

Neither of them spoke. They just lay there together, the only sound the heaviness of their breathing, and the drips that fell from their hair onto the floor below. Between them a pool of chocolate formed and congealed on the cold metal plates of the walkway.

．　．　．

They left a trail of chocolate footprints as they made their way out of the conching room and back across the courtyard. To any onlooker they would have looked grotesque. Sam's hair had turned from blond to brown, and her white blouse had grown a thick brown chocolate crust all over it. Matt looked more like some kind of swamp creature than a businessman—either that or some monstrous Al Jolson impression, his whole body blacked up with only his eyes and teeth shining white beneath it all. Between them they must have been carrying several pounds of chocolate—in their hair, in their clothes, and over every inch of their bodies.

They moved slowly, shuffling rather than walking, with Sam supporting Matt as they went. After a while he pulled away, telling Sam that he could manage on his own, but he still allowed her to take the lead. He was in shock, and they both knew it.

She took him across the courtyard and back down the stairs to the basement. Just past the cafeteria was a set of workers' changing rooms —men's and women's—which she had come across while she was lingering down here earlier. Sam led him into the women's changing room. Two separate shower cubicles were in here, so they could easily shower at the same time without having to be coy about it. Also, a whole pile of neatly folded coveralls was on the bench by the lockers— they could use them not only as clean clothes to change into, but also as towels to dry themselves off after their shower.

She steered Matt into one of the shower cubicles and watched him turn the tap on. He didn't bother undressing first, and she didn't bother suggesting it—his suit was probably ruined anyway, so it wouldn't do much harm. The most important thing was that he keep himself warm under the hot water and clean as much of the chocolate off himself as possible.

Leaving him to it, Sam went around to the cubicle next door and set about getting herself clean. Unlike Matt, she undressed carefully before getting into the shower. She gave herself a rudimentary rinse, before picking up each article of her clothing, one by one, and holding it under the water to wash as much of the chocolate out of it as she could. Only while she was swilling water around in her shoes did she realize that her finger was as bare as the rest of her.

"Dammit!" she swore. "My ring!"

"What's the matter?" asked Matt from behind the partition wall.

"It's my ring. I've lost it. It must have come off in the vat."

"Was it expensive?"

"No—I don't know. It was a present."

She looked at her hand. It looked somehow empty without Cameron's ring, naked. She had been wearing that ring for nearly two years now—in bed, in the shower, always. Except for half an hour the other night, she'd never taken it off. And now it was gone.

"Maybe they'll find it when they empty out the vats," said Matt wearily. "If I hear of anything, I'll get it back for you. Or if you like, I could ask—"

"No, don't worry." She looked at her hand and smiled softly. "It doesn't matter."

. . .

Sam finished her shower first. While Matt stayed in the cubicle, rinsing out his clothes and hanging them over the top of the shower door, she stepped out into the room and changed into some factory coveralls. Then she left the room, telling Matt to shout if he needed anything, and that she would meet him in a few minutes back in the staff cafeteria next door.

For the next few minutes she busied herself in the cafeteria making coffee. She didn't see Matt again until he emerged from the shower rooms, dressed in a pair of white pants and a white factory jacket. He was pale, and he was shivering slightly, but he looked a great deal better than before. Like Sam, he was barefoot, having left his shoes in the shower room to dry.

She passed a hot cup of coffee across the table toward him and watched as he took a sip.

"Thanks," he said.

"No problem. I couldn't remember how you liked it, so I brought some sugar out and some milk." She indicated the creamer and the sugar bowl on the table between them.

"It's fine." He lifted the cup to his mouth once more. After a few moments he put the cup back on the table. "Anyway, I wasn't saying thanks for the coffee."

"Oh," said Sam uncomfortably. "Well, in any case, you're welcome."

"I was thinking about it in the shower—how I really owe you thanks. And how I should be apologizing."

She glanced at him nervously. "Apologizing?"

"Yes. I'm afraid I haven't been very nice to you over the past couple of days. Ever since we got locked in here, I've been cursing my luck. Not just because I'm stuck here, but because I'm stuck here *with you*. I thought that at least if I'd been locked in here by myself, it would have been bearable—but with you here . . . Anyway, I've had some pretty uncharitable thoughts, so I'm sorry for that."

"That's okay."

"It was a different story when I saw your face peering down at me from the top of that vat."

Sam turned away, uncomfortable. Why was he apologizing? Neither of them had been very pleasant, and they both knew it—surely it was better just to forget about it and move on? Something about the intensity of his expression unnerved Sam slightly, as if his experience in the depths of the chocolate tank had changed him somehow. "Look," she said, "while we're apologizing to each other, I should probably join in. I mean, I've had some pretty evil thoughts about you too."

"You have?"

"Yes." She paused for a second. "I was all ready to leave you in that vat, you know—shut the lid and pretend I'd never seen you."

He smiled weakly. "That wouldn't have been much fun."

"I'm not joking, Matt. For a moment I seriously thought about doing it—leaving you there to stew."

"But you didn't leave me. That's the important thing."

"No, I didn't." She looked away from him, avoiding his eyes. "I'm not a very nice person, Matt—you should know that by now."

They sat across the table from each other, each of them cradling a hot cup of coffee. Sam couldn't bring herself to raise her eyes, so instead she buried her embarrassment by raising her cup to her face. As she sat there, breathing in the steam that rose from the surface of her coffee, she felt suddenly vulnerable, almost as if it had been *her* who had suffered a shock, not him. She felt raw, as if someone had just peeled off a protective layer from her body.

"You know, while I was in the chocolate—under the surface, I mean—I had a sort of . . ." He paused for a moment, looking for the right word. "Well, I suppose it was a kind of dream really, but it was incredibly vivid—more like a hallucination. I thought we were on a desert island together, somewhere tropical, off the coast of Africa. I had been captured by some cannibals, and they'd put me in a big cooking pot to boil me up for a stew. I was burning all over from the boiling water, especially my chest, which felt like it was going to burst any second. Then they started beating me to tenderize my flesh, like you do with steak. It was unbearably painful. The only thing that made it all right was the thought that *you* had escaped and were going to get help. You were my lifeline to the outside world. While they were boiling me and beating me, that was all I could think of, that somehow you might be able to get me out of this mess."

He took another sip of his coffee. He looked miserable, hunched over his cup, staring down into the liquid as if it were a well and he was contemplating throwing himself into it. He gave a brief, bitter laugh before continuing. "It's sad, isn't it? You'd expect that at a time like that I'd experience something a little more significant: my life flashing before my eyes, or a vision of the Pearly Gates or something. But all my brain can come up with is some half-baked dream. And a dream full of clichés at that. As a summary of my existence, it's not very reassuring."

"I can't imagine a summary of my life would be much different," said Sam.

"No?"

She looked up at him. "You're not the only person who's afraid of drowning, Matt."

"But that's just it, I'm *not* afraid of drowning—not really. I thought I was about to be *eaten*." He sat across the table from her, staring at her with the same intensity once again, but after a few moments he turned his attention back to his drink. "Anyway, I suppose it's not all bad. At least it's given me an idea about how to get out of here."

"Really?"

"Yeah. I was thinking about it in the shower. What do people do when they're stuck on a desert island? They build a signal fire. I thought we could do the same."

Sam sighed. "But we tried that yesterday. The fire alarms don't work."

"Not a fire to set the alarms off—a *signal* fire. Up on the roof. If we made it large enough, we might be able to attract someone's attention."

She thought about it for a second and couldn't prevent a spark of hope from lighting up inside her. "It *could* work, I suppose."

"It could. But even if it doesn't, at least we'd be doing something together, instead of fighting all the time. Perhaps it will help us start again. As new."

He looked sad as he said this, almost as if he thought the idea was just as unlikely as his plan actually working. For the first time since she'd been locked in here, Sam found herself full of respect for him. However unpleasant he had been in the past, it must have taken guts for him to offer the olive branch like this. Perhaps he wasn't the coward she had taken him for after all.

Returning his gaze, she smiled at him tentatively. She hoped he would understand it for what it was—a signal that she agreed. They had a pact.

Chapter thirty-six

Matt's idea was simple. They would gather all the flammable material they could find and build a fire big enough to be seen from a distance: it would be a sort of beacon—a pillar of smoke by day, and of flames by night. The hope was that someone, somewhere, would notice their fire and call the fire department.

He wanted to get started right away, but Sam convinced him that he wasn't fit to do any heavy work just yet. He was still shivering badly, and every now and then he would cough up a brown, chocolaty phlegm. To help keep him warm, she had gone back to the warehouse where they'd spent the night and brought him back the dust sheets to wrap around himself. Then she took him upstairs to the roof terrace, to sit in the sun while she set about searching for wood for their signal fire.

It was beautiful outside—clear and bright and hot. The sky was the color of cornflowers, and not a cloud was in sight—just the occasional streak left behind by a passing airplane. As Matt sat on the edge of the roof, staring down at his car in the parking lot below, he began to feel much better, and soon he had warmed up enough to unwrap himself from the dust sheets Sam had brought him. He basked in the sunshine, relishing the way it seemed to recharge him.

Meanwhile, Sam was cracking ahead with their signal-fire plan as if their lives depended on it. She scurried back and forth into the factory gathering fuel, and soon a fair-sized pile was forming on the roof terrace: old wooden chairs, wooden shelves, telephone directories, and countless cardboard boxes, which she flattened so that they wouldn't take up too much room. She brought a whole stack of pallets up from the warehouse in the service elevator, and also some old hazelnut sacks. In one of the rooms downstairs she found a large, dusty carpet, which she rolled up and brought upstairs on the grounds that, if nothing else, it would make a lot of smoke.

Her resourcefulness and enthusiasm for the job made Matt smile. He never knew what the woman was going to bring up next. At one point, after a great deal of noise, she came out carrying an enormous sheet of corrugated iron, which she'd seen lying in the courtyard. If they were going to light a fire on the roof, she explained, they'd better build it on top of something nonflammable, otherwise they'd end up burning a hole through the roof and into the factory below. On another occasion she came upstairs carrying a fire extinguisher, "just in case"; and somewhat miraculously she also managed to lay her hands on a can of lighter fluid in one of the warehouse offices downstairs. Matt protested that he should be helping, but she refused to let him. He had to relax, she said, in the sunshine.

While she set about organizing the material into piles, Matt took out his wallet and sorted through it to see how being dunked in chocolate had affected its contents. He kept a lot of important stuff in his wallet—not only his credit cards, but all the business cards he'd collected as well. To his dismay, most of these were now useless, sodden with brown grease, their phone numbers and other contact details illegible beneath the thick cocoa stains. He went through them one by one, checking which ones were salvageable.

Eventually he came upon an old photograph—one that he'd had in his wallet for years. It was a picture of a woman sitting on a wicker chair, and smiling gently toward the camera—and although the image was hopelessly stained, he still stared at it for a while, wistfully.

On the other side of the roof Sam noticed him looking at the photo. "An old girlfriend?" she asked.

"No, it's my mother."

'Your *mother?*"

Matt resented her tone a little—he had no idea that Sam had been through his wallet already, and he didn't see why she should be so surprised at his having a picture of his mother in his wallet. "She died when I was a kid," he said defensively. "I never really knew her, so I keep her picture with me. What's wrong with that?"

Sam came across and peered down at the chocolate-stained photograph in his hand. "She was beautiful," she said eventually.

"You can't really tell from this. It's ruined. I'll probably have to throw it away."

"You still have the negative though, right?"

"My dad does—although I don't speak to him much anymore, so it doesn't really make any difference." He shrugged. "Anyway, it's only a picture. I don't know why I keep it—force of habit, I suppose."

He paused for a second before scrunching the photograph into a ball and throwing it onto Sam's woodpile, along with his ruined business cards. He meant it as a full stop to their conversation, and Sam obviously understood it as such, because she didn't talk to him again for a while.

As she went back to stacking all the things she'd brought up to burn, Matt glanced over to where he'd thrown the picture. He had a sudden impulse to go back and retrieve it, but he knew it was too late—and anyway the picture was pretty much irredeemable. So instead he continued sorting through his wallet for a few minutes, taking out his credit cards and wiping them on the pants of his factory outfit. When nothing was left inside, he opened the wallet as wide as he could, to scrape out as much of the chocolate splatter as his fingers could reach. Some of the smaller pockets proved fussy though, and it was impossible to clean everything the way he wanted. The task was fairly unsatisfying—not at all the purge he had been hoping for.

.   .   .

After a while Sam disappeared downstairs one final time. She returned about ten minutes later with some lunch: a large tray stacked with cheese, lettuce, tomatoes, a giant container of tuna fish, some bread, some mayonnaise, and a carton of orange juice. She put them down in front of him with a flourish and a smile, as if she had just cooked up something impressively elaborate. Matt smiled back uncomfortably. He knew he should thank her or at least acknowledge her efforts, but he felt suddenly self-conscious and for some reason couldn't think of anything to say.

They used one of the dust sheets as a picnic blanket and laid the food out on the roof between them. They were both ravenous, their enormous breakfast already a distant memory.

"When do you think it's best to light the fire?" asked Sam, heaping a pile of food on her plate. "Shall we do it this afternoon, or do you think we should wait until it gets dark."

"I'm not sure."

"I think we should definitely get some smoke going this afternoon. But on the other hand, somebody might take more notice if they saw actual flames—and flames will show up better at night."

"Maybe we can have the best of both worlds: light the fire early this evening, and build it up as it begins to get dark."

"Good idea," said Sam, and then pointed to Matt's side of the picnic. "Pass me another tomato, would you—they're delicious."

She was right—the tomatoes were delicious. In fact *everything* was delicious. Matt was surprised that he was enjoying it so much: compared with the take-out food he had been eating all week, it was incredibly simple—just a couple of basic ingredients thrown on a plate—but it tasted better than any restaurant meal he could remember. For a long while they ate without speaking, each of them savoring the flavor of their food. Not until they were picking at the leftovers did Sam finally break the silence.

"Matt, can I ask you a question? You don't have to answer it if you don't want to. It's just something I've been wanting to ask you ever since we pulled ourselves out of that vat."

"What do you want to know?"

"Well," she said uncertainly, "I just wanted to know what it felt like. When you were in there. What did it feel like to die?"

"Fantastic," he said dryly. "It was a real giggle."

"I'm serious," said Sam earnestly. "I just want to know what was it like. Were you scared?"

Matt sat there for a while without answering, but eventually he turned his head. "No, I don't think I was scared. I was *frustrated,* because I couldn't breathe, and I remember feeling angry with myself for not taking a proper breath before I went under. But I think it all happened too quickly for me to be scared."

"Do you remember what your last thoughts were? I mean, your last *conscious* thoughts, before you had your dream."

"Yes, I remember them clearly. I was sad at what a waste it all was."

"What, that you were dying?"

"No. I was sad at what a waste *everything* was. My job, my life—everything." He took a deep breath and turned back to face the sky. "I seem to spend all my time striving for something—a better job, a better apartment, more money. I strive so hard I never have the time to appreciate anything I've got. It's pathetic really, but that's the way it's always been. I live my life in the future. Except, of course, when I'm living in the past. *Today* never gets a look."

He turned to Sam again. "You and me are the same, Sam. We both spend all our energy working. But do you ever wonder why it is you work so hard?"

"I love my job."

"I'm sure you do, but that's not what I asked. You can still love your job without letting it take over everything you do."

Sam drew back a little. "What are you trying to say?"

"Just that there's more to life than always reaching for something you can't have." He sighed. "All the struggling and the striving—all it seems to do is bury you. That's why I was so angry at myself for not taking a proper breath before I went under. It's typical. It's what I do every day of my life. My dad's exactly the same—married to his work, unable to live life without filling every waking moment with business plans. It's like he's afraid of stopping, like he's scared that if he's not constantly *doing* something he might suddenly wake up to the fact that my mother's not there anymore, that he's alone, with nothing but his store to keep him company."

He broke off, staring sadly into the pile of food before him. Eventually Sam said, "And what about you? What are *you* afraid of?"

"I don't know."

"I mean, why do you work so hard? Are you just following in your father's footsteps, or are you scared you won't measure up—or what?"

Matt thought about it for a moment before repeating, "I don't know."

"No, me neither."

Matt lay down on his back to look at the sky. He felt empty—it was as if he'd coughed up all of his insides along with the gobs of chocolate he'd inhaled, and now there was nothing left—he was hollow.

For the next few minutes he concentrated his mind on the present: the sunlight on his skin, the faint puff of air that occasionally blew across his face, reminding him, gently, that he was outside. It felt good, and for a while he allowed himself to feel relieved, as though some terrible danger had passed without bringing him to harm.

Up above, a single cloud drifted past, high up, and dissolved slowly until nothing was left of it. Higher still, an airplane streaked noiselessly southward. It left a trail of vapor, but soon that too expanded and dispersed, until nothing was left to break the unending blue that stretched across the whole dome of the sky.

Chapter thirty-seven

They lay on the roof until about five, talking occasionally, but mostly just sunbathing. The sun was still fairly high when Sam decided to get up. She wanted to clear away the food they'd eaten and finish preparing for the fire. The bottle of lighter fluid she'd found earlier was almost empty, so she wanted to see if she could find some more—or perhaps some paraffin—anything to make starting the fire a little easier. She stood up, straightening out her factory jacket as she did so. For some reason she felt nervous.

While she set about clearing up their lunch things, Matt stayed where he was, lying on his back watching the sky. He had taken his jacket off and was lying in nothing but a pair of white factory pants. Sam paused for a moment to look at him. She ran her eyes over the contours of his chest for as long as she dared, before turning quickly away. She should be getting on.

"Do you want a hand?" asked Matt lazily as she picked up the tray of leftovers.

"No, I'm okay."

She gave him another long glance, before turning her back and hurrying inside.

. . .

Downstairs she threw away the remnants of their lunch and stacked the plates in the sink. It seemed like ages ago since she was last in this room, washing up their breakfast things—so much had changed since then. Matt had changed. He was softer and more likable now, and she didn't feel the need to be half so defensive any longer. She had changed too. It felt terrible to think of the way she had acted since she'd been locked in this factory: arguing with Matt just for the sake of it, complaining at anything and everything—and then all that self-indulgent angst about Matt's having walked out on her this morning. Looking back on it now, she didn't blame him—in his position she would probably have walked out too. It made her feel ashamed to think that while she had been complaining to herself in this kitchen, Matt had been struggling to stay afloat—struggling for his life—all by himself in that chocolate vat.

As she finished washing the plates, she resolved to try to spend less time arguing with Matt and more time cooperating with him. It shouldn't be so hard. Now that she'd got to know him a little, he didn't seem half so bad anymore—not at all the corporate bully boy she had imagined him to be. Perhaps if they worked together a little more—willingly, rather than with that grudging sense of necessity that had characterized all their dealings together so far—well, perhaps then they might find a way out of here.

Her thoughts turned once more to their fire. That was their best chance of escape as far as she could see, but they were going to need more than just a box of matches and a couple of drops of lighter fluid to get it going. As she dried her hands on the kitchen cloth, she had an idea: T&B made chocolates with liqueurs in them—they could use alcohol to help light their firewood. She remembered seeing a stack of boxes containing bottles of brandy in one of the storerooms upstairs—they were locked away in a sort of metal cage, but there was also a desk in that room, and she might just find the key to the padlock in one of its drawers.

Before she left the kitchen she took an empty box and filled it with a few things to take up to the roof: a couple of glasses, some cans of cola, and a large pack of Trundel & Barr marshmallows that she'd found this morning while they were making breakfast.

For the first time since she'd arrived here, she felt pleased with herself. Matt wasn't the only one who could be resourceful after all. She would make a fire so big it would be visible from the town center. And while they were waiting to be rescued, she would make it nice for them—some marshmallows for them to toast together, and perhaps a glass of brandy each, for the celebrations once help arrived.

. . .

By the time she got back up onto the terrace, Matt had put his jacket back on. He was sitting on the wall by the edge of the roof, staring out across the parking lot and beyond to the southern outskirts of Balti-more. As she arrived in the doorway, she stopped for a moment to look at him serenely sitting there, and she almost felt as if she were intruding. Compared to his stillness, she felt clumsy and blustering.

She wanted to get on with making the fire, but somehow it didn't seem appropriate just yet. Hesitating for a second, she stepped out onto the terrace and put her box of things down. Then she walked slowly over to the edge of the roof and sat down beside him.

"It's a beautiful evening," she said quietly.

Matt nodded. After a few moments, he pointed out some houses on the other side of the industrial park. There were several blocks of them: small houses in rows, their chimneys lined up like dominoes. "I heard that those houses are more expensive than most places in Baltimore," he said. "Despite the fact that it's close by an industrial park, it's one of the most desirable parts of town."

"Why's that?"

"People want to live here because of the smell. The factory has to pump the air out of the conching room through big ventilation shafts, just to keep the place cool. The smell of the chocolate carries for miles. The factory manager here was telling me that on muggy days the aroma gets quite intense. So thick you can almost chew it."

They sat for a while, looking out across the city. The sun had begun its final golden descent toward the horizon, bathing the tops of the buildings and the distant hills in warm yellow light. The houses Matt had pointed out were only a couple of hundred yards away, on the other side of a warehouse building, and yet somehow they seemed far away indeed.

"Do you think anyone will see our fire?" asked Sam after a while.

"I don't know. I suppose there's only one way of finding out."

· · ·

Together they made a pile of some of the cardboard and stacked a few of the smaller pieces of pallet wood around it. Taking the bottle of brandy she'd found, Sam poured a liberal amount over the pile, then dug around in her bag to find her book of matches. The pile took fire immediately, and within a few minutes they had a healthy blaze going.

For the next twenty minutes or so they fed the fire, building it up until it was hot enough to pile on some of the larger pieces of wood.

After a while they threw the carpet onto it, and soon it was smoldering and producing vast plumes of thick, acrid smoke.

Matt coughed. "Do you think anyone's going to notice?"

"Of course they will. But perhaps we should wave our hands or call for help or something, just to make sure."

"Maybe."

Sam looked out across the parking lot. She couldn't see a soul—it was as if the city were deserted. Undeterred, she walked to the edge of the building and began waving her arms—tentatively at first, then more vigorously. "Come and give me a hand," she said to Matt.

"Why? There's nobody there."

"You don't know that. Someone might come past at any moment. Or they could be watching from their window. Come on—come and wave."

Matt wandered over beside her and raised his hands halfheartedly above his head.

"Come on," said Sam, "put some feeling into it!"

She jumped up and down and began flailing her arms even more frantically than before. Matt watched her for a second before turning around and heading back toward the center of the terrace.

"Where are you going?"

"You seem to be doing a much better job without me. I'm going to tend the fire."

Sam paused for a second, watching him walk away—something despondent was in the slope of his shoulders—but then she returned to her waving.

At one point she thought she saw a man wheeling his bicycle on one of the far-off streets. She shouted out to him, but it sounded weak and small in such a big open space. So she opened up her throat and bellowed as if her life depended on it: "Help! Someone—help!"

Shouting like that was strangely cathartic, and though the figure with the bicycle had disappeared from sight behind one of the houses, she still felt a little better. It felt good to scream for help. It felt like something she had wanted to do for years.

.   .   .

The sun went down around seven thirty. Shortly afterward, they built the fire up, piling dozens of thick slats of wood onto it until it was truly blazing. The heat it gave off was immense. It made Matt's eyes water. He began to worry about whether the corrugated metal on which they'd built the fire would be sufficient to protect the roof from catching fire. Picking up a long slat of wood, he poked nervously around the edge of it, flicking any stray embers back toward the center of the fire.

After a while the fire began to mesmerize him. He stood and watched as great tongues of flame licked the air—yellow and orange in the thick of the pile, and a deep, almost transparent purple at the top of the flames. Instinctively he tried to hold each flame with his gaze, but each one was gone before he even had time to register its existence. The fire was changing so rapidly and so constantly that there was nothing for his eyes to catch hold of. He tried staring into its depths, but in the heat of the blaze even the wood itself seemed to be shimmering, as if it too were in flux: the pallet slats, so solid as he had stacked them against one another, were effectively evaporating before his eyes.

He turned to Sam to tell her this, but discovered that she wasn't even looking at the fire. Though she had stopped waving and shouting a while ago now, she was still standing over by the edge of the roof, watching out over the city. He didn't really know what she was looking for. Nothing suggested that anyone had seen them. Nothing suggested that anyone cared if they were here, or even whether Trundel & Barr burned to the ground.

"Maybe it's better if you sit down," he called over to her.

"Why?" she said without looking back. "I thought the idea was to get people's attention."

"That's what the *fire's* for. If people look up to see you standing there, they might just assume you've got everything under control."

She paused for a second before reluctantly stepping away from the edge to join him by the fire. She sat down next to him and settled back against the wall by the doorway that led into the factory. Together they watched the pillar of smoke rise into the early-evening sky.

"Perhaps we'll have better luck when it gets *properly* dark." Her voice was enthusiastic, but Matt could tell by the way she avoided his eyes that she didn't believe it any more than he did. "Once it's *properly* dark the fire will be much more visible."

"What happens if it doesn't work?" said Matt bluntly.

"Of course it will work."

"But what happens if it doesn't? We should be prepared for that. We've had that fire going for over an hour now and I haven't seen a single person walk past down in those streets. As far as I could tell, the place is deserted."

Sam turned to look at him. "Why are you being so pessimistic?"

"I'm not being pessimistic."

"Yes, you are. It was the same when we were stuck in that vat—you didn't think we could escape from there either, but I still managed to get you out."

"Yeah. But only after drowning me." They both fell silent for a minute, before Matt said, "Sorry. That was unnecessary. All I'm trying to say is that we should have some sort of backup plan, that's all. If the fire doesn't work, then we should be ready to try something else—and if there *isn't* anything else, then we should be ready for that too."

He paused, looking at her face. She seemed to be ignoring everything he was saying. She was sitting opposite him turning her head slowly from side to side, as if listening for something. "Sam? What are you doing?"

She held her hand up abruptly to silence him. "Did you hear that?"

"What?"

"I could have sworn I heard a siren."

Matt sighed and raised his eyebrows at her. "Well *that's* wishful thinking if ever I heard it."

She climbed to her feet and stood for a few seconds with her head cocked to one side. "There it is again. It *is* a siren—they've come to get us!"

She strode over to the parapet wall to take a look. Matt was sure she was imagining things, but then he heard it too—the shrill electronic sound of a siren in the distance. It was faint, but getting louder by the moment. Pulling himself to his feet, he walked briskly to the edge of the roof to join Sam. Over toward the west, in among the narrowly packed houses they had been looking at before, was a flashing blue light. It was heading their way.

Sam held her arms above her head and began waving frantically, moving farther along the roof each time the flashing light went out of sight for a moment. Cautiously, Matt joined in once again. The light was still a long way away.

It was tantalizing, watching the progress of that light. For someone responding to an emergency, it seemed to be traveling along a very indirect route, turning from one street to the next in a kind of zigzag toward them. Eventually, like a flashing blue firecracker, it shot out from between two of the warehouses a hundred yards away and swerved quickly onto the road that ran across the front of the factory parking lot. As it did so, Matt lowered his arms instinctively. The siren wasn't coming from a fire engine after all, but from a police car.

"Over here!" screamed Sam, jumping up and down on the spot as she waved.

Matt could see that the car was no longer coming toward them. The tone of its siren lowered slightly, and it sped off up the road in the direction of the city.

"You're going the wrong way!" Sam shouted, running to the end of the roof, almost leaning over the parapet.

Matt sat down on the wall. "It's no use. They've gone."

"But they can't have gone!" She stood there for a while waving her arms desperately. But eventually even she had to give up: as the police car disappeared in the distance, she dropped her hands to her sides.

"They were never coming here in the first place," said Matt. "They must have had some call from the center of town."

"Do you think they saw us up here?"

"I don't know."

"They might come back for us later. Or they might radio one of their other cop cars, or maybe the fire department. There's plenty of smoke up here. It must be worth investigating."

"Maybe," said Matt doubtfully. "If they saw us."

Sam sat down on the parapet wall, utterly deflated. "Why are you so negative? Anyone would think you *want* to stay in here until Monday." And then she put her face in her hands and began to cry.

Matt watched her for a while, unsure of what to do. She was hunched over, crying noiselessly into her hands, her shoulders heaving every now and then with silent sobs. Christ, he thought, she's even tense when she *cries*. Stepping forward, he put his hand on her back, but she flinched and turned away from him. He paused for a second, uncertain whether he should stay with her, but then he took a risk and put his arm around her shoulders. This time she didn't flinch, but just leaned back into his arms as she tried to control her sobbing.

"Come on," he said soothingly, "it's not that bad. We only have to wait another day, and then it'll all be over. In the meantime we have plenty of food. We can find a better place to sleep tonight, where there won't be any mice—maybe we can even sleep up here, by the fire. We've got clothes, and blankets—"

Sam interrupted him by slapping him feebly on his thigh and pulling away slightly. "Oh, Matt, just shut up, will you?"

"Why? What did I say?"

"That's not why I'm crying. I don't care if we have to stay. I just wanted to get something right for a change, and my stupid fire's not good enough."

She sobbed again and clutched her forehead in her hands. Matt didn't know what to say, so he just held her and waited for her tears to subside.

After a while she said, "God, you must think I'm such a damn *girl.*"

"Yes, sometimes. But what on earth's wrong with that? I *like* it when you're a girl."

Sam wiped her eyes, but didn't say anything.

"Anyway," he continued, "I think it's a fantastic fire. It's not your fault if there's nobody around to see it."

Before them, over in the center of the roof terrace, the fire crackled and burned. They could feel the heat of it all the way over at the edge of the roof, and the flames looked bright against the factory chimneys and the darkening sky to the east. Once again Matt noticed the shimmering of the wood in the heat of the pile, although from this distance something was far more constant about the way it glowed.

Sam didn't seem to share his appreciation. Suddenly she was standing once more, saying that she had to throw some more fuel on the blaze. While she hurried off to the woodpile on the other side of the fire, Matt watched her. He felt a wave of sympathy for her, in the same way that he had last night, in the warehouse, when she had been woken up by that rat. She was terribly alone somehow—as if she had never had anyone to look after her, had always been forced to look after herself. Perhaps she was more similar to him than he'd thought.

In the distance another siren sounded, but neither of them bothered to look toward it. It was obviously traveling the same way as the first one, and soon it had petered out altogether in the direction of the city.

Chapter thirty-eight

As dusk deepened into night, they stopped feeding the fire. As Matt pointed out, if they carried on at this rate, they would soon run out of fuel. They faced a simple choice: either they threw everything they had left onto the blaze in one go, made a conflagration so big that it would be seen for miles, or they could tone it down, keep it going for as long as possible in the hope that someone nearby would eventually notice.

In truth, it wasn't much of a dilemma. All the fire and smoke they had produced until now had had no effect whatsoever—at least if they burned it slowly, they would be able to stay beside it into the night. Since nobody else was going to pay any attention to the fire, they might as well enjoy it themselves.

While Matt stacked what was left of the woodpile, Sam arranged somewhere comfortable for them to sit by the fire. Taking the last of the cardboard, she laid it out beside the parapet wall, then folded up a couple of the dust sheets for them to use as cushions. She moved slowly, smoothing out the creases in the sheets with her hands to ensure that they would be comfortable to sit on. She was calmer now. While it had been embarrassing crying like that in front of Matt, she certainly felt a lot better for it. She seemed to have shed some burden that she'd been carrying around all weekend, and at last she could relax.

"Come and sit down, Matt," she said, once the makeshift seat was ready. "You deserve a rest. We both do."

Matt stacked the last few pieces of wood away from the edge of the fire, then came and sat down.

"It's been a long day, hasn't it?" said Sam.

"Very long."

She smiled at him shyly. "I've decided to take a piece of your advice."

"Oh, yes? And what advice is that?"

"Well, yesterday you said that there comes a time when you should stop struggling and just give up, let events happen by themselves."

"I said that?" He looked sad. "Doesn't sound like me."

"I think you were just saying it to shut me up. But anyway, it's good advice—which is why I'm reclassifying this fire. It's no longer a signal fire, but a campfire. And we are now officially on vacation."

"I haven't had a vacation in months."

"Well, you're having one now." She reached into the box she'd brought up from the kitchen earlier. "Marshmallow?"

Matt looked down at the bag of pink and white balls with surprise, then smiled. "Thanks."

He skewered a marshmallow to the end of a splinter of wood, and Sam did the same. Then they held them into the flames alongside one another.

"So," he said after a few moments, "are you going to tell me a story then? That's what people do around campfires, isn't it?"

"I'm afraid I don't know any stories."

"Tell me something about yourself then. I was just thinking, I've been stuck in this place with you for over twenty-four hours, and I still hardly know anything about you."

Sam shrugged. "What do you want to know?"

"Anything, really . . . Tell me about how you became a journalist."

She thought for a few moments, watching the pink skin on her marshmallow begin to bubble and burn. "Actually, I can do better than that. And I've thought of a story to tell you after all. It's not so much about *how* I became a journalist but about *why* I did."

"Sounds good to me." Matt settled back against the parapet wall.

"It's a story about a boy I met in West Africa. I went out to the Côte d'Ivoire a few weeks ago, as part of my documentary. The idea was to see if we could get some footage of conditions on cocoa plantations, and maybe get a few interviews with people who had worked on them."

She lifted the marshmallow to her lips and blew on it before carefully taking a bite. "Unfortunately it didn't turn out to be as easy as that. Nobody wanted to let us film on their plantations, for obvious reasons.

And it was difficult finding anyone who was willing to speak out against the plantation owners, because they were worried about what might happen to them if they did. It was like nobody wanted to trust us. I suppose it wasn't surprising really—we were just a couple of white people flying in to ask a whole load of awkward questions, and then flying out again.

"After about a week or so of not really getting anywhere, Paul and I met up with some people from Unesco. In the absence of anyone else to talk to, we thought we could at least get an interview out of them—they know the country, and they know the conditions. It was better than nothing. But then, after the interview, one of them took me aside and said that if we wanted, he might be able to smuggle us into one of the plantations. And better than that, he knew of a boy from Mali who had recently escaped from a plantation north of Abidjan. He was just about to be repatriated, so there was a good chance he might want to talk to us.

"Anyway, the next day, the man from Unesco took us to the Malian consulate to meet this boy. I have to say that when he introduced me to him, I thought there must have been some sort of mistake. I wanted to talk to some *victims* of slavery, but this guy looked more like one of the *perpetrators*. He was enormous, with shoulders as wide as a bus, and he had a neck like Mike Tyson. Not only that, but he had an evil look on his face—a look of pure resentment, as if he hated everything and everyone. I couldn't imagine anyone bossing him around, and I certainly couldn't imagine him as anyone's slave. It was only when the man from Unesco told me his age that I looked again and realized how young he was—he couldn't have been more than fifteen years old. He was massive, but in the end he was still just a kid.

"So anyway, after Paul had set up the digital camera, I started to interview him. He wasn't very helpful at first. He just gave me one-word answers, as if he didn't trust me and didn't really want to be talking to me in the first place. He told me that his name was Abubakhar. He told me he was from Mali, and that his family was very poor. He told me that he had been working on the cocoa plantations since he was nine years old. But then, halfway through the interview, his attitude suddenly changed. He started to smile at me—a big, beautiful smile that changed his face completely. I don't know what happened—it was like he'd suddenly made a decision to trust me. He became so friendly, and so cheerful, that it was quite a shock when finally he took his T-shirt off and showed me the skin on his back."

She paused for a moment, thinking back to the scene.

"It was horrendous, Matt. His whole back was a mass of scars—there were so many that it was impossible to tell where one scar stopped and the next began. Many of them were recent—bright pink ribbons of scar tissue stretching right across his shoulders. On the plantation, he said, he would be beaten every day—with ropes or sticks or strips of leather. He was awoken every morning with a kick in the ribs, and if he made any mistakes on the plantation, he could expect much worse. For example, when he'd accidentally damaged one of the cocoa trees by cutting the pod too close to the trunk, his boss had punched him in the face with the butt of a machete. He pulled down his bottom lip to show me where two of his front teeth had been smashed in.

"I couldn't believe some of the stories he told me. The worst beating he'd ever got, he said, was after the first time he tried to escape. That's where most of the scars on his back came from: he had been whipped by three men until his whole back was a mass of blood—then flies had got inside the cuts and infected them, making him so ill he almost died. When he recovered, his boss told him to consider it a warning. If he ever tried to escape again, they would kill him. So the next time he *did* try to escape he made sure he succeeded—and here he was to prove it.

"I asked him how he'd ended up a slave in the first place, and he told me that when he was nine years old, his uncle Youssuf had taken him to a rich relative in Timbuktu who said he could find him work. But this relative had simply sold him to a slave trader, who had smuggled him across the border to Côte d'Ivoire and handed him over to a plantation owner. He had worked fourteen hours a day ever since, believing that the money he was earning would be sent back to his parents in Mali. It was only once he discovered from one of the other workers that this wasn't true that he decided to escape.

"I asked him how he had managed to get away, and he told me that he'd dug a hole at the back of the hut where he slept. Ever since his first escape attempt, his boss had started locking him up at night, so he used a knife to cut his way out. Then he'd run through the plantation to the road and spent the rest of the night walking as far as he could to get away from the area. At first he'd wanted to walk northward, in the direction of his home country—but then he figured that was the direction his boss would expect him to go. So instead he walked south. He walked all the way to Abidjan—over two hundred miles. He was too afraid to try to hitch a ride on a truck. He didn't trust anyone. Eventually he'd found his way to the Malian consulate, where they were looking after him while they tried to locate his family.

"When I asked him if he had ever tasted chocolate, he laughed at me and told me that there was nowhere to buy chocolate here, and that anyway it was far too expensive for people like him. So I gave him some, which I had in my backpack, and told him that children in Europe and America ate chocolate regularly. He tried it and said it tasted very good—but then he gave the chocolate bar back to me, saying that he didn't want it. I'll never forget what he said then. He said, 'Take a message back to the children in your country. Tell them they are not eating cocoa, but flesh—my flesh, and the flesh of my friends. Tell them that people have died to make their chocolate.'

"What can you say to something like that? So in the end, that's what this documentary is all about. It's an attempt to honor Abubakhar's request. He was an amazing boy—truly incredible. All he cared about was going home to be with his family. I just hope he made it back okay."

. . .

Sam finished her story and fell into silence for a while, staring into the fire.

"So that's why you're so vehement about this antislavery business," said Matt.

"Yes."

Matt gazed into the flames. "I don't blame you."

"You should have seen this boy's back, Matt. It was still raw. And he's just one child in thousands. The Unesco guy told me that they reckon there are about fifteen thousand child slaves in the Ivory Coast alone."

"On T and B's plantation as well?"

Sam hesitated. "Not quite. I'm afraid I bent the truth a little in order to force your boss to give us an interview. Your plantation does employ children, and it pays them a pittance for working long hours. But technically speaking, they're not slaves."

"But as good as slaves."

"Yes." She smiled sadly. "On the other hand, in some ways T and B is better than many of the other big companies. At least you're accountable. Some of your competitors get as much as seventy-five percent of their cocoa from the Côte d'Ivoire, but they barely even know which plantations it comes from. You can't help getting the impression that they don't really care, as long as the price is right."

Matt watched the firelight flicker across her face. He was overcome by the urge to reach out and comfort her, but he knew he couldn't do it. Too much was separating them. Instead, he distracted himself by saying, "Have you ever been to the T and B plantation?"

"No, but I've been to one nearby."

"What was it like?"

Sam grabbed a couple of slats of wood from the pile beside her and threw them on the fire. "Well, for a start it doesn't look like a plantation. I always imagined a cocoa plantation would be something like an apple orchard—you know, rows of trees all exactly the same distance apart, and no room for anything else. But actually it looks more like a fairy-tale forest. Half the trees aren't cocoa trees at all, but massive jungle trees, covered in vines and great beards of moss—the sort of moss that takes thousands of years to grow. Moisture drips from every leaf and every branch, and the ground is covered in this sort of thick mulch. You can smell it—it smells rich and steamy and organic. There's something really primeval about the place. Against a backdrop like that, the cocoa trees themselves look pretty inconspicuous."

"It sounds magical."

"It is. And it would be lovely too, if you could forget for a moment how bad the conditions are for the workers there. And if it weren't for the insects, of course."

"The insects?"

"Yeah. Apparently cocoa plants are pollinated by midges—as a consequence there are millions of the damn things everywhere."

They sat there for a while, staring at the fire. They were close together now, their backs against the wall of the factory, their shoulders touching. While Sam had been talking, she'd opened up one of the dust sheets and draped it over their legs to protect them from the heat of the fire: it gave them a conspiratorial feel, like two children sitting up in bed together.

After a while, Matt had an idea. "You know, there might be something I could do to help the situation on our plantation."

"How do you mean?"

"If we cleaned up our act a little. If we made a *feature* out of paying good wages on our plantations, made sure we didn't use any child labor—maybe even joined the Fairtrade Foundation—that could become a marketing tool. We could present ourselves as an ethical company. One of the good guys."

Sam sighed and continued staring into the flames. "You're always looking for an angle, aren't you?"

Matt took another marshmallow and skewered it on the end of his stick. He had hoped that she would be pleased with his idea, but instead it seemed to have upset her somehow. It seemed that whenever they ended up talking about what he did for a living, she pulled away from him. He was tired of dancing around this woman. He just wanted them to be straight with each other.

"Listen, Sam, I don't run the company. Accountants run the company, and all they see is numbers in different columns. They'd never authorize a large increase in costs at the plantation, because they know they can get cocoa more cheaply. But if I put it to them as a marketing exercise, they'd be willing to do it. They'd probably even see it as value for money."

"But that's ridiculous."

"Of course it's ridiculous." He shrugged. "It's called playing the game."

"Well, you seem very good at it."

"Yes, I am good at it." He leaned forward and put his marshmallow in the fire. "Listen, I hate all the politics and the bullshit you get when you work for a big company, but unfortunately that's just something that goes with the territory. But it doesn't have to be a bad thing. If you learn how to use it, you can actually make it work for you."

Sam didn't answer him, just stared glumly into the fire.

"Okay," he said at last, "you've told me a story about yourself, so now it's my turn. I want to tell you a story."

"What about?"

"It's about how I ended up with my job. And about how the chocolate industry works—how the whole marketing world works."

"Well," said Sam, "if you're going to tell me all about life, the universe, and everything, I think you'd better pass me the brandy."

Matt picked up the bottle and handed it to her. She unscrewed the cap, held it to her lips, and took a large, unashamed swig, before settling back against the wall to listen to his story.

Chapter thirty-nine

"Okay, before I start, can I ask you something?" said Matt. "Do you believe in ideals?"

"Of course. We have to have ideals, otherwise we won't have anything to strive for."

"But what about in the real world? Do you believe an ideal can ever actually exist? Do you believe anything can ever be perfect?"

"I don't know," said Sam. "I hope so."

"I wish I could be so optimistic." He stared sadly into the fire. "You know what the biggest problem in advertising is these days? Apathy. Everyone is bombarded with so much advertising that they just switch off from it. When you're watching television and a commercial break comes, you switch over or turn the sound off or go and make yourself a cup of coffee. When you're reading a magazine, you flick straight past the ads without even looking at them. People are bombarded with images of perfection everywhere they go—and now they take them for granted. It's like perfection isn't good enough anymore."

He took a sip from the brandy bottle. "I haven't always worked for T and B, you know. A few years ago I used to work for a different chocolate company. It was much, much smaller than T and B. There were only about a dozen other people there, and because there were so few of us, we used to work twelve-, sometimes fourteen-hour days, just to get all the work done. We got paid zip, our offices were cramped, and there weren't enough desks to go around. But the good thing about it was the camaraderie. Everybody worked together as a team. There was none of this separation between marketing departments and sales departments and production and so on—everyone mucked in together, and if any one of us had a deadline to meet, the others would all help to make sure we hit it.

"As far as marketing goes, we were pretty basic. Obviously we didn't have anything like the budget T and B has, so most of the time we just concerned ourselves with little things—special offers and the like. But every six months or so we would splash out on something a little more adventurous. Perhaps we'd have a customer competition: win a luxury weekend break in Paris—that sort of thing. Or we'd pay for a counter display so that storekeepers could show off our products. Every time we did this, we had to come up with a suitable slogan—something catchy, but which got the message across. And that's where the fun started.

"You see, there's an old marketing adage that there are four words which catch consumers' attention more than any other words in the English language. These words are *new, free, chocolate,* and *sex*. I never saw any market research to back up this truism, but it kind of makes intuitive sense. I mean, everybody likes things that are new and things that are free; chocolate is the world's favorite flavor; and, well, *sex* speaks for itself. So whenever we were about to splash out on a marketing campaign, we used to hold a competition in the office to see who could come up with a slogan that contained as many of these words as possible.

"As you can imagine, most of the offerings were pretty lame. We used to get things like 'Our new chocolate is better than sex' or 'Win a holiday, free with our new chocolate!' The thing was, nobody ever managed to come up with a decent slogan which included all four of these words. Sometimes we had three. Sometimes the offerings were so bad that we went with something else altogether. But then one day, when we were planning a poster campaign on the New York City subway, I got fed up with this futile exercise. As a joke, I suggested that rather than trying to make grammatical sense out of these four words, why didn't we simply print the words by themselves and use that as our slogan. To my surprise the others actually thought that was a good idea. In fact, they really liked it. So that's what we did: we made a poster which said simply, 'New free chocolate sex,' with a picture of our chocolate bar under-neath.

"Over the next few weeks, sales in the New York metropolitan area increased by twenty percent. It was the single most successful advertis-ing campaign I've ever been involved in. We started getting orders from all over the place: supermarkets, newsstand chains, all the people who normally wouldn't even stock our chocolate. It was unbelievable.

"Of course, because I came up with the slogan, I got the credit. It was ridiculous really. All of a sudden I was some kind of marketing guru. I got calls from the business press—people who wanted to interview me about how I'd come up with the idea. I kept wanting to tell everyone that I'd just meant it as a joke, that it was all just a big misunderstanding. But I didn't, of course. Instead I spun some bullshit about tapping into the spirit of the age, and in the end I did just as good a marketing job on myself as I ever did on the product. I got my name in the papers—I was something of a celebrity for a few weeks—and then I ended up being offered the job at T and B."

He fell silent for a while, just poked at the edges of the fire with a long stick. Eventually he said, "Of course, with hindsight, I know why the campaign worked so well."

"Why's that?"

"Well, it's what we all want, isn't it? It's not just sex, it's new free chocolate sex. It's like the ultimate expression of instant gratification. Instant gratification without responsibility. It's the consumer's ideal—and maybe also his curse."

Sam smiled quietly. "I don't know. There's nothing wrong with a little instant gratification once in a while."

"Sure. But it's hardly an ideal to strive for, is it?"

He threw his stick into the fire and leaned back against the wall, close to Sam.

"And how about you?" asked Sam. "What are you striving for?"

"I don't know."

"But you *are* striving for something? I mean, aside from all the material stuff—the house, the car, the new stereo."

"I must be," said Matt. "Aren't we all?"

They sat together, staring into the flames.

"Well, maybe that's the curse then," said Sam after a while. "Not the gratification, but the striving for it."

Chapter forty

On the grounds that nothing was wrong with instant gratification after all, they decided to finish the bottle of brandy. They softened it by mixing it with the cola Sam had brought up from the kitchen along with the marshmallows and drank it liberally while they gazed at the fire and chatted.

Neither of them could avoid noticing how close they were sitting. Their legs were touching, their arms were touching—each of them could feel the whole length of the other, soft, warm, almost as if they were melting into one another. It felt both delicious and agonizing: they were neither together nor apart. And for fear that anything might change, that something might somehow wedge its way between them again, or that one of them might make a move too far, they both stayed extremely still.

"This is blissful," said Sam. "Who'd have thought that watching a fire could be so entertaining? Normally I'd be switching the television on about now, or putting on a video. This is much better."

She meant it. For the first time in months she felt utterly relaxed. There was nothing to worry about here: nothing to strive for, and nothing to strive against. She felt none of the trepidation she was used to whenever she'd come this close to Cameron. And she felt none of the pangs of urgency she had experienced on the night she'd tried to seduce Paul. She was happy simply to sit here and enjoy the evening for what it was. It was something of a revelation to her—the thought that she didn't need to do or be anything, but could just let things happen of their own accord. It was such a simple discovery, it made her wonder why she hadn't tried it months ago.

· · ·

Every now and then, during a lull in the conversation, Matt would skewer another couple of marshmallows and put them in the fire. He was feeling more relaxed now too. Ever since nearly dying in the chocolate vat he had been struggling with how meaningless everything seemed: all his striving over the past few years, all his desperation to prove his value to the world—in the grand scheme of things it amounted to exactly nothing. But now that he had admitted as much, it didn't seem to matter anymore. All that mattered was the here and now: sitting by a fire, with Sam by his side, and half a bag of marshmallows within easy reach.

Perhaps it was the brandy warming his bones, but he felt at last like some life had been breathed back into him. The alcohol was certainly doing something to him—since he'd had little to eat since lunchtime, the spirits seemed to have gone straight to his head, and he had the odd but exhilarating sensation of being both light and heavy at the same time. Despite the roughness of the flavor, this was actually the best brandy he had tasted in years.

Or perhaps it was having this woman next to him that made him feel so alive again. It had been such a long time since he had allowed a woman so close, and only now did he realize how much he had missed the feeling.

"You know, Matt," said Sam as she adjusted her position to settle more comfortably against his shoulder, "I think I underestimated you. When I interviewed you last week, I thought you were just some brainless executive who didn't give a shit about anything except company profit margins. I also thought you were in on this whole plantation thing. I would have been quite happy to pin the entire scandal on you. I'm sorry about that."

"That's okay. If I was any good at my job I *should* have known." He paused before saying, "I suppose I underestimated you too. I thought you were some heartless bitch who was out to get me."

"Maybe I was."

"No, I'm sure you were just—

"It's okay, Matt, you don't need to make me feel better. I'm just trying to put things right, that's all. You're a nice guy. You deserve better treatment."

"We both do." Then Matt smiled bitterly. "We're a real couple of fuckups, you know that? The pair of us, we're as bad as each other."

Sam smiled sadly. "Well then," she said, gazing at his lips, "perhaps we deserve each other after all."

The fire crackled and shone before them, lighting up their faces with a strong, golden glow. Beneath the cover of the dust sheet Matt's hand reached tentatively over toward hers and, finding it, gripped her fingers gently in his.

Afterward

One of the most satisfying properties of chocolate is that it melts at body temperature. Not only is this a delightfully sensual experience, but it also greatly helps your body to absorb all the thousands of substances that chocolate contains: liquids are much easier to digest than solids. As you place the chocolate in your mouth, and as your taste buds are coated in waves of both sweetness and bitterness, your body is already preparing to metabolize what you're eating.

Even before the chocolate leaves your mouth, the digestion has kicked in. Enzymes in your saliva have already started to break down the fats and complex sugars in your bar. The process continues in your stomach and your intestines, where even the tiniest particles are broken down further and further, until they are so minuscule, they can pass through membranes, and even into your very cells.

At the end, virtually nothing is left. So efficient is your body at digesting chocolate that within just a few short hours you have metabolized everything—fats, proteins, sugars, even the tiny traces of water and electrolytes. That bar, which felt so solid as you placed it against your teeth, has been entirely assimilated—you and the chocolate have effectively become one.

Chapter forty-one

Sunday morning and dawn was blossoming over the chocolate factory. Shafts of new light spread from the horizon, illuminating the tops of the factory chimneys. From somewhere, far off, the song of a blackbird drifted over the rooftops, and from even farther away the soft purr of a car cruising toward the town center. The air was still and crisp and pregnant with dew.

On the roof terrace Matt and Sam lay entwined beneath a pile of dust sheets and assorted factory clothing. Dotted around them were various objects: a small stack of wood, a bottle of brandy, a half-empty pack of marshmallows, and the remnants of the fire they had lit last night. A rich, smoky tang lingered on their sheets and in their hair. Every now and then a faint puff of wind would lift petals of ash into the air, sprinkling them like confetti upon the sleeping couple before blowing them away again, down into the parking lot below.

Gradually the dawn ripened into morning, and the pale sky became a deep, cloudless azure. The sunlight spread downward from the tops of the chimneys to form a golden pool on the roof terrace. Beneath the pile of dust sheets one of the sleeping bodies began to move slightly. It was just after seven o'clock.

. . .

Matt woke up with Sam's head on his chest. For a moment he was unaware of any other sensation but this. His whole world consisted of her proximity: the heat of her limbs draped across him, the weight of her head upon his chest, the strands of her hair blowing gently across his face. He could feel her breath pulsing on his shoulder, small puffs of warmth against his skin, and only after he had lain there for a while did he realize that he was unconsciously breathing in perfect time with her.

He opened his eyes and they stung, unready for the brightness of the new day. He lay there blinking at the clear blue sky above him and wondering how he had ended up here like this. He had spent so much time and so much energy trying not to like this woman, and yet here he was in a makeshift bed with her, moving when she moved, breathing when she breathed. He didn't know exactly what had happened last night to change things, but in a way he didn't really care. All that mattered was now: the softness of her skin, the heat of her breath, the movement of her breast against his own.

He didn't want to get up. He wanted to lie here, staring at the sky and sharing the warmth of their bed. But his body was stiff. One of his hands was developing pins and needles. His back ached from sleeping on the hard roof, and every part of him that had no contact with the warmth radiating from Sam's body was cold and numb.

Eventually, the fullness of his bladder got the better of him. Trying not to wake her, he slid his arm from beneath Sam's head and pulled back the dust sheets.

"Don't go," she said sleepily, "it's cold without you."

He leaned down to kiss the top of her head. "I'll be back in a couple of minutes."

Swiftly, he made his way through the factory to the bathroom. Parts of the way were so dark that Matt could barely see where he was going, but he was familiar enough with the layout of the place now and he could navigate through the darkness just as well as he could at home. He wanted to run there and back, return to the roof terrace as soon as possible, so that he could climb back into the bliss of their bed once more. But he held himself in check. There was plenty of time, he told himself—there was no need to rush anymore. They had all of today and all of tonight before anyone would come to disturb them.

After he had finished in the bathroom, he splashed his face with water and then looked at himself in the mirror. He barely recognized the man who looked back. It was like meeting someone he had once known, someone he knew he liked but whose name he couldn't quite remember. No professional or social veneer was on his face now. He was half-naked, his hair was ruffled and gray with ash from the fire. His face was dripping, and he had sleep in his eyes. Even a smudge of chocolate was still behind one of his ears. But for all this he looked better than he had for months, because for once he looked relaxed. And though the smile on his face was not so broad, and not so beaming, he knew that it was for nobody's benefit but his own.

When he got back to the roof terrace, Sam was awake.

"Where did you go?" she asked sleepily.

"Bathroom," he said, kneeling down beside their cardboard mattress. He hesitated, and it crossed his mind that he was too late, that he had taken too long inside the factory. Now that Sam had woken up, she would have had time to think about what had happened between them last night. She would have had time to form regrets.

To hide his fears he turned away from her and looked out across the rooftops of the city.

"What are you looking at?" said Sam.

"The sky. It's a beautiful day."

"Come back to bed."

She held the coverings up. With that one single movement, all Matt's doubts dispersed. So he crawled back in beside her.

He could feel her warmth straightaway—she was glowing like an oven—and as she pressed herself closer, it felt as though the heat of her body were radiating right into him. She rolled over and slid her hand across his chest. For a second he wondered if she had done so consciously, but then her fingers began to trace tiny circles across his ribs.

He smiled, surprised at her boldness. "So I take it you're wide-awake then?"

"Yes," she said, raising her mouth to kiss his lips. "Completely."

. . .

Sam was also surprised at her boldness. She made love to him without any anxiety or self-doubt, without even any thought. She was simply following her instincts—and it felt deeply satisfying, like rediscovering an old skill that she thought she'd lost for good. It seemed impossible now that she had ever felt anything but attraction toward Matt. If doubt crossed her mind at all, it was only to register that she had never really been resisting *him,* but herself.

Later, however, she was a little more circumspect. As they were showering together downstairs, she couldn't help feeling surprised that they had ever managed to come this far.

"If you had suggested last week that I would ever find myself standing naked in a shower with you," she said, "I think I probably would have laughed in your face."

He was busy scrubbing the remnants of yesterday's chocolate from her back. His hands felt firm and confident, and she liked the way they occasionally strayed around her sides and down over her buttocks.

"Any regrets?" said Matt as he rubbed soap into the small of her back.

"None at all. Not about *this,* anyway."

"But about other things?"

"Yes," she said, "but now is not the time for regrets. Now is just for us."

His hands slid around her sides to her belly, and he pulled her close to him. For a while they stood like that, hot water cascading across them both. Sam shut her eyes and leaned back into him, enjoying the feeling of being enclosed. His arms were large, solid. She could feel his hardness growing against her back.

"Hey," she said eventually, opening her eyes again, "it's your turn." She twisted herself around and took the soap from his hand. "You were pretty woozy yesterday when you washed yourself—I'll bet you missed a lot."

For the next few minutes she washed and rinsed his back. There wasn't actually much chocolate left there, but she continued washing him anyway. She was enjoying the feel of his flesh beneath her touch.

"You know something," said Matt, "despite the fact that we're washing it off ourselves, I haven't thought about chocolate once so far today. Normally I wake up in the morning and it's the first thing that enters my mind. It's kind of ironic, don't you think, that it's only after I'm locked up with thousands of tons of the stuff that I can finally forget about it?"

"Maybe it was that dunking you got yesterday."

"You think?"

"Maybe. It's called exposure therapy." She ran her hand down the center of his back. For someone who sat behind a desk all day he was surprisingly muscular.

"You know what else I haven't thought about this morning?" said Matt, turning his head over his shoulder. "Escaping."

Sam smiled. "Me neither."

"In fact, I think I like it here."

She leaned forward and kissed him, once, between his shoulder blades. "Perhaps we should move in permanently," she said.

· · ·

After their shower they made themselves a simple breakfast in the cafeteria—some bread, some jelly, and some fruit. And while they ate, they talked about their past lives and past lovers. Matt told Sam about Sophie, about how he had almost managed to convince himself that her bulimia and her obsession with chocolate was normal, about how that night in his father's store had brought the whole pretense crashing about his feet. And in return Sam told him about Paul. At least, she started to tell him about Paul, but she soon lapsed into telling him about Cameron. Before she knew it, she was giving him the whole story— about how they'd met, how Cameron had moved in, and how he'd started to hit her. The words gushed out of her like a confession, and when she finally finished, she felt cleansed, as if she had pricked a boil that had been growing beneath her skin.

"Why did you stay with him for so long?" said Matt.

"Same reason you stayed with Sophie—I thought that if I ignored the problem, it would somehow go away. I'd never been in a relationship like that before. I guess I was pretty naive."

"Did you love him?"

The question threw her, and she had to stop for a moment to try to find the right thing to say. "I'm not sure that *love* ever came into it. He had me in thrall. It was like I was his prisoner somehow: in the end I didn't just split up with him—I escaped."

"Into Paul's arms."

"Not quite. Paul didn't come along until much later. In fact, Paul doesn't know anything about Cameron. I haven't told him."

"Why not?"

"Well, let's just say that Paul's not as good a listener as you are."

She picked up one of the apples she'd brought from the kitchen and took a bite. Rather than turn away, as she might have done yesterday, she held his gaze. "What about you? Have *you* ever been in love?"

Matt smiled. "What, you mean like in fairy tales?"

"No, I mean like in real life."

His smile dropped slightly. "In that case, no, I haven't been in love for a *long* time."

"So you weren't in love with Sophie?"

"I don't know. I thought I was . . ." He looked sad at the memory. After a while he said, "Actually, I don't think I've truly been in love with anyone since my first girlfriend, when I was a kid. I was *besotted* with her. I used to write love poems to her by flashlight under the covers of my bed when I was supposed to be sleeping. I was fifteen, and her name was Tracy Winters."

"So what happened? Did she break your heart?"

"No. It was my father who broke my heart. He didn't approve of her, so he wouldn't let me see her anymore. To be honest, I think he was just jealous. When my mother died, he lost the love of his life—I don't think he could bear the thought that someone else in his house could be happy with a girl, even if it was just some teenage crush. So he put a stop to it. I tried to see her in secret, but in the end she got fed up and went out with one of the boys in the class above."

"That's a terrible story."

"I know. I've never forgiven my father for that."

They sat for a while, staring at the table in front of them and holding hands in defense against the ghosts that circled around them both.

"Do you think we will ever fall in love again?" said Sam after a while. Then she blushed. "I don't mean with each other, I mean with anyone. Do you think love is still *possible* for us?"

"I don't know. I hope so."

"Sometimes I think that love doesn't really exist anymore. Sometimes I wonder whether it hasn't been replaced with something else while we weren't looking. Something more . . . commercially manageable. Like one of your marketing tricks to get us to buy more chocolate."

Matt smiled. "Well, there's a cynic talking if ever I heard one."

"But it's not really so far-fetched, is it? I mean, why do you think we all change partners so often? Why do you think so many people divorce each other only to jump straight into marriage with someone else? It's almost as if love has become disposable—like razors, or paper cups."

"But that's not down to commercialism."

"Maybe not completely, but commercialism must have something to do with it. People are so used to consumer culture that they can't help letting it into the most private parts of their lives. They start treating *everything* as if it has built-in obsolescence: their cars, their homes, their jobs—even their marriages. If something starts to break down, then rather than repair it they just trash it and go and buy themselves a new one."

"I think the problem's simpler than that," said Matt. "I think it's all just a matter of *time.*"

"How do you mean?"

"People don't give themselves the time to be in love anymore—not like they used to. Love is a very selfish emotion. If you're going to make it last, then you have to sacrifice other things in order to nurture it. You can't be in love if you spend every waking hour in the office. You can't be in love if you are always rushing from one place to another. If you're too busy even to sit down and eat a proper meal, then how are you ever going to find time for a proper romantic dinner? Love is a slow thing. Our world is too fast for it."

"You sound like a man who speaks from experience."

"Do I?" He sighed. "Well, maybe I do. Working in marketing is not always conducive to holding down a proper relationship."

"And being a journalist isn't always the best way to keep your faith in human nature."

"So where does that leave us?" said Matt.

"I don't know. Maybe what we need is a world where there isn't any marketing, and there isn't any media. Nothing to distract us from what's important. Just us."

He smiled bravely and gestured around them. "Somewhere like a chocolate factory?"

"Yes," said Sam, returning his smile. "Somewhere *just* like a chocolate factory."

.   .   .

He knew instinctively that this new peace between them would be lasting. Being with Sam felt different today. Yesterday just the sight of her clenched shoulders was enough to make him feel irritable, defensive, and her scowl gave him the impression that she was permanently furious. But this morning all that seemed to have dissolved. She no longer looked angry, even when she frowned occasionally. And though she sometimes made jokes at his expense, they no longer seemed sarcastic, calculated to hurt, but rather playful. She didn't seem half so tense anymore either—not just her shoulders, but her whole body: it was as if she had just been released from a particularly tight corset that she'd been wearing ever since the Chocolate Trade Fair two weeks ago.

Of course, not only Sam was different this morning. Matt recognized several changes in himself too. For the first time in weeks he felt truly and fully in control of himself. If Sam made some derogatory remark about him or his job, he didn't *need* to fly off the handle at her. There was no urgency to prove himself, to come up with brilliant solutions to problems, to hold himself constantly rigid for fear that if he let go for even a second, then everything around him would somehow collapse. He was no longer even frustrated to be locked in here for the weekend. All that was gone. So what if he couldn't find a way out of the factory? So what if he failed? Sam had seen him half-dead and covered from head to foot in chocolate—after something like that, there wasn't much point in being afraid of looking silly.

It seemed faintly ridiculous, and perhaps a little sad, that he had spent so much of the last few days arguing with Sam. It should have been obvious to him that he was attracted to her, but he had become so efficient at cutting himself off from his feelings that he genuinely hadn't realized. This morning all that had changed. This morning he was happy merely to be by her side, sharing a feeling that had been denied him for far too long now: not love, exactly—not yet—but something more basic than that, a feeling of *togetherness*. Each time she touched him, he felt a thrill run through his skin. When she gazed at him over breakfast—long, luxurious glances, totally unabashed—he felt at the same time both desperately weak and incredibly strong. It was as if he were being gradually charged, like a battery, after months of languishing out of sight, at the bottom of someone's drawer. And now, without really even trying, he was becoming solid, strong—*worth* something.

. . .

After they had washed their breakfast dishes together, Sam suggested they go for a walk.

"Where to?"

"Nowhere in particular—just *around*. We can survey our kingdom."

"Isn't that all we've done since we've been here?"

"Yes, but so far all we've been looking for is a way out. I thought it might be nice to look around as though we're going to stay. We might see things a little differently."

Their walk only took them as far as one of the production rooms upstairs. Here, Matt lifted Sam onto one of the factory conveyor belts, and they made love once more, surrounded on all sides by unwrapped chocolate bars. Unlike the tentative caresses of earlier this morning, where each touch had been infused with the gentleness and simplicity of novice lovers, they now abandoned all reservations and took each other frantically among the packaging materials. They tore at each other's clothes urgently, as if the few seconds it would take to undo the buttons on their factory jackets were unacceptable. Boxes, wrappers, even chocolates themselves, were swept aside onto the floor without regard, pants tugged off, legs and arms thrown open and then clasped again insistently around each other's body. All around them cartons lay squashed, and scores of chocolate bars along the conveyor belt were bruised and split. But as the two of them rocked wildly against each other, they neither noticed nor cared.

In the end, it turned out that they weren't quite urgent enough. Long before either of them was satisfied, they were interrupted by an alarmingly loud crashing noise coming from downstairs. It was far too big a noise for them to ignore. They paused for a second, hoping vainly that it was something entirely unrelated to them, and that they would be able to return to their lovemaking once more. But when the crashing noise came again—seemingly from the gates at the side entrance to the courtyard—they were forced to stop. The sound was unmistakable now: someone was trying to break into the factory.

Chapter forty-two

The irony of their situation did not escape them. Just twenty-four hours ago they would have welcomed the sound of someone breaking the door down. They would have run to the gates and done their best to lend help to their liberators. But nobody likes to be interrupted while making love. And even if they hadn't been making love, neither of them really *wanted* to be rescued anymore. Besides, the crashing noise downstairs didn't sound like someone coming to rescue them at all. It sounded hostile, violent.

They climbed quickly down from the conveyor belt, scrambling for their clothes. The urgency with which they had undressed just a few minutes ago had returned, only this time in reverse, as they struggled to get their factory outfits back on as quickly as possible. And as they dressed, the noise downstairs continued, intermittently, like random claps of thunder across the side of the building.

Matt was the first to get all his clothes on. While Sam was still thrusting her legs into her factory pants, he hurried over to the window and looked down at the parking lot below.

A disturbing sight greeted him. Near the courtyard gates, not far from his own car, there was a new vehicle—a large, white, unmarked van, with pieces of cloth wrapped around its license plates. Standing in front of it were four or five people, dressed in jeans and bomber jackets, their faces concealed with dark glasses and baseball caps. One of them was attacking the metal courtyard gate with a crowbar. Every now and then he would stop trying to lever the gate and beat his crowbar violently against the metal lock—this was producing the crashing noise.

After a few moments Sam came and joined Matt at the window. "Who do you think they are?" she said nervously.

"I don't know. Maybe they're after the computers." He gritted his teeth angrily. "Can you believe this? They're breaking the door down in broad daylight!"

Sam looked anxiously around the room. "We'd better hide."

"Look at them! So much for security cameras. They're just ripping at the gates like they don't care *who's* watching."

"I'm scared, Matt." She took hold of his arm. "Maybe we should go up to the roof—or somewhere we can keep a lookout for them. I don't want them to find us."

He turned and looked at her. "I suppose we *could* go to the roof. Either that or . . ." He stopped and turned back to the window.

"Either that or what?"

"Well, I was just thinking that if they break that gate down, then maybe we could sneak out to my car and call the cops."

Sam watched his face apprehensively. "I don't know, Matt. Maybe we should just keep our heads down."

"But this is our chance to get out of here. And besides, I don't see why we should just let them get away with it. This is *our* factory."

They stood there for a second looking at each other. They were both frightened, although they showed it in different ways; but mixed in with their fear was something else—another, more intimate emotion, a sort of sadness. Their solitude had been disturbed, and each of them had a vague sense that something between them had been broken as a consequence. They stood like this for a few moments, looking at one another, their eyes filled with mutual regret. But then the crashing noise came from downstairs again, snapping them back to their senses.

"Come on," said Matt anxiously.

Taking Sam's hand, he led her to the stairs. They descended them cautiously, and fortunately they paused on the landing to look out at the courtyard below, because at this point there was a final crash, and the metal gate to the parking lot clattered open.

Five figures walked briskly into the courtyard and stopped to look about them. Although Matt and Sam could see more clearly now, they still couldn't make out the intruders' faces—they were all wearing dark glasses in an obvious attempt to conceal their identities. Two or three of them were carrying backpacks. One of the others was holding something made of metal at his shoulder—some kind of silver cube—but it was difficult to see what it was because a piece of cloth was wrapped over it.

After a few moments the shortest one of the group, who appeared to be the leader, pointed toward the door that Sam had entered on her first afternoon here. Sam and Matt watched as the group marched across the courtyard, opened the door, and disappeared inside.

"Right," said Matt, "here's our chance."

Together they hurried down the stairs and stepped out into the courtyard, opposite the open gate. Sam ran straight for the opening. She could feel the adrenaline pumping through her, making her heart race —it was exhilarating and terrifying all at the same time, and intoxicating to think that they were finally about to escape from where they had been trapped for so long. Had she been alone, she would have run straight through the gates without looking back and made for the nearest hiding place. But she wasn't alone. When she reached the threshold, she turned to find that Matt wasn't right behind her as she'd thought—instead he had stopped a few yards away and was hesitating by the doorway that led down to the basement.

"What are you *doing?*" she hissed.

"We have to get our clothes. We left them downstairs in the kitchen."

"*Forget* our clothes—let's just get out of here."

"But we have to get them. My car keys are in my jacket."

"Leave them. We can come back for them later."

"No. I'm going to get my keys." Matt turned away from her and disappeared through the doorway.

Sam stood for a few seconds on the edge of the parking lot before cursing to herself. If they got caught now, she'd goddamn kill him. Reluctantly she stepped back through the gateway and followed Matt down to the basement.

They found their clothes downstairs, in the cafeteria, hanging on the backs of a couple of plastic chairs: Sam's chocolate-stained blouse and skirt, and Matt's crumpled suit. By the time Sam arrived, Matt was already pulling off his factory jacket and replacing it with his suit jacket. He struggled to get his shoes onto his bare feet, while Sam set about gathering up her things. She grabbed her skirt, her blouse, and her shoes, and only then realized that something was missing.

"Dammit!" she said, looking about her frantically.

"What's wrong?"

"I can't find my shoulder bag. I think I must have left it upstairs, on the roof."

"We'll have to leave it."

"But it's got everything in it," she insisted. "My address book, my phone—everything."

"Well, maybe we can come back for it later. Or I can have it sent to you when the workers return tomorrow. But right now we've got to get out of here."

He was right, of course—she knew he was right—but she couldn't help resenting the way he suddenly seemed to be in such a hurry *now*, when a few moments ago he was happy to risk everything for his damn car keys. And she didn't like the way he was ordering her around all of a sudden. The playful lover from upstairs seemed to have been replaced with someone altogether bossier. Perhaps it was the suit that did it. Despite all the crumples and the chocolate stains, the sight of him in that suit resurrected all kinds of unwelcome feelings within her.

Anxious and irritated in equal measure, she followed him out of the cafeteria as they began to make their way back up the stairs to the courtyard. They moved cautiously and slowly. Matt was worried that some of the intruders might have returned, and as he pointed out, the last thing they wanted was to be caught on the stairs—there was no escape by running back down into the basement.

At the top of the stairs Matt put his head quietly around the doorway and took a quick look around the courtyard. The place was strangely silent, almost as if the burglars had given up and gone home. From behind him Sam could see the intruders' van through the open gateway.

"Is it clear?" she whispered up to him.

"I think so."

The gateway was beckoning. It was so close to them—a short dash across one corner of the courtyard and they would both be free, just as they had both spent much of the last two days dreaming about. But as they stepped out of their doorway, they were welcomed by a shout from the other side of the courtyard, and suddenly a group of men were pouring through the doorway from the warehouse and marching toward them. Involuntarily they both froze, moving only to turn and face their attackers. There was no point in running now. They'd never make it to the car without being caught.

Sam was full of both anger and fear as the five figures stepped toward them—although, close up they looked far more chaotic and much less sinister than they had from the window upstairs. Also, something was vaguely familiar about the shorter one who was leading them. For the first time Sam realized that this shorter person was not a man after all, but a woman. She had braids in her hair, which were tucked up underneath her baseball cap.

One of the men stepped forward—the one she'd seen carrying the silver cube earlier—and she now noticed that this cube was a digital camera. Now that she looked at him, this person looked familiar too.

"Sam?" he said, walking straight over to where she and Matt were standing. "Sam, what the hell are you doing here?"

The man took his dark glasses off, then removed his baseball cap. There, standing before her, was Paul.

Chapter forty-three

Matt watched in dismay as Paul stepped forward and reached out to enfold Sam in an embrace.

"Where've you been?" he asked.

"Where have *I* been?" said Sam, pushing him away, hard. "I've been locked in *here* for two days. You said you were going to come up with the camera on Friday afternoon. What the hell happened to you?"

"Amy's van broke down. I tried to ring you on your cell phone to tell you, but you seemed to have switched it off." He stepped back a little to take a look at her. "You look a state!"

"I had an accident with some of the chocolate. I . . . that is, we . . ." Her voice trailed off, and she gestured toward Matt.

Paul turned to him, as if only just realizing that he was there. "Ah, yes," he said guardedly. "The marketing guy."

Matt resented the way Paul had his hands all over Sam. He resented that Paul had interrupted their peace with crowbars and strangers in baseball caps. And he resented that the man couldn't even remember Matt's name. Stepping forward to face him, he said angrily, "Do you mind telling *the marketing guy* what the hell you're doing breaking into his factory?"

"I'm not breaking into your factory," said Paul. "These guys are. I'm just here to film it."

Matt turned to face the rest of the group. To his surprise he found he recognized some of them. The leader, the woman with the braids, was the same woman who had planted the cream pie in his face on Wednesday morning. And the tall man, standing near the back, had thrown the first rotten egg at him. *"You!"* he said, pointing at the woman called Amy. "I'd recognize you *anywhere."*

Amy ignored him. "Okay," she said to the group, "let's go. We can't just stand around here all day."

"Isn't anyone going to tell me what's going on?" said Matt, flinging his hands in the air. "What the hell are you breaking into this factory for?"

"Keep your hair on. We're just going to spray a few words on the walls and leave, that's all."

"Antislavery slogans," explained one of the others.

"So," said Amy, shooting an irritated glance in Matt's direction, "if we can just continue . . ."

Matt was outraged. After all this time of having the whole factory to himself, having a crowd of people barge in here like this was very wrong. He had grown to think of the place as a sort of sanctuary, somewhere private to him and Sam, and now strangers were marching through it threatening to cover it in graffiti.

Worse, Sam seemed to be playing along with them. The woman who had fought him tooth and nail less than forty-eight hours ago was now standing aside meekly for these intruders.

"Sam?" he said. "Aren't you going to do anything to stop them?"

Sam glanced at her director and then back at Matt, before averting her eyes uncomfortably from both of them. "I don't think there's anything I *can* do."

"Why the hell not? These people are breaking the law!"

"I know. But they're not going to listen to me. The only reason Paul and I are here at all is to film them—as impartial observers."

"So you're just going to let them get away with it?"

"What else can I do?" Sam looked miserable. "This is my work, Matt."

Matt watched in despair as Paul took her arm and led her after the others. The protesters were filing through the doorway and up the stairs to the production line—the very room where Matt and Sam had been making love just a short while ago. Matt could see some of them opening up their backpacks and pulling out spray cans. The reality of the situation finally sank in: they had broken down the gate, and now they were going to vandalize the place.

"Are you coming or staying?" said Amy from beside him.

"Oh, I'm coming, naturally. I don't see that I've got much more to lose."

"Good," she said. "I'd hate to think you might want to stay down here and call the cops."

Matt followed her to the bottom of the stairs. "Tell me, do you always go around throwing pies at strangers, or have you just taken a dislike to me in particular?"

"It was nothing personal, I promise. You should see what we did to the sales director of Mars."

. . .

For the next ten minutes or so Sam accompanied Paul around the packaging room, observing while he filmed. At first he wanted her to remain silent, so that he could record sound as well as pictures—but since there wasn't much sound worth taping, he eventually decided to abandon their silence and start asking her advice. If they used this footage, then Sam would have to provide some kind of a commentary over the top. Since she was going to have to find something to say about what he was filming, it was only fair that she had some input.

"Do you want me to stick to the action," he said, "or should I take some general shots of the place as well?"

Sam shrugged. "Stick to the action."

Before them, Amy and the others were painting their antislavery slogans all around the walls of the packaging area. Amy seemed to be the most practiced at it. She was working on a row of concrete pillars, spraying CHOCOLATE = SLAVERY in neat red letters down the length of each one. The others were not quite so deft. Their painted offerings looked crude and childish across the back wall of the room: STOP SLAVERY NOW repeated again and again.

At the edge of the room Matt was sitting on a cardboard box, dressed in his chocolate-stained jacket and white factory pants. He was still clutching his suit pants in his hand. For a while Sam watched him, wondering what must be going through his head. The expression on his face was a cross between bewilderment and disgust, and every now and then his eyes flicked to the conveyor belt where they had made love earlier, as if terrified that one of the protesters would start spraying graffiti on it. He looked utterly miserable.

She understood how he felt. Having these people here, invading their private space, was deeply unpleasant. Over the past couple of days she had grown to think of this as *her* place—hers and Matt's—and now it was being desecrated by heathens.

She desperately wanted to go and talk to him and share his discomfort, but she didn't feel that she could. She felt responsible to Paul. Having the two of them in the same room together was extremely awkward. While Matt knew all about what had happened between her and Paul, because she'd told him all about it this morning, Paul could have no notion of how her weekend had progressed with Matt. And now wasn't exactly the right moment to break the news.

"What do you think of getting a close-up on a pile of those chocolate bars?" said Paul, looking up from his camera screen. "It might be a visual way to show the link with T and B."

He pointed over at the pile of Bliss bars that had spilled out of their boxes when Sam and Matt had knocked them over earlier.

She blushed. "Yeah, whatever."

. . .

On the other side of the room, meanwhile, Matt was watching the progress of one of the protesters with a sort of sickened interest. He was a nerdy young man, taller and skinnier than the others, with a long face and acne all over the back of his neck. Extraordinarily clumsy, he stumbled over cartons of chocolates, looking for space to put his graffiti.

Unlike Amy, the leader of the group, this boy sprayed his slogans crudely and slowly, more like a cat marking his territory than a serious protester with a cause to advertise.

As the boy came closer, Matt felt compelled to talk to him. "Is that the best you can come up with?"

The protester looked at him blankly, unsure how to react. "Eh?"

"Well, 'stop slavery now' . . . it's not very catchy, is it?"

The boy shrugged his shoulders. "As long as it gets the message across," he mumbled.

"That's just it—it doesn't. Not really. For God's sake, you're going to be on television doing this. You're going to have exposure to millions of people—the least you can do is get yourself a memorable catchphrase."

"Like what?"

"Well, to start off with, you haven't even got the basics right. The first rule of marketing is that you've got to fix the *brand name* in the consumer's mind. 'Chocolate equals slavery' is too general. It could be any chocolate. How are consumers going to know who to boycott?"

"How about 'T and B equals slavery' then?"

Matt rolled his eyes. It was like talking to a child. "T and B is the *company* name. People don't remember company names—they remember *product* names. What you want is something that identifies a specific, big-name brand as the guilty party. Something along the lines of 'Snickers equals slavery.' Or 'Kit Kat kills.' "

"Hey, that's not bad!" said the youth appreciatively.

"Just remember to use one of T and B's brands, though, won't you? I don't want Mars or Nestlé suing me for giving you ideas." He reached into one of the boxes beside him—pulling out a Bliss bar, he threw it over to the protester. "Here, this is our brand-new chocolate bar. It should be in the news at about the same time the documentary hits television. And if you can't come up with a good catchphrase using the word *bliss,* then you should be ashamed of yourself."

Matt got up and strode across the factory floor to where Paul and Sam were filming the progress of Amy and her spray can. Sam saw him coming and turned stiffly to meet him, a strained smile on her face. He saw her shoot a quick glance at Paul, but her director was oblivious to them both—he was too busy staring into the eyepiece of his camera.

"Look, Sam, how long's this going to carry on for?" Matt asked. "I can't sit around and watch this happen much longer. Look what they're doing to the place!"

Sam smiled at him sadly. "It'll be over soon, I promise."

"Yes, but what's *soon?* And how much more damage are they going to do? I can't be a party to this, Sam. I don't care what T and B has done— I still work for them."

"I know. But there's nothing I can do."

"Well, we don't have to stay and watch, do we? The least we can do is get out of here—now that the gate's open. I can give you a lift home in my car if you like."

Sam shot another glance at Paul. "I don't know, Matt. I should really stay here until they've finished. It's my job."

Matt looked her in the eye for a few moments, and an old, familiar bitterness began to rise within him. He knew that if he said anything now, it would only be something he'd regret, so he decided to leave the conversation there. Turning on his heels, he left Sam where she was and marched across the room toward the stairs.

Nobody paid him much attention as he walked away. Paul was busy filming. Amy was happily spray-painting a slogan across one of the windows, and the spotty-necked youth was still trying to think of a suitable catchphrase. The only one who saw him open the door was Sam. He paused for a second, just to give her a chance to change her mind and join him—but of course she didn't. So he stepped through the door and hurried downstairs.

. . .

It was strange to be able simply to walk out of the chocolate factory. As he strolled through the gateway, he felt as if he would be stopped at any moment—armed guards would appear, sirens would sound, and dogs would bear down upon him from all directions forcing him to go back inside. After all the trouble they had gone through over the past two days, it seemed wrong that escape wasn't just a little bit more difficult. He would have liked some last hurdle to leap or a moat to swim across—then at least he would have been able to feel that he had achieved something. But as it was, he simply strolled through the gateway and across the parking lot to his car. It seemed a bit of an anticlimax.

Perhaps if he had made this walk with Sam, there might have been something to celebrate. All their escape plans over the past forty-eight hours had been schemes they'd worked out together—that he was now getting into his car without her seemed wrong. What was the point of escaping from somewhere if the only person you wanted to be with stayed behind? And what was the point of going home when all that awaited you was a shabby apartment full of empty pizza boxes?

As he opened the door and sat down behind the wheel, he felt cheated. Sam had cheated him. She was more interested in getting a few extra camera shots to round off her documentary than she was in going home with him. She was more interested in staying inside the factory. With Paul. For a moment he considered ringing the police on his cell phone—in fact, he took his phone out of the glove compartment and switched it on—but just as his thumb was hovering spitefully over the 9 button, he found that he couldn't bring himself to do it. Switching his cell back off, he threw it back into the glove compartment and started the engine.

. . .

Sam watched Matt's departure with a mixture of resignation and dismay. Couldn't he see what sort of a position she was in? She couldn't just waltz off with him while Paul was standing right next to her. It was one thing when it was just the two of them locked in here—but things were more complicated now.

Beside her, Paul was becoming ever more enthusiastic about filming the protesters. One of them, a young man she'd not had a chance to speak to yet, was writing a new slogan across one of the walls: T&B'S BLISS IS AFRICA'S CURSE. It brought to mind the story she'd told Matt last night, and she felt a sudden, irrational longing for them to be back on the roof together, tucked up under a blanket beside the fire.

"Paul," she said suddenly, "I've just got to go outside for something."

"Uh-huh?" said Paul, absorbed in his filming.

"I'll be back in a minute, okay?"

"Okay."

Why did all the simple decisions in her life seem so difficult? She knew she should have called Matt back straightaway—she'd even known it at the time—so why hadn't she? What was she afraid of? As she ran down the stairs to the courtyard, she sensed that she was too late, but she had to try anyway. Surely it was better to come late than not at all? If he was still in the parking lot, she might still be able to get him to wait for her—just for a few minutes.

As she hurried out through the broken factory gates, she vowed to be bold from now on, to stop hiding behind her fears and start doing the things she knew to be right. She didn't want to be timid with Matt—if they had any future together, she wanted to be open and honest from the start. But when she arrived in the parking lot, Matt was already turning away through the factory gates. She was just in time to see his car pull out onto the road to Baltimore and accelerate away into the distance.

Chapter forty-four

By the time Sam returned, Paul had finished filming the protesters and had turned his attention to the production line itself. He had managed to switch on one of the conveyor belts and was filming large lines of truffles sweeping down the length of the room.

"This is fantastic!" he said. "I should get some more footage like this before I run out of time on the tape."

Sam watched him as he panned round to all the boxes and boxes of chocolate bars stacked behind him. "Paul, don't you think we should be going now?"

Paul ignored her. "Are all the other rooms in the factory as good as this? It would be great to get some footage of the rest of the production process while we're here."

"I don't know, Paul. The light's not much good in the other rooms."

"What I'd really like would be some shots of the raw stuff. You know—big vats full of chocolate—that kind of thing. Is there anything like that downstairs?"

Right now Sam would have liked to drown Paul in one of those vats. "No, Paul," she said, concealing her frustration. "There's nothing like that. You know, I really think we should get going now. The longer we stay, the more likely it is we'll get caught."

"You think the marketing guy might have called the cops?"

"You never know."

"Okay. Maybe you're right."

He called over to Amy, who agreed that it was time to be going. They had finished what they were doing in here—not a single foot of wall space didn't have a slogan of some sort written on it, and spray paint was on the windows, on the stacks of boxes, even on the conveyors themselves. Amy's three companions were standing on one side admiring it all. The youngest of them, the one with the spotty neck, was halfway through eating one of Matt's new chocolate bars.

A few moments later Amy was geeing them into action again, making sure they gathered together all their empty cans and packed them away in their backpacks. Sam watched impatiently as they walked around the room, checking that they'd left nothing behind that might identify them personally. She wanted to get going. A small, irrational part of her thought that if they left now, they might still have a chance of catching up with Matt on his way back to Manhattan. Without him there was nothing to keep her here anymore. She just wanted to go home.

At last, once all the empty spray cans had been gathered up and packed away, the group made their way back downstairs to the parking lot and bundled into the back of Amy's van. It seemed an odd way to be leaving the factory after all this time. Sam wanted to stop for a moment, take one last look at the building before they drove away, but there was no time for lingering. Once she'd climbed into the back of the van with the rest of them, Amy shut the door behind her, then made her way around to the driver's seat. Within minutes they had left the factory grounds and were on their way to the highway.

. . .

Nobody knows how to celebrate like those who have just broken the law and got away with it. Sam had not really noticed much tension among the protesters while they'd been painting their slogans—and indeed, since Sam had been inside the factory trying unsuccessfully to attract attention for two days, she didn't see any *need* to be worried about getting caught—but now that they were back in Amy's van, it became obvious that they must all have been nervous. Whoops of joy were accompanied by actual screams as the protesters let off steam. Cans of beer were opened and then sprayed around the back of the van. It was like being at some kind of victory festival.

It was difficult not to join in. Paul was shouting along with the rest of them, and even Sam accepted a celebratory can of beer—but in her case it was more of an emollient than a way to join in with the festivities. After all that she'd been through this weekend, she felt that she could do with a drink.

Only after they had left Baltimore and were just about to join the interstate did Paul finally notice Sam's mood. "What's got into you? You're being very quiet."

"It's been quite a strange weekend."

"I can imagine. I don't think I could handle being locked up with that weird marketing guy for *any* length of time. Let alone two whole days."

"Oh, he's okay. When you get used to him."

"Still, you're out of there now. You should be celebrating. Not only that, but it's our last day's filming. Tomorrow we edit, then you record your commentary, and the whole documentary's wrapped up."

"Yeah, it'll be good to get the thing finished." Sam turned away. For a moment there she'd half-expected Paul to ask about her weekend, or even show some curiosity or concern about how she and Matt had coped together—but of course all he was really interested in was the film.

"What say you and I celebrate tonight? We could go out to dinner somewhere—I've recently discovered a fantastic Afghan restaurant in Hell's Kitchen—and then maybe we could go back to my place . . . ?"

"Sorry, Paul, I'm not really in the mood today."

"Oh, come on." He touched her sleeve. "I missed you this weekend."

"If you don't mind, I just want to go home. Maybe have a shower and get to bed early."

He pulled back slightly, letting go of her arm. "Whatever you say," he mumbled. "It was just an idea."

She spent the rest of the journey in silence, watching the traffic over

Amy's shoulder. In the back of her mind was the vague hope that she might spot Matt's car on the road home—but she knew it was highly improbable. Matt's car was far quicker than this rickety old van: he had probably almost reached Manhattan already. No matter how desperately she wanted to catch up with Matt, she knew she couldn't do so simply by wishful thinking.

After a while she gave up and settled back in her seat, listening to the conversation of the others as they reminisced about past protests and spoke excitedly about future ones. It surprised her how *devoted* they all were. They had no reservations about what they were doing, no self-doubt, no hesitation. It made her feel mildly envious: if she'd had just a portion of their confidence, then she would never have allowed Matt to leave the factory without her. She would have told Paul to shove his documentary and gone downstairs with Matt. At the very least she would have tried to make him wait for her, instead of just letting him walk away like that without even saying good-bye.

She was just wondering whether she was ever going to see Matt again when one of the protesters pulled out a handful of Bliss bars that he had stolen from the factory. He offered them around to the others, seemingly unaware of the irony, and each of them accepted, happy enough to be eating the very products they were supposed to be boycotting. When Sam was offered one, she too accepted, more out of curiosity than anything else. After all, if her documentary was going to be sabotaging the launch of this product, then she should at least know what the thing tasted like.

To her surprise it was actually delicious. As she took a second bite, she smiled sadly to herself: regardless of the ethical background to this product, she had to take her hat off to Matt and his company. Whatever their faults, she couldn't deny that they made a damn good chocolate bar.

* * *

Matt arrived home around three. He had driven flat out all the way, only to get stuck in gridlock just a couple of miles from home. It had been all right on the turnpike, when he'd been able to take out his aggression on the passing lane, but once he was caught in traffic, there had been nowhere for his anger to go. So for the next forty minutes it had simply festered inside him: thoughts of Sam ignoring him while her director filmed the vandalism of their factory, thoughts of Paul with his hands all over her when he greeted her, thoughts of his own impotence when faced with a rabble of student protesters. It was all too much. By the time he finally made it back to the apartment, he was miserable, tired, and completely fed up.

The situation that greeted him when he got back was hardly welcoming. He hadn't cleared up properly after his binge earlier in the week, and pizza boxes and open cheese packs were still in the bedroom. In the two days he'd been away, these had begun to go stale, giving the air in the place a sickly sweet taint.

He dropped his keys on the kitchen table and wandered through the apartment looking for the source of the smell, and as he did so, the frustration that he'd felt in the car was transformed into something more like self-disgust. It wasn't even a week since the cleaner had last been around, and yet the place looked like a landfill. He was appalled that he could have let himself go like this. This was the way students lived, not company directors. Not Matt.

Removing his chocolate-stained jacket, he went and found a black plastic sack so that he could start clearing the place up. He threw away everything perishable—cheese packs, stale cookies, remnants of pizza, half-empty cans and bottles—and once that was done, he got a cloth and a pail of soapy water and began to scrub the kitchen.

In a way he was glad that the place was as bad as it was, because it gave him something to do with himself. Normally he would simply have come in and switched on the television—but today he knew he needed more than this to distract himself. At least when he was cleaning he was *doing* something, rather than merely anesthetizing himself.

In only a couple of hours the entire apartment was spotless. He managed to fill another half hour by taking a shower, washing his hair, shaving—and then a further forty minutes or so by rearranging all his clothes. But eventually he was forced to sit down and face what was upsetting him. No matter how much he cleaned and scrubbed and tidied, his apartment was still empty. As he sat and looked around him, he realized for the first time that he didn't really like his apartment all that much. Clean or dirty, it didn't really matter. After two days in an industrial park outside Baltimore, Maryland, it no longer felt like home.

Chapter forty-five

Late that evening, a thick haze began to settle over New York City. The bright fresh day was congealing into an extraordinarily sultry night, and the air was fat with moisture in the way it only ever is just before a storm bursts. Across the city, people were taking cool showers, closing their windows, and turning on their air-conditioning.

Sam went to bed early. She was desperately tired, but despite this she was finding it difficult to sleep. She was hot and uncomfortable and didn't seem to be able to find a position that felt natural. Her ancient air conditioner was noisy, so she had it on low. After two days in the factory, where the only sounds were the ones she and Matt had made themselves, it was particularly difficult to get used to. Sam found herself staring at the ceiling, watching the changing shape of the shadows.

She had a real urge to call Matt at home. She wanted to say good-night, just as she had done in the factory yesterday, and the night before that. But she didn't know if she could just ring him out of the blue: they hadn't exactly parted on good terms, and last time she'd called him, after their interview, he had simply hung up the phone on her. In the end, as she lay there watching the shadows sway across her ceiling, she convinced herself that calling him would only make things worse. He wouldn't want to speak to her at this time of night. In fact, he probably didn't want to speak to her at all. After the way she'd betrayed him this afternoon, he was probably glad to be free of her.

· · ·

A few neighborhoods away, in his loft apartment in TriBeCa, Matt was also finding it difficult to sleep. He was realizing for the first time just how big his bed was. It felt wide and empty, and despite its softness—especially when compared to the hard concrete floors he had shared with Sam over the preceding two nights—it was also somehow uncomfortable. Nothing could replace the comfort of having someone to sleep beside him.

He tossed and rolled from one side of the bed to the other, and all the while he kept thinking about how simple his life had been before he met Sam. He had been perfectly happy a couple of weeks ago, and then Sam had come along, barging her way into his life uninvited, making everything suddenly unstable and complicated. He was too angry to sleep. He wanted his freedom back.

For a while he toyed with the idea of phoning her to ask her what the hell she thought she was playing at, kissing him one moment but ignoring him as soon as her protester friends turned up. It would be simple to call her—he still had her cell phone number and her address, written on that piece of company notepaper that Alex had handed him almost a week ago. But as he lay in bed, he convinced himself that there was no point in calling her now. She was probably spending the night at Paul's place anyway. Or even if she was at home, Paul would still be there with her, sharing her bed. So instead of calling her, he just lay there, torturing himself with thoughts of them together and wondering how long it would be before he'd be able to get to sleep.

. . .

Outside it began to rain. Matt and Sam both heard it—Matt through his quiet, centralized, but erratic temperature control system listened as the first few loud, fat raindrops spattered on his windows; while Sam heard them clunking on the metal box that comprised her air conditioner—but it was not enough to soften the humidity. In the long run it only seemed to make things worse, easing the atmospheric pressure just enough to keep things feeling oppressive. Both of them lay in their beds, listening to the occasional drips and praying that the sound heralded the burst of a storm. But the storm never came, and after a while the rain stopped altogether, leaving them both hot and uncomfortable and more awake than ever.

End

Chocolate contains some twelve hundred different chemical compounds. Some of them, like the various antioxidants, vitamins, and minerals contained in cocoa, are known to be good for us. Others, such as caffeine, are undoubtedly harmful. Over the years scientists have made all kinds of ambitious claims about chocolate: they say it has antibiotic properties that actually prevent tooth decay, they claim it helps us live longer, and that the mere smell of it is enough to boost our immune system. On the other hand, different scientists say it rots our teeth, shortens our life span, and inhibits our immune system.

The truth is that nobody really knows what effect chocolate has on us—not when it is eaten in modest quantities. Most of these chemical compounds remain untested on humans. For all we really know one of them might be highly toxic—or alternatively one of them may turn out to be the elixir of life.

But then, what right-minded person thinks of any of this when he is about to bite through the surface of a block of premium chocolate? Sometimes it is best to forget what scientists say and simply trust our instincts. All of life is a risk. Chocolate, for the most part, is simply one of those small things that makes taking the risk worthwhile.

Chapter forty-six

Monday morning, nine o'clock, and the T&B building in Rockefeller Center had just opened for business. The forty-seven employees of corporate headquarters were beginning to arrive, switching on their computers, checking their emails and their voice mails. The day began as any other, with a few early faxes, an occasional telephone ringing, and the reassuring sound of the coffeemaker in the staff kitchen.

Outside the Walrus's office his assistant was filling seven or eight china bowls with company chocolates. Once she had finished, she set about distributing them around the office to all the different departments. She stopped in each place for a minute or two to say good-morning, and to swap gossip about the weekend. She had observed this Monday-morning ritual each week ever since she'd started working here.

The main topic of conversation this morning was what had happened at the factory over the weekend. Everyone knew that there had been a strike, but it was a surprise when they learned that someone appeared to have broken into the place—the same protesters who had brought the office to a standstill last week. The intruders had spray-painted their slogans all over one of the packaging areas, and then, bizarrely, they seemed to have lit a fire on the roof. For several minutes the news spread across the office floor, eclipsing even the most exciting weekend gossip. But then, gradually, interest fizzled out again as each of the employees turned his or her attention to other, more pressing things.

. . .

Matt didn't arrive at work until after nine thirty. He was groggy and flustered: after staying awake for half the night, he had then overslept and had hurried to work without eating a proper breakfast. His best suit was still at the dry cleaner's, and his second-best suit was hanging over the back of a chair in his kitchen, so he had simply grabbed the first clothes that came to hand—a pair of slacks and a battered old blazer he hadn't worn for years. They made him look slightly scruffy, but somehow more approachable.

The office seemed a much smaller place than it had last week. After the huge, cavernous rooms of the factory it looked poky and cluttered, and as he wove his way between the workstations to his own department, he felt as if he had to take smaller steps to compensate for the lack of space.

"Good morning," said Claire as he arrived at her desk. "How are you feeling? Has your flu cleared up?"

"My flu? Oh, yes! It's much better now, thanks. I've pretty much recovered."

"Have you heard the latest news? About what happened at the factory?"

Matt swallowed hard and tried to look nonchalant. "No," he said slowly, "what happened?"

Claire told him the gossip, and Matt listened attentively, pretending to be surprised at each revelation. After a while he felt compelled to change the subject. "Has anything else happened while I was away?"

Claire shook her head. "Not really."

"And I don't suppose . . ." He paused for a moment, wondering how to make it sound unimportant. "Have any journalists called here for me by any chance?"

"Do you mean Samantha Blackwood?"

"Yes," he said hopefully. "So she *has* called?"

"No," said Claire. "Nobody's called for you since Friday."

Matt turned his back on his assistant to conceal his disappointment, and with a brief instruction for her to put Sam through if she rang, he stepped into his room and shut the door behind him.

· · ·

It was strange to be back in his office. For a while he sat in his chair and stared at the bouquet of flowers in the corner of his room. They were a little wilted now, but were still blooming—it seemed incredible that it had only been a week since he'd bought them. And it had been *less* than a week since he and Sam had argued in this very room, in front of a television camera and several thousand dollars' worth of sound-recording equipment. Five days ago. Matt frowned, irritated with himself. Five days, and he was already acting like some lovesick teenager who'd been stood up on a date.

On the other hand, in a way he *had* been stood up. Sure, Sam hadn't exactly promised to call him yesterday, but she had made all sorts of other promises—they both had. They had promised not to argue, and to be more tolerant of one another. She had promised not to target him in her documentary, and he had promised to look into his company's employment policy in Africa. And that night they had spent on the roof together—that too had been a promise of sorts, a pledge of something more to come. Surely that had meant something to her. Surely that, at least, was worth a phone call?

It frightened him to think that something that had felt so strong just twenty-four hours ago could now appear so utterly fragile. When he'd woken up on the roof next to Sam, he had felt such peace, such unassailable contentment, that in the isolation of the factory it had seemed impossible that anything could destroy it. And yet it had turned out to be far from indestructible—a mere bubble, pricked in an instant as soon as the outside world intruded upon them once more. And all the promises they had made to one another so full-heartedly would now, exposed, simply evaporate into nothing.

A part of him wondered if this was just the way it *had* to be. In the seclusion of the factory it was easy to pretend that their brief affair was something big, something momentous—because that's what he wanted it to be. But in truth, nothing really distinguished it from any other one-night stand. If he was sensible, he would leave it alone, file it away like a vacation romance, to be remembered once in a while with a secret half-smile, and only ever to be mentioned in passing as he told his dinner-party story about how he had once fallen into a vat of liquid chocolate. Pursuing things now might ruin it completely.

He gazed anxiously at the roses in the corner of his room. Perhaps he shouldn't wait for Sam to call. Perhaps he should phone her himself, finish it now while he could still do so cleanly. Tentatively he reached into his pocket and pulled out the folded piece of paper with Sam's number on it, but even as he did so, there was a knock on his door and Claire entered carrying a pile of letters.

"I thought you might want to see your mail," she said matter-of-factly. "There are one or two things left over from last week that look like they might be important."

He smiled sheepishly and slid Sam's number out of sight, under the desk. "Yes, of course."

He glanced up at the large pile of mail in Claire's hands. It seemed that now wasn't really the time to be worrying about making personal phone calls. He reminded himself that he actually had quite a busy day ahead of him—perhaps he should try to push all thoughts of Sam to a corner of his mind, while he got on with the immediate business of the office. Difficult as it might seem, he would be able to think things through much better if he left them till later, after work, when he had more time.

With a frown, he folded the paper with Sam's number under the desk and pushed it back into his pocket. While Claire arranged her pile of papers on the desk before him, he switched on his computer screen and typed in his password. His working day had begun.

· · ·

Later that morning Matt went to a board meeting to discuss next year's budget. Phil was there, along with all the other directors, seated around the long, oval table that filled the boardroom. The meeting was chaired by the Walrus, who was sitting at one end, scowling at each of them in turn, as if daring them to challenge his authority.

Matt didn't say much to begin with. It was not the most inspiring of meetings—the financial director had produced some figures for the company budget during the next half year, and everyone who thought he didn't have enough was here to argue about it. Matt didn't need to argue. For once, miraculously, the projected marketing spend looked more than adequate. But that didn't mean he had nothing to say. In fact, he had an important issue he wanted to raise with the Walrus—he was just waiting for the opportunity to bring it up.

That opportunity came sooner than expected. The Walrus, who had been watching his employees argue, seemed to have noticed Matt's quietness. After shooting a couple of glances in his direction, the great man suddenly turned toward him and bellowed across the table, "Mr. Dyson, *you* haven't said very much today."

"That's because I'm perfectly happy with things," said Matt. "My department seems to be getting what we deserve—no more, no less."

The Walrus eyed him carefully, as if trying to think of something that might throw him off-balance.

"Pray tell," he boomed, "how did your meeting go last week?"

"My meeting?"

"Yes, your meeting with that journalist. You were going to give me a full report. Why haven't you?"

Matt answered carefully, "Because there was not much to report."

"It went well then?"

"I think I did the best damage control that I could. Given the circumstances."

"Good—"

"But," Matt continued, spying his opportunity to speak out, "in the light of some of Samantha Blackwood's criticisms, I would like to suggest we introduce some new measures at our African plantations. In fact, since we're discussing this year's budget, perhaps now would be a good time to raise the issue."

"Our plantations?" The Walrus scowled at him suspiciously. "I believe they come under the heading of production, not marketing."

"Yes, well, that's where I think we're missing an opportunity. If we were to change our employment practices on the plantations, it could be an important marketing exercise. I think we could make a name for ourselves as an ethical employer. If we were to raise the plantation workers' wages and put some community projects in place—"

"Community projects! Such things cost money, Dyson. And what possible benefit could they bring us?"

"Enormous benefits, in my opinion. The ethical market is booming. This could be an easy way for us to take a piece of that action. Conversely, if we *don't* do something about our plantations, then people like Samantha Blackwood will always be popping out of the woodwork. That could not only harm our reputation, but have an adverse effect on sales."

The Walrus paused for a few moments, weighing up the information in his mind. After a while he turned to his sales director and asked his opinion.

"He's right," said Phil. "One or two of our major buyers have already voiced concerns over this issue. It would be good if we could give them some sort of assurance."

The Walrus looked from Phil to Matt, and back to Phil again. "Absolute nonsense!" he bellowed. "I'm not pandering to public opinion just for the sake of it. Tell your buyers that if they'll mind their own business, then we'll mind ours." Pausing for breath, he turned back toward the financial director. "Now, I believe we were just about to get on to our projected sales figures . . ."

. . .

The rest of the meeting was concerned solely with numbers. Matt switched off after a while—it all seemed fairly arcane to him, the discussion of abstracts in the form of millions, and tens of millions. At one point Phil shot him a commiserating glance, as if to say, "Nice try," and Matt smiled bravely back. The battle was not over yet. There would be other meetings, and other opportunities.

Afterward Phil accompanied Matt back across the office.

"Where were you all weekend?" Phil said. "I tried to ring you a few times. I was hoping we could go out together on Saturday—have a few drinks, meet a few girls. But I couldn't get hold of you."

"I was away. I wasn't feeling too good at the end of last week. I thought I'd have a break."

"Mandy's been looking for you as well. She says you owe her a date."

Matt frowned. "Yes, I'm afraid I probably do."

"She told me about what happened in the bathroom, by the way. I have to say, you were a sight that morning. If she hadn't explained it all to me, I swear I would have thought you were, you know, in flagrante delicto—"

"Phil," Matt interrupted, "can you do me a favor and keep Mandy occupied for the next few days?"

"Occupied? I thought that was *your* job."

"You know what I mean. You're her boss—can't you give her a couple of days off or something? I'm sure she deserves it. And I could do with some space for a while, just so that I can get my thoughts together."

"Well, I *might* be able to arrange something . . ." Phil paused for a moment and looked at Matt. "Are you all right?"

"I'm fine. I've just got a few things on my mind. I'll tell you about it another time." Matt turned and headed toward the Walrus's office. He had not yet told the old man about what had happened in the factory over the weekend and was dreading the storm he was about to unleash.

"Okay," Phil called out after him. "If you need to talk about it, you know where I am."

"Thanks, Phil, I appreciate it."

.   .   .

The Walrus's response to Matt's story was not nearly as bad as it could have been. Rather than exploding, as Matt had expected, he had merely huffed a little and then told Matt to go away and sort it out with the factory manager.

The rest of the day was much like any other, and were it not for the gnawing, anxious feeling in Matt's stomach, it would be easy to imagine that none of the events of the past week had happened. Grant and Alex and Maya were all busy putting together the final details for the Bliss launch, and that afternoon Matt made Claire fax a press release about their launch events to all the major newspapers. But Sam still didn't call, and by the end of the day he had given up hope.

That afternoon he left the office at five thirty on the dot: he had made a resolution this morning never to work long hours for T&B again. But as he climbed into a cab, he was forced to acknowledge that without work to fill his evenings he was going to have to find something else pretty fast. The last thing he wanted was to end up like Phil, chasing anything in a skirt in an effort to hide the emptiness in his life.

He was back home just before six. He made himself a cup of coffee and watched the evening news. He flicked through the channels for a while, before switching off and turning to the pile of magazines he had tidily stacked yesterday—but they were all old, and he discarded them one by one, wondering why on earth he hadn't thrown them away.

And then, when he'd run out of things to distract himself, he simply sat there in his living room and began to think.

Chapter forty-seven

Uptown, in a small office inside the New Horizons building near Lincoln Center, Sam and Paul were going through all their footage. They had been here all day now, picking out pieces of film that would fit into Paul's storyboard, editing and reediting until Sam was hardly sure what the documentary was really about any longer. The editor they were working with turned out to be as much a taskmaster as Paul was. But it was now almost seven o'clock, and Sam wanted to stop.

"Can we call it quits now, guys?" she begged. "We've been working without a break since lunchtime."

Paul smiled at her cruelly. "Stop? Now? This isn't the Samantha Blackwood I've come to know and love."

"I'm tired, Paul . . ."

"But we'll be done in an hour or so. The execs want to see something tomorrow afternoon. We're going to knock their socks off with this, but first of all we need to get it finished."

Sam sighed. Paul was trying to bully her, just as he always did—and his workaholic ally sitting beside him simply made it more difficult. But Sam knew she had to get out of here, so for once she decided that she wasn't going to let Paul get away with it. Leaning forward, she said to the editor, "Do you mind excusing us for a moment? I need to talk to Paul outside."

She stepped out into the hallway, and once Paul had joined her, she shut the door behind them. "Look," she said, "can't you two finish off without me? I didn't sleep too well last night, and I'm tired. I'm not going to be much use to you like this."

"But we need to finish—"

"I'll come in tomorrow morning, early, and finish the rest of the commentary then. It'll be fine, I promise. In fact, it will be better than fine. I'll be able to work much more efficiently after a good night's rest."

Paul looked for a moment as if he were about to protest, but then he merely sighed, his face dropping in obvious disappointment. "I suppose you're right. I was just hoping that we'd be able to get the whole thing wrapped up this evening, and then I'd be able to take you out. To dinner."

"It's a nice thought, Paul, but I wouldn't be much company, I'm afraid."

"How about if we *both* stopped now? Would you come out to dinner with me then?"

"I don't know, Paul—I've got things on my mind."

"Well, how about tomorrow then? I could cook you something at my place. We could have a nice meal, forget about work for a bit."

"I can't," said Sam hurriedly, casting around her mind for a suitable excuse. In the end all she could come up with was "I'm . . . busy."

He turned away for a second, as if looking for a place to escape to, but there was nowhere to go except back into the editing room. He turned back to face her and sighed, and as he did so, his whole body seemed to deflate slightly. "Why are you avoiding me?"

"I'm not—"

"Yes, you are. Every time I ask you out, you just make some excuse, like you're embarrassed or something. It's like you want to tell me to back off, but you don't know how to say it."

"It's not that," said Sam uncomfortably, "it just . . . it wouldn't be right."

"Why not? Is it because of what happened the other night at my place? Because I know I was a jerk that evening."

"You weren't a jerk. You were just following your instincts, that's all." She smiled sadly, then said, "I can't say I was exactly happy about you leaving me in bed like that, but as it happens I think your instincts were right."

"They weren't—"

"Yes. They were. You and me make lousy lovers. We've got too good a working relationship for that. When we're chasing a story together, we're dynamite, but when it comes to the everyday stuff . . . Well, we'd soon get bored with each other."

"So this is it then? You're calling it off?"

"Yes."

Paul lowered his eyes. "I suppose you're right." He smiled awkwardly. "We never really got started in the first place, did we? And anyway, I know you've had your mind on someone else . . ."

He paused for a second, as if giving her the opportunity to deny what he was saying, but Sam simply looked back and didn't say anything.

"Listen, Sam, I'm not entirely stupid, you know. I realize that something must have happened between you and that marketing guy over the weekend. It was pretty obvious, the way you were acting with each other when I turned up at the factory. And the way he stormed out without saying good-bye. In fact, I'd say he's got it quite bad. Nobody acts like that unless they're really into someone—not even a weirdo like Matt Dyson. And you've been so damn distracted today that it's fairly evident you like him too."

"Yes," said Sam quietly. "I think I do."

"Well, I suppose you could do worse than him. I mean, he's not exactly short of money. And he seems like he could be okay. Weird, but okay." Paul shrugged. "No hard feelings, eh?"

"Yeah. No hard feelings."

Paul took hold of the door handle. "Now, I'm going back to work. I'm going to finish this damn documentary tonight if it kills me. And I'll expect you in here by nine tomorrow morning at the latest. Just because you're going early tonight, I don't want you thinking you're being let off easy—you're going to have to work like a dog tomorrow if we're going to get it all done in time."

He opened the door and stepped back inside the office to rejoin their editor.

"Paul," she called after him before he left her. "Thanks."

He turned back for a second with a broad smile—a little *too* broad to be entirely convincing—then closed the door behind him.

. . .

Sam walked away down the hallway and caught one of the elevators that led to the lobby below. When she arrived downstairs, she stopped for a moment. She didn't feel like going home yet. Though she was tired, she had a buzzing, restless energy within her that made it difficult to concentrate on anything, and she had the feeling that if she went home to her empty apartment, it would only get worse. So instead she stepped through the security turnstile and made her way over to one of the soft chairs near the reception area.

She sat down and rummaged around in her shoulder bag until she found her cell phone. She wanted to check her messages, just in case Matt had called her during the afternoon. He hadn't, of course. All she had was a text message from her friend Rachel inviting her out to the movies later in the week, and a voice message from the protesters asking when their documentary was due to air. Disappointed, she erased both and made a mental note to answer them later, when she was a little less preoccupied.

For a moment she kept the phone in her hand, wondering whether she should call Matt. If he hadn't phoned, then maybe it was up to her to do so. It would be easy. She could do it with the touch of a button.

She hesitated, staring at the menu on the phone's display, but after a few seconds she began to feel unbearably nervous, so she quickly switched the phone off again and buried it back in her shoulder bag. Why should *she* be the one to call? Wasn't that supposed to be the man's responsibility?

She sat back in the chair and looked around her at all the people walking in and out of the lobby. She recognized a couple of them: people she'd had to negotiate with in the early stages of producing this documentary. She also recognized one or two executives from the trade magazines: the kind of people who held television's equivalent of Matt's job. But most of those passing through were complete strangers—trainees, secretaries, junior staff—unbearably trendy young things with expensive haircuts and an air of unbounded confidence. It amazed her that this building could house so many of them.

She looked up at the metal and glass balconies above her: six or seven floors of them, all bustling with people. They jutted out flimsily over the lobby, as if there wasn't quite enough to hold them up. Beneath them, enormous steel wires fanned out toward the glass front of the building—it looked as though the whole structure were held in place by tension. As she sat here looking at it, she found herself thinking the same thing she always thought: What would happen if one of these wires were to snap? She had the feeling that all she needed was a pair of strong wire cutters, and she could bring the whole building down around her ears.

Fuck it, she thought, why shouldn't she phone Matt? She was a modern woman—she didn't have to wait around for days to find out whether a man liked her. If he wasn't prepared to take the initiative, then why the hell shouldn't she?

Reaching into her bag once more, she picked out her cell phone and dialed his work number. Her heart was pounding as she held the phone up to her ear and listened to it ring—once, twice, three times, ten times —but in the end there was no answer. She switched off her cell for a second before turning it back on, determined not to allow herself time to change her mind. She still had Matt's home number in her phone from when she'd called him last week. Scrolling down through her phone list, she found it and pressed DIAL. Her hands were shaking.

She listened to Matt's home phone ringing at the other end, but once again there was no answer. She told herself that he must be on his way home. Perhaps he had gone out after work, joined his colleagues for a few drinks. Or maybe he had just decided not to answer his calls. Whatever the reason, it was terribly frustrating after all this time not even to be able to leave a message. Why didn't the son of a bitch have a message service?

She left the phone ringing for what felt like five minutes, but in the end she had to concede defeat. Switching her cell phone off sullenly, she threw it back into her shoulder bag. She felt drained. She was tired of speculating about Matt—perhaps it was time she simply gave up. Swinging her bag onto her shoulder, she left the comfort of her chair. She stepped out through the great glass doors of the building and began to make her way wearily toward the subway station.

Chapter forty-eight

Matt sat in his apartment, turning over the events of the past week in his mind. There were a million reasons why he had to end it with Sam. She didn't fit in with anything in his life. She loathed his job, and she was fundamentally opposed to everything he stood for. And she already had a boyfriend—that was a good enough reason to steer clear of her on its own. Matt had never had an affair with someone else's girlfriend before, but the thought of skulking around, trying to snatch a few clandestine moments together, was more than he could bear. He just wasn't ready for something like that.

The longer he sat, the worse he felt. After a while it felt like sitting at the hub of a carousel: all the same thoughts kept returning again and again, whirling around his head until he began to think they'd never stop. What had he got himself into with Sam? Hadn't he learned *anything* from his last relationship? Why did he always end up falling for women who were so . . . difficult?

If his head was confused, then his heart was a mess. He was used to his emotions arriving one at a time, but today they seemed to be coming all at once. Just the thought of Sam was enough to make him feel angry and happy and sad and horny all at the same time. And jealous too. It had been unbearable last night, lying in bed, imagining her together with Paul—the memory sent a wave of misery washing through him.

It was no good, he couldn't carry on like this. He had to end it as soon as possible. Getting out of his chair, he stepped over to the desk where he'd left Sam's number. His original intention was to call her, but when he saw her address on the piece of notepaper, he changed his mind: some things were better done face-to-face. Besides, a part of him desperately wanted to go and see Sam again, just one last time. So he folded the piece of paper into his pocket, and moments later he was walking through his front door, his heart pounding with a mixture of uncertainty and anticipation.

She didn't live far—probably no more than a mile—and before long he was strolling down her block, checking building numbers against his piece of notepaper. By the time he found her brownstone, it was just after seven o'clock. The sun had dropped below the roofs of the buildings opposite, and the color of the light was turning from a rich golden yellow to the gentle blue of evening.

Matt climbed the short flight of steps and rang her doorbell. There was no answer. With a resigned sigh, he turned and sat down on the top step. He had no idea how long it would be before Sam returned, but he didn't really care. So he just sat there, in the gathering dusk, and waited for her to come home.

. . .

It was about an hour before she finally arrived. She didn't see him at first. She was ambling slowly down the block with her arms folded, gazing sadly at the sidewalk beneath her feet—but then, just a few yards from the door to her building, she did finally look up. When she saw Matt she stopped, an expression of confusion covering her face. She glanced nervously up and down the street before climbing the steps to join him.

"How did you find out where I lived?"

"Same way I found out your phone number—the paper gave it to me." He shifted along the step to make way for her. "You should talk to them about that, you know. They shouldn't just give out your details to strangers."

Sam sat down beside him. He thought for a moment about suggesting they go inside, but that felt presumptuous. If she wanted him to come inside, then it was up to her to invite him.

"Have you been here long?"

Matt shrugged. "A while. I've been getting funny looks from your neighbors. They're not very friendly—I said hello to a woman who lives in the next-door building, but she just went in without saying anything."

"She probably thought you were Cameron. He used to hang around a lot. Last year."

They sat side by side for a while, not speaking. He suddenly felt foolish for coming here like this. Why hadn't he simply phoned her? Perhaps if he'd called, then they could have said what they needed to and got it over with, but instead he was just sitting here, feeling awkward. Sam must be feeling awkward too. The poor woman probably just wanted to go inside—she had her door keys in her hand right now.

He could sense the gap between them—just a few inches of air space between her body and his, which shrank and then expanded again every time either of them took a breath. He couldn't help thinking that if they were to inhale at the same time, if both of them took just one really deep breath, then their bodies might touch.

He hesitated for one final moment before saying quickly, almost impatiently, "Sam, we need to talk. I would have called you, but I don't seem to be much good on the phone with you."

She smiled hesitantly. "Last time we spoke on the phone together, you put it down on me."

"Did I?"

"You remember. After the cream pie."

Matt frowned. "Listen, Sam, I don't think this is going to work. You and me, I mean. I don't think we should see each other anymore."

"Oh . . ." Her smile rapidly faded. "Do you mind me asking why?"

"Isn't it obvious? You already have a boyfriend. And even if you didn't, there are still a thousand other reasons why you and me are a bad idea."

"There are?"

"Of course there are. Just look at us. All we ever do is argue with each other. One minute we're getting along fine, and the next minute we're fighting again. It seems that as soon as I think I know what's going on, something changes—it's driving me crazy."

"You make it sound like it's all my fault."

"Of course it's not your fault. It's both of us. But that's just my point: we disagree about everything—politics, chocolate, those protester friends of yours. We couldn't even agree about the flowers I sent you." He turned away from her, trying to hide his increasing agitation. "And then what about our jobs?"

"I don't know, Matt," she said, her voice turning suddenly bitter, "what *about* our jobs?"

"Well, they're not exactly compatible, are they? You're investigating my company, for God's sake. How can I get involved with you when there's still a part of me that wonders if the things I tell you in bed are going to end up being the subject of a TV documentary?"

"I'm glad you think so highly of me."

"Oh, come on, Sam! If I were to tell you something really secret about my company, don't pretend you wouldn't be tempted to broadcast it. You're ambitious, I know you are. And while we're on the subject, how do you know I'm not just trying to be friends with you so that you won't make me look bad in your documentary? I can't even be completely sure of *that* myself."

"Great. So in other words I fucked you to get more information out of you, and you fucked me to make sure I'd stop criticizing you."

"That's not what I said."

"But it's what you meant." She let out an exasperated sigh. "I thought we sorted all of this out over the weekend. So *what* if we've got different jobs. And so what if we disagree occasionally. None of that matters as long as we trust each other."

"Well, maybe that's the problem. I can't trust you."

"Why the hell not? Jesus, Matt, where's all this coming from? I thought *I* was supposed to be the cynical one. If you want to split up with me then fine, but at least give me a proper reason."

"I've given you a reason."

"No, you haven't. All you've given me is a whole load of bullshit about our jobs. And you say we argue all the time, but actually we'd pretty much stopped arguing. So why don't you tell me what this is really about?"

Matt felt the heat rise to his cheeks. Until now he had been feeling vaguely numb: all the confusing thoughts from earlier seemed to have settled like a sediment at the bottom of his mind. But now here was Sam, stirring them back up again like some kid with a big stick, and it made him feel unbearably resentful. How dare she do this to him! He had to clench his jaw, just to stop himself from raising his voice.

"Okay, you want to know what this is about? It's about *you*, Sam. It's about the way you make me feel. Nobody's ever treated me like you do. You beat me up, and then you virtually leave me to drown. You fight and you scratch, and it takes days to calm you down—and then just when we're beginning to get somewhere, you completely abandon me. As soon as Paul turned up yesterday, you just went off with him and left me out in the cold."

"Well, what did you expect me to do? It wasn't exactly an easy situation, having you both in the same room together."

"You didn't have to ignore me completely. You could at least have called me when you got home."

"Sure. Or you could have called me."

"But it shouldn't be up to me. You were the one who left me standing. You're the one with the boyfriend."

He stopped, and the word *boyfriend* dropped between them like a lump of stone. He glared at her. To his surprise, Sam wasn't glaring back. Her face had suddenly softened, as if she finally understood what was going on. "Is that what all this is about? My relationship with Paul?"

"Isn't that enough of a reason?"

"It didn't seem to bother you when we were in the factory. You knew all about Paul then."

"Yes, but things were different in the factory. We were in our own safe little bubble there. Now we're in the real world. I can't live like this, Sam. I can't spend my whole time wondering if it's safe to phone you, or if I might be *interrupting* something."

Sam sighed and said enigmatically, "Well, there's not much chance of that happening."

"What do you mean?"

"Paul and I split up. I finished it this evening."

Matt was stunned. "Really? I mean . . . why?"

"Why do you think?" She shrugged. "To be honest, we were never exactly an item in the first place—not properly. I thought I made that obvious yesterday. But it seems I was wrong."

Matt didn't know what to say. He hadn't expected this, but actually it was typical: just when he thought he had a handle on the situation, Sam did something that totally changed things. For a few seconds his mind switched between different reactions to the news: part of him was overjoyed that she was free again; part of him was angry at the way she'd just sprung this on him out of the blue; part of him just wanted to run away, give himself some space to think about things. But mostly he just felt like a fool. Why hadn't she told him about this earlier, when she'd first sat down?

"Look," he said, flustered, "just because you've split up with Paul, that doesn't make it all better. You can't just wave a magic wand and expect everything suddenly to be okay."

"So . . . does that mean you still want to call it off?"

"No. Maybe. I don't know."

Sam folded her arms and leaned back against the doorframe to look at him. "I've noticed something about you, Matt. As soon as things start to get difficult, you try to run away. You did it on the telephone when I called to apologize the other day. You did it in the factory when we had that argument in the cafeteria. And now you're doing it again. Well, I can't keep running after you—it's not fair. If you really want to break it off between us, then let's get it over with. Just get up now, and leave. Otherwise let's stay here and try to sort this thing out, like adults. It's your choice."

For a moment Matt hovered on the edge of the step, energy flowing through every cell in his body. Why shouldn't he go? After all, wasn't that the reason why he'd come here this evening—to finish it? It would be so easy—all he had to do was stand up and walk away, and he would be a free man again. But then another part of him resented the implication that he was a coward and didn't want to give Sam the satisfaction of proving her theory right. And besides, deep down he knew that freedom wasn't something he particularly wanted anymore. He had been free ever since Sophie walked out on him, and all it had ever brought him was unhappiness.

He returned Sam's stare. Something defiant was in her eyes, almost as though she were willing him to take her up on her challenge. For the first time it crossed his mind that perhaps a part of her wanted him to go. Perhaps she wanted to finish this too, return things to the way they were before they'd met. It would certainly make things a lot simpler.

Eventually he turned away. Slumping back against Sam's front door, he let out a deep sigh. Who was he kidding? He wasn't going anywhere until they'd sorted all this out.

"You confuse the hell out of me, you know that?" he said.

"The feeling is mutual."

"When I came over here this evening, I had it all worked out. I had reasons for everything. But now I don't know *what* I'm doing."

They sat for a while on the doorstep together, in silence. Sam was staring at her right hand, looking at the space where her ring had been before she had lost it back in the factory. Matt looked at it too and noticed for the first time that her finger was ever so slightly crooked, as if it had once been broken.

Before them, on the sidewalk, the first of the streetlamps began to flicker on. It illuminated the block with uncertain flashes of light, reflecting sharply off the top of the parked cars, before settling down into a steady glow. Matt suddenly became aware of the things around them: the smell of the lavender wafting down from Sam's window boxes, the faint kiss of the breeze on his cheeks, the dark silhouette of the railings at the bottom of the steps—all the things that were not his own voice, saying the things he should be saying.

"You should be wary of being with me," he said after a while. "I'm not very good at relationships. I've never had one that lasted beyond six months—the average is more like three or four weeks."

"That's better than nothing. Isn't it?"

"Maybe. It depends what those three or four weeks are going to be like. Sophie told me the last few weeks of our relationship were hell."

Sam took hold of his hand. He looked up at her face and saw tears on her cheeks now. The sight made him feel wretched. To hold down the lump in his own throat, he said, "So what happens now?"

"I don't know. I suppose that's up to you and me."

"We'll probably fuck it all up, won't we?"

She laughed and wiped her eyes clumsily. "Probably."

She let go of his hand and stood up. Sliding her key into the lock, she opened the door. Matt followed, relieved at last to be going inside. There was much more to be said between them, but at least now they would be able to do it in the comfort of Sam's living room.

Behind them a second streetlamp turned itself on, and then a third— but no one was there to see it now. The street was empty. The only sound to interrupt the distant roar of traffic was the click of Sam's front door closing tight. And the only movement was the gentle swaying of the tree outside Sam's bedroom window, whose leaves threw a camouflage of shadow patterns on her curtains, like a patchwork of ripples, constantly changing with the breeze.

Chapter forty-nine

New things do not stay new forever. Matt knew from experience that customers, like children, soon tire of new toys. No matter how exciting a product seems when it first comes out, within a short time it begins to lose its shine, and gradually people start to look around for something else to amuse them. If you want to stay ahead of the field, you have to reinvent yourself constantly. You have to find new ways to dazzle and entertain, grab the headline, seize the imagination. If you can't always be new, then you must at least *seem* it. Otherwise the world will turn its ever-shortening attention span toward someone else, someone who plays the game just a little bit better, and you and your product will be forgotten.

Six weeks or so after the International Chocolate Trade Fair, the enormous sculpture that had been its centerpiece had already faded from people's memories. It had been so big, and so elaborate, that few people had truly been able to understand it in its entirety. The one or two pictures in trade magazines didn't really do it justice. One of the newspapers gave a detailed description at the time, but it read too much like a shopping list and hadn't done anything to capture the wonder of the piece itself. After several weeks, those who had joined in the scramble to pull the sculpture apart were hard-pressed to recall anything much about it, beyond the random slabs and chunks they had been able to take home. Even the sculptor himself found it difficult to remember exactly all the details he had constructed. What he really remembered was how time-consuming it had been to make, and how little money it had earned him—and since it had been too short-lived even to enhance his reputation, he vowed never again to make anything quite so elaborate, and so ultimately ephemeral.

For a few people, however, this sculpture had been more than just a curiosity. To Samantha Blackwood it represented all that was wrong with the world: greed, needless excess, and sheer wastefulness. It still haunted her dreams occasionally, providing a backdrop for all the nameless fears that she was only just beginning to come to terms with.

The chocolate universe even cropped up in her journalism once or twice. This afternoon, for example, she was writing a column on the destructive nature of Western culture. She wanted to use the way the sculpture had been torn apart as an example of how destruction had been elevated to an art form—like stamping on a sand castle, but on a grand scale. But in the end it didn't fit in with the other ideas in the article, and she was forced to delete it.

For Matt the chocolate universe also lived on. To him it represented a warning—a reminder that ideals are not always healthy, and rarely achievable. Rightly or wrongly, he remembered it as a flawless sculpture, perfect in every detail and truly wondrous to look upon. But he also remembered the feeling he had had when standing before it—it wasn't a pleasant feeling at all, but rather a sense of inadequacy, and loss.

While Sam was writing her magazine piece, he was lying on her bed in the next room, describing the sculpture to his father on the telephone. It was the first time he'd spoken to his father since Sophie had left him, and given the old man's passion for elaborate window displays, Matt figured it would be a good way to break the ice. Later he would talk to him about what had happened to Sophie, and how he had got together with Sam, and perhaps even ask a few questions about his mother, and how his father had coped with her loss all those years ago. But these were all delicate topics to broach. So for the moment he kept to the relatively safe subject of work, and the enormous sculpture that he'd seen at the Chocolate Trade Fair.

. . .

Outside, the sun was shining. Despite its being early June, the temperature was a pleasant seventy-five degrees. In the yard next door, a couple of Sam's neighbors were sunbathing—their radio was playing, and the DJ was predicting more agreeable spring weather. Farther along the block, on the corner, the owner of the mini-mart was doing brisk business in his chocolate stocks. Two blocks away, however, the basketball players had their shirts off. One of them was telling the others, as he bounced the ball between his legs, of a TV documentary he had seen the other night about slavery in the West African cocoa plantations. He vowed never to eat another chocolate bar, before executing a tight turn and lifting the ball cleanly into the net above him.

South of the city, Amy and her protesters were celebrating once again—this time with the help of a few bottles of wine, and a sound system balanced precariously on the roof of Amy's van. They had just heard the news that while T&B remained unrepentant over its human rights record, several other chocolate companies had banded together to condemn the use of slavery in cocoa production and had announced measures to try to combat the problem. The protesters were joined this afternoon by Paul, who under the influence of alcohol, and perhaps also the intoxicating effect of Amy's smile, was standing on the hood of her van, dancing in time to the music.

Farther south still, outside Baltimore, Maryland, a fleet of trucks was leaving the T&B chocolate factory laden with boxes of the company's new chocolate bars. Repeat orders had been unexpectedly high, and the factory had been forced to step up production to cope with demand. Despite the recent strike, conditions at the factory still hadn't changed—and didn't look as though they were ever going to. There were some vague rumblings about holding another strike, but there wasn't much enthusiasm for it. Nathan Trundel had threatened to move production abroad, and the workers were afraid that, as far as the Baltimore factory was concerned, the writing was already on the wall.

·   ·   ·

After Matt had finished on the phone to his dad, Sam came in and joined him on the bed. She settled against his chest, and for a while they lay together in silence, gazing through the window at the tree outside.

After a few minutes Sam raised her head. "Matt, do you think we'll ever get bored of each other?"

"I don't know. I hope not."

"So you're not planning to wait for a couple of years, and then trade me in for a younger model?"

"Give me a chance! I've only known you a few weeks." He turned to look at her. "What's brought all this on?"

"*In Style* has just asked me to write a feature on 'speed dating.' They want me to go to one of those parties—you know, where you get to talk to each man for just five minutes before moving on to the next. I have a feeling that my faith in human relationships is about to get a battering."

Matt laughed. "Perhaps I'm the one who should be worried. What happens if you meet someone else there?"

"Don't worry, I won't. It sounds like my idea of hell. When I say you get five minutes with each man, that's actually the maximum. With some agencies you only get three. Apparently five minutes is too long for some people—they run out of things to say."

"So this is the next crusade, is it? Last week it was chocolate market- ing, this week it's speed dating."

She shot him an angry glance. They had agreed not to mention the subject of chocolate. For the past ten days Matt had been running an advertising campaign for the Bliss bar on billboards, TV channels, and radio stations across the country. In reply, Sam had published a string of articles to highlight T&B's human rights record—with the word *bliss* as a counterpoint for the word *misery* in her headlines. Keeping their work and their relationship as separate as possible seemed the only way to avoid arguments.

"Since you mention it," she said, trying not to be too annoyed, "as far as I'm concerned, they're both just symptoms of the same problem. Everybody wants a quick fix, and damn the consequences for the rest of the world. Three minutes! What does that say about our attention spans?"

"Three minutes is much longer than the average time people spend reading each newspaper article before they move on to the next."

"Touché," said Sam, and allowed herself a brief half-smile.

"If it's any consolation, I agree with you on this one. I don't see how anyone can find their soul mate in just three minutes. It's taken me weeks even to start *liking* you."

"Gee, Matt, you sure know how to compliment a girl."

He smiled at her. "Well, it kind of answers your original question. If it has taken me this long just to scratch the surface, I don't see how I could possibly get bored with you. In fact, you've been full of surprises ever since I first set eyes on you."

They lay for a while in silence, gazing through the window once more. Eventually Sam smiled and said, "Do you want to see something funny?"

"Yes—what is it?"

She hesitated. "Okay, I'll show you, but you must promise not to gloat."

"Sure. I promise."

She got up and left the room. A few moments later she returned, carrying a copy of one of yesterday's tabloids. "I was going through the newspapers this morning when I came across this. They say it's the latest form of viral marketing. Take a look."

She opened the paper and handed it to him. Matt found himself looking at a story entitled "Diamonds Are Bliss." Apparently a thirty-six-year-old mother of two from Philadelphia had bitten into one of T&B's new Bliss bars and found a diamond ring inside. There was a picture of her, smiling as if she'd just won the lottery, and holding up an unusual-looking ring made of two silver bands wrapped around a yellow gemstone.

"That's not *your* ring, is it?"

"Yes! Only they got it wrong: it's not a diamond—it's just a citrine."

"Jesus, we're lucky she hasn't tried to sue us!" He looked back at the photo in the paper. "Are you going to try to get it back from her?"

"No, it'd be a shame to ruin a good story. And besides, look at the woman's face. I'm sure the ring will give her more pleasure than it ever gave me."

Sam lay back down on the bed beside Matt. After a while the sun dipped below the top of her window. It streamed over the bed, forming a pool all around them, and when Matt put the newspaper down, she had to shut her eyes against the brightness.

She remembered the last time she'd lain in the sun with Matt, on the roof of their factory four weeks ago, entwined beneath a pile of dust sheets. It seemed like months ago already. Everything had felt so brand-new that morning, so fresh, as if she'd just been unwrapped for the first time. It was sad to think she'd never feel quite that way again with Matt. But at the same time she couldn't help feeling that it was probably a good thing. Already, the way his hand reached out to touch her waist was somehow familiar, and the familiarity made her feel solid.

Outside, in the yard next door, she could hear her neighbors' radio tuned to a golden oldies station playing love song after love song. Somewhere in the street a car engine stopped, a door slammed, a set of keys dropped to the sidewalk. And beyond, though she was no longer really listening, there was the sound of children playing.

Author's Note

I am deeply indebted to Green & Blacks, and especially to Cluny Brown, for answering all my questions about chocolate marketing, and for keeping me supplied with the finest Fair Trade chocolate I have ever tasted. There is much inspiration to be found in a bar of Maya Gold! Thanks must also go to ICAM for having the generosity to let me wander around their chocolate factory in Lecco, Italy, and specifically to Marisa for all her hospitality. I have had a variety of editors during the creation of this book, and I must thank Kirsty Fowkes, Katja Scholtz, and especially Andy McKillop for their brutal honesty when things weren't going quite right. Also Greer Hendricks, George Lucas, and Suzanne O'Neill, who did a fantastic job in creating this American edition, and Simon Trewin, Dan Mandel, and Nicki Kennedy for all their enthusiasm over the past couple of years. To those friends and family who haven't seen me for months at a time, thank you for saving me from madness by dragging me out of my study at various intervals. But the last word, as always, must go to Liza, who has put up with more than she deserves to. Without her support this book would never have come close to being finished.